DEAD ENDS

Jeffery Deaver is the No.1 internationally best-selling author of more than forty novels, four collections of short stories, and a nonfiction law book. His books are sold in 150 countries and translated into twenty-five languages. His first novel featuring Lincoln Rhyme, *The Bone Collector*, was made into a major motion picture starring Denzel Washington and Angelina Jolie. It has also been adapted into a blockbuster television series called *Lincoln Rhyme: Hunt for the Bone Collector* starring Russell Hornsby. Jeffery Deaver has received or been shortlisted for a number of awards around the world. A former journalist, folksinger, and attorney, he was born outside Chicago and has a bachelor of journalism degree from the University of Missouri and a law degree from Fordham University.

You can visit his website at www.JefferyDeaver.com

@JefferyDeaver

/JefferyDeaver

Also by Jeffery Deaver

NOVELS

The Colter Shaw Series

Hunting Time
The Final Twist
The Goodbye Man
The Never Game

The Lincoln Rhyme Series

The Watchmaker's Hand
The Midnight Lock
The Cutting Edge
The Burial Hour
The Steel Kiss
The Skin Collector
The Kill Room
The Burning Wire
The Broken Window
The Cold Moon
The Twelfth Card
The Vanished Man
The Stone Monkey
The Empty Chair
The Coffin Dancer
The Bone Collector

The Kathryn Dance Series

Solitude Creek
XO

Roadside Crosses
The Sleeping Doll

The Rune Series

Hard News
Death of a Blue Movie Star
Manhattan is My Beat

The John Pellam Series

Hell's Kitchen
Bloody River Blues
Shallow Graves

Stand-alones

The Broken Doll
The October List
No Rest for the Dead (Contributor)
Carte Blanche (A James Bond Novel)
Watchlist (Creator/Contributor)
Edge
The Bodies Left Behind
Garden of Beasts
The Blue Nowhere
Speaking in Tongues
The Devil's Teardrop
A Maiden's Grave
Praying For Sleep
The Lesson of Her Death
Mistress of Justice

Short Fiction Collections

Trouble in Mind
More Twisted
Twisted

Short Fiction Individual Stories

The Rule of Threes
The Deadline Clock, a Colter Shaw Story
Scheme
A Perfect Plan, a Lincoln Rhyme Story
Cause of Death
Turning Point
Verona
The Debriefing
Ninth and Nowhere
The Second Hostage, a Colter Shaw Story
Captivated, a Colter Shaw Story
The Victims' Club
Surprise Ending
Double Cross
Vows, a Lincoln Rhyme Story
The Deliveryman, a Lincoln Rhyme Story
A Textbook Case

Original Audio Works

The Starling Project, a Radio Play
Stay Tuned
The Intruder
Date Night

Editor/Contributor

The Chopin Manuscript (Creator/Contributor)
The Copper Bracelet (Creator/Contributor)
Nothing Good Happens after Midnight (Editor/Contributor)
Ice Cold (Co-Editor/Contributor)
A Hot and Sultry Night for Crime (Editor/Contributor)
Books to Die For (Contributor)
The Best American Mystery Stories 2009 (Editor)

JEFFERY DEAVER

DEAD ENDS

HarperCollins*Publishers*

HarperCollins*Publishers* Ltd
1 London Bridge Street
London SE1 9GF

www.harpercollins.co.uk

HarperCollins*Publishers*
Macken House,
39/40 Mayor Street Upper,
Dublin 1
D01 C9W8
Ireland

First published by HarperCollins*Publishers* Ltd 2024

1

A catalogue record for this book is available from the British Library.

ISBN: 978-0-00-835482-4 (HB)
ISBN: 978-0-00-835483-1 (TPB)

Set in Janson Text LT Std by Palimpsest Book Production Limited, Falkirk, Stirlingshire

Printed and bound in the UK using 100% Renewable Electricity
by CPI Group (UK) Ltd

Contents

The Babysitter

"Your move," Kelli said.

She and the two children sat on the sumptuous oriental carpet in the family's game room. On the walls were posters of Las Vegas and Atlantic City. Nearby was a six-sided table for card games. A bar too, presently locked tight.

Kelli Lambert, seventeen, was in jeans and pink Hollister sweatshirt. Her blond hair was pulled back tightly into the ponytail that made her look all the more like the cheerleader that she was.

"No, me!" said William. The five-year-old, also blond, was fidgety. He'd sat still in one place for nearly ten minutes, which was maybe a record. His father was sure he would grow up to be an ace soccer player.

"It's your sister's turn," Kelli said to the boy. She nodded to Mab, seven. The girl had given herself the nic, no one knew from where. Her given name was Barbara. Her parents had no predictions or expectations about her future career, athletic or otherwise—beyond growing up to be a woman as beautiful as her mother.

"Me!" William said firmly and with a frown.

Kelli cocked her head. "You won the last game," she explained. "Another player goes first now. The player to your left. That's your sister." They were sitting in front of the colorful board game Candy Land.

He made a face and said to the babysitter, "That's not in the rules!"

"It's in *my* rules." She gave him a kind, but firm, look through her blue-framed glasses that made her pretty face appear studious. Her braces matched the shade.

The teen was sitting across from her charges, in the lotus position, and her knees rose and fell. After the children were asleep she sometimes did yoga until the parents returned.

Cards were drawn, the plastic gingerbread men advanced. Mab won this game and then the next.

William sat back glumly. "She cheated!"

"Did not!"

"Yes, you did."

"William," Kelli said sternly. "No talk of cheating."

It wasn't even clear how anyone *could* cheat at Candy Land—especially given that the babysitter watched the board the way the eye in the sky at Vegas casinos scanned the tables. "You're going to apologize right now."

"No."

"I didn't cheat!" Mab was on the verge of tears.

"William." Kelli's voice was ominous.

He said nothing.

She added evenly, "Bed for you right now. No Disney, no cookies."

A debate. Then: "All right, sorry." He didn't mean it but no matter.

"Thank you. Mab, accept his apology."

"I accept."

"Good. You guys tired of Candy Land?"

"Yeah, kinda," Mab said.

"Your parents have any other games?"

"I guess," Mab said. She was looking around. "Something . . . pin . . . Pinocchio."

A smile. "No, not for us."

William frowned and thought for a moment. "Dad plays Poke Her."

Kelli blinked and stared.

"With his friends. They come over. They play it with cards and chips."

She laughed. "Poker. Not for us either. A few years, maybe."

The tall, lanky girl rose and looked in the closet, then the drawers in the game table and a buffet. "Nothing here."

Next door was the office. She walked inside, flipped on the overhead light then the one on the cluttered desk. She looked in that room's closets too. She returned to the game room. "No luck. Sorry, guys. I'll bring some other ones next time."

"Monopoly Junior!" Mab called.

"Okay, I will. Now, let's get cookies and—"

• • •

:—milk. And we'll put on Disney. What're you two in the mood for?"

The screen went dark.

Rachel Winston stepped back from the computer keyboard and stood with arms crossed over her chest. She and her husband both continued to stare at the monitor that had been showing the security video of the babysitting session earlier that evening. Their luxurious home was seeded with cameras.

Erik fidgeted like his son might do.

She snapped, "I told you she saw."

"Shit," he muttered.

"Why on earth would you leave them out?"

He said nothing. His tongue slipped from his mouth and touched his lip. A nervous habit that she found repulsive. Snakish.

Rachel tapped the long, red nails of her right hand on the opposite arm's bicep. Her shoulders were raised and rigid.

The Winstons might be described as beautiful people. Thirty-eight, nearly six feet tall and voluptuous, Rachel resembled an actress who sometimes won awards but whom few people could actually name. Erik was an inch or two over her height and still had the physique of the baseball player he'd been in college. Attractive too, with thick dark hair that could be unruly; he'd had to become an expert at taming it with comb and spray. At the event where they'd met it had been his hair that drew her to him, across the crowded room, at the same time that he gravitated toward her because of her abundant chest. Only later did they learn they had a few substantive interests in common.

Rachel muttered, "She looked at it. She looked right at it." She'd made her point but her fury pushed her to repeat herself.

"Looking isn't seeing."

She sighed and closed her eyes momentarily. "And that means what?"

"You know how you look at something and don't see it. Like ads in magazines. You look at them but you don't focus. It doesn't register."

"How could it not register? You want me to run the tape again?"

The "it" was a diagram of the Golden Luck casino, located on a Native American reservation about thirty miles from Gardenview, the suburb in which this palatial home was located. In exactly one week an "accidental" electrical fire would break out in the basement of the casino, resulting in its near-total destruction.

The absence of a casino would throw the residents in this part of the state into abject panic. But not to worry; the syndicate that

Rachel and Erik headed would leap in and fill the gap—miraculously in a matter of weeks. Their casino, known as the Half Moon, would be located in a nearby resort and up and running before the ashes of the Golden Luck had cooled. The prep work had already been done on the sly and the right money had gone to the right officials on the Gaming and P&Z Commissions.

In a final coup, Rachel's idea, the employees from the Golden Luck would find new employment at the Half Moon, making a much higher salary. This would not only supply staff for Rachel's and Erik's venture but would leave the Roberto organization, owner of the Golden Luck, with no employees trained in the art of separating gamblers from their life savings.

A brilliant plan . . .

Except for one glitch.

A goddamn seventeen-year-old cheerleader had now glimpsed the blueprints—with the big, bold printing on top: *Golden Luck*.

Which for some reason her goddamn husband had not thought to tuck away into a drawer.

When the story of the fire hit the news, the girl would think, "Hey, Mr and Mrs Winston had this map or something of that same casino. Holy cow!"

Or "Holy shit!"

Or whatever teenagers nowadays said.

Rachel shivered with rage.

Erik said delicately, "Really, honey, it's not so bad. First, we're not sure she actually saw it. And even if she did she'd have to watch the news to hear about the fire, and what kid nowadays does? They're on their phones and doing Tok-tik or whatever and Facebook and shit. And even if she *does* watch the news she'd have to watch it at exactly the same time as the story about the fire's on. And you know how short TV stories are. What're the odds?"

Rachel said nothing. Her mind was clicking, as it tended to

do. This was a gift. She didn't like to get her hands dirty in their projects but she could come up with a dozen different smart ways to solve problems. She'd hand those solutions over to somebody else and get started on something new.

"So, it'll be fine," Erik concluded breezily, looking her way with fragile confidence. "Anyway, what is there to do about it now?"

His wife scoffed, as if he'd asked the stupidest question in the world. "What there is to do is we kill her." She pulled out her phone.

• • •

To him, they were not people.

They were Objects.

Some of those in the profession thought of those they were hired to kill as Targets. Or just Them. Some actually liked to think of them by their names—but they tended to be the emotional ones, the sadistic ones and, driven by the thrill of taking lives, didn't last very long in this business.

Michael himself had settled on Objects, and that worked for him.

They weren't male, female, black, white, any nationality or creed, whatever creed was. Objects.

Replaying in his mind Rachel Winston's phone call, the hulking man, with a sallow complexion and sunken eyes, stepped off the bus in the Mapleton section of town. While the city itself was for the most part gray and tough and gritty and industrial—which is where he handled most of his jobs—the outlying areas could be pretty. This 'hood didn't have the mini mansions of Harper or the sleek and chic high-rises of Wilmington but the residents here kept up their unpretentious homes nicely and tended their trim lawns and gardens.

Michael appreciated their efforts regarding the gardens in

particular. Those who knew his professional specialty might be surprised that he himself enjoyed pulling on work gloves and knee pads and puttering about in the small yard behind his colonial home. He raised mostly vegetables. Some of these he gave away but many ended up in the dishes he prepared. Minestrone soup, breaded eggplant, ratatouille. He wasn't a great cook but the food he prepared was hearty and flavorful. Rich with oil and butter and salt. He didn't care about cholesterol or blood pressure. He figured his lifespan was limited, due not to physiology but factors like the criminal justice system and the guns that the Objects occasionally possessed and were not reluctant to use. So his circulatory system worried him zip.

Michael began walking west from the bus stop through the cool, overcast autumn evening. He owned a nice car but he traveled almost exclusively by bus when he was on a job. No tag numbers to trace and city conveyances did not have very good security cams, if at all.

In this business it was important to blend in. He didn't wear a porkpie hat or camo gear or long coat that might conceal an automatic weapon. Today he was in a tan sports jacket, black slacks, blue dress shirt and burgundy tie: a middle manager at an insurance agency, a supervisor at Outback. No one paid him any mind. He might be heading home to any one of these houses from a busy day at work.

Home to hug the wife and children. To water his green beans and Italian parsley.

Michael was thinking of his most recent job. The Object was a labor organizer. Had Michael's client's business unionized, as the Object was attempting to accomplish, profits would have plummeted, and so the man had to go. Michael had spent some days working up a plan to make the death appear accidental.

He was successful. Everyone bought the drunk-driving scenario (the Object had certainly done his part). The hit was clean, it was elegant and, most important, it didn't get much scrutiny by the law. Cops here were overworked, understaffed and more than happy to accept a mishap at face value, and move on to busting inner city kids for selling drugs and the brown-toothed cookers for supplying them.

This job didn't permit that kind of sophistication. For one thing, the death had to happen fast. Also, the murder of the Object would raise many an eyebrow, and even the best-organized apparent accident wouldn't put suspicion to rest. So, the plan was a quick shooting, and let the chips fall where they might (quite the ironic metaphor, he thought, given that a casino was at the center of the job).

The police would go into gear and investigate. So what? Michael thought, let them. He would melt the clear plastic gloves he wore when shooting. The weapon had been stolen from a gun show and the suppressor he was going to use he'd made himself, all of which meant the ballistic profile of the bullet would lead investigators nowhere.

But fast didn't mean impulsive or careless. He'd plan out the time and the place with his typical care. There'd be considerable surveillance work to do.

He now paused beside a particularly nice garden—filled with autumn flowers in abundance and zucchini ready to harvest and tomatoes red as fresh blood—and looked across the street to an unassuming, white-sided bungalow.

It was Kelli Lambert's house.

He saw the girl walk into the front room, carrying a glass of milk or soda or something. A moment later the lights dimmed, replaced by flickering blue. In his household, growing up, children didn't watch TV on school nights. But Michael had come to learn that it was a very different world nowadays.

• • •

The round, handsome woman of about fifty, looked her over in a particular way.

It was the gaze mothers gave babysitters. Part friendly greeting, part probing analysis.

Kelli was used to it.

"Good evening, dear."

"Hello, Mrs Bailey."

They were in the entryway of a cluttered but clean house in Harbor Grove, a neighborhood popular because of the school district and the view of Ambrose Lake.

"Come on in."

The woman led her into the family room and they sat on a couch that you sank down into.

This was a try-out. Some parents didn't want to commit to an entire evening with a new babysitter, even those who had references like Kelli's, but would schedule an initial session for an hour or two while they visited with neighbors up the street or had a fast bite at a neighborhood bar. Any emergencies could be resolved in minutes. There were, Kelli had learned, a whole bunch of rules and arrangements in the babysitting business. These were called "protocols" in the business world, her mother had explained— Clara Lambert was a senior planner in the shipping company her husband had founded.

Kelli liked it that she'd learned a new word.

Protocol . . .

She shifted on the squooshy sofa, feeling a twinge in her joints. In cheer, the team was trying a new routine that launched a student high into the air. Kelli had volunteered to be the "volleyball," as she'd joked. Fine with the others; no one was really up for trying it. The move had gone pretty well the first couple of times but on the third, she'd spun a bit too far and, when she landed in the arms of the girls on the floor, it was on her side, not back. A muscle somewhere got pulled. Then she'd insisted she try it once more, even though her coach said she didn't need to. The final move had gone perfectly.

Only a bit of ache remained.

"So, honey," Mrs Bailey said, "your references are wonderful. Mrs Arthur said you straightened up her kitchen when you didn't need to."

"Just cleaned a little."

"Well, you don't have to do that for us. Oh, and I liked the notes you included from the children you've sat for."

Kelli never asked, but sometimes the kids wrote her something. Mab Winston, for instance, had written a glowing review and drawn a picture of Kelli, which was not half bad. (The little demon William had offered neither praise nor a portrait.)

"You live nearby, right?"

"Mapleton."

"Pretty there."

"It's nice."

A pause. Mrs Bailey's face grew still. "You live with your mother, right?"

She nodded. "My father passed away."

Which was the question that Mrs Bailey was really asking.

The topic had come up because it suggested that Kelli would take her job seriously; without the main breadwinner in the family, the girl would need money to help her mother and to save up for important things like college tuition. She wouldn't risk her babysitting reputation by sneaking boys into the house or drinking the parents' vodka and refilling the bottles with water.

"I'm so sorry."

"Thank you."

Then Mrs Bailey sat back, nodding. "Well, I think the girls are going to like you just fine. I'll go get them."

The woman rose and stepped out of the room. Kelli looked

around. It was hard to avoid the wall decorations. Mr Bailey was a hunter. There were a half-dozen deer heads mounted on plaques, the creatures' glassy eyes staring into the room. Directly at her, it seemed.

Creepy.

Something else caught her attention too: a large wooden cabinet with glass doors. Inside, four rifles sat with their ends pointed upward. She rose and walked to it. The guns—of dark brown wood and glistening blue-black metal—were impressive, like the works of art the Winstons had scattered throughout their mansion. Mr Bailey must have spent a lot of time caring for and polishing them.

She tugged at the door. It was securely locked. But looking up, she saw a small piece of metal protruding from the top. Hearing that Mrs Bailey was still upstairs, Kelli reached up and took the key. She tried it and the door opened. Inside, on the floor of the cabinet, was a large, dusty box. She lifted the lid carefully and found some pistols. She closed the lid. And relocked the door.

Her father had owned guns and they had always fascinated her. She'd wanted to go shooting with him but he'd said absolutely not.

"Please?" Drawing out the word the way teen girls were so adept at doing.

He'd used that line that infuriated her. "When you're older."

Now, looking at the deer, she thought: could I ever really shoot anything? She tried to imagine it. Like anybody who had the internet or TV, she knew how guns worked.

Pulling that slide thing back . . .

Lifting the gun . . .

Squeezing the trigger . . .

All cool.

But actually taking a life?

Without seriously considering the question, she returned to the couch. She pulled from her backpack the board game, with its colorful images of the happy characters sprinting through the fantasy landscape.

Candy Land was the perfect game for young children. Kelli had looked into it. Totally G-rated, the game had been developed by a retired teacher in the 1940s, recovering from this really bad disease, polio. She found herself in a ward filled with school kids who were recovering like her. To distract herself—and the children—the teacher came up with the idea of a game that involved a journey through a land of candy, were the players tried to be the first to the Candy Castle. The worst danger was getting stopped on a square of sticky candy until you drew that same color of the space you were on. Even Lord Licorice, who looked a little weird, didn't pose any real danger.

It was not, Kelli had thought, Grand Theft Auto with a sweet tooth.

She'd read that more households with young children had Candy Land than had chess sets (though she wondered if, after the streaming TV show *The Queen's Gambit*, that was still true).

As she was laying out the board, two twin girls about six charged into the room. One shouted, "Candy Land!"

Kelli smiled and said hello to Monica and Marion as they sat down across from her.

Mr and Mrs Bailey appeared in the doorway and, after the typical recitation of departing parents—bedtimes, snacks, tooth-brushing and which were the preferred stuffed animals to accompany the girls to sleep—they departed.

Without even looking at the gun cabinet.

Much to Kelli's great relief. If they had, they might've noticed that the key was no longer on top of the piece of furniture and wondered where it might have gone.

Never guessing that it sat deep in their babysitter's back pocket.

. . .

Removing an Object is mostly about research and preparation.

The fatal shot would take only a few seconds. The time leading up to it would require days or weeks.

Michael sat in a coffee shop—a non-chain establishment, one with a fake security cam over the counter (he knew all the brand names). An ear bud was plugged in. Never use wireless; hacking and eavesdropping via Bluesnarfing and Bluebugging are so easy that even a fifty-year-old can do it, Michael had once joked.

He liked music, classical mostly, light classical, not weird classical, and now, with a slowly vanishing cappuccino in front of him, he might have been listening to Bach inventions or Mozart's "Queen of the Night" aria as he was preparing for a presentation or studying an important spreadsheet.

However, he happened to be listening to surreptitious recordings of a half-dozen conversations and staring, somewhat blankly, at a map of the city on his computer. Later he would turn his attention to that. Now, his whole world was listening to the words.

Some recordings had been made via X-treme883 Shielded pickups, which were very sensitive, though they distorted the tone (it rendered Kelli's voice higher than it naturally was). In other recordings, conversations had been vacuumed up via a SoundStealer, a two-thousand-dollar microphone that could pick up a human voice from hundreds of feet away. The early models were dangerous. Say you were listening to someone on the other side of the street and a motorcycle with a bad muffler shot past. The decibels in your earphone might shoot from eighty to one hundred and thirty in a second. That could blow your eardrums out and Michael knew one man in this business who that had happened to. He never recovered fully.

The new models, though, contained software that muted the sound instantly when the dBs rose to a dangerous level—like the shooting earmuffs that activated only when you fired the gun; you could carry on a normal conversation until you pulled the trigger.

Michael was jotting notes. He preferred to plan jobs on paper. Paper could be burned; paper could be soaked and wadded up and pulped in a garbage disposal. In this day and age you couldn't escape bits and bytes but if he had to communicate electronically he used Department of Defense-level and Pretty Good Privacy encryption, which despite the modest name could have been called Really Damn Good Privacy.

Always aware of his surroundings as he worked, he had noted that a woman nearby, in a dark skirt and white blouse, kept looking his way. She was a little younger than him, maybe mid-forties. She was attractive, a bit heavy. The looks were mere glances—but not too quick. Once or twice she lingered. Michael got this some. He was a good-looking man with a full head of salt-and-pepper hair and he was, as he had to be in this job, in good physical shape. He did not acknowledge her look, of course. While he certainly felt that tug, low in his gut, he would never pick up anyone in a venue like this, or at a time like this. His attitude was not out of fidelity to Anita, of course (she was presently off-shift from the Good-Night Gentlemen's club and was probably making several thousand dollars in the nearby Day's Inn). No, it was purely for security. Never mix lust and work.

The woman was merely pretending to read her novel—she'd flipped pages once in the past five minutes. Maybe this was because she'd come to Joe's in hopes of meeting a man.

But she might also be part of an operation. Meet Michael, go home with him, look for evidence.

Or shoot him in the back of the head.

Such was Michael's life.

Always risk.

But reward too: the satisfaction of using his God-given skills and removing Objects from the earth. While making a great deal of money.

The conversations on the recordings ended and he studied his notes. He had enough. He wiped the SD card and, when no one was looking, dropped it into his napkin, where he broke it into several pieces with his powerful hands. They went into his pocket; he would later pitch them into the roadside grass on his drive home.

He sipped some of the cinnamony beverage and he turned his attention to the map, moving his mouse to the venue that he'd heard mentioned on the tape.

Ameri-Mall was a large indoor shopping center/entertainment spot about five miles from downtown. It was quite the attraction. There were the typical stores you'd see at such a place: from cheap to glitzy. One of the big draws was the rides—a portion was actually a mini amusement park, with a small roller coaster and Ferris wheel and bumper cars and arcades. Especially popular with teens.

After ten minutes of studying the map—and examining some architectural drawings he'd scored—Michael sat back, eyes on the stained acoustic tile ceiling. It would be impossible to do the job in the mall itself, of course; the place would be far too crowded—and the killing had to be at peak hours, to escape safely afterward. But one advantage about the venue was the maze of underground parking. Much of it was patrolled and covered by security cameras but there were many blind spots.

He was satisfied. Barring a turn of bad luck, the hit would work.

After downing his drink, cold but just as tasty as when it was steaming, he rose. Michael was halfway to the door when he heard a voice.

"Excuse me."

He turned. He was looking at the woman in the white blouse. She was smiling.

His unresponsive, almost cold, eyes did nothing to deter her.

"I knew it! I saw you at Fitness Is Us. The spinning class Tuesday. Don't tell me I'm wrong."

He had no idea what a spinning class was. "No."

"No, I'm not wrong? Or no you weren't there?"

"I wasn't there." He noted that her blouse was one button less secure than it had been five minutes ago.

"Are you sure?"

How could that possibly be a question?

"Okay. Maybe you don't spin, but you sure work out." She scanned his body.

"I have to go."

"Sure I can't buy you another cappuccino?" she asked. So she was all-in, no coyness present.

Which he respected.

"No. I have to get home. Sorry." He added the last word not because he was, but because it was something that one said at a time like this. And he needed to appear normal.

"Maybe I'll see you in here again."

"Maybe."

Michael walked outside into the cool evening air, reflecting that, no, it hadn't been an LEA op. No undercover cop in the world would be that clumsy.

Nor was she one of those pushy people who might just stand up, walk out the door with him and, inundating him with one-sided conversation, accompany him in the direction of his home.

This was particularly good news. It would have been a considerable inconvenience to kill her.

. . .

A dilemma.

Erik Winston paced in his office.

The office where he'd left out in plain view the damn documents about the plan to torch the competitor casino.

Of *course* the babysitter hadn't appreciated anything incriminating in what she'd seen—if, like he'd told his wife, she'd seen anything at all.

He'd once watched a TV show in which an audience was shown a scene of a streetside scuffle between a couple of men. While it was going on someone in a gorilla suit walked by in the background, stopped and waved. Ninety per cent of the audience never noticed the creature.

It was the same in Kelli's case. She was so focused on looking for a game for the kids, the diagrams didn't even register.

Besides, there was a practical risk in killing her. What if investigators found that the victim had babysat for the very couple opening the casino that replaced the Golden Luck? A sharp cop might start to make connections.

The *lesser* risk was to let her live and take the slim chance that she had seen the casino's name.

He now rubbed his eyes. He was no saint; he'd ordered hits before and had come close to carrying out a few himself. (The two jobs his father sent him out on didn't work out, but that wasn't his fault. It really wasn't.)

No, Erik Winston didn't care about taking adult lives . . .

But a kid?

That was bad.

But the plan was already in motion. His wife had found a pro willing to tap a teenager. Rachel had always been more brutal than he was. They'd met at the funeral of her cousin, an enforcer of the organized crew that her uncle headed up. Erik ran a small numbers and gaming operation that paid a cut to the uncle's operation. Their marriage was traditional in one sense—the wedding night lasted three energetic hours—but was also a business arrangement. He merged his operation into hers, sort of a reverse dowry.

He was grifting and scam, not guns and blood, his wife's preferred approach.

But this was too much.

No, it was wrong and dangerous to kill the girl.

What to do about it, though?

He poured another Scotch and sat back, considering the quandary.

Well, maybe there *was* a solution.

Erik considered himself an expert at human nature. He knew his wife. She was good at coming up with schemes and plans—solid ones, profitable ones—but once she'd done so, her attention jumped to the next job and the next. The earlier schemes faded from her mind.

He knew the psyche of hit men too. They were stone cold, and in the business for one thing only: money.

A plan formed. Their hit man was making fifty K for the job. Erik would contact him and offer one hundred K, cash or bitcoin, to get sick the day of the hit. Something gut-wrenchingly bad, puking, high fever. So bad he was laid up in bed.

Rachel would try to find another hit man but given that she was focused on other projects and that it was hard to find a suitable killer before they burned down the Golden Luck, the hit would end up in the back of her mind. The arson would happen, the story would run but Kelli would never hear about it. The whole problem would go away.

Erik walked into the front of the house and looked through the curtains. His wife's car was not in the circle.

He pulled his phone from his pocket and texted the killer, laying out his plan.

There was a delay of only ten seconds.

I keep the original 50?

Erik debated. This seemed unfair since the man was being paid a bonus to *not* finish the job, which meant he was avoiding any risk of jailtime. But he saw no other option.

Okay.

And the reply.

Deal. Cash. McMurtry's one hour.

Erik told the man he'd meet him there. He drained his glass and hurried to his car. He had to be gone by the time Rachel returned.

• • •

Kelli pushed through the thick doorway from the parking garage and stepped into the light. It was so bright she blinked.

She headed to the rendezvous spot, where Tiff and Joanne and Kisha and Sha'ana were clustered together. Two of the girls she knew from cheer, one from the cafeteria and one from Computer Club. They were sitting in mesh chairs, leaning forward, huddled and holding phones.

Tiff held hers up, to the "Awws" of the others.

It wasn't of a boy, Kelli knew. That would have been a

different tone of *Aww*. This would be of a cute cat. Maybe a baby goat.

Kelli strode up.

"Yo!" Joanne said.

They nodded and smiled greetings.

"Drop some screen, girl," Kelli said to Tiff.

She'd been wrong about the vid, but close. It was a puppy doing a TikTok dance.

"Aww," Kelli echoed.

"I need jeans," Joanne announced, and this would be quite a project because she was so tall and thin. But her crew, Kelli included, was up for the challenge.

They rose from the chairs and started down walkways. Kelli had no doubt that they'd be successful. You could find anything you wanted at Ameri-Mall, the Emerald City of shopping centers.

• • •

At McMurtry's, in the business district, Erik ordered a smoky Lagavulin and watched some of the more attractive women in the place. It was a watering hole for businesses in the area and most of the female clientele had jobs in the tall office buildings that created dim canyons in this part of downtown. But stepping inside here was like slipping into a different dimension. Jackets came off, buns got undone, fresh makeup was applied. There was definitely Tinder action going on here, figuratively as well as literally, and Erik knew that hooking up at McMurtry's invariably meant good sex . . . and even, he'd heard, the occasional marriage. He took pleasure in observing the turgid jousting around him, even if he was no longer allowed to play.

He looked at his watch.

The killer was five minutes late.

He had a fantasy that the man had had another job before he

was to meet Erik, but something went wrong and he got shot dead. That would take care of the dilemma right there. Not only would Kelli the babysitter survive but he'd save his hundred K.

Win, Win.

He had just lifted the sweet, pungent liquor to his lips when a woman's voice said in a snarling whisper, "Are you out of your mind?"

Shit and a half.

He closed his eyes momentarily.

Rachel lifted his glass out of his hand. She set it loudly on the bar.

"He told you?" Erik whispered.

"Of *course* he told me. He's a murderer but he's honorable." She pointed a finger at her husband's chest. "A deal . . ." A painful poke with the long nail into his breastbone. "Is."

Poke.

"A."

"All right, I got the message."

"Deal!"

Poke.

"Ouch."

"Shut up. And our money?" she asked snidely. The pronoun was a reminder that, in a way, he'd tried to rob *her*.

He handed over the envelope. She pocketed it.

She leaned close and he smelled some floral scent, a delicate one. It went perfectly with her arresting, sensual physique. It did not, at all, match her icy, hateful eyes.

People around them had turned, surely registering her scary face and harsh words. She glared back and they resumed their drinking and flirting. She whispered to Erik, "Do you like what we do at night?"

Oh, hell, this again.

He nodded.

"Do you *really* like it, Erik?"

"Yes."

"Am I creative? Do I know what you enjoy?"

"Yes. But it's just I kept thinking, she's a kid, she's a kid."

Rachel said, "Whips or kid. You choose."

"Honey, I love—"

"Whips or kid?"

"All right," he muttered.

"There's my boy." She picked up his whisky and downed it, then strode out the door, saying, "Pay up and let's go. I want this over with."

• • •

Kelli looked at her phone to get the time.

No kids wore watches anymore. Older people gave them as birthday and graduation presents but they ended up in drawers. A phone was everything, a clock, a calculator, a newscaster, a game, a camera, a lifeline.

Having said goodbye to her friends (the jeans mission successful), she walked along the brightly lit hallway of Ameri-Mall in the direction of the parking garage. Here was Claire's, full of trinkets. Here was Justice, full of Chinese shirts and jeans covered with American logos.

Unlike some friends, Kelli was not addicted to shopping and had no need for retail therapy but sometimes it was just good to be in a place that was a bubble away from the outside, the real world. A place that was undeniably cheerful, where you could find a new outfit, friendly people, a mochaccino with whipped cream—a place where you could forget, momentarily, that you'd be returning to a home without a father.

Something now caught her eye—in the window of a store just past Justice. A hairclip in the window. It was in the shape of a feather and would go well with her hair when she wore it up, which she did at cheer so she didn't get blinded during a spin or twist routine. It sparkled and shone—it seemed to "call her name," an expression of her father's when he'd noted she saw something she liked.

Oh, go ahead, girl, splurge.

She did, and a moment later was walking to the exit, swinging the small shopping bag in her hand.

She stepped through the double doors and into the dark stairway that led to what she called the "secret" portion of the garage, always deserted, so there were plenty of places to park. It was spooky, with the dimness, the dripping pipes, the groans, the rat droppings, the graffiti—why tag a wall here, when only a few people would see it?

Spooky . . .

Of course, it wouldn't be, she thought, if you had a gun in your pocket or purse.

Any threat she'd pull it out, aim it and—if he didn't back off—start firing.

But that wasn't going to happen.

She had no weapon on her.

Sure, when she'd found the guns in the cabinet at the Baileys', she'd thought about borrowing one, taking it into the woods and trying it out. He probably wouldn't even know, considering that he didn't seem to open the dusty box very often.

She'd satisfy that urge she'd had to go shooting with her father.

Well, she *was* older now.

But Kelli had decided, no. A gun wasn't for her.

Besides taking it from a client, even to borrow, was clearly breaking the babysitting protocols.

And that was something, Kelli had decided, she simply could not do.

• • •

Michael was in the garage beneath the Ameri-Mall.

Hiding in one of the spots he'd identified in his research. This part of the facility wasn't near the main entrance, and the stalls were mostly empty.

He'd been following the Object in the mall—certain he hadn't been seen—and was now near where the hit would take place. When he got within about fifteen yards from the kill zone, he stopped.

He'd created the shooting solution in the coffee shop and rehearsed it in his head a dozen times.

Research and preparation . . .

He pulled on the clear latex gloves and took his gun from his back waistband (the best place to stow larger pistols; they invariably displayed a profile when in a holster on your hip or even under your arm). The SIG-Sauer was a fine weapon, more complicated than a Glock but, in his opinion, more accurate. The caliber was 9mm and, compensating for their medium size, caliber, the slugs were hollow points that expanded upon hitting their target, devastating organs and muscles.

From his pocket Michael took a suppressor. He screwed the tube onto the muzzle. Pros like him objected to the word "silencer." For one thing, it was inaccurate; no gun would ever be silent. Also, hit men didn't like filmmakers and actors portraying them referring to the accessory inaccurately. It made them seem amateurish.

Suppressors over the years evolved from crude devices, tubes filled with rubber baffles, which lasted only three or four uses and fired out bits of material that the police could trace. Today, they were far more sophisticated, containing rings in carefully designed shapes, scientifically mounted in the tube. They worked by catching the hot gas from a gunshot and dispersing it slowly, so that the huge sound becomes an audible but quiet *thunk*.

Michael took one more item from his jacket: a C-clamp, the sort you can buy at hardware stores around the country. This he affixed to a pipe running from floor to ceiling. He rested his gun on it and aimed toward the target area. When he was tagging an Object with a firearm, he always used a rest. No pro shot freehand.

He looked at his watch.

How long would he have to wait?

Only seconds, it seemed.

The Object stepped into view at that very moment.

Michael had earlier chambered a round in the SIG. Firearm safety dictated that you not mount a suppressor on a loaded gun, and under other circumstances he would have followed that rule. But here, he couldn't risk mounting the suppressor first and then pulling the slide to chamber a bullet. The noise would be too recognizable; even someone who'd never touched a gun knew the distinctive metallic snapping from TV.

He would shoot three times. To effectively kill, you needed to obliterate your target, not risk merely wounding. He rested the weapon on the C-clamp and controlled his breathing. In, out. In, out. He increased pressure on the trigger.

Aim, breathe, squeeze . . .

Now!

Thunk, thunk, thunk . . .

The gun kicked hard. Blood and tissue sprayed everywhere.

• • •

Rachel Winston barked a scream and threw her hands up when the bullets blew apart the head of the man she'd been talking to, spattering her with gore.

Her husband screamed too.

The man, whose name was Larry Markus, had been counting

the money she'd just handed him when he collapsed. Bills fluttered everywhere.

"Jesus," Erik gasped. A pistol appeared in his hand and he swiveled around, crouching.

"No," came a whisper from the shadows.

Without a moment's hesitation Erik dropped the gun.

Sighing at her husband's cowardice, Rachel, not a bad shot, eyed the gun and debated scooping up the weapon.

"You too, lady" came the voice from the dark. "No." Whoever it was had seen her eyes—and therefore her intention.

She slumped.

A large man, pale, with thick salt-and-pepper hair, walked into the light. He was holding a suppressed gun, which was pointed toward them.

Rachel began, "Listen . . ."

"Shhh. Turn around."

"We didn't do anything," Erik whined. "We were just shopping. We—"

Rachel told her husband, "Shut up."

"Turn around," the man muttered, like a parent irritated at a difficult child. Just how they talked to William.

They turned around.

In the corner of her eye she was aware that the killer was bending down and collecting things. Probably Erik's and Markus's guns and the money.

He'd had them turn their backs so he could shoot them more easily if one of them made a move. She couldn't help but admire professionals, even at a time like this.

"All right," the killer said.

They faced him.

She said, "If you're from the Roberto organization—"

"Don't talk."

Erik began babbling. "We won't. We won't say a word, you let us go and—"

"Shut up." This time it was the shooter who'd snapped at him. The broad man now looked around carefully. He said, "It's good."

"What?" Rachel asked.

"I wasn't talking to you."

Another person stepped from the shadows and joined them. Rachel gasped.

It was Kelli Lambert, the babysitter.

"Hi, Uncle Mike," she said to the gunman and kissed him on the cheek.

• • •

Kelli looked down at the body.

"Who is he?" she asked.

Her uncle held up the man's wallet. "Larry Markus. I've heard of him. Trigger man out of Detroit. He'll tag anybody. Children, the elderly, the disabled." The tone of his voice made it clear how he felt about that.

She then looked over the married couple standing in front of the body, both of them spattered with blood and other icky stuff. Mr Winston's face was totally comical. It was a smile in a way but kind of distorted. She guessed it meant he was way freaked out. Was he going to puke? Kelli stepped back. It was so gross when people did that.

His wife's expression was calmer but it was still: WTF?

Kelli said, "We don't have a lot of time. You know." She glanced at the blood running down the floor toward a drain. Soon it would be out of the shadows and visible. "So, like, let's get to business."

"Business?" Mrs Winston muttered. Her face was growing red. Confusion had turned to anger.

Her uncle took over. "We know you're going to burn down the casino that Roberto and his crew owns and then start up one yourself."

Mrs Winston grimaced and lifted her palms toward her husband, like she was saying, "Told you so."

"We have it all on a tape. Do you want to hear it?"

"That's not necessary," Mrs Winston muttered. She looked at Kelli with a cold smile. "I assume when you were *pretending* to look for your goddamn games, you left a bug."

"Pretty much."

Michael continued, "And we heard the call of you arranging to take my niece out. And meeting here to pay Markus." Generally pretty calm and cool, he was now mad. And having Uncle Mike mad at you was not a good thing.

Kelli squinted as she recalled listening to the tape. "You said there was a nosey little bitch you needed dead. I.e., me." She smiled brightly. "Hey, I just learned something in school. Want to hear? 'I.e.'? It's Latin for *id est*. It means, 'That is.'" Latin was her favorite class, after coding.

Her uncle said evenly, "You can go ahead and burn down whatever you want. We don't care. But if you don't transfer two million into this bitcoin vault, a copy goes to the cops, FBI *and* the Roberto organization." He set a card on the concrete between them and stepped back. Mrs Winston nodded for her husband to collect it.

Mr Winston scurried forward. "But we're only clearing one mill. Where are we going to get—"

Uncle Mike said, "Not our problem."

"Shit." He collected the card.

Kelli said, "You know I think we need another million. That 'little bitch' part. What do you think, Uncle Mike?"

He was nodding with approval. He added to the couple, "Midnight tonight."

Mrs Winston whispered, "Three million? Impossible."

Kelli stared at her coolly and thought it was really neat when the woman looked away first.

A sigh. "All right. We'll get it."

Uncle Mike said, "Go on home. I'll finish up here." A nod toward the body and the hundred-dollar bills littering the garage floor. "And say hi to your mom for me. We'll be there Sunday for supper."

"Bye," Kelli said brightly and kissed his cheek once more. She started away but then turned back, looked toward the Winstons. "Oh, by the way: a five-dollar tip, for a whole *evening* babysitting? Seriously?"

• • •

Kelli Lambert sat at a metal table with rounded edges. It was bolted to the floor, as was the chair she was in. She was bored. She didn't have her phone with her and there was nothing to look at. No windows. Nothing on the walls, which were painted green and were scuffed. She would have painted them. She was pretty good with a roller and brush. She'd done her own room when she and her mother moved into the new house.

There was a shadow outside, in the corridor.

Her heart beat a little faster and she smiled when the door opened.

The guard let the man inside. He was fifty-two and had broad shoulders and a thin waist. He wore a gray jumpsuit with short sleeves. His arms were thick and his left forearm bore a tat in the shape of a dagger.

"Daddy!"

"Honey!"

Contact was against the prison rules, but they didn't apply when you were Tomas Milandic, the most powerful mob boss in the state. Anyway, also against the rules, the guard had left them alone, so who was to notice any infractions?

"You're too thin," he said, frowning as he stepped back and studied his daughter.

"Dad. I eat like a horse. I'm just at cheer practise five times a week, and we have a game every Friday night."

"Eat more."

"Then they couldn't catch me when I do an aerial. I'll be too big."

He glanced at her hair. "Hm. Nice. I like that."

She touched the feather clip she'd bought at the mall—at the store next to Justice: Tiffany's. It had cost five thousand dollars. Sometimes you just needed to splurge—especially when she was going to make the family seven figures that night.

She asked, "How's it going with the doctor?"

"It's working out good."

The prison offered psychological counseling. Her father was in group therapy with some cons diagnosed with antisocial personalities. They'd been convicted of all sorts of serious crimes, hijacking, robbery, assault and, some of the younger ones, hacking and cyber stalking and ransomware attacks. They were all recidivist offenders, and the prison officials were hoping to turn them around.

Her father, however, was not there to cure himself . . . or help cure anyone else. He wanted to make contacts he might use when he was released in four years and returned to the helm of the syndicate that *his* father—Kelli's grandad—had created thirty years ago.

"The Eagles?" he asked.

She grimaced. "Lost our second in a row." The John Adams High Eagles were not a stellar team.

"So, when I call my bookie?"

She thought for a minute. "They're playing Travis City. I say Travis. And the spread? Make it eight."

"I'll do it. How'd the babysitting gig go?"

She held up three fingers. "In the vault."

Her father beamed. "Three? One mill extra. You put together a good one. But then you always do."

Kelli had known from a young age what her father did—he'd had to tell her at ten or so that there were certain things in their life she couldn't talk about, to anybody. Money in the basement, certain visitors who arrived in limos with thick, tinted windows, the guns hidden behind books on the shelves.

He'd even told her there was a chance that "certain people"—i.e., the police—might catch him.

Which is just what happened last year. One of the lower-level runners in her father's company had turned them in. Her dad and some key friends in the crew were locked up for conspiracy.

Part of the sentence was forfeiting most of the family's money.

Young Kelli had liked the intrigue of his career outside the shipping business he ran . . . and liked the fact that her father had entrusted her with his secrets. She'd never participated, of course, but had quietly observed how he conducted business, whom he had over to the house, what they said and what plans they'd made.

After he was arrested Kelli, then sixteen, had done a lot of thinking about the situation. She'd come to visit him and said she had an idea. She was a popular babysitter. What if, on a job, she were to find something about the parents that was incriminating? They could blackmail them.

"Absolutely not," was his stern response.

At her next job, though, she'd left a plush bunny in the basket stuffed full of the children's toys in the family's living room. The cute thing had huge, floppy ears, a sweet smile, a round puffy tail . . . and, inside, a digital recorder. She'd collected the device a week later on another assignment at the house and listened to the ten hours of recorded conversations.

She told this to her father on their next visit.

"You did what?" he said angrily. "I said not to."

She lowered her head contritely. "I'm sorry, Daddy." But then she looked at him quizzically. "What's insider trading?"

His face softened. "Explain."

The bunny had caught the man using that phrase, along with the words that they had to be "really careful or we could get ten years."

Which told her that he was doing something that he wouldn't want anybody to know about.

And that he'd pay to keep quiet.

Her father had thought for a moment then said, "Have my brother get you a bug that's shielded from scanners. Mike knows where to go."

"Oh, they make those? That's neat."

The next few recordings captured the man's plan to use information to buy stock illegally. Uncle Mike had visited them and played some of the recordings. The shocked man had immediately transferred $250K to a bitcoin vault that Kelli and her uncle had set up.

Kelli and her mother moved to their new house in Mapleton. Going by her mother's last name and claiming her father had passed, she'd amped up her babysitting business, trying to get jobs in the homes of men and women like the Winstons—from a list that her Uncle Mike had supplied, people he and her father knew were engaging in criminal activities, and who had young children who would need babysitting occasionally.

On a job, Kelli would search the house for incriminating evidence, on the pretext of looking for games, and would plant the bugs. Her uncle followed up with the collection, making sure she stayed out of harm's way.

It would have been the same with the Winstons.

Except for hiring somebody to tag the "little bitch." Once her uncle learned that the hit man was going to be paid at Ameri-Mall, he'd told Kelli about it. She'd met with her friends beforehand and then headed down to the garage to wait until Uncle Mike had killed Markus. Then she'd confronted the pair and together they'd shaken them down for the three mil.

Her dad now said with a frown. "Mike told me, the latest job? They were going to tag you?"

She shrugged. "They hired some asshole from Michigan."

"Language," he said in that voice that parents sometimes use to correct their children when they don't really believe in the rule they were enforcing.

"Sorry. But it was cool. Uncle Mike's always there, right behind me."

"Just be careful. A father worries."

"I will. Promise." Then, "Oh, there's something else I want to do. I babysat for this family, the Baileys?"

"Are they on Mike's list?"

"No, this was a real job. They had this gun cabinet in the family room. Locked. But the kids could climb on a chair and get the key."

"Idiots," her father said, a dark expression on his face. He had very firm opinions about gun safety and youngsters.

When you're older . . .

"After they left, I opened the door and got a picture of the twins standing in front of it. I locked it up again and kept the key."

"What're you thinking? A hundred thousand to keep the pic off social media?"

"No, they're not bad people. They're just like, yeah, idiots. I thought I'd send them a copy of the picture and a note saying, 'Child Protective Services.' They'll get the message."

"That's my girl," he said, wearing a proud expression. "But they'll know it came from you. You'll never get a job from them again."

"No problem. Always a demand for babysitters with games and fresh-baked cookies."

The door opened. "Time," the guard said uneasily.

"Sure thing, Joey."

Father and daughter hugged again.

"See you next week, Daddy."

The man led her father into the hall and Kelli sat back down to wait for the escort to take her back to prison reception.

Forgotten

A Colter Shaw Story

I

"He's going to die in there. I mean, it's only a matter of time. My boy . . ." The man's voice choked. "There's a gang inside. Friends of the man that got killed."

Listening on his mobile, Colter Shaw noted the passive construction of the sentence. He didn't say: Friends of the man that Jude was *convicted* of killing. Though that was what had happened.

"They're out to get him. I know it! He's afraid to walk outside in the prison yard. He's afraid to eat meals."

"Can't they segregate him?"

"No. Or they won't."

"Has anyone else called about the reward?"

"A couple people," Arnie Sterling told him. "They didn't know anything about the case. They just wanted the reward money. And said they had alibis for Jude's whereabouts at the time of the murder. But it was just bullshit. They didn't know anything."

Exploiting tragedy. Colter Shaw had learned this happened often.

"You've tried private eyes?"

"One or two. They weren't interested. And I can't afford them anyway, not the good ones. It was all I could do to scrape up the reward. I mean, it's nothing, I know. But it's all we could think of to do."

"Let's get together. I can be there the day after tomorrow."

"Really?"

"Give me your address."

"Oh, thank you, sir! Bless you."

Shaw was spending this muggy June evening at his house in Florida. It was his fixed residence, though he spent little time in the place. The large, rustic craftsman home, on a lake, had plank oak floors, wormwood walls, leaded glass windows. The siding was natural shake shingles. It featured four bedrooms, a study, a kitchen built for someone who was a far better and more eager cook than Colter Shaw. Eclectic assortment of furniture. Ancient maps were his main decorations—he collected them.

The favorite feature was a long lake-facing porch for sipping coffee in the a.m. and beer ten hours later (where he presently was, and what he was presently drinking). People envied him, having such a homey, stylish place. He thought he should appreciate it more. Shaw was known in his family as "the restless one," and his abode tolerance was about thirty days, tops. It was then time for the road.

Shaw walked into the den, which was awash with brilliant light; the June sun was low in the west. He googled "Jude Sterling" and was surprised to find only three brief articles about the boy in the *Valley Register*, which covered the Ohio county where he lived. One was about his winning a long-distance foot race for his high school last year, setting a record. The other two were about the shooting.

Hanson Valley Resident Charged
In Shooting Death of Drug Dealer

January 14. Jude Anthony Sterling, an unemployed nineteen-year-old resident of Hanson Valley, was arrested yesterday and charged with second-degree murder and related offenses in the shooting death of Daryl Williams, twenty-nine, on January 12.

Williams was shot to death at the Mason Gravel and Rock Quarry off Pemberton Road. According to a Steuben County Sheriff's Office spokesman, the quarry is known as a place for drug sales among local youth. Authorities in Canton, where Williams lived, reported that he had a history of drug offenses in that city and in Akron.

The County Sheriff's Office spokesman added that drugs and cash, traceable to Williams, were found in Sterling's truck, immediately after the killing. The alleged murder weapon was also found in Sterling's truck.

Sterling was suspended from high school several times for fighting and drug possession, according to Department of Education records.

Arraignment is scheduled for tomorrow.

Colter Shaw turned to the second story, which was even shorter. It struck him as almost an afterthought.

Quarry Killer Found Guilty

May 17. Hanson Valley resident Jude A. Sterling was convicted today of second-degree murder in the death of Daryl Williams, twenty-nine, on January 12 of this year. He was also convicted of possession of controlled substances and larceny.

Williams, a known drug dealer, was shot in the back of the head by Sterling at the Mason Gravel and Rock Quarry. Sterling also robbed Williams of drugs and cash.

It took the jury three and a half hours to reach a verdict.

Despite pleas for leniency by his parents and some family members reading character statements, Judge Hanley Warwick Walker sentenced the defendant to twenty-five years to life.

2

Colter Shaw arrived in Hanson Valley, Ohio, at ten in the morning, after fourteen hours on the road. He'd made the journey in his gray, thirty-foot-long Winnebago, whose odometer registered just over 139,000 miles upon his arrival.

Shaw had owned four other RVs, similar to this one, over the past ten years. Two he traded in, according to his own admittedly arbitrary rule of thumb: when the odometer reached a quarter-million miles—ten times around the circumference of the earth at the equator. One camper was totaled in a crash in Colorado, in which he was injured, though not badly. The fourth was destroyed in Oklahoma City when a man threw a Molotov cocktail at it. The improvised explosive device didn't breach the windshield, but the flaming gasoline flowed into the body and burned the vehicle to the rims in twenty minutes.

Shaw, who was inside the RV at the time, escaped with most of his belongings. Six feet tall, and with a muscular build, he had been a champion wrestler at the University of Michigan and learned grappling—also known as street wrestling—from his father. When he located the bomb-flinger who had thrown the device, it took only five minutes to convince the man to turn himself in, which he did, though only after a brief stop in the emergency room to treat the man's dislocated shoulder.

In Hanson Valley, Shaw parked outside of the Sterlings' bungalow, located in a tattered section of town. They obviously weren't a family that could easily spare the $2,600 they were offering to anyone who could prove Jude was innocent of the murder. Arnie worked for the power authority doing line maintenance work; Jewel was a checker at Foster's, a local grocery store that had been in business for sixty-two years, a mom-and-daughter operation.

Shaw always met offerors—his term for those posting a reward—in person. This gave each party a chance to size the other up. He'd need their cooperation and that meant they'd have to be comfortable with him. He, too, always made sure the offerors were people he wanted to do business with. Once, he'd declined a forty-thousand-dollar reward for a runaway teen. He'd walked into the father's living room, noted the Nazi flag dominating one wall, and turned around and left, thinking to the teenager: Keep running, son, and good luck.

Arnie Sterling was a wiry man in his forties, with thinning flyaway reddish hair. His wife was heavy and her face was pinched, as if fraught with constant worry. They warmly welcomed Shaw into their cluttered kitchen and Jewel poured coffee. He declined baked goods.

"He got into a fight last night. This prisoner was baiting him. They finally broke it up but the guards don't really care."

Jewel added: "And there was a knifing yesterday, he told us." She was tearing up.

Shaw said, "Let me tell you how this'll work. You don't pay a penny of expenses. That's out of my pocket. If I find proof Jude is innocent, *and* he's released, then you owe me the money. But not until then."

The husband and wife regarded each other. He said, "Seems fair."

"More than fair." Jewel dabbed her eyes.

Arnie said, "We might be able to add to it, the reward, I mean. A cousin of mine is—"

"No, the reward's fine. Twenty-six hundred's what you offered. That's what's on the table."

The husband gave a perplexed look. "You got a funny way of running a business, Mister."

Shaw smiled. He produced a notebook and his favorite fountain pen, an Italian model, black with its trademark three orange rings.

For an hour the parents talked about their son and the case, and answered Shaw's questions, during which time Jewel kept the coffee mugs filled and Arnie would step outside every so often for a smoke. Shaw took copious notes, writing in small elegant letters, with each line perfectly horizontal although the notebook was not ruled. This was not a skill he worked at; he'd inherited it from his father. Curiously, his sister, Dorion, and brother, Russell, did not get the calligraphy gene.

Slowly a picture of the young man emerged.

Jude didn't do well in school. He suffered from attention deficit disorder. "He was hyper a lot of the time," Jewel said. "Just going, going, going. All the time. It could be exhausting to be around him. Of course, this frustrated him, too, and made him angry. He'd tend to act out a lot."

The school counselor recommended therapists, but the Sterlings were unable to afford anyone other than a strip-mall psychopharmacologist, who saw Jude once every two months to prescribe and monitor his various medications. Success with the drugs was hit-or-miss.

Shaw asked about the newspaper report on the boys' troubles in high school.

"That was such bullshit, that story. Why'd they write that?" The father's cheeks flushed. "Jude got into some fights in school. Like we all did, like everybody did,"

He was suspended a few times because of it. Only once, in the ninth grade, were the police called. It was a bad fight and the other boy was bloodied. But the prosecutor declined to take the case to trial and Jude was let go. He faced several trespass and shoplifting charges but there was never the evidence—or maybe the energy— to pursue those cases either.

"And the drugs?" Jewel scoffed. "A little pot. And that reporter, you ask me, he hasn't been in *any* high school in the twenty-first century. Half the students smoke something. And pot's the least of it."

While his grades were not good, he showed talent in art and talked often about creating a superhero comic book series or writing graphic novels. (English and art were the only courses in which he ever received a grade as high as a B.) He didn't do well at team sports but competed successfully in track and field; his sport was long-distance running, and for a year he held his school's record for the ten-thousand-yard run. He still jogged regularly.

Shaw could only imagine what living in a ten-by-ten cell was like for a fleet-footed young man like Jude.

After graduation, Jude worked at a series of odd jobs—landscaping, fast-food, sorting packages at an international parcel delivery warehouse, stocking at an auto-parts shop.

When he was between jobs, which was often, he'd just sit home, watching horror and superhero films, sketching in notebooks, smoking pot.

"And after high school? Drugs?"

His father told Shaw, "Never meth or coke, anything like that. It's just that pot'd calm him down. He gets . . . Okay, I'll be honest, Mr Shaw. He gets angry. He's got that side to him."

"Angry about what?"

The mother shrugged. "Stuff. Can't get a job, not a good one. And the ones he gets, he gets laid off. Not just him, but everybody around here."

Hanson Valley, Arnie explained, had been a busy mill and dairy farming town in the nineteenth and early twentieth centuries, but as had happened in countless locales of similar size and economies, the fortunes of the town plummeted with the loss of industrial work overseas and the edging out of local producers by mega-farms. "Unemployment in his age group? Was thirty per cent last year."

Jewel said, "And he gets mad about what happened to his brother."

The Sterlings' younger son, Frank, fifteen, was disabled. Eight years ago, the car in which he was riding was struck by a pickup that crossed the centerline, the driver hotdogging and passing on a curve. No one else was badly injured but Frank Sterling's resulting brain trauma left him emotionally and cognitively disabled. The boy was in the public school's Special Needs program. The driver was a county official's son and got only a ticket. This continued to infuriate Jude.

"But whatever you hear people say, he's not so mad he wants to hurt anybody."

Finally, Shaw capped the pen and rose. "I think I have enough to get started with."

Arnie walked Shaw to the door. "Bless you, sir. You're the only one listening. We just couldn't believe he was convicted of murder. We tried to talk to the lawyer, the police, the press, the parents of the kids who were at the quarry that day. They wouldn't pay us any mind. Nobody cares. Just like that"—he snapped his fingers—"the whole world forgot about him."

3

Over the next few days Shaw approached nearly forty people in and around Hanson Valley, about one half per cent of the population of Steuben County, looking for information from friends of Jude and his family, classmates, co-workers, teachers, other family members.

The majority of them declined to speak with him, but fourteen people were willing to talk, some over coffee or a beer or, in several instances, a meal Shaw paid for. The interviews were largely nonproductive; the folks he spoke with offered opinions like, "Oh, I couldn't believe he'd do it." Or: "He has a temper, I've seen it. He gets all scary."

Colter Shaw's father, a former professor turned survivalist in California, had compiled a lengthy list of rules, most of which began with "Never."

Never assume October ice is thick enough to walk on.

Never assume a mother bear is more than ten seconds away from her cubs.

Ashton Shaw formulated some more general rules too, one of which was: *Never make decisions based on opinion, only facts.*

And it wasn't opinions about Jude Sterling's character that Shaw was presently after. He wanted *facts*: details, even if second hand, about what might have happened on January 12 at the quarry, the days leading up to the events, and the days following.

He spoke—by phone—with the author of the *Valley Register* pieces but the man couldn't offer any other specifics. Arnie and Jewel had spoken to him and asked if he could look into their son's arrest, but he wasn't, he explained, an investigative journalist. He was a police blotter reporter who also handled the classified advertising department.

He spent a half hour with Jude's attorney. Arnold Cummings was a fifty-year-old general practitioner in Hanson Valley who— Shaw had learned from a private eye he used occasionally (and whose fee often ate up much of the reward)—was the town's main criminal lawyer, though he handled mostly DUI, domestic abuse and minor drug possession offenses.

Cummings, a big man wearing a rumpled seersucker suit, was clearly overworked and distracted. His desk was piled high with folders. When Shaw explained about the reward and his role here, the lawyer was, curiously, not defensive that someone was revisiting the conviction. Shaw's impression was that Cummings believed he'd done an adequate job for the fee he'd been paid—probably bargain basement. The case was done, and he had no more interest in the forgotten boy.

"What're you, a private eye?"

"Like that."

"And they offered a reward . . . Well, it's a waste of your time and their money. He did it," Cummings said. "Classic case. Kids, not working, hanging out, drugs, guns."

"Did he admit it?"

"No, but who does?" The man swept off his glasses and cleaned them on the tail of his blue and white sport jacket. "Tough about the sentence, have to say. But Judge Warwick's a hard-ass. I'd've thought you whack a drug dealer, you're doing a community service. Ten to twelve would've been good. But the back-of-the-head thing was a problem for him, I guess."

"You have a copy of the transcript?" Shaw asked.

This was public information, not subject to the attorney client privilege.

"You can get one at the courthouse," Cummings muttered, then looked coyly at Shaw. "Course, they'll charge you fifty cents a page." He cocked his head. "From me, it'll only cost you a quarter."

. . .

Shaw piloted the Winnebago to Watkins, the site of the medium-security prison where Jude Sterling was incarcerated.

The place was a nondescript, one-story facility, gray and sterile, outside of which flew two flags: one American and one Ohioan. Shaw had a familiarity with prisons—the inhabitants often being good sources for information on his reward jobs. He had also pursued rewards offered by department of corrections officials for escapees, though those didn't happen as often as TV and the movies might suggest. He called older prisons "Brick-and-Bars" and the newer ones "Windows," referring to the ubiquitous inch-thick impenetrable glass. Watkins was one of the latter, constructed probably ten years ago.

Shaw sat in the pungent interview room, musty, for five minutes before Jude was brought in. The narrow-faced boy was six one and skinny. He had shaggy reddish hair, his father's shade. His complexion was pale, and that pallor was accentuated by the orange jumpsuit, which was too big for him.

His dark eyes were cautious.

Shaw introduced himself with a smile. He needed the boy at ease and had to show he was on Jude's side. They were not allowed to shake hands, and the boy nodded and sat with a jingle of cuffs.

"Your father and mother've offered a reward to see if anybody can maybe find some evidence or a witness that you're innocent."

No response.

Shaw was looking at the back of the boy's hand. "What's that?"

Jude held it up and shrugged. "Wasp Man."

It was a drawing of a creature—a man from the waist up, below that, a wasp, a superhero, Shaw guessed. It was well done.

"From a movie?"

"Naw. I made it up. It's not a tat. I drew it."

"It's good." Shaw remembered his aptitude for art and his love of comics.

The boy stared at the drawing. He made a fist and straightened his fingers out.

"I know some things about what happened in January, Jude. I'd like you to tell me your side."

In fits and starts, backing the narrative up and pushing it forward—and with stops for Shaw's questions along the way—the young man told his story.

Twenty minutes later he sat back.

"What do you think, sir?"

"You've given me a lot to work with." He rose.

There was motion outside the window in the door and Jude and Shaw looked up. A guard was walking with a compact, dark-complexioned prisoner, who stared at Jude with a cold grin and fierce pinpricks of black eyes.

Jude startled Shaw by actually shivering—not in fear but in rage. He shouted, "Asshole!" The guard wagged a take-it-easy finger toward Jude and he sat back. Was this the prisoner he'd had the dustup with?

He inhaled and exhaled deeply, then calmed. "Can you get me out, Mister?"

"It's hard to overturn a conviction." Colter Shaw knew this. He had considered law school at one point and had done some paralegal work. A good field for a restless mind, bad for a restless body.

"But I'll do everything I can."

4

Back in the camper, which was parked in a Walmart lot, Shaw brewed a cup of Kenyan coffee and, after adding some milk, sat down at the banquette and reviewed the trial transcript and his notes. He reconstructed what had happened on that freezing cold day in mid-January.

The story began about 2:30 p.m. on January 12. Jude was planning to pick Frank up at school, as he often did if their parents were working. But an accident on the Klamath River Bridge stopped traffic. His brother did not have a cell phone, so Jude called the school to say he'd be late, and a secretary said she would tell Frank that his brother was on his way.

When Jude arrived, though, he learned the message hadn't been delivered and Frank had taken a ride with some students. They were a sophomore, Erik; two seniors, Travis and Carli—all attending Frank's high school; and a freshman at a nearby community college, Michael.

In her statement to police, Carli said that the four students had told Frank they would take him home but had to run an errand first—driving to the Mason Gravel quarry to meet Daryl Williams to buy drugs. (Shaw was surprised at the candor—until he saw a prosecution memo in which it was decided to waive any narcotics charges against the students at the quarry that day, in exchange for their cooperation. He guessed the prosecution could run a drug case anytime it wanted in a county like this one; homicide would be a rarity—and a conviction a feather in the cap of a small-time DA.)

"Michael had this idea we could say we had this sick kid we were taking care of and Daryl'd maybe give us a better deal on the stuff."

When Jude arrived at the school and learned who it was that Frank had left with, and where they were going, he "stone cold freaked." He thought about calling the Sheriff's Office but if his brother was arrested it would have been a disaster for Frank to be held in detention even briefly.

Jude sped to the Mason Gravel quarry to look for the students and his brother.

The quartet told investigators that when they got to the quarry they knew Darryl Williams was there too; they'd been in touch with him on their mobiles. But they weren't sure exactly where he was. The grounds were huge; the deep, shadowy pit was surrounded by thirty-five acres of forests and fields.

Carli said, "It was like 'We're under these three big trees and there's a hill on the right, and a rock.' And he's like, 'It's all fucking trees and hills and rocks. Be like more specific, or something.'"

The students split up into two groups to look for him. Carli, Michael and Frank went in one direction. Travis and Erik went in another.

"We found Darryl first," Carli testified. The dealer was in one of the clearings, angry because he was cold and that the students were by then a half hour late. The deal couldn't be completed yet, though, because Travis had the money. Carli called him and told him where they were. He said he'd be there in five minutes.

At that moment Frank Sterling had a panic attack, which wasn't uncommon when the boy was in stressful situations. He began screaming and grappling with Michael and the dealer, who shoved him away and stepped back, shouting for him to calm down, which only made Frank more upset. That's when there was a gunshot from the trees and Williams dropped to the ground. The two students, Carli and Michael, fled, leaving Frank curled in a ball, still hysterical, staring at the dealer's body and screaming.

A few minutes later, Michael slipped back to the clearing again, looking for Erik and Travis. As he did, he saw Jude holding the gun. Michael found the two other students and they hurried to the car and left. Travis and Erik had seen nothing of the shooting. They were near the two-hundred-foot-deep quarry pit itself, which wasn't fenced, and were concentrating on both looking for Williams—and watching where they stepped.

Jude Sterling's account was this:

After he arrived at the quarry he drove over the truck paths until he noticed a car. He drove to it and parked. The car was a Subaru Outback, Williams's. He saw no one inside the vehicle. After walking the grounds for about five minutes he heard voices in a clearing thirty or so yards away. Jude started in that direction. A moment later he heard screaming—his brother. Then he heard the gunshot. Panicked, he ran toward the sound. On a path that led into the clearing, he found the pistol on the ground and picked it up.

"I, like, didn't know what was going on. Maybe somebody else had a gun."

In the clearing, Jude was shocked to see Williams lying there, he said, but concentrated on calming Frank down—and looking around for a threat. "I didn't know what was going on. It was just all so weird." Finally he got Frank under control. They were about to leave when Jude bent down and went through the dealer's pockets and took a half-dozen bags of marijuana and four hundred dollars in cash. "I shouldn't've, I know. I just, I was pissed Frank was upset, so I took it. And I was thinking maybe those assholes from school would come back and I didn't want them to get the stuff and the money."

He and his brother returned to the pickup and drove home. On the way he told Frank not to say anything to their parents about what had happened. The brother said he wouldn't.

The actual crime was much more complicated and nuanced than the tale contained in those two brief newspaper articles Shaw had found online, which made it sound that Sterling meant to murder Williams for his money and drugs.

But this did not surprise Shaw, who had been press fodder on a number of occasions in the reward-seeking business.

Never accept any story on its face . . .

He wondered how many jurors had read the brief article and, in their minds, voted the boy guilty even before opening statements had begun.

5

Shaw assessed the trial, which seemed to him to have proceeded very quickly; the transcript was quite brief for a criminal trial.

On the prosecution side, the convenience store clerk testified about seeing Jude's truck. He had in his possession the murder weapon and drugs and cash traceable to the victim. The DA conceded that the gun was not Jude's—there was testimony that he'd never owned a weapon, had no interest in them—but he told the jury that Jude had found the Smith & Wesson in Williams's Subaru; it held traces of Williams's DNA.

As for motive the DA offered the theory that in addition to stealing the drugs and money, Jude believed Williams was threatening his panicking brother. "The defendant simply lost control." One prosecution witness testified that he had seen Jude lose his temper in the past, especially when his brother was in jeopardy. He'd once badly beaten a student who was bullying Frank. This was the assault that got Jude arrested.

Another student testified that Jude had once said if anybody "hurts my brother, they're dead."

Michael testified that he'd seen Jude with the gun in the clearing.

The defense case wasn't stellar.

Attorney Cumming pointed out there was no gunshot residue on Jude's hands, but that was countered with: he'd thrown away the gloves he'd worn or scrubbed his hands thoroughly when he got home.

He argued that the shooter could have been one of the other four students, intent on robbing the dealer. They had been startled by Jude's arrival and fled, leaving behind the drugs and cash, but the DA pointed out the absence of their DNA and fingerprints on the gun and of gunshot residue on their hands or gloves (though the same argument about pitching the gloves and washing hands would apply to them too, a rebuttal, though, that Cumming did not offer.)

One witness who did not testify was Frank. The prosecutor understood the boy's disabled condition and both sides stipulated that he need not appear at trial but be deposed. The boy said that he didn't remember anything of the shooting. He had a "bad moment," apparently his term for a panic episode. He recalled lying on the ground, curled up, trying to picture his "safe space."

It took the jury three hours and twelve minutes to convict Jude.

• • •

Shaw walked into the Steuben County Sheriff's Office, where he asked to see Detective Sonja Malloy.

As he waited in the small entry hall, he thought: Odds this'll be productive? Ten per cent tops.

Still, the woman, in her thirties, handsome, eyes still and unsmiling, came to collect Shaw and escort him back to her office.

He had not worn his concealed weapon because when you go to police stations, that causes all kinds of high-blood pressure.

Malloy seemed sharp, well-organized, conscientious. The folders on her desk—all closed when he arrived in her small, cramped office—were laid out according to date, presumably in order of priority. There were a lot of them, and more on the credenza behind her. It told Shaw that the department was overstretched—like lawyer Cummings's firm. Not much incentive to look too deeply into a—literally—smoking gun case. Take the fast and easy ones when you can. Close them quickly and move on.

Shaw explained to Malloy that Sterling's father had offered a reward for information that would lead to his son's being exonerated either by identifying another individual as the killer or uncovering facts that would prove Sterling was innocent of the crime. Shaw had come to town for that reward.

Unlike the lawyer, Malloy was clearly defensive at his presence. She told Shaw that he would have no access to police reports, statements or other documentation, only information that was already in the public record. Shaw confirmed that he understood this. He said, "I'm sure it was a righteous investigation. It's just that the parents will feel a lot better knowing that everything was done for their boy. His life is over with."

She didn't seem moved. He wondered if she had children herself. Shaw had noted no wedding band and there were no pictures of husband or offspring on the desk, but this was often true about law enforcers. Since suspects—some murderous, some psychotic—were occasionally in their offices, they tended to avoid displaying evidence of their families.

"You do this for a living? Rewards?"

"That's right."

Now she seemed less defensive—because, he sensed, she wasn't taking him seriously. He got this some.

"What do you want to know?"

"What's the story with Daryl Williams?"

"High-level dealer. One of the main sources of meth, fent and oxy in this part of the state. I will tell you, Mr Shaw, I'm not troubled he's no longer with us."

"Was this his turf?"

"Steuben County's a free trade zone. We get some peddlers from Akton—that's Akron and Canton. Nobody as big as Williams usually, though,"

"So he'd have rivals."

"You're thinking somebody drove down here, shot him during a deal and left the gun. Make it look like the sale went bad, or the buyers tried to perp his supply?"

"Just considering options."

"Except Williams sold wholesale too. He had solid suppliers from out west. A retail dealer wouldn't take him out. They'd need his product—the quality and quantity were too good."

Shaw said, "What about the just-plain-crazy factor? One druggy takes out another one because it's Throwback Thursday."

He thought that might earn a smile.

It didn't.

"Just one more thing and I'll leave you to it. Inventory of Williams's Subaru?"

She hesitated. This was edging into not-public-info territory. Then she turned and dug a file out of the cabinet behind her. She found a document. "Front seat. Fast-food wrappers, Burger King sixteen-ounce cup of cola, unwashed socks and a T-shirt. Six dime bags of pot, five one-gram bags of meth. A hoodie."

"Anything in the trunk?"

"Six-pack of Budweiser. A box of Fiocchi 9mm slugs. Two of Remington .380s. Look, sir, from what you know about the case, I assume you read in the transcript that Jude threatened to kill anybody who hurt his brother."

"It's an expression. How many times have you heard people say, 'I'm going to kill so and so'?"

"In my line of work, pretty often. And sometimes they mean it. Let me ask you a question: How much is the family offering?"

"That's for them to tell you."

"Well, it's probably more than they can afford. Be a shame if somebody pitched the idea of their boy's innocence just for the sake of taking their money."

"I don't get a penny unless Jude walks."

This brought her up short. Then she added, "Did you know, Mr Shaw, that when Michael saw Jude in the clearing, he cocked the gun and pointed it at Daryl Williams's head? He was going to shoot him again."

Shaw paused. "That wasn't in the transcript."

"Judge struck the testimony."

"But he *didn't* pull the trigger, did he?"

"No need to at that point—he realized he was aiming at a dead man." Then the patience was gone. "Now, sir, I have some active cases to get to."

6

In the morning, Shaw sipped coffee as he looked over an email from Mack McKenzie, his PI. She had sent him a dozen images—surveillance and mugshots—from some of the more powerful organized crime figures in the Canton–Akron area. He transferred these to his phone.

Then, he fired up the camper and went in search of the four students who'd been at the quarry on January 12.

It didn't take much time to find them. Their names were in the transcript, and Hanson Valley was a small town. He first tracked down Carli Trent and Michael Nagler, who happened to be together at the place where she worked.

Carli was a slim blond, with a tasteful tat of a porpoise on her neck. There was undoubtedly more ink elsewhere but in keeping with today's fashion, she was in layers of garments, the outer a long-sleeved sweatshirt. Michael was a good-looking jock, with longish hair, also blond. A blue jeans and T-shirt kind of guy. This particular garment was printed with a tour poster of a band Shaw had never heard of, which was most of them in the history of pop and rock music. Michael seemed pleasant enough, though Shaw recalled it had been his idea to exploit the disabled Frank to try for a discount from Williams.

Carli was behind the counter of a dingy coffee shop on a side street in downtown Hanson Valley. Michael was hanging out between classes. It wasn't a coincidence they were here together; from their conversation Shaw could tell they were dating.

He asked for a cup of "South American Import." Given that the place smelled more of Lysol than rich, roasted beans, he was expecting stale Folgers, but in fact, it turned out to be a pretty good brew (though he identified it as Guatemalan, not from the lower hemisphere, as the chalk-board menu promised).

He added some milk and, when she was between customers, said to both of them, "I'm in town helping out Jude Sterling's parents. I'm looking into the case about a possible appeal. Can I ask you a few questions?"

Shaw was in a sport coat and dress shirt; they probably put him down as a lawyer or legal assistant.

"I guess." From Michael.

Carli said, "I never liked him, Jude, I mean. His brother was sweet, poor kid. But Jude, always kind of weird."

"Freaky," Michael said.

Again, no interest in opinions. "You didn't actually see him shoot Daryl Williams, right?"

Michael shook his head. "No."

"Uh-uhn." Carli was enthusiastically wiping down the cappuccino machine.

Shaw said to Michael, "I understand you came back to the clearing, looking for Travis and Erik."

"Not in the clearing. I walked past it."

"But you saw Jude cock the gun and point it at Daryl."

"Yeah. I thought he was going to shoot him again but he didn't. Then I found Trav and Erik, and we booked out of there."

"You don't know how long it was between the shot and when Jude walked into the clearing."

With a glance at her boyfriend, Carli said, "Man, after the shot, we just ran."

"I want to show you some pictures. These are some dealers from Canton and Akron. Did you happen to see any of them around town on January 12?"

He turned his phone so they could see the pictures he'd downloaded that morning. "I've got this idea that one of them followed Williams to the quarry and killed him. Then left the gun to make it look like it was a deal gone bad. Jude just happened to find it"

They examined each shot carefully as Shaw scrolled through the images.

At the end, Carli shook her head and tugged at one of her—hard to count—dozen or so earrings. Michael said, "Nope. I mean, I guess somebody else *could've* done it. But we didn't see any other cars there." He looked at his girlfriend, who continued the negative shake.

Shaw thanked them and said, "Good coffee by the way."

Carli offered a slightly confused glance. He guessed compliments on the products were few and far between.

Shaw returned to the camper.

Because Erik Summers was under eighteen, Shaw placed a call to his father and asked if he could have a conversation with the boy—in the parents' presence. The man said, "What, you think Jude's innocent?" He gave a cold laugh.

"I'm just looking into the case, for his parents."

"Erik didn't do anything wrong. He got sucked in by those older assholes."

"I just want to show your son some pictures. See if he recognizes anyone. They're men who might've had a motive to kill Williams."

From the phone there came another harsh laugh, raw, almost unhinged. "You crazy? Jude Sterling's a psycho. Of *course*, he killed that dealer. You stay out of my way. You try to talk to my son, you don't know the crap you'll be in."

The tone suggested he kept a shotgun near the door.

Shaw asked if he could at least leave a number in case he changed his mind.

The father hung up on him.

The fourth student, Travis Lanford, was willing to talk. Shaw met the lanky blond young man outside a Lions Club, where he'd just attended an AA meeting.

The boy—a star football player, Shaw had learned—said, "The quarry, what happened there, it fucked me up. I started meetings the next day." He explained that he'd been hooked on meth for more than a year. He was ruining his life but he couldn't do anything about it—until the "wake-up call": the shooting. He'd been sober since then.

"Good job," Shaw said. "It's tough, I understand."

"Yeah. One day at a time."

Shaw asked if he'd seen Jude in the clearing.

"No. Erik and me, we didn't even know it was Jude with the gun until we were in Mike's car and booking out of the place. We heard the shot and it was like, shit, and we just took off."

Shaw explained his theory that another dealer might have killed Daryl. He showed him the pictures of the dealers, and Travis looked them over closely. "No, never seen any of them. Sorry."

"Appreciate you looking."

"You don't think he did it?"

"Just getting facts. Don't have any opinions yet."

He nodded back to the Lions Club. "There's this Greater Power thing in the program. I don't know if Jude's into it. I don't really know him. But if he does believe, maybe you're the answer to his prayers."

• • •

The drive to Canton took forty-five minutes. Shaw had made a reservation at an RV camp named Bide a Wee (Scottish for "Stay a little"—one of the most common names for camper parks). He bought a hookup spot and parked the Winnebago. Occasionally he used his Yamaha motorbike on jobs. But for this one, he chose to rent a sedan. For one thing, cycles are conspicuous and he needed to be as invisible here as spring air.

For another, someone driving two wheels is a lot more vulnerable than someone driving four.

After leaving the Avis lot, Shaw drove to a nearby diner. He pulled into the parking lot, walked inside a place decorated in the style of the Fifties—there was a cutout of Marilyn Monroe on the wall—and sat at the counter. He ordered coffee and a tuna salad sandwich.

Shaw once again read the profiles Mack had prepared of the local crew members. One seemed more promising than the others. His name was Orin Trimbeaux and he was a mid-level drug and gun dealer who'd been detained for selling weapons in Steuben County, though he'd been released.

Trimbeaux was a short, wiry man of mixed race, Black and Anglo. He had spent nearly a quarter of his thirty-eight years inside prisons or detention centers. Drug offenses, weapons, assault. He'd also done time for domestic abuse (two different girlfriends were the complaining witnesses, and the offenses happened within days of each other—which was probably a record of some sort).

The reports that social workers, defense psychiatrists, and parole officers submitted for Trimbeaux's various appearances in the judicial system were consistent: he was of above-average intelligence but had been diagnosed as suffering from borderline personality disorder, was given to paranoia and bouts of temper and presented with extreme narcissistic tendencies.

Trimbeaux's current address was a rental in a run-down

neighborhood in Canton. Shaw parked across the street from the two-story, single-family house, a hundred years old, and waited for the dealer to appear. He knew someone was inside, because of the flicker of a TV screen, and he soon could detect that Trimbeaux had several visitors, two men and two women. Shaw kept up the stake-out for six hours straight, with only one break to use a restroom and buy food and drink.

At eight that night Trimbeaux emerged, disheveled and appearing tired or maybe drunk in his unsteady gait. Shaw followed him on foot to Washington Street, a four-lane commercial avenue lined with bars, fluorescent-lit restaurants offering functional food, nail salons, shops selling wigs and hair extensions, payday loan businesses, delis.

Shaw tailed the dealer into Erin's Tavern, a scuffed and pungent bar. Above the door was a sign informing patrons that it had been founded in 1972. Shaw didn't doubt it. The cobwebs in the corners and grime on the walls and ceiling were credible evidence.

After waving to the bartender, Trimbeaux sat at a table with four other men, who greeted him with fist bumps and bro hugs. One was Anglo and about twenty-five, two were Black and in their thirties and one appeared to be Latino and was in his forties or fifties.

When he was working, Shaw favored black jeans and dress shirts and dark sports jackets, as he'd worn earlier today. Now, though, he'd picked a shabby black windbreaker. He had not shaved in two days, an intentional choice. He wore too a logo-free baseball cap. He'd muddied his Ecco black slip on shoes. He blended.

At the bar he ordered a Jack Daniels and a ginger ale, in separate glasses. He sipped the soft drink, not the bourbon, and pretended to examine his iPhone screen while watching Trimbeaux and the others in the dark mirror behind the bar.

They were laughing, gesturing to the greasy TV screen occasionally, complaining to the bartender about the temperature, and one-upping each other with stories about street exploits. Trimbeaux's mood would change abruptly, from giddiness to anger to paranoia. Most others at the table were clearly afraid of him. Shaw noted that the Latino was not. He wasn't one of the crew; Shaw guessed he was with another gang or a supplier.

There were few other patrons and Shaw noticed that several of the men at the table, including Trimbeaux, glanced his way occasionally. Shaw had wanted to stay longer but decided it was prudent to leave.

Never assume your enemy isn't suspicious . . .

He finished the ginger ale, poured the whisky into the taller glass, to hide that he hadn't drunk any, and paid and left.

As a reward seeker, Shaw did a great deal of surveillance. Which meant that he also had a sense of when *he* was being followed. Now, in the deserted streets of this harsh portion of Canton, he believed someone was tailing him. After unbuttoning his jacket to ease drawing his concealed-carry Glock, he aimed his phone, in selfie video mode, behind him. He stopped and looked at the vid. Too dark, too hard to tell for sure, but it was possible that a figure was following, sticking to the shadows.

He returned to his car near Trimbeaux's, climbed in and made a quick U-turn. There was no one that he could see, but if the person had been following, he could have slipped into a narrow alley between a restaurant up for bankruptcy sale and a vaping store. He drove past Erin's and glanced in the window.

Trimbeaux and most of his crew were still there. The Latino was not.

A half hour later, in the Winnebago, he shut the interior lights out and studied the RV camp grounds. He didn't see any surveillance. He locked the door, showered and went to bed.

His Glock was on the table beside him.

Before he fell asleep, his phone hummed.

"Hello?"

"Mr Shaw." The man's voice was urgent. "It's Arnie Sterling. There was a fight. He got stabbed, Jude. One of the prisoners—a friend of Daryl Williams."

"How is he?"

"They won't tell me! Just that it was bad. He's in the prison hospital. I asked if he could go to the city ER, but they won't do it." The man was near tears. "What've you found?"

"I have one lead. I can't say that it'll pay off. If it doesn't then I don't have much else that'll help him."

"The prisoner who stabbed him is in solitary but there'll be somebody else. Maybe they can get into the hospital and finish what they started."

"I should know by tomorrow."

A pause. Arnie's voice choked as he said, "If it's not too late."

7

The next day, in a brown leather baseball cap and sunglasses, Shaw followed Trimbeaux, again on foot, from his house to a dive of a pizzeria, where the dealer met once again with the Latino from the night before.

Even in new clothes and the shades, Shaw didn't want to risk getting made as the suspicious man in the bar last night, so he waited across the street, sipping coffee in an outdoor café, from where he could watch the men through the pizza place's large, smeared plate-glass windows. They split a large pie and halfway through the meal, when the counterman and other patrons weren't looking their way, Trimbeaux slid the Latino a thick envelope and received in return a slip of paper, which the dealer pocketed without glancing at.

Shaw knew transactions like this. The supplier—the Latino— had received cash in the envelope and, in return, he had given Trimbeaux the address of where the product he'd just purchased was hidden and ready for pickup. Maybe a safe deposit box or a locker at a local bus station.

The two men left. Shaw didn't follow them. As soon as they turned the corner on a side street, he entered the pizzeria and sat on an unsteady chair at the table next to where the two men had been seated.

The counterman moved in with a gray bin to bus the dishes.

"Hold on there a minute, will you?" Shaw stopped the sweaty, heavy-set man, who blinked in surprise.

"Yeah?"

Shaw said in a low voice, "You have two options."

"I'm sorry?"

"One, call your lawyer and tell him you're about to be arrested on a RICO charge for using your place of business for illegal organized crime transactions."

He blustered, "The hell you talking about? I—"

"Shhh. Listen to option number two."

The blustering stopped.

"You take this three hundred dollars." Shaw proffered the bills. "And tell me the name of Trimbeaux's friend. Latino. Wearing a black and gray shirt."

"I don't get what game you're playing, Mister, but you're looking for trouble."

Shaw had heard some bad lines flung his way from time to time. This was one of the worst.

The man was big, yes, but not muscle big, fat big. Anyone can bluster, anyone can threaten. The danger is in the five per cent who don't, the five per cent who simply look you over and silently proceed to hurt or kill.

The counterman was squarely in the ninety-five per cent.

Shaw continued, "Option one or option two?"

The eyes filled with dismay. "You don't know what you're doing, buddy. Nobody fucks with Orin Trimbeaux."

Another bad line.

Shaw cocked an eyebrow. "Two hundred more if you give me the Latino guy's *address* too . . . Or should I just call the Organized Crime Division of the County Sheriff's Office."

Shaw wondered if they actually had one.

The man looked around, as if there were anybody here to come to his rescue. Nope. He was on his own. Finally, a whisper, "Eduardo Garcia."

"And he lives where?"

"I don't know! Not exactly. I think Miller Street, near Eberhardt Square."

It was good enough. Shaw gave him the full five. "I need something else too."

"What?"

"A to-go bag."

"You want a slice?" Nodding at the congealing pizzas behind the counter.

"No. Just a bag."

. . .

In the mid-afternoon, Shaw, piloting his rental, followed Trimbeaux once again from his apartment. This time the man was in a black Cadillac Escalade. He drove to a storage locker outside of town, near the interstate. This was presumably where Eduardo Garcia's wares had been stashed.

Shaw watched Trimbeaux emerge with two heavy suitcases. Which he stashed in the back of the Caddie. The dealer fired it up and steered onto the highway. A half hour later, the SUV turned into the weedy parking lot of an abandoned factory. Continuing past it, Shaw pulled into a neighboring property. After he parked, he climbed from the sedan and walked to a stand of trees where he had a good view of Trimbeaux in the parking lot. It wasn't long before two cars showed up. One was a dusty gray pickup, an F250. The other a tricked-out muscle car, big-spoke chrome wheels. Its color was dark red.

Shaw started recording a video on his phone and set it against a tree, the lens facing the parking lot. Then looking through Swarovski binoculars as he nestled prone, in dry grass, he watched the transaction. Three men from what Shaw guessed was a white supremacist group—visible tats were a swastika and a confederate battle flag—bought a dozen handguns and what seemed to be several small machine guns, maybe H&Ks.

This was good enough for Colter Shaw.

• • •

As dusk approached that night, Shaw was driving down a deserted country road outside of Canton. The Avis was not a bad car. Customers always drive rentals with heavy feet, and the fifteen K on the odometer was really more like thirty. But the shimmies and rattles and thuds were minor irritations.

Shaw knew it wasn't the car's fault when there came a loud pop and the Malibu veered to the right, onto, then over, the shoulder. It came to rest in boggy land, about two feet shy of an ash tree that would have turned the front end into a thing of the past. He'd been going sixty.

The rapping on the window was loud. The man had used the grip of a gun as a knocker, then turned the muzzle his way. The other hand gestured him out of the vehicle. Shaw lifted his right hand—no threat—and with his left unlocked and opened the door. He stepped out and looked over the man who had shot his tire out.

It was Travis Lanford, the handsome varsity football player—the man who had also, Shaw now understood, murdered Daryl Williams on that cold, cold day in bleak January.

8

"You have a gun. I saw it."

"I do," Shaw told him.

"Take it out and give it to me . . . No, I don't trust you. You probably know karate or something."

"I don't." Which was true, though there was no reason to mention the champion wrestling thing.

"I don't care." Travis looked up and down the road. It was deserted. "Take it out and throw it on the ground."

He did as instructed. The gun landed in a clump of grass. Travis picked it up and pocketed it.

Shaw said, "You were following me. I knew there was someone. I thought it was one of Trimbeaux's crew."

"You're just full of bad decisions, Mister. I saw that reward. Twenty-six hundred? You risk everything for that?"

"How're you going to explain the shot-out tire?" Shaw nodded at the front end.

He laughed. "Trimbeaux's crew did that. Yeah, I followed you—

and saw you following *them*. They got suspicious and came out here have a talk with you here. Shot your tire out."

"And then shot me?"

Travis said nothing. He was sweaty and his mannerisms twitchy. Shaw understood that the AA was for show; he was still a tweaker.

"Why'd you kill Williams?"

"Shut up. I'm not here to talk. *You* are. I saw you take something out of that pizzeria. I want it. What is it? Evidence? A video or something?" When Shaw didn't respond, he said, "And I want to know where those fucking notebooks are. All the stuff you were writing down that I told you. You talked to Mike and Carli too, and Erik. Right? I know you did."

"Travis. Things like this have a way of unraveling. Sooner or later. It's best if you just give yourself up. You make a plea deal, help the DA make a case against Trimbeaux and Garcia for weapons dealing? That'll go a long way. I know how these things work."

"Notebooks. Are they in that camper of yours?"

"No. I learned a long time ago that's the first place people look. I keep them hidden somewhere else."

"Where?"

Shaw didn't reply.

Travis's edgy voice rose in volume as he said, "I'll start shooting! Your foot, your knee." He raised the gun.

Colter Shaw was a man who lived to rock climb, to ride his motorcycle just at or over the edge, who, on reward assignment, occasionally grappled with escaped felons or murderous suspects. The idea of a catastrophic injury like a shattered knee or ankle was horrific.

"You really should think about my offer," Shaw told him.

Travis glanced at the gun in his unsteady hand. "And you should think about mine."

It was then that a loud electronic bleat filled the night and a voice on the loudspeaker called, "You, with the weapon, drop it now! Or you will be fired upon!"

Instinctively Travis turned, giving Shaw just enough time to lower his center of gravity and charge forward. He dropped low and gripped Travis's left ankle, then executed a simple John Smith single-leg takedown, a classic wrestling maneuver. In a matter of seconds Travis was on his back, the breath knocked from his lungs and his gun ripped from his hand. Shaw tossed it aside fast.

Never a good idea to hold on to a weapon when the police are training theirs on you.

This wasn't one of his father's rules but, to Colter Shaw, it just seemed to make sense.

· · ·

As he took back his license and concealed-carry permit from the trooper and stowed them in his wallet, Shaw was listening to the man.

"So. We got a call from somebody reporting an assault on the road here, mile marker thirty-four. Somebody named Travis Lanford had attacked a Colter Shaw. What exactly is going on?"

Shaw didn't explain that, in anticipation of the attack by Travis, he had been live-streaming the drive via a body cam to his resourceful private eye, back in Washington, DC. The minute the tire was shot out, Mack had called Tom Pepper, Shaw's friend and retired FBI agent, who had contacts within the Ohio State Police. He'd called in some favors and OSP had a team sent here.

"What's this all about, sir?" the trooper asked, less patiently this time.

"For the time being I'm pressing charges against Travis for assault with a deadly. You can add an illegal weapons charge too, and there'll be some drugs somewhere. I'll come to the station tomorrow for the interview. But now there's someplace I have to be."

"Well, sir," the trooper with the ramrod-straight posture said, "I'm afraid that's not possible. You'll need to stay here until we get everything straightened out."

Shaw thought things *were* pretty well straightened out. He said, "Could you call this number." He smiled. "As a favor."

The trooper hesitated and then placed the call. It seemed that he stood to attention when the voice answered. He said, "I'm at a crime scene with that man, Colter Shaw and . . . Okay, sir. Yessir."

He disconnected. He looked at Shaw and said, "You're free to go. And I personally would be more than happy to help you change that tire."

9

He looked down at the young man in the hospital bed.

Jude Sterling looked up at him groggily. Weariness defined him.

"How're you feeling?"

"Got cut bad. They use glass. 'Cause of the metal detectors. You'd think the guards'd, you know, figure that out."

"You'd think."

"Gets infected."

Not surprising. The hospital ward was wretched. There were a few too many bloodstains on the walls and yellow stains on the floor. The lighting was as green as the tiles and the pallor of the patients and the medicos alike.

"You'll be okay?"

"They say so. Scar. They don't do plastic surgery here."

"Women like scars on men. Think they're sexy." Some did. Shaw knew this for a fact.

He noted that Jude was shackled, hand and ankle, to the sturdy metal frame. He wondered why both were necessary.

"You said you found who really shot Williams."

"Travis Lanford."

He blinked. This intelligence took a moment to settle. "How'd that work?"

"I'll tell you about it later. You should get some rest. But there's a question I have to ask."

He nodded.

"Did you cock the gun in the clearing and point it at Daryl, after he'd been shot."

"Yessir, I did."

"Why?"

Jude shrugged. "It might sound funny, but I thought of things I've seen in movies. The killer, whoever, he looks dead. But then you get close and he jumps up and has a knife or something, or axe. You know now I didn't shoot him to save my brother. But I would have. I'd do that in a minute."

Shaw nodded.

"You really think I'm getting out?"

Shaw explained there would be procedural issues and the fact that he'd stolen drugs and money—even if from a drug dealer—might mean continued time in the system. But his lawyer would be working hard to get him absolved of the most serious crimes.

Jude appeared grateful, but at the word "lawyer" his face fell.

"I've got somebody better than Arnold Cummings."

They shared a smile.

"Can I see my parents?"

"I don't think so. Not yet."

A guard approached and whispered something to Shaw, who nodded. He said to Jude, "I have to go. But get some rest. People will be in touch. You'll be looked after here."

After Tom Pepper had spoken to a captain at the Ohio State Police, he had also talked to the director of the Department of

Prisons. Jude was now probably the safest prisoner in the Warwick Correctional Facility.

Shaw turned and followed the guard out of the hospital wing, through a half-dozen corridors, as gray as the medical facility was green, and finally out of the lock-down portion of the prison to the general public reception room. The massive door clicked shut behind him. He handed his ID badge to the receptionist and received back his gun.

He turned to Sonja Malloy, who frowned deep furrows into her attractive face and said, "So?"

. . .

The two of them walked outside into the fine June night. Crickets vied with bullfrogs for attention, with the amphibians winning, hands down—if, Shaw reflected, one could put it that way, given their biological morphology.

The breeze was a gentle breath, perfumed by jasmine.

Malloy had interesting eyes, dramatically lit in the outdoor overhead light. The pupils black and yellow. Cat's eyes.

They leaned against her unmarked car. Shaw said, "Something was off. Instincts told me Jude Sterling wasn't a killer—*probably*. Oh, he was angry, he'd been in fights. He wanted to hurt. But there's a Grand Canyon between hurt and kill.

"I put it at fifteen per cent he pulled the trigger. How much of a threat to Frank could Williams've been? Decided I'd go on the assumption that Jude was innocent. If he wasn't the shooter, then who? Rival dealer? Possibility, of course. But, say, thirty per cent."

"You do this percentage thing a lot?"

"I do."

"Why no more than thirty, with a rival?"

"What you told me yourself: Williams was one of the bigger

suppliers of meth in the area. Killing him would be a disruption in the supply chain. Not good for anybody. And even if somebody wanted to take him out, why drive fifty miles on a freezing day all the way to Hanson Valley and kill him in the middle of a deal, with witnesses around?"

"Even with your Throwback Thursday factor?" Now, a bit of a smile.

"Even with that."

"That leaves fifty-five per cent."

"What?" Shaw was confused.

Malloy said, "Fifteen per cent Jude did it, thirty per cent some triggerman from a crew did it. That totals forty-five. Who's the fifty-five per cent suspect?"

It took Shaw a moment. "No, the percentages don't have to add up to one hundred. That's not how it works."

"Oh."

"So let's take Jude and a rival out. Where do we go from there? The guns interested me. The murder weapon was the .38 Special. It had Williams's DNA on it so everyone assumed it came from his car, the Subaru."

"What we thought, yes."

"But in the trunk there was only ammo for a nine mil and a .380. Okay, Williams might've also had a .38 Special. Many dealers collect guns—"

"Like baseball cards."

Shaw frowned. "Like what?"

She looked over his face. "You don't know about baseball cards?"

"No."

In the wilderness enclave where Shaw and his siblings were raised, their father—given to bouts of paranoia—would not allow television, much less the internet, on the property. Shaw had very few cultural points of reference, particularly sports.

Malloy explained that her own father collected them. "I inherited about five thousand. I keep hoping to meet a man who'll appreciate them."

Filing that in the bottom drawer, Shaw continued, "So, sure, Williams might've had the Smittie. But the odds of having *three* guns—and one without a couple of boxes of ammo in the trunk?"

"Twenty per cent." Malloy was apparently getting into the number game.

"I can live with that. So, here were my assumptions. One, the gun *wasn't* Williams's and it wasn't Jude's. Two, Williams was top end in the business. He wouldn't come to Hanson Valley for a penny-ante deal. He'd be carting a major supply, planning to meet dozens of clients and suppliers. Remember, he was pissed off that the kids were late. Probably meant he had other meetings."

She nodded.

"So my theory was: somebody at the quarry found his car and popped the trunk. Saw a motherlode of meth, fent, oxy. Who knows how much? A hundred K? More?"

"And it was this 'somebody' who brought the Smith & Wesson with him?"

"That's right."

"You suspected Travis."

"He was the front runner. He was a meth addict and that's a hard life. You hang in bad places, you're on the street, hustling. Likely he'd have bought himself a cold gun or two. I put it at seventy per cent."

She shook her head. "Why don't they have to add up to a hundred?"

Shaw repressed a sigh. "Okay. There's a race, bunch of runners. Sam's one of the best. He's got a ninety per cent chance of winning. Fred's good, he's got a sixty per cent chance of winning the race, and Tom has a fifty per cent chance of winning."

"Oh. Sure."

"Now back to Travis. Erik was with him at the quarry. Erik's father was adamant I not talk to him, which told me Erik had said that something bad happened that afternoon, and Travis threatened him to keep quiet about it."

"So Travis was the prime suspect." Malloy was nodding while she twined a strand of hair between short-nailed fingers. Those eyes . . . they were really quite captivating. "And then you needed to prove your theory."

"I showed all the kids, except Erik, some pictures of dealers from Canton I said I was going to investigate. I started tailing Orin Trimbeaux. Travis started tailing me. He was afraid I'd make the connection between Trimbeaux and him."

"And this PI of yours had surveillance on you?"

"Right."

"You still took a chance."

He thumped his chest. "Body armor. I minimized the risk."

"And, on January twelfth? How did it go down, you reckon?"

"Travis and Erik were making their way to the clearing to hook up with the others. Travis sees the Subaru, unlocked. He finds the stash in the trunk, filled with Williams's supply. It's a gold mine. He comes up with the plan. He takes his own gun, the Smittie, wipes it down and then rubs Williams's soda cup on it. For the DNA. He goes to the clearing, hides in the brush so nobody can see him. He shoots Williams and drops the gun on the path. He tells Erik that if he says anything he'll kill him too. He buries the drugs and his own gloves somewhere and then takes Erik's. When they did the GSR test on the four kids, Erik was the only one not wearing gloves, I'll bet."

"I think you're right."

"The kids leave and go back home. A day or so later Travis goes back to the scene and collects the drugs. He then signs up for AA to make it look good."

A flash of lightning in the distance. A leisurely rumble arrived.

This seemed to silence the bullfrogs for a moment, though perhaps it was a coincidence. "Oh, here's a bonus." He reached into his backpack and handed her the to-go bag from the pizzeria where Trimbeaux and Garcia had lunched. It contained their beverage glasses. He'd wanted to get samples in Erin's bar the night before but the boys in the crew were getting suspicious, so he'd left early.

He explained, "DNA samples. Trimbeaux and his main gun supplier—Eduardo Garcia." He gave her the man's residence, which Mack had narrowed down to an address on Miller Street. "Probably'll match that DNA your forensic people found on the slugs in the Smittie. I'll come by the office tomorrow and sign a chain of custody card. Oh, and I'll upload a video of Trimbeaux selling to some neo-Nazis."

Malloy exhaled a laugh of surprise at this. "Were you ever law enforcement?"

"No."

She frowned as she looked him over. "You *want* to be law enforcement?"

Shaw smiled.

"Ohio's flusher than some states. The county's got a good pension plan. And two weeks' vacation. After one year of service, of course. Paid maternity leave too." A pause. "Or paternity. For what it's worth. I'm just saying."

• • •

Three days later, Shaw was back in Florida.

He bypassed the elaborate appliances in the kitchen and dropped a cut-up chicken and pieces of onion and orange into a crock pot and added a half bottle of cabernet. He was having Teddy and Velma Bruin over for dinner that night. He'd just turned the knob to "low" and had a sip of beer when his phone hummed.

It was Arnie Sterling, who told him in an excited voice that Travis Lanford had accepted a plea bargain: twenty years in prison, no parole, and the state would not seek the death penalty.

The same day a judge signed an order releasing Jude Sterling and expunging his record in the Williams case. The prosecutor declined to bring a case on the theft from Williams and the possession of controlled substances.

Shaw had also heard from Detective Sonja Malloy, who'd phoned with the information that Trimbeaux and Garcia had been arrested for illegal arms and drug sales. They'd pled not guilty. He told her he was more than happy to return to Ohio to be a witness at the trial. He floated the idea that he might arrive a day or so early and they could discuss the case over dinner. She offered the refinement: that she'd cook. Apparently he was destined to learn about baseball cards firsthand.

A triple-note chime sounded. It was from his Atlas radar intrusion system on the driveway. True, it might have been an actual intruder—Shaw had scores of enemies—but since this was the time of day when the mail person arrived, he figured he didn't need to fetch his Glock.

He met the woman halfway down the walk and collected the bills and flyers and an envelope measuring about nine by eleven. Inside was a package wrapped in gray tissue paper. He tore it open and found himself looking at a framed drawing, done in color pencil on off-white construction paper.

Shaw had to laugh. The image was of Jude's Wasp Man, the half-human, half-insect superhero. The curious creature, wearing an old-time leather helmet, was standing at the mouth of a deep pit—maybe a quarry. The sun was rising, or setting, behind him, and he struck quite the pose, head up and his arms (all four of them) were raised to the sky. Light beams radiated from his head. His uniform was a blue jumpsuit, and on the chest were two letters in gold: *C.S.*

At the bottom of the picture were the words in careful script: "Thank You."

Shaw walked back into the house to find a hammer and some nails. There was an empty spot on his den wall where he thought the sketch would fit perfectly.

Hard to Get

"So, Lessing . . . *Doctor* Albert Lessing, right?"

"Well, technically, I guess. PhD in poly sci. I sometimes say 'Doctor' when I try to book a table at Le Grand Toque but it never works."

The lean, balding man whom Lessing was sitting across from just stared blankly. Lessing reminded himself: no. No jokes. Not with *him*.

"So. There's a situation. You've been attached to CEE for two years now."

The man's question really wasn't one. Spies—especially someone at the level of the director—know all the answers. But the other man's remark was a way to ease into a discussion of the "situation," Lessing assumed.

"Yessir. And before the Central and Eastern Europe desk—"

"You were on Russia."

"Yes."

"And before that you were a professor."

Dr Lessing.

The director looked down at an open folder and read. The papers were marked with the words "Top Secret." You'd think somebody would have come up with an esoteric classification system like *X-1* or *ClassCon A*. But why get fancy? Those two words made the case just fine.

Albert Lessing looked out the window and saw, overlaid on the view of autumn trees in Northern Virginia, his own reflection. The thirty-eight-year-old, pale of complexion, was a bit narrow-shouldered, a bit under six feet, a bit under his ideal weight, his mother to point out the last. He'd been told he was handsome in a Minor League Baseball shortstop sort of way. Whatever that meant.

The view from here was impressive. Lessing's office, shared by four other analysts, was several floors below this one, and in a different wing. You opened the door via an old-fashioned combination dial, like a safe. Again, nothing esoteric.

The director had absorbed what he needed to and looked up. "Now, Tony Kauffman's been injured. You know him?"

"No." The Central Intelligence Agency employed over twenty thousand people, which was larger than the population of the town in Illinois where Albert Lessing grew up.

"Heard the name CS?"

"Right." Clandestine Services. Undercover spies. Lessing was an intelligence analyst—it was his division that took the intel that people like Kauffman and the local assets whom he ran would send here to headquarters for dissection.

"He'll live but he'll be out of commission for a while," the director said. "Ran off the road on the autobahn near Munich."

"Was it . . . ?"

"No, a real accident. Deer."

So, the Russian SVR, the foreign intelligence successor to the KGB, or another spy agency or a stateless terrorist cell hadn't tried to kill him.

The director continued, "For the past eight months Kauffman's been putting together an op to take down the Cincinnati Network. Or at least put a dent in it. You familiar?"

"Not too much," Lessing said. "Just the US is the target. Some bigwig in Moscow put it together a year ago."

"Rostikov," the director muttered, with a twitch of lip. The expression suggested he and this Rostikov were longtime adversaries . . . and that the Russian was winning the game.

The director explained that the Cincinnati Network was an agent-in-place operation. The Russians scoured websites and blogs for disaffected US citizens and foreign nationals and recruited them. The people they targeted weren't traditional assets—agents who'd send the Russians classified information, à la Aldrich Ames or Robert Hansen. Named after the city because the original controller was based in Ohio, before he slipped out of the country, the operation represented a subtler approach to the post-Cold-War Cold War. The traitors' assignments were to do whatever they could to destabilize the country, through legal or quasi-legal means. "Basically, lobbying, writing papers or articles for social media and the traditional press to undermine democratic values: like getting bigoted, incompetent or corrupt politicians into office."

Agents with the Cincinnati Network were believed responsible for getting Ku Klux Klan members into several state senates, he told Lessing, thumping the file folder angrily. They inflamed tempers at Black Lives Matter rallies. They encouraged anti-immigrant riots and supported university officials who turned a blind eye to student rape and sexual assault. When a sheriff in New Mexico was arrested because he had used his office to blatantly harass immigrants, even documented ones, Cincinnati Network provocateurs mounted a fierce campaign to discredit the judge hearing the sheriff's trial.

"Now, Tony Kauffman was injured on his way to southwestern

Poland. He'd found out from a deep source that one of Rostikov's men and his brother will be in town there in two days. A hunting trip. Deer season." The director gave a laugh. "Ironic, no? *Deer* . . . He'd found out where the men'll be staying. Kauffman was going to stay in a hotel nearby and hang out in their bar and, somehow, make contact."

"He'd be a dangle."

"Exactly. His cover was just the sort of guy they'd want for the Cincinnati Network."

Lessing nodded, impressed. "So Rostikov would fly in from Russia, and, bang, rendition."

"No. For one thing, Rostikov never gets into the field. Too risky. But it wouldn't matter anyway; we can't kidnap anybody on Polish soil. Warsaw's very clear on that. Bulgaria, Czech Republic, Slovakia, we would work a snatch. But not in Poland. No, we would've been happy if Rostikov's man just recruited Kauffman. We'd run him as a double. We figure we could keep the op open for a year before they caught on. We could penetrate enough of the Network to bring down, thirty, forty per cent of it."

The director looked Lessing over carefully. "Now, you've probably guessed what you're doing here?"

Lessing had not—until that question. The implication stunned him. "You want me to take over." His heart began to pound.

"Kaufmann's cover is he's a professor at Potomac University and moonlights for a think tank in DC. He's already published some anti-American op-ed pieces in the papers and on some fringe blogs. You've been a professor and written plenty of academic pieces. And I've read your reports here. You can put sentences together. And you're fluent in Polish and Russian."

After a pause, Lessing said in a somber voice, "I'd be NOC."

"That you would. Can't get around it."

This was the most dangerous form of clandestine work. Official

Cover meant you were attached to a government organization, most likely the State Department. But instead of doing what your job title or affiliation suggested, like Agricultural Attaché, you were really a spy. With OC operations, you worked largely within the embassy and had the security forces watching over you most of the time. In a Non-Official Cover op, you were on your own. No armed marines in obvious view, discouraging anyone from taking a pot shot at you if your cover was blown.

And NOCs had no diplomatic immunity.

Which meant once arrested, you could be "tried" at midnight and shot at dawn, with or without a blindfold.

"So?"

Lessing thought about his sedate life here. His cubicle. His tiny house. His two goldfish, one named after a philosopher, the other after a writer.

But then he thought of two other names: James Bond. Jason Bourne.

"I'm in."

The director stood and shook Lessing's hand. "Welcome to Clandestine Services."

• • •

Two days later Albert Lessing was landing at Prague airport.

Well, technically, according to his passport, credit cards and other documents, he wasn't Al Lessing at all, but Peter Crenshaw.

Crenshaw was a talented professor at Potomac University in Washington, DC, and a skilled writer of position papers and research pieces for a prestigious (though completely fictional) think tank. But he was having some hard times. He was twice divorced, and being taken to the cleaners by not one but both ex-wives. And he was an alcoholic.

In other words, the perfect bait for Rostikov's agent.

The plane landed and Lessing disembarked. He approached Czech Passport Control, uneasy. His first time fooling an official about his identity. But he'd arduously memorized his fake name and the fabricated details of his life, prepared for questions. But the young officer simply stamped the document and nodded him into the country.

After he'd gathered his suitcase and exited through the green "nothing-to-declare" door at Customs, he was met by a local officer. Stan Smiles was a former Delta Force member who'd moved on to Military Intelligence and then joined CIA. He was OC, attached to the embassy in the Czech Republic as an economic development liaison, but in fact he ran clandestine agents and local assets throughout Eastern Europe. Though they'd never met, Lessing felt he knew the man well, since Smiles had been the source of terabytes of solid intel, which Lessing had spent many long hours analyzing.

Smiles was about what you'd expect of a government agent: a lean, grizzled man with a crewcut. He was in his mid-forties. Lessing noted that he never, well, *smiled*—maybe because that expression had been retired, due to his name. He was, however, endlessly enthusiastic. Lessing's impression was that whatever he did, running spies or attending soccer games or eating borscht, Smiles loved doing it.

"Here we go." Smiles nodded at a large sedan, a make of car that Lessing wasn't familiar with. Inside was a sullen, dark-complexioned man. Smiles tossed Lessing's bag into the trunk and they got in, then sped away from the airport.

"This is Vlad."

"Hi. How you doing?"

Vlad said nothing. He just drove.

Smiles asked, "What'd you think of the boss?"

"The director?" Lessing wondered if this was a test. He cast a glance at Vlad, who spotted his eye in the mirror. In a light

Slavic accent, the driver muttered, "Don't worry. I've got higher clearance than you two put together."

Smiles said, "He doesn't but it's high enough."

Lessing said, "To be honest, I was surprised he called me. I'm pretty junior."

"Don't be offended but you'd probably be his last choice. There's an art to clandestine work. People train for years and only then do they get a plum assignment like this. But the Cincinnati Network is a thorn in his side. When Kauffman broadsided Bambi, and ended up in the hospital, the director just about had a stroke.

"Great. Thank you. I didn't feel enough pressure already, Stan."

"Ah, nonsense. Sometimes it's better to have a fresh mind. Before you get all jaded and start overthinking everything. Now, we'll be at the border in about three hours, and Kostka is about five miles past that."

Lessing said, "Any border crossing issue?"

Poland and the Czech Republic were both European Union. But with immigration problems plaguing Europe and the Mediterranean states, some countries were reinstating border controls.

"Not here. Not yet." Smiles continued, "Now, we've confirmed that Boris Bukharin, Rostikov's number one, got to Kostka this morning. His brother knows what Boris does but isn't a player. He runs an import business."

"In Poland to hunt."

"That's right. They're staying at the Chopin Lodge downtown, though it isn't much of a downtown. The whole town's about five thousand people." He looked out the window and said softly, "Peter."

Lessing fired back with, "Yes?"

"What's your second wife's name again?"

"Andi. Short for Andrea. She lives at one oh seven South Maple

Drive in Cary, North Carolina. I know because I send checks there in the amount of three thousand forty-one fifty a month."

Smiles nodded. "Good." Then he dug into his briefcase and displayed pictures of Russian agent Boris Bukharin and his brother. Lessing studied them.

Then, turning further around in the front seat, Smiles looked over Lessing carefully. "Now, I know you're sharp and, yeah, you've got a good command of cover. Don't you think, Vlad?"

"Oh, he is star. That what I call him. Mr Star."

"But there's one thing you can't memorize. What I said earlier: the *art* of spying."

"Art."

"Yes. And in this op, the most important tactic is playing hard to get."

"Go on."

"You've pretty much got what they're looking for, for the Cincinnati Network. But they're going to be—"

"Suspicious because it's *too* much like what they want."

"Exactly. We've really kept a lid on the fact that we know Bukharin'll be in Kostka. Rostikov and Moscow won't be expecting us to make a move here. But these people're naturally suspicious— it's kept them alive and successful for years. These are the heirs to the KGB and the NKVD. The best spy soldiers in the world. They'll be intrigued by you, they'll be tempted. But at the first sign that you're interested, their shields go up, Scotty."

"Play hard to get. Okay."

"Once he gets the hang of it, it won't be that hard, will it, Vlad?"

"Is piece of cake, Mr Star."

"You've got our cell numbers memorized."

Lessing spouted them back.

"Good. Oh, one more thing: at Langley, the suicide pill? Which one did they give you? In your tooth?"

"*What?*" Lessing glanced up frantically.

A moment passed. Vlad smiled in the rear view: "Is messing with you."

Smiles laughed, sat back and began to text.

Lessing wondered if the two men could hear his heart beating.

After a winding, three-hour drive through farmland, hills and forest they arrived at Kostka, a medium-sized town filled with blocky, dirty-white concrete buildings from the Soviet era and fewer, some charming, Bavarian-style wooden-and-stucco structures.

"We'll drop you off here. Before the CCTVs can pick us up. If anybody asks, you took a car service from Prague. It's longer than flying into Krakow but a popular trip. Prague is the new Paris and a lot of travelers to western Poland stop there first, for the sights and restaurants."

Smiles pointed. "There's your hotel." It was an American chain. "Why're you staying there?" he quizzed.

"I don't speak Polish and I was afraid I couldn't be understood at a local place."

"Good."

"Now, across the street is the Chopin, where Bukharin and his brother will be. See it? Just hang out in the restaurant."

Lessing regarded the sign. *Pstrąg Pływanie.*

It meant "The Swimming Trout" in Polish. (As opposed to what? The Walking Trout? The Jogging Trout?)

"Good luck."

He climbed out and took his suitcase from the trunk. Then started up the sidewalk.

Smiles called out, "Hey, Albert?"

Lessing just kept walking.

Vlad shouted, "Good job, Mr Star."

The car sped away.

The panic didn't hit until he glanced back and saw the sedan vanish down the road. He thought: What the hell am I doing?

• • •

Lessing's confidence didn't return when he walked into the neat but well-worn lobby of the hotel. The desk clerk, in a suit, was on the phone and continued to speak to the person on the other end as he looked Lessing over suspiciously. It was not a glance but an examination, as if Lessing were a job applicant. The gaunt, sandy-haired man finally hung up. "*Tak?*"

"I . . . I'm sorry. Do you speak English?"

"Yes, I suppose I can."

"Do you have a room for two days?"

"Let me look."

Lessing knew there was a room, since Smiles had called. The hotel was nearly empty. "Only one left. It is the most expensive, but that is all we have."

"Fine. I'll take it."

"Passport." The man held his hand out, took the booklet, read it carefully and flipped the pages. Then read it again. Lessing had traveled internationally and had never seen a hotel clerk pay such attention. The man then made a photocopy of the booklet and dropped it on the counter. He made a show of searching for the registration sheet.

A round-headed employee, about twenty or so, walked into the lobby from the back room. He was in dark slacks and a white shirt with a narrow floral tie.

The manager turned to the younger man and snapped, in Polish, "What are you wearing? That tie! You know what I tell you? Do you want to be fired? Do you want to end up on the street, meeting men like your sister does?"

Lessing forced himself to display no reaction to the cruel

words, since Peter Crenshaw wasn't supposed to speak the language.

The boy said, "It is all that I have clean."

"I will accept no excuses. Go buy a more respectable tie. A solid color."

"I . . . I cannot afford one."

A scowl. "Wear that for today, but if you show up in it again, or one like it, you will lose your job."

"Yessir. I'm sorry." The blushing boy continued on his mission, vanishing into a door that appeared to lead to the hotel's restaurant.

The manager turned back to Lessing. "Such an attitude today's youth have! The things he just said to me!"

"Is that right?"

"Yes, it is right." He offered the registration sheet to Lessing and pointed out where to sign.

Lessing filled out the form, signed it and handed it back, prepaying the two nights with cash in Polish zlotys. Though the country was in the EU, it had not accepted euros as the currency.

The hotel manager took the sheet and reviewed it carefully. Lessing had an absurd thought: he was back in school and about to get a C-minus for his penmanship.

Handing over his room key, the manager said, "The dining room is open from eighteen hundred hours to twenty-three hundred."

"Thanks, but I'll be eating someplace else."

A sigh of disappointment—as a potential source of revenue vanished. The manager shrugged, pointed out the elevator and, without another word, turned away and began to type at the computer behind the desk.

As he pressed the Up button, Lessing glanced back at the front desk and noted that the manager was jotting something down on his registration card.

What did it say? Lessing wondered. He had an idea: "At break-fast seat this guest by the kitchen and make sure his coffee is tepid."

Or maybe: "Make up his room at five a.m."

. . .

By the time he got to the Swimming Trout restaurant and lounge at seven that evening, Lessing had cast aside his concerns. The room at his hotel was not bad and it featured a mini bar stocked with a half-dozen tiny bottles of liquor and snacks. He'd cracked open some buffalo grass vodka, mixed it with orange soda, and drank it down as he ate a packet of nuts, then slept off some of his jet lag.

A shower, a shave, fresh clothing . . . and he was ready to spy.

The bar of the restaurant was large and woody and dark. There were photos of wildlife on the walls and, though smoking was prohibited, the place smelled of tobacco, and the glass in the picture frames was tinted yellow.

As soon as he entered, Lessing had spotted Bukharin and his brother, along with two other men—apparently hunters (they wouldn't be SVR; Smiles would have reported if there were other agents in the area). They were at a round table in the center of the place, drinking what looked like vodka with beer chasers.

Most of the people in the bar were sturdy men, and a few women, still tinted with the remnants of summer tans. Judging by the faint aroma of body odor, not everyone had bathed recently. Slim, pale Alfred Lessing stood out, and he momentarily drew the attention of the husky denizens here. But the conversations—about the day's hunt, or a past year's, or a fishing trip—resumed immediately.

He said to the huge, balding bartender, "Uhm. Please, a *wódka i piso.*"

The man roared. "*Piso!* You want *piso!*" In thickly accented English.

Several others, include Bukharin, turned.

The man said in Polish to the others. "He ordered *piso!* That's English for pee."

The others laughed.

Lessing was blushing.

In English again, the bartender said, "Ah, I make no offense. You asked for vodka and pee."

Just as Lessing had intended, the man had mistaken *piso* for *piss*. Well, he had wanted to draw attention to himself.

"I'm sorry, I mean—*wódka i pivo*."

"Yes, yes! And I will give you that. And it will be complimentary on me, because you have been a good man of humor."

The glasses banged hard onto the scarred oak bar. Lessing settled onto a barstool, lifted the shot glass to his benefactor and tossed down the burning vodka. Then sipped the beer.

His phone rang; it was the alarm, not a call. He looked at the screen, grimaced and shut the tone off, then pretended to have a conversation with someone on the other end of the line.

"Yes, I got your email. Why should I answer?" He gestured to the bartender for another vodka and then tossed it down and said, "How could you ask for that? . . . You think I'm made out of money? . . . Yes, because you spent it on Jake! Right? . . . No, he's not just a friend. You're sleeping with him . . . It's not a terrible thing to say if it's true . . ."

He tried not to overact. Closing his eyes briefly. "*Lawyer's* bill? Why should I pay your goddamn lawyer's bill? We're divorced . . . I don't owe you anything except alimony. And even that you don't deserve . . . Another *wódka!* . . . What? . . . Poland, on business, that's where I am . . . Oh, because *I* work for a living." He tossed back one more drink. Poor Peter Crenshaw was, of course, an alcoholic. "And if you think—hello? Goddamnit!" He pretended to disconnect and drew back the phone as if to fling it into a wall.

Bukharin and the men at the table leaned away from the trajectory. Then Lessing controlled himself and put the phone away. Another hit of beer and he sat back down at the bar, shoulders slumped.

A moment later, he felt a shadow over him and turned to see Bukharin leaning against the bar next to him. "You are American, Mr Piso."

"Yeah, yeah, very funny."

"Ha, I joke. Who has not made mistaken words sometimes, in a different language? Once, in London, by mistake I told a girl she had nice breasts."

"What did you want to say?"

"Tits."

Lessing had to laugh.

"I am Boris."

"Peter."

"Your ex-wife, did I hear?"

"Yep. You have one?"

"I have a present wife but I have ex-girlfriends. I am knowing how things go."

"Well, mine cheated on me. Then sued *me* for divorce."

Bukharin frowned. "Your . . ." He gestured low on Lessing's torso. "It works okay?"

"What? Oh, that works fine. No, her complaint was that I wasn't rich enough for her. She married a professor. What'd she think, I was a real estate magnate?"

Bukharin said to the bartender, in Polish, "Another bottle." Then to Lessing: "You are here for the hunt?"

"Hunt? No, no. I'm writing a paper on economics and development. American companies want to partner with Polish ones.

We need to—we've screwed up our economy so badly." Bukharin cracked open the fifth of vodka. He refilled Lessing's glass.

He had to *play* drunk. He didn't have to *be* drunk. Still, here he was making a connection with his target. He couldn't risk the man growing suspicious. He tossed down the fiery drink. Bukharin took a swig directly from the bottle. No one in Eastern Europe sipped.

"So, you're all hunters?" Lessing glanced back at the table where Bukharin had been sitting.

"Yes, yes. And it was a good day. Five stags between us. You hunt in America?"

"No. I've always wanted to."

Maybe they'd invite him out tomorrow. Hell, the one time he'd fired a gun was at CIA training. The only animal he'd ever killed was a squirrel and the weapon had been a '98 Honda Accord.

Bukharin was saying something. Lessing wasn't sure what it was. The entire room was swimming.

Ha, the Swimming Trout.

No, the Drunk Trout.

Lessing held his glass up. Bukharin filled it but said, "Ah, be careful with Polish vodka, Peter. It can be very dangerous if you aren't used to it."

"I survived five years with that bitch." He tapped the phone in his pocket. "I'm not afraid of a little vodka."

And he threw up on Bukharin's shoes.

• • •

The next day, Lessing awoke late in the morning with a hangover that seemed to be a creature in itself. A Frankenstein's monster. A Dracula. An orc.

He lay in bed until one o'clock and finally made a call to

Smiles. They went through the encryption procedures and then had their conversation. Lessing reported he'd made contact with Rostikov's man, Boris Bukharin, and had given away a bit about himself, but not too much.

"Definitely played hard to get."

Without explaining how.

The vomiting incident of last night had not, it seemed, jeopardized the mission. Bukharin had taken things well; he had the attitude of a man who was no stranger to heavy drinking. He'd cleaned himself up and seemed genuinely pleased by Lessing's embarrassed offer to buy him dinner the next night, to make up for the faux pas. He would have to see, though; tomorrow they were venturing further out into the countryside and might not be back until the day after; they were taking camping equipment with them, just in case.

Lessing told Smiles only the latter part of their conversation and added that Lessing would be in the Swimming Trout bar from seven till closing tonight just in case the men returned.

Lessing spent the afternoon wandering the chill streets of Kostka, to get some exercise, then returned, showered and changed clothes. As he was leaving the hotel he noted again the cynical gaze of the manager and wondered once more what the man had written on his registration card. Across the lobby was the young skinny hotel employee who'd been berated by the manager yesterday for his flowery tie. He was carrying some trash bags out a side door.

Lessing stepped outside and joined him. "Hello."

"Hello."

"You speak English."

"Yes, I watch the shows. We study in school, but we also watch your TV. And Sky from England. We learn more of how people really talk, doing that."

Lessing looked around. "Your boss doesn't like me."

"And he doesn't like me. And *I* am his nephew."

"Really?"

"Yes. He doesn't like many people, in the family or out of the family. He is strange. His is rec . . . rec . . ."

"Recluse? He keeps to himself?"

"Yes, yes."

"And suspicious?"

"Of everything and everyone."

Lessing's voice lowered. "Can I ask a favor?"

"What?"

"You know those cards the hotel uses for each guest?"

"Yes?"

"Well, I saw him write something on mine. I'm thinking he changed the room rate to a higher fee."

"Oh, Uncle Stav would do that. Yes, I would think he might."

Lessing dug into his pocket and handed him a hundred dollars' worth of zlotys.

"Oh, my. Oh. Well, look."

"Could you do me a favor? Could you take a picture of that registration card with your phone and send it to me? Only if it's safe to do that, though. So you won't get caught."

"Yes, yes. And if he is going to cheat you, then we can send it to the police, get him put in jail. The family would like that."

Lessing smiled. He typed the young man's number into his phone and let it ring a few times so that they would have each other's number.

Then he said good night and headed off to the restaurant, reminding himself that there would be no vodka tonight.

No *piso*, either.

• • •

A new bartender was on duty at the Drunken Trout, as Lessing had dubbed the place. She was an attractive blond woman with narrow cheekbones and arching brows.

She looked up as he took a seat at a barstool. *"Tak?"*

"Coca-Cola."

"With rum or with whisky?"

"With ice."

Present were a few hunters, along with two middle-aged couples, both Polish, he could tell from their conversation, and at the bar, a drunk elderly man and a woman in her thirties, in a business suit, sipping wine, lost in her computer screen.

Lessing began reading a day-old edition of the *International New York Times.*

By 9 p.m., Bukharin and his brother had not shown. Lessing assumed they were spending the night in the countryside after all, and he decided to have dinner here. It was early by his circadian clock but he was hungry. Thinking wryly: Wasn't much in the mood for supper last night. Staying firmly in cover, he struggled to ask the bartender in English mixed with broken Polish if he could have dinner at a table here, in the bar, rather than in the restaurant proper. She frowned, cocking her head.

The woman patron at the end of the bar looked up. "You are wanting a table?" she asked in accented English.

"I do . . . But that's not what I asked for, I'm assuming."

"No, you asked for a piece of steel."

She turned to the bartender and spoke in Polish.

The bartender said, "Ah, yes. You can be sitting anywhere you are liking. Here there will be a menu." She pushed one toward him.

"Steel?" he asked the customer.

She replied, *"Stal* is steel; *stół* is table."

"So a steel table is a *stal stół.*"

She laughed. "It would be *stół ze stali.* But, yes, that is much what you said."

Lessing thanked her. She smiled and turned back to her computer. Then grimaced. Lessing could just see the screen. He noted a box reading in Polish: *Cannot find server.*

In Polish the woman asked the bartender if the internet had gone out. The answer was: "I'm surprised you could get a signal at all this time of night. When everyone is home, it overloads the servers. People are on Facebook or YouTube or looking at dirty movies." The women laughed and the customer glanced Lessing's way. He noticed and glanced back, but kept a neutral expression on his face.

She said nothing about the bartender's off-color comment but gestured to the Dell laptop and said to him, "The internet is out."

Lessing tapped the newspaper. "You know, this's a revolutionary new idea. You don't need a server. You don't even need batteries."

"Ah," she laughed and gave another smile, revealing a row of perfect white teeth. "You should make a patent for it. Become a billionaire. Move to Silicone Valley."

Lessing struggled not to laugh at the word choice. He held up the menu. "Can I ask you to help translate? I'll pay for it with stock options in my battery-free computer company."

She gestured to the stool next to hers. He walked to it and sat. Now that he was closer, he revised his assessment of her age upward, seeing wrinkles around the blue eyes and her full lips. She was not model beautiful but had an earthy sensuality about her—the near-Asian Slavic face and voluptuous figure.

"I am Alexandra."

"Peter."

She was a sales representative for a housewares company, based in Warsaw. This part of the country was her territory. Lessing explained what he did. Alexandra wasn't too familiar with position papers and think tanks, but she had enjoyed her years at university, in Gdansk, and asked him about that side of his career and how he liked teaching.

He told her about life on campus and described Potomac University, which he'd been to a number of times and could describe from memory.

"It must be beautiful this time of year."

"Yes, it is. Autumn term is my favorite."

Her daughter would be starting school in Warsaw next year, she told him. And showed him on her phone a picture of a pretty blond dressed in a dark blue school uniform.

At the reference to the girl, Lessing glanced at her left hand, and she noticed. "My husband is no longer my husband."

"We're in the same boat."

"Boat?"

Forgetting idioms didn't always translate.

"I'm divorced too."

"Oh, boat. Like *Titanic*."

She kept a straight face for a moment and then they both laughed.

Lessing was in no mood to drink but recalled that he was an alcoholic. He needed to stay in character. But no vodka. He ordered white wine. He gestured for Alexandra's glass to be refilled.

"Ah, with this wine, you have paid for my menu translation services now. It is a better arrangement, as I suspect your company will not do well."

They clinked glasses and she pulled the menu closer and translated the dishes for him.

Everything seemed heavy and was served in sauce with starchy sides.

He shrugged. "Thanks but, fact is, I'm not that hungry."

"You don't want anything?" Alexandra asked.

"Well, I do." And, on impulse he leaned forward, hesitating just a moment to gauge whether or not he had license. Her eyes lowered and she leaned into him.

Lessing kissed her. She kissed back.

He nodded toward the door. She nodded back. He paid for the drinks and they donned their coats. They stepped outside into the brisk autumn evening air. She slipped her arm through his and they strode toward the hotel.

And why not?

He was James Bond, he was Jason Bourne.

He was a spy.

• • •

The sun rose through a notch in the hills to the east of Kostka and shot into Lessing's hotel room, striking him and Alexandra directly on their faces. They both stirred.

He stumbled from the bed, snagged his jockeys and pulled them on, a T-shirt too, and then returned to bed, sliding under the blankets so that he could lie against her warm body. She eased closer yet.

Lessing replayed the passionate evening in detail, then once again. Then his thoughts returned to his assignment and he wondered if he'd hear from Bukharin today. Would he have to go back to the Trout tonight? He was aware of Alexandra stirring, stretching, reaching to the bedside table to check her phone, and then settling back against him.

"Peter?" she whispered.

"Yes. You thinking about breakfast?" His eyes were still closed.

She didn't answer him. Instead, she said, "Peter. I wasn't honest with you."

He looked toward her.

Hm, something sexually transmitted?

The ex is not completely an ex?

"I don't sell pots and pans, and I'm not Polish. I'm Russian. I'm an officer in the SVR."

"You're . . ."

"Are you familiar? It's the foreign security service. It's like your CIA in America."

"*What?*" he whispered.

His breath came fast as machine-gun bursts.

She added, in a barely audible voice: "And my name isn't Alexandra. It's Valentina. Valentina Rostikov."

• • •

Well, I'm not dead.

This was Lessing's first thought.

If she knew he was an agent she could easily have poisoned his drink last night when they returned to the room, or shoved some clever Russian skewer, disguised as a pen, into his ear in the middle of the night.

And how do I handle it?

A thought occurred. Lessing began to laugh. He said, "Russian agent? Don't you want to be Mahatma Gandhi?"

"Be . . . what?" she asked, a frown crossing her handsome face.

Hell, he'd got it wrong. "I mean, *Mata Hari?* The spy who was the sexy seductress, the temptress. That's kinkier than some Russian." Lessing's hand wandered over her belly.

She took his fingers and stopped their gentle motion. In a voice that wasn't chastising but that nonetheless made clear she was serious, she said, "I'm not making a joke."

He withdrew his arm and sat up. "I . . . I thought this was some kind of, I don't know, role playing. You know, pretending to be spies in bed. Handcuffs, blindfolds."

"You Americans," she scoffed.

"You're serious? You're a Russian spy with the SRV."

"SVR."

"Whatever. I mean. Jesus." Lessing was stammering. Partly

because he felt his role demanded it. Partly because he couldn't control it. "I think I have to report it to somebody. Don't I?"

"I'd rather you didn't. At least not yet."

Lessing sat up, pulling the sheets closer around him.

Alexandra said, "Let's go outside, to the square. We can talk better there."

Twenty minutes later, they'd showered and dried, coiffed and bundled. They went downstairs and out the door of the hotel. They walked to the café she indicated, with her arm through his.

"You're shivering," she said.

"I've never done too well with cold," Lessing told her.

Or with firing squads at dawn.

She selected a table outside. They moved the chairs into the sun, which tempered the cold, and sat opposite each other at an unsteady table whose leg Lessing propped up with a stone shaped like an arrowhead. When the waitress appeared, they ordered coffee and bread and sausages.

When she walked away, Rostikov said, "The other night, there was a man you vomited on."

Lessing frowned. "How did you . . .?" His eyes grew wide. "He's an associate of yours. You're both spies?"

"He was not here to work, but on holiday. He found you interesting. He called me in Moscow and I flew into Krakow to come look for myself."

"Found me interesting?" Lessing gave a sour laugh. "Nobody finds me interesting." He grimaced. "Except you, last night. Or so I thought."

"No, no, that was not part of any plan." She smiled. "I wanted that very much. After all, I could simply have told you last night what I'm going to tell you now."

"Really? You mean that."

"Yes." Her steely blue eyes met his.

He supposed he believed her. Though getting into his room, as she had, would've given her more of a chance to check him out, see if he was legitimate. New to the game, Lessing didn't know when spy mentality stopped and man-woman mentality began.

He squeezed her arm. Then said, "But what is all this?"

"Boris learned that you have been having a difficult time with your ex-wife recently."

Lessing gave a sharp wave of his hand, "No, I've been having a difficult time with my ex for many years. *Recently*, I've been having serious money problems because of her. And the one before her."

"Two?"

He shrugged.

Rostikov started to speak but just then the waitress returned with their food and beverages, and she fell silent.

Lessing sipped some coffee and helped himself to a piece of black bread spread with a seasoned white spread. It was very good. He looked at the whipped concoction, trying to figure out what it was.

"Lard," Rostikov told him.

Ick, he thought. But then finished the slice and fixed himself another. "You?"

"No." She sipped coffee and asked, "Are you patriotic? . . . Oh, I see you're confused. And understandably concerned. But, please, just answer my question."

"To a degree. Probably like most people."

"Would you lay down your life for your country?"

"I would lay down my life for certain countrymen. Or countrywomen."

"Well said. I like that. I've read some of your writings, Peter."

"You have?"

A laugh. "As it turns out they were on my computer last night in the bar. I downloaded them after Boris told me about you. You are critical of your country."

"Aspects of it, yes." He cocked his head and put down the lard bread. "Nothing is perfect."

She sipped coffee. "I used to smoke. I miss it every day. Especially in the morning. Now, here's the long and the short of it—an English expression, whose literal meaning I cannot grasp. I have a great deal of money at my disposal. And by this, I mean a lot. Seven figures, in dollars or euros that I can pay you. And you have something that is valuable to me."

Lessing had to be careful not to let on that he knew what she was fishing for—joining the Cincinnati Network and publishing articles and position papers tactically to undermine the country.

Hard to get.

He said, "I doubt that very much."

"Oh, but you do. You have access."

He frowned.

"Did you know that next year, your president's son will be attending Potomac University?"

Lessing felt as if he'd been kicked in the gut.

"I didn't."

"What I'm going to say is very inflammatory, and very risky. But I'm taking a chance because years of instinct are telling me that I can say it to you and you will not go running immediately to the authorities."

"And, if you're who you say you are, I'd probably get shot in the back if I tried to run to anybody."

Lessing was very aware that she didn't laugh this off. "For your fee, I would need you to make sure you are a professor and advisor to the president's son. What you'll do in that position is pick his brain on aspects of his father and mother and other people in the government. Maybe he can bring you materials from the White House. Maybe he can remember conversations."

"Because you want to assassinate the president!" Lessing said in disgust. He shoved his chair back with a screech and rose. "I don't think so."

Rostikov smiled. "No, no, Peter. Sit. Please. We are way past that. The fact is even in the days of the KGB such action was never on our list. This is not to hurt people. That will never happen. We want to simply have a better chance economically. Our country is not healthy in that way, as yours is."

Slowly he returned to his chair. Thinking: Played that one just right.

Lessing knew this was an even better grab than the original scheme. Hiring him to write fake position papers would mean his handlers would be low-level grunts. But running him as a double with access to the White House would mean involvement of senior covert Russian assets in the US and Moscow. Once he had the names, he'd hand them over to the FBI domestically and to CIA and military forces overseas.

Of course her reassurance that nothing violent would come of spying was ridiculous. This was not about interest rates and factories. It was about geopolitical power and nationalistic domination. But he tried to make it seem that her words had comforted him.

Think, he told himself. Imagine you're in your cubicle, analyzing data. What do you do? You let the ideas come. Let them flow spontaneously like an endless stream of intel.

Lessing cocked his head. "I could create an after-school club, a political club. No, not political. That might seem suspicious. I'll find out what he likes. Photography, languages, the yearbook, maybe cooking . . ."

Rostikov touched her chin, frowning slightly. "This is very clever, yes."

Eyes straying around the square, he said slowly, "I think sports may be a good way to go too. You know, the president was a champion football player. But he's changed his mind about the game, especially with young players. Because of the head injuries."

"I have read about that—the injuries."

"Every college boy wants to play a sport. I'll talk to our athletic department and see if I can get involved coaching. And . . ." Then he frowned. "But, no. What the hell am I saying? I can't do this. I can't betray my country."

She rested her hand on Lessing's arm. "Peter. You aren't betraying anything. You are assisting two countries to peacefully coexist. No one wants destruction and death. But knowledge is the way to peace."

No, knowledge is the way to power.

Rostikov was smiling the broad, beautiful and sexy smile he remembered from the night before, in bed. "My God. In merely a few minutes you have found some very good ideas."

"And," he said, ignoring her comment. As if his mind galloped ahead without any intervention on Lessing's part, he blurted, "The boy has a brother too, you know. In a younger grade."

"Yes, but we didn't think there would be any way to get close to him."

"Maybe. But if we think about it, there'd have to be times when they were together, the brothers. Maybe I could arrange to be there too. And think about this: the president and his aides might be reluctant to talk in front of a seventeen-year-old—college students have minds of their own. But a boy who's nine or ten? They might not think twice about sharing state secrets when he was around."

Rostikov digested this. "Yes, excellent."

It was then that his phone vibrated with a text message. He glanced down. And when he saw the screen it took all his will-power to keep from uttering a gasp—if not passing out.

There was no written message, just an image: a photograph taken with the phone's camera. It was from the crewcut boy at the hotel, the manager's nephew. The image was of Lessing's registration card, as he'd requested. The notation the desk clerk had made on the card, near Lessing's name, was "CIA."

He felt his stomach drop. No! How had he found out?

Lessing glanced at Rostikov. She was looking him over with curiosity.

He took another sip, hoping that the cup would hide his expression of fear. He understood now that the surly man's suspicion was more than his general nature; he must be an undercover agent— probably for the Polish state police. Somehow, either Lessing had made a mistake and given himself away or the agent had called on some good resources to ferret out who the guest was.

Or, someone he'd met since his arrival in the country was a double agent.

Vlad, the driver of the other day?

Smiles himself?

Lessing's head throbbed with blood as his heart pounded.

"Important?" Rostikov asked, nodding at his smartphone.

"The ex again." Thinking fast. "She's sent me a bill for braces. She's thirty-eight years old and wants braces."

He slipped the phone away in his pocket. That Rostikov hadn't reacted, other than giving a faint smile, confirmed for him that the hotel manager was probably a Polish, not a Russian, agent. Still, it was only a matter of time before the information went from Warsaw to Moscow and then to Valentina Rostikov.

Rostikov had started speaking again. He tried to concentrate. She was explaining about the payment arrangements. How the money would be placed in a bank in Geneva, under the guise of payments for consulting fees. "You will declare it and pay taxes in Switzerland. Sad. But that's a small price to pay."

Lessing nodded. He asked a few pertinent questions. But his only thought was how to escape. He might have only minutes before she learned who he really was.

"You're having second thoughts?" Rostikov said, noting his troubled eyes.

"No, no. Just . . . actually not feeling too well. Where's the restroom? Do you know?"

She hesitated. "Well, I don't." She was looking around.

"I'll find it. I'll be right back." Lessing rose and smiled at her then stepped into the restaurant. He glanced back, noting that she was looking at her own phone. He had to assume she'd just gotten a text about him from SVR headquarters.

He stepped into the tiny, garlic-scented kitchen of the place, then he was out the back door. In the alley, he turned away from the restaurant and jogged to the closest street. A line of four cars queued, waiting for the light to change. Like most cars here, they were small, dark-colored sedans. He stepped to the first. The driver, a young woman, glanced his way and frowned, seeing his troubled face. He wasn't looking at her, however, but at the gear shift, which was a manual. He didn't know how to operate one.

Some James Bond.

Same with the second car. The third, however, was an automatic. He rapped harshly on the window, quickly flashing and putting away his Virginia driver's license before the round, balding driver could see it clearly. Lessing snapped in Polish, "I'm an officer with Agencja Bezpieczeństwa Wewnętrznego. We have a state emergency. I need your car!"

"But I—" The man's face revealed concerned surprise.

"Here." Lessing thrust two hundred dollars' worth of zlotys into the man's hand and opened the door. "Wait at that corner. I'll be five minutes."

The man climbed out, counting the money. "Well. Five minutes only. But let me see that ID once again."

"There is no time!" Lessing dropped into the driver's seat, slammed the door shut and hit the accelerator. He skidded into the opposite lane and headed for the nearest road that seemed to lead out of town. He had no idea where it went but it was paved and he suspected—prayed—it didn't dead end at an old coal mine or factory . . . where his bones might be found twenty years from now.

Glancing back in the rearview mirror, he could glimpse the café table where he'd just been sitting with Valentina Rostikov. She had leapt to her feet and was gesturing to a car, which skidded to a stop in front of her. Lessing saw its driver lean over and push open the passenger door. It was Boris Bukharin.

Suddenly, behind them, Lessing saw the driver whose car he'd commandeered running up the street, pointing his way and shouting. Lessing floored the gas. He glanced up in the rearview mirror. Bukharin and Rostikov's car suddenly swung around and burned rubber in his direction. They sped after him.

Lessing looked ahead.

Soon they were racing along the two-lane road, which was surrounded by dense trees. Completely deserted.

No need for a coal mine or abandoned factory for my bones, he reflected. A body buried in this wilderness would never be found.

The flat road meant they could easily hit seventy or eighty miles an hour without straining the cylinders. It was still too warm for ice or snow but the asphalt was damp in places and several times Lessing's car skidded badly. With luck and some skill he controlled it and continued on.

A few miles along, the trees became sparser and soon they were in open fields.

Lessing grimaced. There was little cover and if Rostikov and Bukharin, only thirty yards behind him now, wished to brake to a stop and pull out guns to shoot, they could easily disable his little car, if not hit him directly through the back window.

Still, what was there to do?

He gripped the wheel and shoved the accelerator to the floor.

The wheezing engine protested but, to his amazement, the shivering vehicle sped up further.

Ahead was a stand of trees and a curve after that. At least the pines would provide some cover and might give Lessing a chance to duck down a crossroad.

He took the curve at close to sixty.

It was true that the trees cut off Rostikov's view of Lessing.

They also had blocked Lessing's view of the cow.

A large, oblivious bovine was standing half on the shoulder and half in the middle of the right lane, looking for another patch of grass to dine on. Lessing was an animal lover—he was truly fond of his goldfish—but he would nonetheless have sacrificed Bossy in an instant, had she not outweighed his car. He spun the wheel, segueing around her, missing the creature by inches.

After a split-second nose-to-nose mutual examination, he caromed off the highway and bounded into a field.

The infrastructure on the undercarriage of the vehicle snapped and cracked and after a brief airborne moment, the car slammed into a ditch half-filled with manure.

Silence.

Lessing stayed conscious, though his face hurt from the enthusiastic airbag, his arm too. He took an assessment; nothing seemed broken. He glanced back toward the road. Nothing. Maybe the Russians and the cow had met unpleasantly.

But, no. Bukharin had braked in time. He and Rostikov were now out of the car and running toward him. He popped the seat belt and shoved the door open as far as he could, stepping over the brown mass into which the car had crashed. He leapt onto solid ground and promptly cried out as he fell, his foot entangled in a vine.

He watched the Russians getting closer, slowing.

"Peter! What are you doing?" Rostikov cried.

He wondered about the procedure, upon capture. Give them only his name, rank and serial number?

Well, he was a civilian. So: name and job title and employee ID?

They walked up to him, carefully avoiding the manure. Lessing sat up. Bukharin remained behind and Rostikov stepped in front of him. Neither had drawn their guns. Of course, they wouldn't shoot him yet; they'd wait till after the torture.

"Why did you do that, Peter? Why did you run?"

"Um, excuse me?" Lessing swallowed hard.

Curious. Could it be that they *hadn't* yet learned he was CIA? But they soon would. He decided to stay in his role a bit longer. "Conscience. I couldn't do it."

"Ah, Peter, come back with us. I'll take care of driver. We'll pay him off." Rostikov nodded at the wrecked car axle deep in manure. "You have such an excellent mind. Your ideas for our project are exemplary. And you were tempted. I could see it! Just let me talk to you a bit longer. Just the two of us."

His shoulders slumped. It was hopeless . . .

Just then a voice from behind startled them all. "You are not to move." It was English, heavily accented with a Slavic intonation. All three turned quickly. Two men in suits and overcoats, burly and unsmiling, were standing in the road. Both held dark pistols, aimed vaguely toward the threesome.

"It's all right," Rostikov said, reaching for her pocket.

The older man said, "No, no. Hands will not move."

"We are officers with the SVR." Rostikov looked at them the way one would regard an irritating gnat.

The older one said to his associate, "Klaus, see."

The shorter and younger man strode forward and took the Russians' IDs. Without a glance, he handed them to his boss, who read through them. He put them in his overcoat pocket.

"No. I want them back." Rostikov said.

The older agent ignored her and said, "You, the American. Come here." Gesturing to Lessing with his pistol.

Lessing understood now. These were *Polish* secret police. He'd been right. The hotel manager worked for them, and he'd informed them that Lessing was CIA. He wasn't going to end up in a Moscow prison at all, but one in Warsaw.

He climbed to his feet and dusted his hands together. Then he walked to the two agents, who looked him over with grim expressions.

Behind them, Lessing could hear a vehicle approaching. A dark van pulled up behind the Polish agents' unmarked sedan on the shoulder of the road. The door opened and four tactical officers climbed out, jogging to the cluster of people in the field. They were armed with machine guns.

They need four soldiers to take me into custody?

But, to Lessing's shock, the officers ignored him and surrounded Rostikov and Bukharin. They bound the Russian agents' hands behind them with plastic restraints and searched them, removing a pistol from Bukharin's jacket pocket.

In a threatening tone, Rostikov sputtered, "Are you mad? You cannot do this! Did you not hear? I'm SVR. We have an arrangement with Agencja Bezpieczeństwa."

The older plainclothes agent said, "Madam Rostikov, that is surely the truth. But it is true also that we are not with Agencja Bezpieczeństwa."

Another figure emerged from the van and made his way over the grassy field. It was Vlad, the sour man who'd driven Lessing and Stan Smiles from Prague.

Vlad eyed the scene, studied Rostikov for a moment, then Bukharin. He said to Lessing, "These gentlemen are with the ÚZSI."

One of the Czech security agencies.

"We're in the Czech Republic?" Valentina Rostikov gasped.

She looked around at the landscape. Apparently they had missed a border marker sometime back, in the pursuit . . . if there had even been one.

In Czech, Vlad said to the tactical troops, "Get them to Mladoboleslavska."

Lessing knew this was a Czech military air base near Prague. The CIA and other US forces sometimes used it as a transit point for prisoners and suspects bound for interrogation sites around Europe and Africa.

The older of the Czech agents nodded to the tactical troops, two of whom extracted black hoods from their pockets and pulled them over the heads of the protesting Rostikov and Bukharin. They were roughly dragged across the field and flung into the back of the van, which sped forward and disappeared down the road to the west.

"Phone?" Vlad asked.

Lessing said, "What?"

"Your phone?"

"Oh." He reached into his jacket pocket and produced it.

Vlad removed the battery and flung it in one direction, the phone in another. The cow stared at the spot where it landed. Then returned to eating grass.

"I—" Lessing began.

"We should go," Vlad said, and began walking to the Czech agents' sedan parked alongside the two men.

Lessing considered his luggage at the hotel. "Back to Kostka?"

Vlad frowned. "Hey, Mr Star. You thinking that a good idea? Really?"

• • •

"How the hell did you do it, Lessing?"

"Well," Lessing said. And fell silent.

"You're a modest one." The director's smile filled the laptop screen.

The slim, sallow man was four thousand miles away, in Northern Virginia, speaking to Lessing and Stan Smiles, who sat in a secure conference room in the US embassy in Prague. They were talking to each other via a system that was like Skype but of course not Skype.

The director continued, "Rostikov's on her way to a black site. Don't worry." He was probably looking at Lessing's furrowed brows. "No extreme interrogation. We'll cut a deal with her. She's not a stupid woman." A shrug. "Or we might just offer to trade her back in exchange for the Cincinnati Network names . . . and a few others. We were hoping to take down forty per cent of the Network. We'll roll up the whole thing, thanks to you."

"You didn't tell me she was a woman," Lessing said.

The director grumbled, "Never occurred to us that she'd leave Moscow. Hardly ever does."

Smiles said coyly, "But good thing for you she's that gender. Considering the other night."

"But, really," the director persisted. "How'd the idea occur to you? To lure her to the Czech Republic?"

"I . . . well . . ."

It seemed that Smiles, with Vlad nearby, had set up a safe house on the other side of the border and were monitoring the operation, visually when they could and by the signal coming from Lessing's phone when they couldn't get close. When he'd stolen the car and fled, with Bukharin and Rostikov in pursuit, Smiles had realized what was going on and called Czech security services to help put together a snatch op.

Preferring not to say that his courage broke, that he'd turned tail and run, Lessing told them: "Just occurred to me. Improvised, I guess you could say."

Smiles said, "Well, it was smart. You made yourself real attractive to the Russians—all those ideas about how to exploit the president's sons. And then, bang, changing your mind, fleeing. You took hard to get to a new level. They *had* to come after you."

The director said, "Another officer might've pushed her, to commit to something, but, no, you knew she'd believe you only if you ran."

"Well, I suppose . . ." Lessing sighed. He decided he couldn't keep the deception going any longer. He had to tell them the truth—that he'd run from the Russians not to lead them over the border but because he thought his cover had been blown by the hotel manager. He opened his mouth to confess.

"Listen—"

Before he could, though, Smiles said, "Now, some practical things. We'll burn your cover. We'll shred the Peter Crenshaw passport. And the credit card." He added to the director, "He covered his tracks well—paid for the meals with zloty and at the hotel, he was cash in advance."

"But listen."

The men glanced at him closely.

Then Lessing actually gasped.

Oh, my God.

Cash in Advance.

CIA.

That was the notation on his registration card!

His "brilliant" strategy, which led to the rendition of a top Russian agent, was based on a complete blunder.

"What were you saying, Lessing?"

Don't be stupid, he told himself. This is not the time for confessions. "I just wanted to tell you that the fact is I couldn't've done it without you guys backing me up."

This didn't seem to be the sort of thing intelligence officers said.

"Yes, well." The director looked off for an awkward moment.

"I've got a meeting. So, Lessing. We've got a Clandestine Service training session opening in a few weeks. Say the word and we'll get you into the program. There'll be travel. Could be tough work, dangerous, but we could use somebody like you. How 'bout it?"

A slideshow went through Lessing's mind: the air trip to Prague, the excitement of getting through Customs with a fake ID, outthinking the surly hotel manager, the passionate night he'd spent with a beautiful Russian spy, the car chase.

Then he thought: Cash in Advance.

Lessing said, "I'll have to pass, sir. I don't think I'm cut out for it."

"You sure?"

"I am."

The director eyed him closely. "You're sure you're not just playing hard to get?"

A chuckle. "Not this time, sir."

"Very well. We'll get you home on the next transport. And thanks again."

The screen went black.

The Writers' Conference

"Got a plum for you, Jim. A round and ripe plum."

"That right, Stan? The Bennett case? Tell me it's so."

Friday noon in the Santa Rosa County Sheriff's Department, in beautiful and some said historic Ocean Shore, California.

Perched on a hill crowned by scrub oak, succulents and pine, and dusted with fine sand, the Spanish-style ranch building dated to the Sixties and indeed featured a view of both ocean and shore. That is, Chief of Detectives Stan Mellers's office did, where the two men now sat. Deputy Jim Handle's desk was on the other side of the structure and his scenery was parking lot and shrubs.

"Aw, Jim. Again? You don't want that case. I keep telling you."

Handle settled his lanky frame into the chair in front of Mellers's desk. It was a beige scene, all around. The rattan chair, Handle's uniform, and his hair. Complexion would've been part of it too, if the detective's face and arms weren't so sun-ruddy.

"You know what, Stan? I *do* want that case. Want it a lot."

"I'm sorry, Jim. But—"

"I know. I'm on the force only three years, not that long. But I've run homicides. Corpse to conviction."

"Gangbangers using each other for target practice. Not *CSI* grade, Jim. Those're what you could call Hondas. The Bennett case's your Lexus. Or even higher ticket than that."

Handle wasn't sure Mellers should be making light of a twenty-five-year-old woman abused and murdered, her body weighted down in the bay. But he wanted onto the case bad, so he kept mum on the taste issue.

Mellers shifted in his chair, also rattan but a swivel model. The chief was six four and outweighed Handle by sixty or more; the furniture protested.

Handle: "I've told you, I've read every psych book and forensic text on serial killers they've got in the county library and on the internet. Most of them, anyway. I—"

"Well, I know, Jim. I'm impressed. Really am. But, see, that's a problem. Sally Bennett was one victim. Solo. *Nada* serial."

"There was that other missing girl. A year ago."

"She ran off. Everybody says so."

"But Sally," Jim persisted, "her death fits a profile. The pattern of the cuts, the sexual assault, the—"

"Just can't make a determination. Not yet. Body was a mess and a half, y'know."

Sally had been in the ocean for a week before she floated to the surface. The fact that her parents had something to bury and the SRSD had proof of a murder was close to a miracle. She might never have been found but for some sea creatures chewing on the ropes binding her to the concrete blocks sixty feet down.

Though, as Handle had told his boss, at least the cold water of the Pacific had had a preservative effect. Corpses dumped into the balmy Caribbean, for instance, were often reduced to an indistinct food group in a few days. This fact was from his homework. Jim Handle frequently thought: I truly intend to get my head around this serial killer thing. I'm going places.

"Just give me a *piece* of the case, Stan."

Mellers himself was running the homicide, as he did all important cases, but he could, and did, dole out portions of the investigation from time to time.

The chief, it seemed, was genuinely troubled he couldn't help Handle out. "Staffing, and everything . . . Wilkins gone with that heart attack, the budget. The Squid Festival, the car race. I just don't have the manpower I'd like to take you off other cases."

This was true. Everybody knew it.

Handle had debated asking their ultimate boss, Sheriff Joaquin Del Rio, if he could get onto the Bennett case. But Mellers had run the Detective Division for twenty years, longer than Del Rio had been in office, and he was a good cop. Handle didn't have either the ground or enough bad judgment to go around Mellers.

Handle gave up on Bennett and asked, "Plum assignment, you were saying?"

"Yesiree, Jim. You're going to like this one."

"What is it?"

"A do at the convention center. And you, yes, you, my friend, get to head up security." As in most cities nowadays, the convention center, and its attached hotel in Ocean Shore, was considered a potential terrorist target, and a Santa Rosa deputy was frequently assigned to meetings there, supplementing the center's security staff.

In reaction, Handle gave a tiny nod like the bobble of a bobble-head dog on the dash of a smooth-riding car, a Caddie—or, okay, a *Lexus*—idling at a stoplight.

"Security."

"Don't look so hangdog, Jim. It'll be like a vacation. You won't have anything to do but stroll around the air-conditioned halls and sip soda and eat funnel cakes. The convention? It's a bunch of writers. How much trouble can they get themselves into?"

. . .

At 2 p.m. Jim Handle parked his squad car in the convention center lot and made his way through the hot Santa Ana wind toward the front door, over a path beside the half-mile gray-sand beach, presently being caressed by waves from a Pacific Ocean living up to its name, which it didn't always do.

As a detective, Handle usually dressed down—jeans, collared shirt and sports jacket. But the rule for security detail was to be obvious. There was some debate about the wisdom of this requirement. One theory was that seeing a uniformed officer would discourage a terrorist from even starting an attack.

The other theory was that the terrorist would know whom to shoot first.

Handle found the director of the facility, a harried-looking man juggling the typical issues of events of this sort. He didn't have much time for Handle, which was fine with the detective. He'd been concerned the man might micromanage and that was one thing that didn't sit well with Detective James Handle.

Then there was a fast meeting with the security staff in their office and, after that, the detective wandered off to check out the writers' meeting.

The convention center in Ocean Shore could hold only ten thousand souls, give or take, which meant the big conferences went elsewhere; there'd never been an AMA or high-tech get-together here. The organizers of a cosplay anime event gave it a shot but there were too many Sailor Moons and Pokémons per square foot and the county fire marshal had to close the gathering down.

But a bunch of authors? They didn't fill up but an eighth of the center. This was largely due, Jim Handle supposed, to the fact that the attendees were part of a specialized group: they were all *crime* writers.

Handle didn't read much. Didn't have the time, for one thing. He tended to put in long hours on the job and he had a family, which kept him plenty busy. Becky was taking a few years off her job as a nurse to raise their boy and girl, seven and five, but Handle spelled her when he could. He also spent time out on his fishing boat, Pacific-worthy, pursuing his favorite hobby.

And when he did read, it was usually for his own edification—like the criminal profiling and forensic books he'd reminded his boss about, trying again to talk his way onto the Bennett homicide.

Still, even if he didn't know much about the world of fiction, he enjoyed walking around the writers' conference, looking at the exhibits and bookseller stalls and sticking his head into a session or two.

He got a kick out of some of the titles. "Killing Your Baby," for instance, which wasn't, as he initially thought, about infanticide, but a panel of writers griping about how Hollywood had made bad movies of their good books. He was going to ask a question—"How many of you sent your checks back in protest?"—but, being an outsider, he decided not to.

Another was "What *Fifty Shades of Grey* Can Teach Mystery Writers About Sex Scenes."

He passed on that one.

Handle did, however, make a beeline for "Serial Killing Update," which presented the latest forensic and profiling trends on the subject. The lecture was by a former FBI agent from the Bureau's behavioral profiling division, and Handle found him well informed and a gifted speaker. Even though the presentation was for laypeople, Handle learned a few things, jotting notes on a pad provided by the organization hosting the event.

Then back to work, cruising the hallways, looking for potential terrorists or robbers, noting that the concession stand was closed, no soda, no funnel cakes.

Around 5 p.m. Handle noticed many attendees gravitating toward a large room off the main corridor. Inside, he saw people queuing in front of a lengthy table at which sat three men and two women. He turned to the attractive brunette he found himself standing beside and asked, "Excuse me, you connected with the convention?"

"Me? I'm just attending. I'm a literary agent."

"Scouting out new talent?"

"And meeting some of my existing clients. Deborah Tailor." She stuck out a hand.

"Jim Handle."

"As in the composer?"

"As in the drawer pull."

She eyed the uniform. "Anything I should be concerned about?"

"Just routine."

"Oh yeah? That's what Sergeant Joe Friday used to say just after the body appeared."

He smiled. "What's going on here? This's a book signing?"

"That's right. This's the nominees' session. Those five'll all have been nominated for the Tombstone. See, on the table there?"

Handle looked where she was pointing and noted a black ceramic gravestone mounted to a wooden base.

"That's an *award*? That people *win*?"

"The biggest writer's award of the year."

"It come with any money?"

"Nope. All about prestige. But you win, you'll usually sell more books. Use it for publicity."

"When's the winner announced?"

"The banquet tomorrow night."

"And those folks, the nominees, I'm curious, they famous?"

"Not like movie stars or athletes. But they're pretty well known in our world."

Tailor identified them and gave a little bio for each.

Joe Devereux, early sixties, wrote a popular series of thrillers about a blind forensic detective in New York City. Seemed a little far-fetched to Handle. But who was he to talk about credibility in entertainment? He and Becky enjoyed *Phineas and Ferb* with the kids.

"He's got the longest line. He the best writer?"

"No. But he plays the game the best."

"The game?"

"Sure," she said. "The game. All the same. Writing fiction, art, movies, business, Washington. And probably the cop world. Pressing flesh, speaking, hitting the media circuit."

Handle understood. "You got that right."

The game . . .

Beside Devereux was middle-aged Lawrence Sharp, a former journalist best known for a historical thriller about a plot to murder one of Hitler's henchmen in 1930s Germany.

"Good book," Tailor said. "Sold well overseas but didn't last long on the charts here in America. I heard a story: when he was touring, apparently a bunch of readers in their teens and twenties came up to him and asked him how he'd thought up that guy Hitler. 'Epic bad guy, man,' one said. 'Better than Freddy and Jason.'"

"Not a joke?"

"Sadly, no."

Sharp hadn't written anything historical since.

The next author at the table was Joan Wilson, a sexy but twitchy thirty-something with a centipede tattoo on her arm. A native Californian, she spent as much time blogging as she did writing fiction, sharing her vehemently anti-pharma, anti-fracking, anti-pipeline views, anti-a-bunch-of-other-stuff views with the world. Her novel series featured a woman cop on the Central Coast who was a kinesics (body language) expert. Rumors were Wilson inundated popular TV crime show producers with emails and tweets, accusing them of stealing her plot ideas. No lawsuits had ensued, however.

Next to her was Frederick James, a dapper man of about forty-five in suit and tie. Tailor explained that James wrote a series of espionage thrillers about a British superspy. His most recent book had gone nearly to the top of the *Times* of London bestseller list but was beaten by Joe Devereux's latest title by a mere eighty-seven copies.

The last author was Edith Billingsley. She was in her late sixties or early seventies, slim, with carefully coiffed white hair. She wrote a popular series of murder mysteries featuring a quirky young woman who lived in Manhattan named Ruth Ursula Nancy Evans.

"Her books're in the cozy category. No explicit sex or violence. Her bad guys swear by saying, 'Heavens!' And they don't kill people. They 'dispatch' them."

Handle nodded. "'Dispatch.' I like that. I should use it in a report. 'A witness stated he saw Hector Gomez, of the M-13 gang, *dispatch* Alonzo Gutiérrez at three thirty a.m. on Alvarado Street by firing ten forty-caliber rounds into his head.'"

Tailor smiled, an expression that faded as she regarded the older woman author, who was at that moment signing a devoted fan's book. "Edith's been nominated for the Tombstone seven times. Never won it."

Handle, who hadn't been to a book signing before, was interested in the phenomenon. He noted that some authors shook fans' hands heartily, some ignored the outstretched palms. Fredericks fist-bumped. Laurence Sharp was a shaker, but he used antibacterial spray after each grip, which seemed a bit insulting. Some authors agreed to have pictures taken with the fans, others didn't. Some signed all the books a fan had bought, while others limited the signing to five or ten, or only the hardcover edition.

The authors were, as a rule, friendly but reserved, displaying a caution that bordered on the paranoid. Joe Devereux, for instance, firmly explained to a fan—a young man wearing a narrow-brimmed fedora—that he wasn't able to accept the unpublished manuscript offered him.

Tailor told Handle, "He wants Joe to give him a blurb—you know, a recommendation—so he can show it to publisher. But you can run into legal troubles doing that if the book's not already under contract. The author could claim he stole ideas from him."

Handle watched the fan grimace and walk off unhappily, his many-page manuscript in hand.

And he noted that Joan Wilson turned down an offer by a husband and wife—clearly people she'd never met—to "come on back to our trailer with us and do some soakin' in the hot tub."

Frederick James declined to sign a fan's breasts with the same Sharpie he'd just used to inscribe her book. Handle noted, before telling himself to look away, that the author could probably have written a whole paragraph on the proffered cleavage.

"Kind of a three-ring circus," he observed.

"Oh, it can be," Tailor said.

"Who's gonna win that ugly award, you think?"

"Oh, I know who it is. The committee chair's a friend of mine. But I'm not allowed to tell."

"I'm a cop."

"And you have the uniform to prove it."

"We're good at keeping secrets."

She debated, he noted. Then in a whisper: "It's Devereux."

"Which, I sense, you're not too happy with."

"Not really."

"All that game-playing of his?"

"Aw, he's not so bad. Just, I was rooting for Billingsley. All those times nominated and never a win. And it was a close call, the votes. But Joe nosed her out by just one or two."

"There's always next year," Handle said. "Well, thanks for the inside scoop." He shook her hand and walked through a doorway to the second floor, where the book store was located, made a purchase or two (serial killer tomes, what else), then headed downstairs and out to his car for his dinner break.

He returned an hour later and made the rounds. He conferred with the conference center's security guards and checked video cameras. No al-Qaeda cells seemed poised to punish infidels here. No armed robbers were planning heists. No stalkers lurked.

Which wasn't to say there were no issues that required his attention. How much trouble could a bunch of crime fiction writers and fans get into? Well, a fair amount, it seemed, especially now that the bar was open.

A screaming domestic erupted when a wife learned that her author husband had carelessly said he'd liked the escort he'd had recently on tour. After Handle separated them, it turned out he wasn't referring to a sex worker; *escort* was the term used to describe a media representative hired by publishers to accompany authors to and from book signings.

One author was nabbed sneaking into the closed book room to rearrange the displays, putting his own books on top of those of his fellow authors. A non-criminal albeit embarrassing offense.

The most violent occurrence: a fist fight broke out when one author criticized another for referring in his book to a Glock pistol's safety catch—that gun doesn't have such a lever. The same thing happened ten minutes later with two other writers, this argument being about the proper use of "magazine" versus "clip" to describe the part that holds ammunition in rifles. Handle reflected that the incendiary argument about Second Amendment rights to keep and bear arms was positively tame compared with the uncompromising passion over getting the facts concerning deadly weapons right.

But these incidents and a half-dozen others were simply grist for every law enforcer, and Handle took care of them with stern humor, minimal intervention and no handcuffs.

It was the murder that truly complicated his weekend.

· · ·

When the front desk clerk got a call near midnight, composed of unintelligible but desperate gasps, she assumed the guest in room 305 needed a Heimlich intervention.

Two young members of the bell staff sped to the room, ready to expel the offending olive or grape. They brought along a defib, just in case.

Opening the door with a master key, they stopped fast, looking down, both no doubt thinking: Damn good thing resuscitation procedures no longer recommended mouth-to-mouth.

The volume of effluence and vomit that had erupted from the guest was quite astonishing.

A fast check, though, clearly revealed that no life-saving techniques need be employed.

Joe Devereux wasn't coming back from the dead.

Jim Handle strode into the room, accompanied by the night manager.

"My God," the skinny suited man gasped. "All that, from choking?"

Handle regarded the rictus on the victim's face, the fierce grip of the fists, the pale residue on the writer's face, the cocoon posture. "Didn't choke. He was poisoned."

"Oh. My. Well." The manager said this while staring at the food cart on which sat half the hamburger that the celebrity writer—soon to be even more famous, if considerably less productive—had been enjoying before he died.

Handle leaned down and smelled the air near the victim's mouth. Stood again. He said to the manager, "You can relax. Wasn't your kitchen killed him. Pretty sure he was poisoned intentionally."

"*What?*" the manager blurted.

"I could smell—"

One of the bellboys nodded knowingly. "The scent of almond. I saw that on *NCIS-LA*. Cyanide, right?"

"Nope," Handle replied. "The smell's pear. Chloral hydrate. Probably concentrated, to cause death so fast."

"How'd you know that?" the manager wondered.

"Research. The Jonestown Massacre? The crazy cult leader Jim Jones used chloral hydrate, mixed with some other stuff, in the Kool-Aid to kill his whole village. Now, this room's a crime scene. I want everybody out now."

Handle called the office to report the incident and asked CSU to get there pronto. He stationed a security guard outside Devereux's room to seal it and then did some preliminary investigation. He returned to the room at the same time that the Sheriff's Department crime scene unit arrived.

"Hey, Jim. You drew this one, hmm?" Scott Shreve, the lead forensic tech, and the deputy were good friends.

"Didn't so much draw it," Handle explained. "It drew me." He gave a synopsis of what he'd learned so far, and he and Shreve walked through the room, the tech photographing the scene from all angles. Shreve then leaned down and sniffed at the bottle of single-malt Scotch on the hotel-room desk. "Yep, like you said, chloral hydrate. Somebody spiked his whisky. And there, under the table, that glass? Looks like he dropped it after taking a slug or two."

Handle was looking around. "And that gift bag, the sort for bottles."

The tech nodded. "So the killer brings the bottle over and gives him the present. The visit. The perp drinks something else, something safe, and Devereux downs the fatal whisky."

"I'd guess. But more likely, the killer left the gift on the door handle, knocked, and then skedaddled."

Shreve said, "Bet he didn't knock. Just left it. Or called from a lobby phone and told the vic he'd left a present. Anonymous."

"Makes more sense," Handle said. "And look at that. A gift card. Under the bag."

Shreve pulled on blue gloves and opened the gold-colored card, which had the words "You're the Best!!!" printed on the front.

"Blank inside."

"Never make it easy for us, do they?" Handle said. He'd learned the value of handwriting analysis in solving crimes.

"Whatta you got?" said a firm voice behind them.

Handle turned and found himself looking at Chief of Detectives Stan Mellers.

"Stan."

"Jim, Scott. So?"

Handle noted two TV reporters lurking near the security guard holding back the crowd to the left. Cameras were pointed their way.

Handle and the others retreated further into the room and in low voices, he and Shreve told Mellers what they knew about the dead author and the likely poison delivered via an anonymous gift.

Mellers asked, "What about motive? He ruffle any feathers? Put his you know what where he shouldn't have?"

"Nothing yet, Stan. Jumping out."

Mellers stepped out of the room and looked up and down the corridor, where other hotel guests, most dressed, some in bathrobes, rubbernecked. Word had spread fast and the hall was crowded. Mellers sent guards to keep them away from the scene.

Handle and Mellers found themselves staring down at the body.

"A shame about this," Handle offered. "He was going to get that big award tomorrow."

"Award?"

"That the conference gives out. Best Book of the Year, something like that."

After a moment: "I read one of his books," the chief of detectives said. "Was okay. Had a big twist at the end. That's all I remember. Couldn't tell you what." He clapped his gloved hands together. "So. Let's get to work."

• • •

The next morning, Jim Handle was back on security detail, though he found himself with little to do except tell the scores of conference attendees who asked that he didn't know anything about the murder.

This was Cop 101 about being reticent to share details of a crime. It rarely ended well if you did. Word got back to the suspects. Who fled the jurisdiction.

Or—if it was easier—shot you in the head.

He was amused at the number of people who came up to him with theories on the crime. Wouldn't have happened at an accountants' or engineers' convention. But most of these people made their living, or a part of it, from crime, so to speak. When it happened, he'd nod studiously and listen. But didn't jot a single note.

The hours dragged by. A pall had settled over the convention center, thanks to the death, and Handle didn't need to play schoolmarm, as he had the day before, with petulant or argumentative writers. Everybody seemed to be on his best behavior.

Afternoon turned to evening and he was pleased when the literary agent Deborah Tailor tracked him down and offered him a ticket for the banquet and award ceremony. With the other officers here, looking into the murder, Mellers had given him the okay to take a few hours off on dinner break, and he decided to join the agent, rather than have Kentucky Fried in his car.

Together, they headed into the cocktail reception, he still in his uniform, Tailor in a classy black number with an uneven hemline. Handle thought his wife would have liked it. The banquet hall lights shot a dozen colors off the dress's sequins.

They hit the bar. She got a martini, he an on-duty iced tea. They tapped glasses.

"Don't worry," Tailor said.

"I wasn't. But about what, just for the record?"

"I'm not going to ask you about the case."

"Little early to speculate."

They talked about the fervent gossip surrounding the death that had filled the halls that day. How some authors led their presentations with a prayer for the victim and his family. Some eulogized. One or two told jokes that landed like cannon balls.

The lights dimmed, announcing dinner.

"Not many people've gone home," Tailor noted, glancing around at the at-capacity banquet hall. "You'd think after the murder, nobody would want to stay."

"No, that'd seem suspicious."

"You think the killer's here?" Her eyes danced around the room. His, too.

"Wouldn't be surprised."

"This a one-time murder? Or part of a serial killing thing?"

"Happens I've made a study of serial killing," Handle began. "This isn't one. That's a very specific, and rare, psychosis and Devereux's death doesn't fit the profile. Besides, poison's rarely a serial killer murder weapon; ruins the chance you can chow down on your victim . . . Oh, sorry, shouldn't've brought up cannibalism at dinner."

Tailor creased her brow. "Don't worry about that. I haven't eaten the rubber chicken at these things in ten years, and I'm not going to start now. Salad and rolls only."

Handle laughed. They greeted the other attendees at their table. Everybody wanted to ask about the case, but nobody did. Handle sipped his tea and enjoyed the banter. Although Tailor had told him about the jealousy among the nominees, these folks—working-class authors, midlist, he'd heard they were called—were amiable and easygoing. Smart too.

The food was as inedible as Tailor had predicted, though Handle was hungry and ate every last morsel of the chicken impersonator, along with the potatoes and, the star of the event, the key lime pie. After came some speeches and then the honoring of a lifetime achievement winner, whose subsequent remarks would have been a cure for insomniacs around the world.

The awards ceremony went on as planned.

The male and female presenters strode onto the stage and read from a sheet of paper, a writers' conference version of the teleprompter, while photos of the nominated authors and the jackets of their books appeared in sequence on a large screen behind them—all except for Deveraux's, since apparently the organization's bylaws did not permit the award to be presented posthumously.

Finally, the woman presenter tore open the envelope, paused with suitable drama and said, "And this year's winner of the Tombstone Award for Excellence in Crime Writing is . . . Edith Billingsley."

Everyone on their feet. Applause, cheers.

The elderly woman, a shocked expression on her face, walked to the stage, a picture of elegance in her long, layered deep-blue gown.

Handle glanced around the room to find the other nominees. The conference organizers, in their infinite wisdom or as a stab at cruelty, had seated them all at the same table, prominently placed nearest the stage. Larry Sharp, Joan Wilson and Frederick James were on their feet and applauding a little too enthusiastically, Handle thought. All shared the identical expression: a Goddamn-it-I-have-to-seem-happy smile bolted onto their faces.

When the applause died down Billingsley gripped the award in one hand and pulled the microphone down to her mouth—she was only a little over five feet or so.

"My goodness," she began, breathless. "My goodness. I hardly know what to say . . ." She gazed down at the ceramic award. Then set it on the podium. She pulled off her pink, glittery reading glasses and said, "Before I thank those who have helped me along the way in my career as a writer, I must first give voice to the thoughts that are on all our minds at the moment. The tragic loss of Joseph Devereux. I was thinking about his death and his contribution to our profession all day and I'd like to share with you some of my reflections."

She never got started, though.

At that moment, Chief of Detectives Stan Mellers stepped briskly from the wings, accompanied by a burly detective Handle knew by the nickname the Hulk, and the two men arrested Edith Billingsley for the murder of the man she was about to eulogize.

• • •

A half hour later, after the author had been booked at headquarters, Stan Mellers was back, holding a press conference in a meeting room off the front hall of the convention center.

There were many more reporters than before. Edith Billingsley's arrest had been picked up by every news outlet from TMZ to CNN to the *New York Times*. YouTube benefited the most: hundreds of smartphones had recorded the stage of honor being turned into a perp walk.

Viral, big time.

Mellers and his boss, County Sheriff Joaquin Del Rio, took to the podium. Del Rio was broad as a tree trunk, part Anglo, part Mexican, with mahogany skin. He didn't say much on the job and he didn't say much now, leaving communication to his chief of detectives.

Handle wasn't onstage, which was fine with him. He wouldn't have anything to say anyway. He sat beside Deborah Tailor. The room was packed. Handle noted the fire department rule, as set forth on a wall sign, limiting occupancy to fifty. There had to be twice as many in the room.

Mellers looked out over the cameras and the microphones and at the audience. He read from a prepared statement. "The Santa Rosa Sheriff's Department today arrested Edith Billingsley, a resident of Ridgefield, Connecticut, for the murder of Joseph Devereux. We believe she removed the seal on a bottle of whisky, added poison, replaced the seal and then left it in a gift bag hanging from Devereux's hotel-room door. The whisky was Glenmorangie, which Devereux has said was his favorite Scotch. The bottle and bag and a gift card contained traces of Ms Billingsley's cosmetics and hand cream, as well as strands of her hair and fibers from her clothes."

Scott Shreve's team was really, really good.

"We also found a fingerprint of hers on the ground-floor doorknob to the stairwell that led upstairs—and by which you could gain access to Mr Deveraux's room on the third floor. Ms Billingsley's room was on the tenth floor, and it's extremely unlikely that a woman of her age would have taken the stairs to get to her room, unless the elevators were broken, which they were not. It would make sense for her to walk up to Devereaux's room because there were no CCTVs in the stairwells, but there were in the elevators.

"Internal phone records show that late last night someone

placed a call from the house phone by the tenth-floor elevator to Mr Devereux's room. The call lasted just one minute. It wasn't recorded but we're sure it was Ms Billingsley calling to tell her victim of the present hanging on his doorknob.

"I should add that from reading through her novels we've learned that the accused is familiar with poisons and administering them, including the substance that has been determined to be the cause of the victim's death. Chloral hydrate."

"Stan," a man called from the back, "what was the motive?"

"We believe Ms Billingsley learned that she was the runner-up to the Tombstone award, given by the writers' conference. She had been nominated a number of times and never won. She knew that if the intended recipient died before the ceremony, the honor would go to the next highest vote winner."

"Detective Mellers," one woman reporter called out, "has Ms Billingsley made a statement?"

"She denies the charge and claims she was by herself at the time of the killing, walking on the beach, thinking up ideas for her next book. No witnesses saw her, though. We know she's lying."

It was then that Handle cocked his head with a frown.

"What is it, Jim?" Deborah Tailor asked, noting his expression.

"I'll be back in a few minutes." He rose, and left the room, pulling his mobile out of its holster, where it sat next to his Glock 17.

• • •

Fifteen minutes later, Deborah Tailor was growing bored with the press conference. She looked around. Jim Handle, whose wry humor and easygoing nature had been one of the high points of the conference so far, still had not returned to his seat. She'd give it a few minutes more and then head up to the room.

Standing out among the horde of reporters, a blond in a fiery red dress and clashing yellow scarf asked Detective Mellers stridently, "Stan, you actually think winning an award, especially one that has no cash prize, could be a motive for murder?"

"Guess it was, Tiffany. Look, it's what happened. We got a dead author . . . These creative sorts. Big egos. Easy to get rubbed the wrong way."

Noting they were in the world of CNN speculation at this point, Tailor decided to leave and return to her room for a Kahlua and a streamed episode of *House of Cards*. She got as far as the door of the meeting room when two gunshots from someone inside the hotel, not far away from where they were gathered, shook the walls and sent most of the attendees diving for cover.

Del Rio, Mellers and the Hulk went into *COPS* mode. They drew their black weapons and headed out the door.

Hot on their heels were the journalists, ditching caution and, no doubt, hoping against hope that the gunfire wasn't over and that they could, for once, live up to the name plastered on their vans and videocams, "Eyewitness."

• • •

Jim Handle stood in the corridor outside the door to room 124 in the hotel attached to the convention center. He'd used a chair to wedge open the self-closing door.

His grim face turned toward the lawmen, who were approaching.

"I've cleared the room," he called, noting their drawn guns. "Nobody else inside. No weapons, no shooters."

"What happened, Jim?" the sheriff asked. The three slipped their weapons back into their holsters.

"Take a look."

Everyone stepped inside. A table was turned over and a man of about thirty years of age lay on his back. He had two gunshot wounds—one in the chest and one in the middle of his forehead. A hipster fedora, spattered with blood, rested near the shattered head.

Mellers asked, "Who is he?"

"An attendee. A fan. His name's Josh Logan. He's from Portland."

The Hulk grunted, as if the man's city of origin explained the carnage.

"What's the story?" Sheriff Del Rio was looking around the room, squinting, trying to figure it out.

When Handle hesitated, Mellers said, "Well, Jim? Out with it."

Another pause. Then: "Fact is, Stan, I'm sorry, but I had a bit of a problem with your case against Ms Billingsley."

"Problem?"

"Go on, Jim," Del Rio said.

"Just didn't sit right."

"What're you talking about," Mellers snapped. "The evidence's all there. Hair, fingerprint, fibers, shoe print."

"He planted 'em." A nod at the body.

"But the print," Mellers said testily. "How could he have planted that?"

Handle grimaced. "No, he didn't. But that was on the door that all the attendees used to walk upstairs to the book sales room, if they didn't want to wait for the elevators. Which sure take their time here."

Nodding, Del Rio asked, "He snuck into her room to steal the evidence. How?"

"Here." Handle used a tissue to lift a hotel-room key card from the table by the window. It was completely blank, unlike the ones issued to guests, which bore the hotel's logo. "Dollars to donuts it's a master key. Stole it from the security office. There's one missing. I asked." Because there were guards nearby, he added in a whisper, "They're not the most buttoned-up rent-a-cops in the world."

Mellers remained defiant: "But the poison? Chloral hydrate. It was in her books. She knows what it does. How to administer it."

"Which tells us," the sheriff snapped, "that she *wouldn't* use it as a murder weapon. Too obvious. But somebody who wanted to frame her might. Jim, assuming you're right, how'd this boy come by it?"

Handle said, "I talked to Narcotics. You can buy chloral hydrate on the street; it's not too strong, it'll give you a high. You concentrate it, you've got a deadly poison."

Handle pointed to a hotplate and a small pan on the floor in the room's closet. A whitish residue crusted the sides and bottom.

"I . . . uh," Mellers said and then stopped trying.

The sheriff asked Handle, "Why'd you suspect him, Jim?"

Handle didn't look Mellers's way as he said, "I haven't been much included in the case, so it was a surprise when I heard Ms Billingsley didn't have an alibi because she was walking on the beach at the time the poison was delivered. I called our tech people and they got in touch with her cell phone provider. She didn't make any calls or send texts around then, but her GPS showed that she *was* on the beach.

"Sure, it's possible she gave the phone to somebody to carry, to make it look like she was on the beach. But that wasn't a reason to give up looking for another suspect. Then I remembered that yesterday this fan tried to give Devereux a manuscript. He got mad when Devereux said no. I asked around and got his name."

"That's him?" Del Rio asked. Another glance at the body.

"Right. I came up here to talk to him. He didn't want to let me in, but I told him I'd get a warrant and that'd look worse for him. He agreed finally, but closed the door—like he was going to unhook the chain—but he didn't do it right away and I heard some noises inside. Like he was hiding something. When he let me in, first thing I did was open the closet door and saw the pan and hotplate and a copy of Ms Billingsley's book. And her hairbrush too . . . He must have known I was on to him because he grabbed that." Handle gestured toward a steak knife lying on the floor beside the dead man's hand. "He came for me." A shrug. "He wouldn't stop. I didn't have much choice, Sheriff."

"It's all right, Jim. You know the rules. Have to suspend you with pay for a couple days, while there's an inquest. It'll go fine."

"Sure, Sheriff."

Del Rio looked outside in the hallway and noted that the reporters were hovering like frenzied baitfish. He said in a low voice, "You get to work on your statement now, Jim." His eyes swiveled to Stan Mellers, who was looking everywhere but back at his boss. "And Stan, you and me, we need to talk."

• • •

At 11 p.m., Jim Handle was sitting outside the convention center on a bench facing the beach. The tide was coming in gracefully, the ocean still friendly.

Handle had given up smoking years ago but he felt like a Marlboro at the moment. It had been that sort of day.

His phone dinged with a text. It was from Becky.

CONGRATS!!!!!!! Luv U!!!

She was generally a pretty laid-back person but she could go hog wild when she texted, her joy or anger given voice through punctuation and case.

There was a reason for her enthusiasm. Her text was in response to one he'd sent a few minutes ago. Handle had shared the subject of his most recent conversation with Sheriff Del Rio. Starting tomorrow, Jim Handle would be the new chief of the Detective Division of the Santa Rosa Sheriff's Department. He would also be taking charge of the Susan Bennett murder case. His salary wouldn't puff up very much, but that didn't matter. Money never did when you were doing what you loved, what you were meant to do.

Good news all around.

Everything going as he planned.

So sorry, Stan, he thought to his former boss. You just weren't cut out for the game.

At least not playing against me.

Handle nearly, but not quite, felt guilty setting Mellers up to arrest poor Edith Billingsley in front of both the audience and the carnivorous media. He thought back over the past twenty-four hours. He'd come up with an improvised but workable plot:

He learned all about the writers' conference and the people involved—the manuscript-toting fan Josh Logan, the jealous nominees, how the judging for the Tombstone worked and who the winner and the runner-up were. Then he planned out the next steps.

On his dinner break last night he'd bought and read Billingsley's novel to find a suitable means of murdering Devereux, one she'd be familiar with.

Ah, perfect, chloral hydrate.

Handle had stopped in the barrio and scored some from a gangbanger, then reduced it down to lethal strength and added it to the bottle of Glenmorangie Scotch—Devereux's favorite. He'd returned to the convention center to steal a master key from the laughably inept security staff. Then broke into Billingsley's room to pick up some physical evidence—hairs, cosmetics—to plant in and on the gift bag and the whisky bottle.

Then he'd left the bottle dangling from the author's door, taken the elevator to Billingsley's floor and called Devereux, saying he was the bell captain and had left a gift from the hotel on his door.

Next, one dead author.

Then, with a little guidance from Handle, even Stan Mellers could conclude Ms Billingsley was the culprit.

As soon as the chief of detectives announced the arrest, Handle went to Josh Logan's room, shot him, pressed a steak knife into his hand for the fingerprints and planted the hotplate and pan and the rest of the evidence.

Success! The chief of detectives was gone. Jim Handle had his job.

And most important, he was at last safe.

Now his eyes took in the scene before him tonight: the cool yellow moon's fluttery reflection on the Pacific's surface. Ah, so beautiful.

Just like the night about a month ago, that moon nearly full, as well. The ocean, close to this calm.

A perfect night.

Handle recalled kneeling in the stern of his twenty-foot fishing boat.

Seeing that delicate moonlight on the teak deck.

On his bare arms.

On the blade of the knife he gripped.

On Sally Bennett's naked white body, so smooth, so pure. She'd been bound hand and foot, duct tape. Thrashing in terror, but not going anywhere.

Handle had admired the light on her flesh for a few minutes more. Then he got to work. With her jaws taped shut, as Handle did with all his victims, Sally couldn't muster any significant volume of screaming. This method of taping was one of many facts he'd learned from all his research into serial killers—a subject he studied so diligently, not to catch predators but to avoid being caught.

When this particular diversion was your hobby, you had to be just as informed as those who would pursue you.

Evading detection was also why he'd married Becky. The profile of serial killers is that they are loners, rarely with spouses. So he'd found somebody pleasant enough to seem a suitable mate, insecure enough not to ask too many questions about his whereabouts when he took his "fishing trips" and eager to have kids (being a father pushes you further into the "no" column when cops analyze serial suspects).

And if he wasn't much aroused by his wife, that was no problem. Every few months he'd spend a day or two with a victim like Sally Bennett, and that would satisfy the great need within him.

Then had come the close call—the inconsiderate school of fish gnawing through Sally's rope, her body floating heavenward. Handle had been careful, but having the woman's body surface was bad. Very bad. He'd tried to get onto the case to destroy evidence and misdirect the leads, but Mellers wouldn't cooperate.

So Handle needed to destroy Mellers's career and replace him.

Thank God the writers' conference had come to town. It offered everything he needed.

"Detective?" A woman's voice cut through the night.

It took all Handle's willpower not to jump. He turned slowly. His hand strayed to his Glock.

Deborah Tailor was walking slowly down the streetlamp-lined sidewalk. She carried her shoes. She would've been walking on the beach.

"Hi," he said, relaxing.

"Join you?"

"Sure."

"Nice tonight. The heat broke."

"Think the Santa Anas're gone for the year. And no wildfires. We were lucky. So. All these writers' conferences as exciting as this one?"

She laughed. "Usually it's mostly passive-aggressive behavior we see. Not aggressive-aggressive."

Handle noted her quick eyes, looking him over. She was sharp, observant. He hoped there wasn't going to be a problem.

"Got a question for you," she said after a moment.

"What'd that be?"

She asked, "You ever write anything?"

"Write anything? Police reports is about all."

Tailor said, "I heard how you figured out Edith wasn't the killer. And how you tracked down the real one."

"All in a day's job."

"Interesting you mention that. It's exactly what I'm thinking of."

"How's that?"

"Would you be interested in writing a series of first-person crime novels with somebody like you as the protagonist?"

"You're joking."

"Nope. Not at all. You've got a voice."

"Voice?"

"I don't mean speaking voice. I mean thinking voice. A personality voice. What about it?"

Handle laughed. "Oh, I don't know."

Though he was thinking: one of the aspects of serial killers—that research again, all those books—is that they avoid activities in which they're public personalities. If he were to become a published author, that'd tamp suspicion down a bit further, after he went on his next fishing trip, which he was already looking forward to.

Still, he had to be realistic. "I've got my college degree, but, fact is, I don't know much about style and grammar and all that. English wasn't my strong suit."

"You'd have copyeditors and proofreaders to handle that. The only thing they can't help you with is plots." Her eyes scanned his face once more. "But I have a feeling you'd be good at plotting, Detective Handle."

He considered this a moment, then said, "You know, I think I would too."

"We have a deal?"

And Jim Handle firmly shook her outstretched hand.

A Matter of Blood

One

Thursday, November 8, 1888

The man in the leather waistcoat quit his rooms and began his short walk to a news vendor on Aldgate High Street.

The early morning air chilled the slim man, save for when he passed through one of the bands of sun slipping through gaps between the low buildings here in the East End. The neighborhood was, however, congested as a hive and those moments of warmth were few.

At the vendor's kiosk he bought a number of newspapers and, venturing to a dismal shop, he purchased some bread and pickles and cheese. He then walked south and east, eyeing the crowds around him with some suspicion, in a circuitous route that eventually led him back to his rooms, a not unpleasant living space on the short and dark and, fortunately, quite private Somerset Street. Entering and locking the door, he hung his jacket and unbuttoned his waistcoat. Then he made a cup of tea and sat at the unsteady table to read the news of the day.

When he found no reports of developments that might alarm him, he located his shears and clipped some articles, as souvenirs. These he arranged into a stack which he set on a second table, beside a much larger collection of stories, sliced from the *London Daily News*, the *London Standard*, the *Daily Mirror*, the *Police News* and the *Manchester Guardian*, and from some smaller papers from around the British Isles, as well as from America, the Continent, Australia and even one from Singapore.

Prominent among them was perhaps his favorite news account from a London broadsheet:

GHASTLY MURDER

IN THE EAST END

DREADFUL MUTILATION OF A WOMAN

This headline and the accompanying article were not what so pleased him, though. No, what was deliciously agreeable was a small graphic box contiguous to that news account. An advertisement:

WARNER'S

SAFE

KIDNEY AND LIVER CURE

The irony of the juxtaposition was not lost on the man in the leather waistcoat, whose given name was Jacques.

Sipping his tea, Jacques fished his pocket watch from the brown vest and regarded the time. He was disappointed to see that it was still many hours till nightfall. His impatience swelled. But he was a man who could contain his urges and so, he told himself, he would simply have to wait. Better to be smart.

He unwrapped his cheese and opened the jar of pickles. Then

began to slice the bread with a knife that was, to him, dreadfully dull.

. . .

Erasmus Nathan Wentworth used a brass tool to scrape clean his pipe and refill it with tobacco imported from America, cherrywood tinged. After tamping it, he lit the bowl and drew the relaxing smoke into his mouth. Let the vaporous ghost escape ceilingward.

The hour was 10 a.m. and he was sitting in his dim office at Metropolitan Police headquarters. His facility was on Great Scotland Yard, not Whitehall Place—in one of the buildings into which the organization had just expanded from the private residence that had housed the police for more than five decades.

His eyes settled on a newspaper front page, the *Daily Advertiser*.

BLOODY SUNDAY!

**TWO THOUSAND POLICE CLASH
WITH SOCIAL DEMOCRATIC FEDERATION
AND IRISH NATIONAL LEAGUE**

THREE DEAD, HUNDREDS INJURED

The incident had happened one year ago and Wentworth had received a commendation for attempting to calm the rampaging officers. He had also received threats upon his life for the very same heroics—from constables who were not pleased to have their antics censured. But Scotland Yard periodically went through paroxysms of crisis, during which the old and the corrupt were winnowed out—like so much chaff.

Wentworth had kept the newspaper, which his wife had mounted in a gold-painted frame, as a reminder that policemen were stewards of the people; they were not overlords, they were not criminals.

He had, however, only to look upon the landscape of sheaves of paper on his desk to be reminded: I am hardly a very good steward at the present moment.

Wentworth, accordingly, added to himself: And where might you be, Jack? And more to the point, *who* might you be?

It had been more than one month since the Whitechapel killer had so viciously murdered victims three and four, who like the first two, were unfortunates—prostitutes—in that harsh, hardworking part of East London. Elizabeth Stride and Catherine Eddowes had been killed on the same day. Miss Stride's body had been found in Dutfield's Yard, off Berner Street. Miss Eddowes's corpse had been discovered in Mitre Square. Unlike the other three victims, whose bodies had been horrifically mutilated, Miss Stride had suffered a "mere" (the press reported, with some disappointment, Wentworth assessed) slash to the left side of her neck. There was some speculation that she had been the victim of another murderer, not Saucy Jacky, but Wentworth thought not. His examination of the wound told him that it was most likely caused by the same blade—and passersby had caused Jack to flee before the dissection could begin.

Detective Inspector Wentworth was one of dozens of officers within the Metropolitan Police's Criminal Investigation Division working full-time or partially to identify and apprehend the Whitechapel murderer. He, along with Frederick Abberline, was based here in the Central Office. Others were in H Division Whitechapel. In addition, detective inspectors from the City Police were assisting and, to stir the stew even more hotly, a private organization—the Whitechapel Vigilance Committee—

was prowling the streets of East London, causing more trouble with false leads (and unwarranted "arrests") than providing assistance.

Looking at the photographs of the savaged victims (save Miss Stride's intact corpse), however, Wentworth could hardly blame the citizenry for their concern.

Somewhere in this city of four million souls was a demented human being bent on performing the most heinous acts imaginable . . . and Wentworth and his fellow law enforcers had been unable to stop him.

He rose and put another log on the fire. He was a lean man, eleven stone, and tall—five foot ten. He was adversely affected by the cold, and today was particularly damp and chill, despite a bold sun. His office was hardly insulated from the elements.

Just as he settled into his chair once more, a figure appeared in his doorway, a constable, a flaxen-haired man, young (although to Wentworth, well into his fourth decade, the newcomers were younger every year). He said, "Two men have arrived to see you, sir."

He was not expecting anyone. Perhaps, he hoped, it was some intelligence that would bear on the Whitechapel affair—that is, some *useful* intelligence; Scotland Yard daily received dispatches and accounts in person, purporting to have information about Jack's identity, his motive, his whereabouts, his ancestry, his relations and any number of other bizarre revelations (such as one sworn statement that the killer transmogrified from wolf to human, at will).

The two men entered. Both were dressed well and were close to Wentworth in age, though perhaps a few years older. One walked in a stilted fashion, assisted by a modest wooden cane.

They sat.

"Detective Inspector Wentworth, I am Henry Gladbrook," said the taller of the two, who turned to the man with the infirmity.

"And this is Dr Richard Adams. May we smoke? Or, I alone, I should say. The good doctor here does not partake."

The doctor gave a good-natured laugh. "Had enough smoke in Kandahar to last me all my years—that is, from our Martini-Henrys and the muskets of Ayub Khan. Assorted cannon too, of course."

Wentworth lifted his pipe and puffed. "Please, sir."

Gladbrook removed a battered case from his breast pocket and extracted a cigar. He scratched a match to flame and inhaled. "Now, I'll get to the matter at hand. And I do hope you will forgive my forthrightness."

"Certainly."

"I am a personal advisor to Lord Ashton, who is in turn—"

Wentworth nodded. "An advisor to Her Majesty the Queen." This was well known.

"Her Majesty has had a word with Lord Ashton and he with me. Hence my appearance here today. *Our* appearance, I should say."

"Pray continue, Mr Gladbrook."

"I will say, Detective Inspector, that you are held in high regard at the Palace."

Wentworth raised a brow. This was so? He had not thought that this was the case.

"The Bloody Sunday riot, of course. And you've been instrumental in concluding a number of investigations. The Bedford murders, the Leeds Station robbery, the Yates abductions. To name but a few." Gladbrook exhaled and the cigar smoke joined the pipe's. "But it's my duty to tell you that Her Majesty is displeased the Whitechapel matter has gone unresolved for as long as it has."

This, however, was *not* news. Or at least Wentworth could easily have summoned the supposition of Her Royal Highness's concern. Indeed, he had been one of the CID officers who'd worked on a possible lead to the killer that Queen Victoria herself had suggested: that Jack was from the Continent, a worker familiar with butchery, arriving on one of the cattle boats that docked every week in the East End. That strain of investigation, however, had not been successful.

"No one is more troubled than I, sir. And I would be pleased if you could tell Lord Ashton and perhaps Her Majesty herself that the officers on the case are working round the clock to see this fellow brought to justice."

"Please, Detective Inspector, rest assured that there is no enmity toward you in particular in the Palace or Houses of Parliament or on Whitehall Street. But it is the belief that we must find a resolution to this matter forthwith. Hence my visit here—in the company of Dr Adams. Whose presence you must surely be wondering about."

"In truth, yes."

"Are you familiar with the character Sherlock Holmes?"

"I am not."

"He's the creation of a gentleman who has written a novel for a general audience about the solving of a crime. This Holmes, a resident of London, is a consulting detective. The novel is *A Study in Scarlet* and it was published last year in *Beeton's Christmas Annual*."

Wentworth was familiar with the publication. Popular stories, many serials. The sort of magazine that Dickens might have published one of his tales in. When his son and daughter, now grown, were young, Wentworth would read to them from such publications and they and his wife delighted to hear him attempt the various voices of the characters, asserting that he was as good as Charles Kean himself.

"The book is quite enjoyable and I understand the author, a fellow named Doyle, is planning more fiction featuring this Holmes. I bring him up because his speciality is using deductive reasoning from obscure facts to come to a conclusion. I know officers such as yourself do that quite frequently."

"It is part of the detection process, yes, sir."

"And that is exactly what my colleague Dr Adams is well known for—in medical circles. But, perhaps I'll let him explain."

"Yes, surely," Adams said. "Inspector, I am a lecturer at the Royal College of Physicians and maintain a private practice as well. One of my areas of expertise, as Mr Gladbrook has stated, is to use deduction to ascertain the cause of a rare or hitherto unseen malady and determine what might be the best way to treat it: surgery, medicine, relocation to a different climate and so forth. Your villains are human beings; mine are foreign bodies, pathogens—what we are now calling 'germs'—and other, sometimes obscure, phenomena that threaten lives. Mr Gladbrook does me far too much a favor to compare me to this Holmes. Whom you really must read, sir."

"I will do." Wentworth added, "When time permits."

The doctor continued, "I understand from Mr Gladbrook that a police surgeon has provided some insights into the killings."

"Yes, Thomas Bond. His opinion was that the murderer had no special skills as a surgeon or no particular knowledge of anatomy. The dissection after the murders—three of them—was haphazard at best. Mr Bond suggested certain insights into the killer's nature a solitary man and one motivated by erotic mania, that is, satisfaction from the killings. I will say that I myself was not swayed by his way of thinking. I believe the killer's motive is, as yet, unknowable."

"I am not, Inspector, a doctor of the mind. I am a doctor of the body. Physiology—the function of the body. And morphology— its structure. I have considerable experience with the effects of trauma upon the human corpus. Treating, as I did, soldiers in the Second Afghan War. Even if this fellow has no particular medical skills, there may be something about what he has visited upon his victims that might tell us something about him. I am here in all humility. I have no experience with crime or investigations. But I stand ready to help."

Wentworth reflected: More to the point, the Palace stands ready to *force* me to allow you to help.

Still, he was not dismayed by the men's presence. "Well, Doctor, I can't see that anything untoward would come of your assistance. Indeed, after these difficult weeks, I would welcome a new perspective. Are you free now?"

"I am."

"Then I suggest that you come around to the room where the evidence and our notes and photographs are assembled. You will see things that do not make it into the press accounts. We are rather circumspect in what is released."

Adams glanced toward Gladbrook and nodded. The palace's advisor said to Wentworth, "Excellent. I will report to Lord Ashton the outcome of this meeting and take my leave. Good day now."

The three men rose and hands were shaken once more. At the door, Gladbrook turned. "Detective, one question has occurred to me. It has been more than a month since the most recent killings. Do you think there is a chance that Jack has decided to cease the carnage? Or even more felicitously, has himself been murdered?"

Wentworth glanced at his desk on which sat one of the photographs of a corpse dismembered by Jack the Ripper. "With a man like this, sir, I have little doubt it is merely a matter of time until the madness comes over him again."

• • •

Together Westworth and Dr Adams strode through the warren of offices and hallways until they descended into what had been a cellar. The dingy room they entered, one of the larger in the building, was damp and chill.

Wentworth recalled Police Commissioner Warren's first visit here. A young constable had said to the imposing man, "'Ere's the room where we're conducting the Ripper investigation, sir. You might say it is in the *bowels* of the building." And offered a laugh.

That constable was now assigned to Tongue, a small—very small—town in the Scottish Highlands.

Wentworth jotted some instructions to one of the junior inspectors, as the doctor hung his greatcoat on a hook and, assisted by his cane, made his way to a large table covered with documents and a few objects taken from the rooms of the victims or, if they'd been discovered outside, the street or alleyways surrounding the bodies.

The inspector joined him.

"The last killing was when?" Adams asked.

"The thirtieth of September."

"Yes, the double murders."

"That is correct."

Adams walked slowly up and down the room, examining the pictures, the diagrams, the objects of evidence. He read the missives that supposedly had been sent by the killer.

"The correspondence he sent is real?"

"We believe so. Some contain information that only the real murderer would have knowledge of. And the handwriting seems to match, so that all three were inscribed by the same man."

The killer or someone purporting to be the killer had sent two letters and a taunting postcard. The first, with the salutation "Dear Boss," was signed with the name "Jack the Ripper." The valediction on other was "Saucy Jacky."

"Yet the grammar and spelling," the doctor pointed out, "are not consistent. And one contains serious errors."

"We believe that is done intentionally, to throw us off."

"So he's perhaps not a slavering madman, as the press suggests."

"I think not. He's clever."

"Now, tell me everything you can about the murders."

For a quarter hour the inspector ran through the now exhaustingly familiar details of the killings. Then he pointed out articles of clothing of the victims, weapons located in the vicinity of the poor women that might have been used in the killing, statements by witnesses.

"We have learned to be skeptical, though. The damned press is paying such sums that people who were in Glasgow or Leeds on the nights of the killings are claiming to have seen the actual slaughter."

Adams returned to the photographs and diagrams of the scenes where the four women were killed.

"Tell me, Doctor," Wentworth asked him, "do you ascertain anything from what we have here that might aid us?"

"I think he is a slight man. And not particularly strong. This ligature here? I know from post-mortem work that it is not difficult to cut through." He was pointing to a partially dismembered arm. "But as you can see, he had to readjust his grip on the cutting tool several times. There were two or three false starts. And the angle suggests he was not towering over the body when he cut."

Wentworth could indeed see that this was the case. He was impressed at the doctor's deduction.

"And the victims were all dead before he began his butchery."

"Yes, our surgeon concluded the same."

The surgeon had fallen silent as he regarded the pictures once more. Without looking up, he said, "I see here that organs have been removed. I recall from the press that he took certain organs with him."

"That is right."

"And he claimed to have eaten part of one."

"So he said, when he mailed back a portion of a kidney. Purportedly from Catherine Eddowes."

Adams tapped a photograph. "May I see the garments of the victims?"

The inspector walked to a wooden box and removed two dresses, a blouse, a shawl, a bodice, a skirt and several petticoats, all of varying hues but with one thing in common: they were stained dark brown with dried blood. Adams took them and examined each carefully. Wentworth was curious but said nothing. He was intrigued to watch the doctor's narrowed eyes study the garments with the intensity of a wolf choosing from the flock. The doctor then, curiously, lifted piece after piece to his nose and smelled. He gave a brief smile. "I think, Wentworth, that I do indeed have an insight."

"What, Doctor?"

"I noted from the photo stains on her clothing that were not dark enough to be blood. I wondered what they were and now I've come to a conclusion."

"What are they?"

Adams continued, "In my profession, of course, we are not always successful. I am familiar with medicines to treat patients. I am also familiar with those chemicals we use to preserve organs and samples from the bodies we are not able to save. If I'm not mistaken, this stain . . . You see it?"

"Indeed."

"It is from a type of preserving fluid that is rarely found anymore. A crude form of ethanol. The smell is quite distinctive."

"Which he would use to preserve the flesh he takes with him."

"Yes . . . And that fact, by the way, suggests that he is *not* a cannibal; that suggestion, I believe, was intended to shock. He would not dine on anything that was steeped in Fitzgerald's Preserving Fluid. That would be as lethal as one of his knives.

Indeed, that's why it is little used. It's exceedingly inexpensive but the fumes have made many an undertaker or surgeon's assistant pass out." He paused and put down the garment. "Now, you believe your killer inhabits essentially the East End."

"We think it likely."

"There are a half-dozen chemists or funeral parlor provisioners who still sell the liquid. I think it worth our while to pay them visits and inquire about recent purchases."

"Good. The hour's late but we must begin our search immediately."

"Now?" Adams asked. The day had vanished and it was now close to 6 p.m. "They'd be closed."

"Then we shall waken those who sleep above or behind their shops. And send other officers to rouse the ones which live elsewhere."

The inspector whom Wentworth had sent on assignment earlier now appeared in the doorway and nodded to his superior. Wentworth joined him and read the piece of foolscap the man proffered. He nodded and slipped it away, then turned again to Adams.

The doctor gave a faint laugh. "Inspector, may I inquire? You said 'we' must begin our search. Myself too?"

"Indeed. You are in a position to ask questions about the preservative, and perhaps other matters, that I am not."

"This is rather far afield from the surgical suite," the doctor said, though Wentworth noted his eyes gleamed. "But I'm game to play detective. If for no other reason than to live up to Mr Gladbrook's characterization of me as this famous Sherlock Holmes." Then Adams frowned. "One question occurs to me, Inspector."

"And what might that be, sir?"

"You have no idea what this fellow Jack looks like, his age, his station in life, his race?"

"Some unreliable witness accounts not worth tuppence."

Adams smiled. "Did you not worry that I or Mr Gladbrook might not be the killer, or perhaps the both of us, come here to win your confidence, lead you to some alley and dispatch you like a sacrificial lamb?"

"Of course it did," Wentworth said.

The doctor at first seemed to think he was making a joke and smiled. The expression soon leveled, as Wentworth extracted from his pocket the sheet of paper that had just been delivered to him.

"My associate has spent the past several hours looking into that very question. And he has verified that you and Mr Gladbrook were accounted for on the early morning hours of the thirty-first of August, the eighth of September and the thirtieth of September. I had him interview those intimate with Lord Ashton too and he, as well, could not be our Jack. As to the *Lord's* employer"— Wentworth's voice fell to a whisper—"I'm satisfied with taking it as a matter of faith that Her Majesty is a most unlikely suspect. Don't you agree?" Without waiting for an answer, he said, "So, shall we get on the trail of our killer, Doctor?"

• • •

Seven p.m. of a dank and grim evening.

The sun was long gone, and mist and fog had coalesced over the East End of London.

But Jacques LaFleur, fair haired and sturdy, felt a warmth deep within him.

Ah, there she is. Yes, yes, yes.

Jacques had had his eye on this one for some time.

Something about the way she sauntered, about the way she sang Irish songs as she walked unsteadily, drunkenly, down the street. About the way she would glower and launch her spittle temper at those who caused offense, real or imagined, on the sidewalk.

Jacques now saw her walking on the opposite side of the street. Not slim, not fat. More comely than the others, although that didn't matter to him in any way. What mattered what was inside of her, he laughed to himself.

The woman, wearing a brown brocade dress and decked with a shawl, and—as always—no hat, strolled along Chicksand Street. She paused, engaged a man in conversation. Their words ended and she continued on her way.

Jacques had a pet name for her: she was his Little Heart. This, because she seemed like someone a boy—Jacques, for instance, in his teenage years—would form a youthful but deep affection for.

He walked in the same direction as she, remaining, though, over the road. For a time he was lost in thought. Jacques had experienced an arduous journey to arrive here—both in London and at the level of satisfaction he had now achieved. Growing up a milliner's son in Oldham, outside Manchester, he had not distinguished himself in that work-a-day city. This had perplexed him. True, he had not been a pretty boy, nor a handsome young man, nor a talented student, nor driven at commerce; he was, though, sharp and charming and he could never fathom why he was not held in higher regard. This concerned him and angered him, and resentfully, he had quit the region of his birth and traveled to London.

Initially Jacques fared no better here than in the Midlands, securing fitful employment at menial labor. This further stoked his ire, and he regarded those in better circumstances with eyes he'd been told burned like a tiger's. Carting sacks of coffee and tea for an importer and staves for a cooper and skeins for a weaver, sweeping sawdust at a butcher's shop, shoveling coal for Hogg's Foundry . . . the list, and the jobs, interminable, and his life as bland as blancmange. Even the occasional girl, for pay or charm, did little to stimulate.

Until one day an urge led—no, forced—him to step across a line.

From good to bad, from legal to not.

A drunken gentleman—by his clothes, of means—had stumbled and fallen on a deserted street in the East End. The man had come to the district for the principal vice for which men of means traveled here from the western part of the city. He had finished his business at a bawdy house up the road, and was now seeking a hansom to take him back into the bosom of his wife and children. Jacques suspected he could honestly say to his woman that he had not dallied—because surely he was so drunk he wouldn't remember having done so.

Jacques had relieved the man of his wallet and gold watch and a small revolver (which told him that if he were to continue along these lines he would have to remember to be very, very careful).

From that day forth, Jacques had a new calling.

That included being a mutcher—when he stole from drunks— and a mug-hunter (or the new parlance, a "mugger") when he stole from someone else.

Burglary was always good, too.

This life suited him indeed. The old Jacques was gone, the new one born. Yes, there had been a bit of a diversion to Newgate Prison, but that was behind him now and he was sitting pretty. More content than he'd ever been.

He now turned his attention back to the cold streets before him.

Will tonight be the night for us, Little Heart?

Oh, Jacques hoped so, he prayed so.

Ah, but now, what was this? A man had stopped his Little Heart in her wanderings. A portly man in fine jacket and bowler hat. They began a conversation. He was not, of course, asking for the most expedient route to St Paul's.

Jacques watched as words continued to be exchanged and business negotiated.

No matter. He certainly felt the urge. But Jacques LaFleur was someone who had learned that patience was the only virtue worth embracing.

Two

Friday, November 9, 1 a.m.

For hour upon hour, Wentworth and Adams made their way around the East End, inquiring among chemists about the purchases of Fitzgerald's Preserving Fluid.

Midnight had come and gone and the men were incurring abuse from both the cold and the shopkeepers whom they awakened, some liberal with their oaths.

Finally, his bones were so cold that Wentworth decided he had reached the boundary. He would interview one more chemist and then flee to his home and wife. Dr Adams too was showing signs of fatigue and ill effects from the chill; his limp was more pronounced than earlier.

But it was fortunate that Wentworth had chosen to awaken the owner of Merry's Chemists, because it was there that at last they found a lead to Jack the Ripper.

The owner, a huge, glowering man who at their knocking had thrown a shabby greatcoat over his white—better said, dirty *gray*—

nightshirt and thrown open the door. He had a lined face, muscles like a teamster's and a balding pate with a half-dozen hairs striving for heaven from his shiny scalp.

The man listened to Wentworth's appeal and then, to the surprise of both the inspector and, it seemed, the doctor, said in a growling baritone, "Think I know 'oo you mean, Inspector."

"Who bought some Fitzgerald's?"

"Right you are."

"You have a name of this fellow?"

"No. Only came in once, I think. Recently."

"Around the thirtieth of September?"

"Could've been. Easy could've been."

The doctor and the officer regarded each other and then the chemist. "What'd he look like?"

"Lor', I can hardly remember now, can I? Get lots o' customers here. Normal fellow, I recall. Moustache?" He frowned. "Can't recall that one, governor."

Wentworth sighed. "Pale, dark?"

"Was a white man, not African. I don't think."

He doesn't think? Wentworth thought cynically. Witnesses were useless as often as not.

"Accent?"

"What'sat, governor?"

"Did he seem foreign?"

"Oh, you mean like from Prussia or France?"

"Anywhere."

"Not 'at I can say."

"Describe him, if you would, Mr Merry."

"Slightly built, shorter'n you," he said to the inspector. "Weaselly face." Merry thought for a moment. "Though I never seen a weasel up close, 'ave I?"

"Wearing?"

"Greatcoat. Brown."

"Did he seem to be a man of means?"

"'Ow would I know, governor? Smelled of some flower. Lavender. If that 'elps you."

"Did he appear to have any knowledge of medicine?"

"'E come in, paid 'is coin and left."

Meaning no, Wentworth assumed.

Adams held up his hands, which were nicked and stained, from his work as a surgeon, presumably. "You surely saw his hands when he handed the money over."

"I suppose I did."

"Were they like mine?"

"No. They was like a lady's 'ands, they was. What's this boy wanted for?" Finally some animation in the dull, hostile eyes. "Is 'e Saucy Jacky? 'E is, ain't 'e?"

"Was he alone?"

"Yes, 'e was."

"What happened after he paid?"

"Not a thing, Inspector. 'E just left—after 'e give me the address."

"What?" Wentworth asked, aghast.

Merry continued: "Fitzgerald's only comes in five-gallon jars. He 'ad somewhere to be, so I 'ad me boy deliver it that night. Yes, yes, yes. Let me see." The massive clerk dug through a jumble of documents and scraps.

"'Ere we go." He handed over a sheet to Wentworth, who displayed it to Adams. It was an address on Anthony Street, about a quarter mile away, an even shabbier district of the East End than where they now stood.

Wentworth thanked the man and turned to go.

But Adams lingered. "One question, Mr Merry. Did he ask you for Fitzgerald's specifically?"

"No," Merry offered. "Just wanted some preserver."

"And you sold him Fitzgerald's but charged him for better-quality fluid?"

The chemist's eyes evaded theirs. "And if I did, governor? Man's got to look out for 'imself, don't 'e?"

"No, no, Mr Merry. Take no offense. I am merely thinking that your tactic of scamming the fellow may be the single most important fact in getting London's worst murderer in recent years in darbies and onto the gallows."

"Blimey. That right?" The chemist beamed.

Wentworth said, "Let's pray it is the case."

. . .

Their hopes for finding the killer from the chemist's intelligence were not immediately fulfilled, however.

The two men hurried on foot to the address on Anthony Street which the hulking clerk had given them. Wentworth peered through a broken window of the warehouse, his police whistle in hand—a Hudson, the latest version, with the pea inside, which could almost split the eardrum of anyone nearby and would summon compatriots from a quarter mile away.

But he slipped the sound piece into a pocket and shook his head. While Saucy Jacky might very well have taken delivery of the Fitzgerald's Preserving Fluid in this warehouse, the small, decrepit facility was empty.

The inspector kicked in the door and they entered. Wentworth found an oil lamp, which he lit. The men examined the place. In truth, it contained very little: broken-down boxes, staves, nails and bolts, bottles discarded by the unfortunate and wretched who had succumbed to the scourge of alcohol, a man's boot, a jacket, old newspapers and periodicals, scattered receipts and bills of lading.

And in the corner, the can of Fitzgerald's.

"Well, this was perhaps his den," Wentworth said. "But he doesn't live here, obviously. He must have used this venue to prepare for some of the assaults. This is roughly midway between them." Much had been made of the location of the killings; lines drawn between them created, some said, a mystical symbol; this was, to Wentworth, nonsense and distracted from the true course of the investigation.

Wentworth panned the lantern over the floor and the men observed that someone had, in fact, been here recently. The dust had been disturbed by footsteps—one man's only, it seemed.

Adams examined the marks. He followed the footprints into the corner. "Here!" He was smelling a rag he'd found. "More Fitzgerald's!" The doctor's eyes were wide. "And, Wentworth. It's damp still. He has been here today!"

The inspector's face, he was sure, revealed the dismay he was feeling. "So perhaps he's out on the hunt as we speak. But where, where?"

"We too must keep hunting!" Adams renewed his search of the dim quarters. The inspector joined him.

It was fifteen minutes later that Wentworth made a discovery. "Doctor!" He lifted a scrap of newspaper on which was written in pencil an address. It was on Barker's Row. About ten blocks away.

"But did the villain himself write it?" Wentworth mused.

"Does the handwriting look familiar?"

"It might. I cannot say."

Adams lifted the paper to his nose and said, "Look at these finger marks. They are redolent of Fitzgerald's fluid. I would say, yes, this could very well be the address of his next victim."

"Come, Doctor. We must hurry!"

Outside, Wentworth oriented himself. "This way!" He sprinted to a nearby police signal box—those booths, first established in Glasgow, where police could use a telephone to communicate with the Division headquarters—here that would be H, Whitechapel, on Leman Street. (The kiosks were also topped with a blue beacon to summon officers patrolling to the box to receive communiques from their superiors.)

As Adams joined him, moving more slowly because of his wounded leg, Wentworth rang headquarters and reported that constables should proceed to the address on Barker's Row immediately; the Whitechapel killer might be there murdering another victim. He was assured by a voice on the other end of the line that an alarm would be raised and officers en route soon.

Wentworth put the mouthpiece down and stepped to the street with Adams beside him, looking for a hansom, of which none was to be found in this luckless portion of the city.

• • •

Now, at last, at 2:30 a.m., his Little Heart was alone.

She had finished with her customer and had recently been in the company of various men and women of the street. Carousing. Trying, it seemed, to borrow some money. Harsh words had passed when she'd apparently been denied the coin she asked for. Then she'd repaired to a friend's boarding room—troubling Jacques that she might be bedding for the night. But apparently the stop was merely for a drink or two. She left the quarters ten minutes later. Walking unsteadily down the deserted street, she began singing in a not unpleasant voice. An Irish ballad. "The Parting Glass."

Jacques smiled to himself that she had picked this particular song, one of farewell.

The street was not entirely deserted, even at this early hour, but Jacques would not let the opportunity pass. Too many days had gone by without a truly satisfying reward. He needed this. And immediately.

He approached, smiling.

"Evening, m'lady."

"I'd say morning now." Her momentary caution vanished and

she became coy. Buxom, and comelier up close than from a distance. Her age was in the middle twenties, he estimated. He gauged her accent to be Welsh.

"Right you are."

She looked him over, fore to aft. He was scrubbed and buffed and assembled in garments with few wrinkles. His waistcoat was dabbed clean. He could see her eyes relax. Most men in this part of the city did not come in quite this pleasant bundle. And, more to the point, someone as charming and as well spoken as he could hardly be the a danger, let alone someone as evil as the Ripper.

His appearance, and the LaFleur charm, had gotten him breath-close to the others, too.

"Isn't the inclement night they'd been thinking it might be," he said, looking up at the sky.

"No, sir, it isn't." She was drunk. That would make his efforts easier. "But then, I always wondered who 'they' is, didn't I? 'They' say the Queen is bloody cross at France. 'They' say the price of coal is going up. Who the hell is 'they'?"

He could not help but smile.

"I'm Henri," he said.

"Marie Jeanette."

He took her gloved hand and kissed it. "If I may be so bold."

A drunken laugh.

"I've an hour free," he said.

"Have you now, governor? Are you French? You said En-*ree*. Not Henry. You don't sound French. I lived there for a time, didn't I?"

Jacques said, "I'm not. But *they* say that I have the charm of a Frenchman."

She laughed once more. "What would *they* say about your purse?"

"That there's some coin in it."

"Lord, it's late. I'm tired. Tuppence upright?"

Jacques frowned. "On a night like this? It's inclement enough. Let's retire inside. A nice warm bed."

"Ach, I'm a tired one, aren't I?"

"Would a florin rouse you?"

Her eyes grew wide. "Two bleeding shillings? Let me see it!"

He dug into his pocket and showed the coin, a Jubilee from last year, Victoria's stern face looking to the left.

"Lor'."

The general rate for unfortunates in the East End was five pence (two for the upright, which she'd suggested, standing in the alley).

He handed the coin over. She slipped it into her purse.

Then she added, "I have a room, small, small. And shabby, perhaps too much so for a gentleman like yourself."

"I'm sure it will be lovely."

In fact, he knew it wasn't lovely at all. For he had already had a look himself. He extended his arm. She hooked hers through it. He said, "Lead on, my lady."

They turned and began to stroll along the sidewalk. She whispered, "You know what *they* say? You're in for a good ride tonight."

Jacques smiled because the masquerade called for the expression, though he didn't feel like smiling.

Michelangelo, Jacques was certain, hardly smiled when he dabbed the final brush stroke onto his depiction of God creating Adam high, high upon the Sistine Chapel.

All great artists took their work as matters of the utmost gravity.

• • •

"Where the devil are the constables?" Wentworth muttered as the hansom was reined to a stop before the address on Barker Street, where he hoped the Whitechapel killer was at that very moment.

He and Adams leapt out, the inspector tossing coins to the

cabbie. They looked about and located the building whose address they had found in the warehouse on Anthony Street.

"Ah, there's one now." Wentworth waved at a tall, slim uniformed officer.

Wentworth identified himself.

"Sir." The constable tipped his hat.

"Where are the others?"

"On their way, sir. A half-dozen constables."

"Tap for more, don't whistle. We don't want to give away our presence."

"The Whitechapel killer's inside?"

"Tap, man, tap!"

Scotland Yard supervisors carried a staff, like a walking stick, which could be used as a truncheon or a horse prod but was more often used to strike the sidewalk, sending a distinctive sound that could be heard for blocks; it meant that any officers nearby should hurry to the tapper's assistance.

The sergeant did this now.

Adams said, "I don't think we can wait, Inspector. He might've heard the hansom pull up."

"Yes, yes. Let's go. But, Doctor, you stay here."

It was then that two other constables approached, running. They pulled up, breathing heavily, and Wentworth summoned one to join him and the sergeant and told the other to remain with Adams.

The three police officers burst through the door of the two-story flat.

• • •

Ten minutes later Wentworth walked down the stairs of the dingy structure and onto the sidewalk, preceding the uniformed officers—now five of them—who had responded to the alarm.

He glanced at Adams and said through grim lips, "Whatever his interest in this place, if indeed he was interested at all, there is no indication that he was ever here. All four rooms—and a suite of two—are occupied by ordinary citizens: pensioners and working people. No one has ever seen a stranger, much less anyone suspicious or who might be a killer. And there is no rear door, so even if he had been here, you two would have seen him as he tried to pass us on the way out."

The inspector gazed about him, at the streets gauzed by smoke and fog. "Well, it was a reasonable chance. That is the nature of police work, of course. Most seeming trails to your villain are dead ends. But that cannot stop you from pursuing them all. And we have men watching the warehouse on Anthony Street and will have here as well, so perhaps we will have him in irons soon." He took out his pocket watch and gave it a glance. "My, the hour is late. I propose we retire for the evening."

"Yes, I must be getting home," Adams said.

"And I to my wife." The inspector ordered the constables to arrange for a watch from an alley nearby.

As Wentworth and Adams walked to a wider avenue, in search of hansoms, the inspector said, "Say, Doctor?"

"Yes?"

"Though we did not find our prey, we've made good strides. Thanks to you."

Adams considered this for a moment and said, "I think the success has been due to both of us. We make, dare I say, a good partnership."

"That we do, Doctor. Now, you can come round tomorrow, or later today, I should say, perhaps noon?"

"I will be there, sir. Good night to you."

• • •

The reunion of Erasmus Wentworth and Dr Richard Adams later that day was, however, delayed because of circumstances neither man had envisioned.

Though it was not at the address on Barker Row, the Ripper had indeed struck once more, killing his fifth victim.

At about 1 p.m., Friday, Wentworth arrived via police carriage at a residence in Spitalfields. He nodded to the half-dozen constables and inspectors present and proceeded as directed to Miller's Court, through a covered passageway off Dorset Street. Outside Number 13, he greeted Superintendent Thomas Arnold of H Division, a striking man in full beard, and another superior officer, balding Robert Anderson, from Central Office, who had run the Ripper investigation, but—after taking an unfortunate trip to the Continent at the time two of the victims were killed—had been demoted to a secondary role.

"Where is she?" Wentworth asked in a subdued voice.

"Inside there," Arnold said, nodding up the dark corridor. Wentworth started in the direction indicated. He paused as Anderson said, "Steel yourself, Inspector."

Wentworth regarded him and then continued to the designated door. Inside he found other officers standing outside a twelve-foot-square room, which was smoky and hot, despite the chill of the day. The place was furnished with a bed and a few other pieces of furniture, but Wentworth paid little mind to the appointments—or his co-workers.

His attention was solely on the human being—or what remained of a human being—in repose on the bed. The three Ripper victims who had been mutilated did not compare to this carnage. This woman had been savaged beyond recognition. Her breasts and a number of internal organs had been sliced free of the body and rearranged. Much of the skin had been flayed.

The heart was missing altogether; it was now clear what the Ripper needed the Fitzgerald's Preserving Fluid for.

"Ah, Wentworth." This from Frederick Abberline, Inspector First Class. His office was just up the hall from Wentworth's.

"Another." Wentworth sighed.

"Indeed."

"What carnage. Who is, *was*, she?"

"Mary Kelly, twenty-five. She preferred the name Marie Jeanette."

"An unfortunate?" Wentworth asked.

"Yes. Worked most of her life on the streets."

Wentworth glanced at the print, titled "The Fisherman's Widow," hanging above the fireplace, in which embers of what seemed to be smoldering cloth still glowed.

Abberline saw Wentworth's eyes. "We believe it took him an hour and a half to two hours to complete his surgery, if you will. He wanted more light and had only her clothes to burn."

"What was the time?"

"Between two thirty and eight this morning, the surgeon estimates. But we'll know better after the inquest. Her landlord sent his man around about a quarter to eleven, for the rent, and he discovered her."

"Witnesses?"

"Several. But some observations seem suspicious, if not wholly unreliable."

A shadow appeared in the doorway, cutting off the glare from Miller's Court. "Inspector?"

"Ah." Wentworth turned to see Dr Richard Adams. His eyes were on the victim.

"Well," Adams said, his eyes on the figure on the bed.

"Come in, Doctor, please."

Introductions were made and Wentworth described Adams's role to the others present, and explained further about finding the chemist who had sold the preserving fluid and where that discovery had led. "I have constables watching that shop, the warehouse we discovered and the flat but they've reported no reappearance."

"Well done," Abberline said. "We appreciate any assistance you might provide, Doctor. I'll stand outside and let you examine the corpse." He left the two men alone.

"A prostitute, like the others?"

"Yes." Wentworth cleared his throat. "So, Doctor, do you think this is the work of the same man? The carnage is much more severe."

Adams looked over the corpse. "I have no doubt. The thrusts and sawing patterns suggest as much. I think the madness that comes over him varies—one night he is content to be more . . . deliberate, you might say. This?" He pointed to the corpse. "His fit possessed him to utterly destroy the poor creature. God only knows why." Adams frowned. "The heart?"

"Missing."

"May I?" Adams asked, nodding toward the body.

"Of course."

The doctor stepped forward, leaned down and regarded the wounds. Using a handkerchief, he lifted the victim's right hand and examined it. There was a knife gash on the palm. He manipulated the appendage and then replaced it. He did the same with her feet. Then he studied the body cavities and portions of the skin that had been removed.

Finally, he stepped back and looked down at the Ripper's handiwork.

"Any conclusions?" Wentworth said.

Adams offered, "I may have. The scars suggest the use of a new instrument. I will need to look into the matter more. Perhaps we can stop by a surgical supply company."

"Yes, we will do." The inspector looked down upon the body. "Why, Jack? Why do you do this?"

Adams said, "I'm afraid the doctor within me is flummoxed, Inspector. The religious man, however, has an answer."

"And what that might be?"

"It's the work of Satan."

"Ah, but we will have a difficult time bringing *him* before the Queen's Bench. So let us continue on our secular investigation."

. . .

Inspector Wentworth returned home at close to 8 p.m.

The bad morning had turned into a worse afternoon and evening. His superiors were clamoring for answers, citizens were demanding a suspect and reporters were crying out for details.

He was unable to provide satisfaction to any one of those needy parties.

Wentworth washed in the bathroom and returned downstairs. He sat at the dinner table and struggled to put his cares aside— and all the while wondering where Saucy Jacky might be at this very moment.

Still, he put a smile on his face and nodded as the slim, young serving girl set dishes before him and his wife. "Wonderful, Jenny! You have prepared quite the sumptuous repast, as you always do."

"Thank you, Inspector."

Supper was lamb and potatoes, a small dish of haddock and grilled tomato.

Mrs Wentworth, a handsome woman of a certain age, gave the girl a coy look. "And Mr Hedrick's son slipped some buns into the package of bread today. And he winked at her."

"Ma'am."

Wentworth turned to the blushing Cockney girl. "You could do worse than to marry into a baker's family, Jenny."

Edith said, "And he's a nice boy and good-looking too, Ras. You remember him?"

In fact, Wentworth had no idea who the young man was. But

his wife had a keen eye and he knew she had passed an accurate judgment on the potential suitor.

He added, "And a hard worker, for sure. Though he won't be forced to work the hours of a detective inspector. He will get home to you in the evenings." This was said with a glance toward his wife.

"Please, sir. I hardly know the boy." The housekeeper's fiery face was, however, smiling.

The girl retired and Wentworth and his wife ate, speaking of her visit to their daughter-in-law in Islington and a new millinery shop that had opened up the road. She reminded Wentworth that they had committed to a trip to Leeds, where they would join friends on a canal boat excursion that weekend.

He began to say, "I shall try with all my heart," but the word took him right back to the horrific murder of Mary Kelly, who had been robbed of that very organ.

"I will try, my dear."

"I know of the new killing. I understand. It's him?"

"Yes, there's little doubt."

"Are you any closer to finding who it might be? The papers are full of speculation."

"All of it spurious. He's quite the elusive one. Most criminals make the error of *trying* to be clever, though in fact they aren't, and that approach trips them up. This fellow we're after is either indeed clever or, not being so, makes no attempt to try. And thus he blunders his way along, engaging in behaviors that don't give rise to clear evidence or witnesses."

"Lucky, then."

"Lucky in part, yes. The fact that there is no motive for the killings—other than butchery itself—that is perhaps the most arduous obstacle." He lowered his voice; Jenny could be nearby. "There is no apparent sexual activity. He does not rob them. He's claimed, if the *Dear Boss* letter he sent be truly his, that he wants to kill prostitutes, but even the most fervent moralist would never cause such carnage because of an unfortunate's profession. For heaven's sake, that part of the city is infested with such poverty that I'm sure if my circumstances placed me in such a locale I too would turn to crime to put bread in the mouths of my family. And those poor women have no other choice."

He sipped from a water glass, his tongue locating the chipped spot to avoid it. Then sighed. "If we knew why, we could then find who. But, sadly, his purpose remains a mystery.

"Although I will tell you we have had some help from an unlikely source." He told Edith about the famous doctor who was assisting them. "Brilliant fellow. Made a connection, thanks to his medical skills, to where the killer might have stayed for a time. Nothing came of it but I've stationed men nearby to see if he returns." He lowered his voice. "A Dr Adams. He came at the recommendation of the Palace. Her Majesty's advisor himself."

"No, Ras!" Edith was delighted at this news.

"Yes." Then gave a dark smile. "Rather at the *insistence* of the Palace. That this fellow remains free is putting the royals and the government in a rather bad light not only here but on the Continent. Even in America too."

"It is a difficult time for Her Majesty," Edith pointed out.

This was certainly the truth. There was the burgeoning controversy of Victoria's recently making Abdul Karim, the Munshi, an Indian Muslim, her most trusted confidant, to the exclusion of most of the court. Then, just months ago, the beautiful Princess Alix, sixteen, the Queen's granddaughter, had faced death from a horseback riding incident. Then there were the perennial problems of the socialists, the Irish, the poverty . . . and Her Majesty's frustration at finding a suitable Prime Minister.

"You're doing all you can—"

Suddenly, rapping on the back door of the flat.

"Who could that be? At suppertime?" Edith asked. Then she called, "Jenny, could you please see who's calling?"

"No," Wentworth said, dabbing his face with his linen and standing. "I will go." In a louder voice: "Jenny, I will attend to it. You go about your chores."

"Yes, sir."

He strode through the kitchen and down from the first floor to the ground. The mews where the Wentworths' home was located was decent and generally safe and it was possible that the visitor was nothing more than a beggar, hoping for food. But London was London and this was hardly Mayfair; it could be a lurker with criminal designs. Hence, his attending to the caller.

Wentworth approached the back door, undid the dead-bolt and lifted the bar. He pulled the door open.

The empty alley greeted him.

Curious. He stepped outside. No one.

But ten yards away, something small sat on the cobblestones where the alleyway turned a corner. The evening was foggy, as it often was at this hour, and he could make out only a shape about eight inches in size. The color was gray, but so was the hue of almost everything here at this time of night in this bleak month.

"Hallo?" he called out.

No response save for his own echoing voice.

Wentworth squinted through the mist. Curious. The object seemed to be a purse. Who could possibly have dropped it here?

He looked around him once more.

• • •

Jacques LaFleur—the Ripper, Saucy Jacky—waited around the corner from the back door of the home of Detective Inspector Wentworth. A lovely blade was gripped tightly in his hand. Not a surgeon's knife but a proper one, more than a foot long.

He'd found the man's house with little difficulty. That morning, the hour approaching noon, Jacques had been in Dorset Street, across from Mary Kelly's room, and he had watched the policeman walk from the front door of the flat where he'd created such a beautiful object in blood.

The slim officer, in a tweedy suit and no overcoat against the chill, had called over several constables and sent them in different directions. Jacques deemed it best to repair to his own flat at that time. He had all he needed, anyway: in his mind an image of the detective inspector who was pursuing him.

Later, sitting at his table in his Somerset Street rooms, surrounded by close on one hundred newspaper and periodical articles about the Whitechapel killings, Jacques had skimmed them quickly, regarding the illustrations only. And soon he'd matched the face he recalled with a name. Erasmus Wentworth. One publication, the *Police News*, gave the inspector's address.

Now he listened carefully and heard the Yarder's footsteps cautiously approaching the purse he'd left as bait.

From Jacques's observation of the goings-on in the inspector's home that evening, he had noted that there might be several permutations that could unfold following his knuckles greeting the oak of the door. The pretty young servant girl might open the door and see the purse and step forward, hoping it would contain a few pence or shillings, or even a sovereign or two. Or the older woman, who he guessed was the inspector's wife, might do the same.

Slitting their throats and then ripping open bodices to swiftly remove their maternal breasts, or slice their bellies, smooth the one woman's, wrinkled the other's, would have been delightful too.

But the outcome he truly hoped for was that which was now unfolding.

The copper himself.

Jacques heard the officer say, "Hm."

He'd be wondering who would have rapped on his door, then dropped a purse. He might be concluding it was revelers in their cups.

From the sound of footsteps, gritting on the alleyway, he was almost to the shadows where the bag lay.

Jacques inhaled a deep breath and tensed his legs, picturing the inspector's terror as the Ripper he'd been seeking lunged forward, slashing slashing slashing, painting a beautiful crimson design upon the scaly cobblestones.

Ah, another pleasing thought: the copper would, of course, not die immediately but would scream for assistance.

And his wife, perhaps the servant girl, too, would appear.

They, as well, would contribute to the canvas of blood.

Imagine *those* news accounts!

The footsteps stopped. Wentworth would be standing over the purse now.

Steady yourself. One . . . two . . .

Jacques stepped forward one pace.

And then: "No," came a firm whisper near his ear.

He turned fast, raising the knife.

There, leaning on his cane, was Dr Richard Adams. An Enfield revolver was in his hand, pointed at Jacques's heart.

The Ripper smiled and lowered the blade.

The doctor led him back into the shadows, away from the alley and toward the street. He whispered, "There's a constable not twenty feet from here. The officers investigating the Whitechapel killings all have a guard. And there is a regular patrol not far, as well. Give me the knife."

Jacques turned it handle first and passed it over.

Hiding behind an evergreen, and obscured by the mist, they could just make out Inspector Wentworth, picking up and examining the bag, which was empty. He called out, "Hallo," once more. And when there was no response, he turned and walked back to the house.

Adams gestured toward the street with the pistol and said sternly to Jacques, "You'll come with me. Now."

•   •   •

The smell in the small, exceedingly damp room was of fish. The place was shadowy. Electric lighting was becoming popular in London—Dr Richard Adams had it in his practice and soon would in his home near Grosvenor Square—but this was the East End and some said electricity would not come here for ten years. Other said it never would.

The illumination in the warehouse tonight came from an oil lamp, not even gas.

Adams looked outside then pulled the burlap curtains together and turned back to Jacques LaFleur. He pointed to a chair. The killer sat. Adams noted that he was dressed well, the garments pressed and clean. He was in a white shirt and ribbon tie. Beneath his checkered suit was his trademark leather waistcoat.

The door opened and Henry Gladbrook entered. The advisor to the royal court also eyed Jacques and then turned away, hanging his own greatcoat. He sat down on an unsteady chair, looked down. Removed a match from a box and slipped it under the chair's short leg.

Jacques said to Gladbrook, "Well, sir, the good doctor here found me. Tracked me down, didn't he? Won't tell me how he did it. But here I am."

Adams, assisted by his cane, hobbled to a bench, dusted it with a handkerchief and then sat. "He was about to eviscerate Inspector Wentworth."

Gladbrook shook his head. "We've been having a rather difficult time because of you, my friend," he said. "You didn't quite follow the plan, now, did you?"

Jacques—Jack the Ripper, Saucy Jacky, Leather Apron—gave a faint shrug.

The plan . . .

Not long ago, Gladbrook and Adams found themselves in need of a dangerous man, one not afraid to use a knife to kill. A man with no family, no friends . . . an invisible man.

Discreet inquiries among gaolers had led to the fellow before them now. He was in Newgate for murdering a solicitor in London during a robbery. Gladbrook had spoken to him and decided he would suit. A word to the Crown Prosecutor and he was released (on the claim that he was wanted in Ireland, and was being handed over to authorities there for political expediency).

And so Jacques LaFleur was set free to help the men on their mission.

Yet the instructions were that the hound was to tree one fox and one only.

Mary Ann Nichols.

Gladbrook reminded LaFleur of this and added, "But suddenly you vanish and we open the broadsheets and learn that you've decided otherwise, despite having taken our guineas. You went on to slaughter *four* more women."

"No, no, no. Three only. Miss Stride I was interrupted during. Only had time to slice her. Still piqued by that, I must say."

"Are you mocking us?" Gladbrook raged.

"No, sir." Jacques fell silent.

"One killing and the incident would have been noted in the public eye for a day or two and then drifted into obscurity. But four others? What would have been a minor crime has gone on to become the talk of the world!"

Adams asked bluntly, "Answer us! Why did you keep killing?"

"Just what you said, governor," Jacques said, eyeing Gladbrook.

"The talk of the world." His eyes blazed. He reached into his pocket and withdrew a number of folded sheaves of paper.

Adams could see they were newspaper and periodical accounts.

Lovingly the killer spread them out on a nearby table. "Look! Look at this! They are telling my story! I'm the hero of all of them."

Hero? thought Adams.

The small man, his face indeed weaselly, looked up to the two men fiercely. "I was nothing as a boy in Manchester. And I was nothing coming here. I could work only menial jobs . . . I even was condemned to mundane crimes in the Chapel. Mug-heading, pinching, flying the blue pigeon—stealing roof lead! That murder I was in Newgate for? It was thanks to my clumsiness I dropped the pistol I was robbing the old barrister with and we both leapt for it. It went off by itself! Lor', there's a twist for you!

"I knew I was smart. I knew I was meant for greatness but nothing ever came my way. It was damned unfair! But when I killed Mary Ann? Why, the very next day I was the king of London."

"And the bloodier the crimes, the more your star shone."

"That's right." His face darkened. "Oh, governors, the truth is I hated the blood, hated the cutting, hated carting back this part and that part. That's why there was a gap. The acts overwhelmed me. I had to stop."

Adams laughed coldly. "And that's why you sent the taunting letters. When interest flagged, and the scribblers moved on to other stories, you stirred the pot."

"Ach, I'm telling you, Doctor, murder's hard work. Unpleasant work. Much easier to write a letter. And, suddenly, guvs, I was on the front page again."

The articles had given Gladbrook and Adams considerable cause for concern. They had sleepless nights, many of them, worried that their killer was going to tell all in a subsequent missive. Notably: who was truly behind the killings.

"But even the letters weren't enough," Adams said.

"And so Mary Kelly."

"My Little Heart."

Adams blinked at the appellation, recalling the organ the Ripper had taken with him.

"Which is why you butchered her more viciously than the others. To garner bigger headlines."

"That's a fact, governor."

Gladbrook said, "And using the name 'Jack.' And 'Jacky'? We thought you were mad to pick that, so similar to your own. But it's clear now. At least a version of your name was in the public eye."

LaFleur nodded to indicate that this was on the mark.

"All right, Jacques," Gladbrook said. "What's done is done. But now you *must* retire. You've had your notoriety, you've had your sixty days of fame." Gladbrook scooped up the clippings and handed them back. Then he reached into his coat pocket and handed over an envelope, which contained a steamship ticket. Then a heavy leather purse.

"And here's fifty gold sovereigns."

"Blimey."

"Outside there's a hansom to take you to the dock."

"But—"

"You leave now. Jack the Ripper transmogrifies back into Jacques LaFleur tonight. You'll go to France and thence wherever you like. But you are never to return to England."

LaFleur looked into the bag. "Well, yes, all right. As you wish." He hefted the bag and pulled on his greatcoat. "I've answered your questions. Now you answer mine, if you would be so kind."

"What might that be?" Adams asked.

"You never told me why you wanted her killed, Mary Ann Nichols. Was it because she had a client you didn't want the world to know about?"

Gladbrook looked at Adams. The doctor answered, "Yes, that's what this was about."

Jacques eyed them, one then the other, closely. "Well, you're subtle birds, both of you. I sport there's more to why she died than some husband being where he should not have been. But the answer's between you and God. Or more likely the devil. Good night to you both now. And thank'ee."

The man left through the warehouse door and Gladbrook closed it behind him. He poured a whisky for himself and the doctor and both men sat. They heard the horses' hoof falls and the clack of wheels on cobblestone, as the killer was driven away.

Gladbrook said, "So, Doctor, thank God you found him. It appears our plan worked."

After the killing of Mary Ann Nichols and Jacques's rogue descent into slaughter, the two men, desperate to locate him, had come up with a scheme to infiltrate Scotland Yard and discover what the police had learned. They would combine that with what they themselves knew about LeFleur. This they hoped would provide sufficient insights so they might track down their renegade killer for hire. And so Gladbrook, taking his cue from the Conan Doyle novel, had suggested that Adams offer his services as a "medical detective" to assist the police.

They knew full well, for instance, LaFleur's appearance, his cologne, the restaurants he frequented, his clothing and the tobacco he favored. Working with Inspector Wentworth, Adams had learned other facts. He could tell from their posture in repose, and the smell of the garments, that the four later victims had been chloroformed before they were murdered. He also noted from the rent blouse he had examined, as well as the photographs, that both a particular type of knife and surgical saw had been employed—though he was not, as the police surgeon had concluded, a medical man.

And at the Mary Kelly murder scene, he had observed that

there was blood and bits of skin beneath the victim's fingernails. This would not be hers but LaFleur's, for she would have collected the crimson stains fighting with him to save herself as he pressed the chloroform-soaked rag over her mouth. (Adams had used his handkerchief on the pretext of examining the wound in her palm in order to remove some samples of the killer's blood and flesh.) After quitting Mary's room and returning to his laboratory, he had tested the blood and skin and learned something about Jacques they had not known. He suffered from the great pox—syphilis. Adams deduced this from large amounts of mercury, the current treatment of choice for the disease.

So he and Gladbrook had gone their separate ways, started making the rounds of East End chemists and medical clinics, inquiring about a man who fit the description of the killer, who had purchased chloroform and certain surgical implements and who was being treated for the pox.

It was Adams who landed the trout, narrowing the search to Aldgate High Street and, eventually, to shadowy, grim Somerset Street. Just as Adams arrived at the rooms, however, Jacques had stepped outside. The doctor could not, certainly, summon a constable, so he'd pursued the killer himself—directly to Inspector Wentworth's home, where LaFleur was prepared to murder the inspector himself and possibly his wife and maid, as well.

"And Wentworth suspects nothing?" Gladbrook asked Adams.

"I'm sure not. He believed I was truly trying to help . . . and he was genuinely impressed by my powers of deduction, if you will, in locating the chemist who'd sold Jack the preserving fluid."

The "discovery" of the chemist, which led to the warehouse on Anthony Street (and the flat on Barker's Row), had been a magician's illusion. The real Owen Merry, the chemist, had been impersonated by a hulking associate of Gladbrook's, who sent Adams and the inspector to the warehouse where the Fitzgerald's

Preserving Fluid had been "delivered" (that is, set there earlier in the day by Gladbrook's man). Wentworth marked down Jack the Ripper's absence to unfortunate timing, but he was nonetheless impressed by Adams's contribution and convinced of his authenticity and value.

"And you will now proceed as we thought?" Gladbrook asked Adams.

"Indeed. I think it's a wise course."

Adams would continue to assist Inspector Wentworth by providing insights and interpretations of the evidence to point the finger of guilt toward one of the suspects already in the sights of Scotland Yard and the City Police. There were several who seemed likely—though, of course, as both Adams and Gladbrook knew, completely innocent.

Would that person ever be found guilty? The British system of justice was as sophisticated as any in the world but it was not infallible. Perhaps, yes, someone would hang for the killings. Or maybe the mystery would remain unsolved for, who could say, a hundred years or more, at which time some investigator, or even some author, might take a fancy to the ancient case and would himself, or herself, try to solve the riddle.

A rap sounded on the door and Gladbrook called out, "Enter."

In walked Gladbrook's aide, the muscular Cockney who had impersonated Merry the chemist. He took his hat off, revealing his largely bald scalp, perfectly round with a few renegade hairs.

"S'done, sir." He handed the bag of sovereigns and a steamship ticket to Gladbrook.

"Potter's Field?"

"Yessir. 'E's six feet down. Unmarked grave. 'E'll never be found on this earth."

This had been Jacques LaFleur's fate from the start. He would have died, murdered by this large man, right after Mary Ann Nichols's murder, had he not vanished. Adams felt no guilt for the man's death; he would have hanged for the solicitor's murder in the event.

Gladbrook fished into the bag and dug out three sovereigns. Handed them over to LaFleur's assassin.

"Crikey, sir. Thank you." He tapped his huge pate, as might a soldier, which he had been, and turned on his heels and left.

Adams and Gladbrook each drained their whisky.

Gladbrook asked, "When are you going to Osborne House?"

"Sunday."

"Please cable me what you learn."

"I will do."

The men rose. Gladbrook donned his top hat and overcoat. They left, stepping out onto a foggy sidewalk. Gladbrook locked the door. He fished a cigar from his case and cut and lit it. "It has worked out to our advantage but make no mistake, this has been a sad, sordid matter," he muttered.

"A matter of blood, you might say." Adams turned his collar up against the damp chill, and, relying on his cane, started off down the street.

Three

Sunday, November 11, 2 p.m.

Osborne House, on the Isle of Wight, was the country estate the royal family most favored.

Located in East Cowes, the Italian Renaissance structure—complete with two belvederes—had been designed largely by Prince Albert, consort and husband to Victoria Regina herself. The other designer, and builder, had been Thomas Cubitt, whose firm had also constructed portions of Buckingham Palace.

Dr Richard Adams now eyed the splendid place from his seat in a brougham, as the horses slowed to a stop. The carriage was comfortable enough, though the uneven ground had toyed cruelly with his war-wounded hip. He now descended stiffly to the ground and, relying on his cane more than he normally would have, followed a doorman into the house and thence to a sitting room on the first floor. The view overlooked the gardens in which Victoria's and Albert's children had grown vegetables, which they "sold" to their father and later cooked up themselves in the kitchen in Swiss Cottage, not far away on the grounds.

A butler appeared with a tea service and Adams took a cup. As he left, the man said, "The princess will be here in a moment, sir."

"Thank you."

The princess . . .

Victoria's granddaughter: Ducal Highness Princess Alix Viktoria Helene Luise Beatrix of Hesse and by Rhine, known throughout the empire as Alix.

It was this innocent child—sixteen years of age—who was the cause, albeit unknowingly, of the death of Mary Ann Nichols—and, Adams now knew, to his shame, of the other four unfortunates murdered by LaFleur.

I sport there's more to why she died than some husband being where he should not have been. But the answer's between you and God. Or more likely the devil . . .

In August the girl had been injured in an equestrian fall and suffered a cut in her thigh.

For most people, such an accident would not have had serious, much less life-threatening, consequences.

But the princess was not like others; she suffered from the Royal Disease.

The malady, known to doctors as hemophilia, was a rare but horrific scourge, in which a flaw in the blood prevents its clotting. Even the most minor injuries can result in the victim's bleeding to death quickly. The informal name, "Royal Disease," arose because Queen Victoria carried the proclivity for this condition in her blood and passed it down to her heirs.

Hemophilia is a condition that affects the male descendants most seriously—Princess Alix's uncle, Leopold, bled to death at thirty, while her own brother, Frederick, died at two.

But females are affected too and the seepage from her wounded leg would, sooner or later, have taken her life as well, if not stanched.

The Queen's aide John Ashton summoned Gladbrook with instructions to do whatever was necessary to save the girl.

Gladbrook had, in turn, called upon Adams in his chambers.

The suave man of court had implored, "Doctor, we need your assistance as a matter of highest concern to the Crown."

"Yes, of course, sir. How may I assist?"

He had described the princess's imperiled state.

"Yes, I'm aware, from the press, of her riding accident. But I did not know she suffered a bleeding wound."

"It is being kept quiet. The court physician feels she can survive two weeks at best." After a pause, the man continued, "We of course pray for the child's recovery, for her sake, and for those close to her, her grandmother in particular."

Everyone knew that Her Majesty had never fully recovered from the death of her beloved husband, Prince Albert, nor of their daughter, Princess Alice, Alix's mother. Victoria also still mourned Leopold's death and that of her infant grandson, nicknamed Frittie, Alix's brother.

To lose the charming and vivacious Alix would be a catastrophe for the Queen.

"But," Gladbrook had added, lowering his voice, though they were alone in the doctor's quarters, "her survival is important for a broader reason. For the empire itself to thrive, it is vital that England form allegiances with other countries on the Continent. Treaties pale in comparison to the more durable bond of marriage.

"The princess must survive so that she might marry into a royal family, ensuring that that country's fate is entwined with that of Mother England. Now, to my mission here, Doctor. We have heard of your work and it is in that capacity that we seek your help."

Adams was, as Gladbrook had told Detective Inspector

Wentworth, one of the most pre-eminent physicians in England, though not, as stated, for his Sherlock Holmesian skills at deduction. No, he was renowned for research into diseases of the blood and internal organs. He had indeed studied hemophilia and was working to determine what the flaw contained in Victorian blood might be and, once identified, how it might be neutralized.

Gladbrook had said, "I've heard of this treatment you are performing. Transfusions."

Adams had pioneered the practice—taking blood from a healthy individual and injecting it into the veins of an ill patient, who had lost blood from a wound or lesion.

There was one obstacle to this treatment, however, deriving from the nature of blood itself. The crimson elixir that flowed through one person's veins might be of a different sort than that flowing through another's. In order for a transfusion to work, the blood from the donor had to match the blood of the recipient. Without this compatibility, the introduction of a donor's blood would be fatal. At present it was possible, before performing the transfusion, to combine two persons' blood samples on an examination slide and, by observing the resulting mixture under a microscope, determine if the donor and recipient were compatible.

Yes, in theory transfusions could save a life under some circumstances, routine surgery or war wounds, for instance. However, with hemophilia, there was an additional—indeed, insurmountable—impediment to the treatment. Adams had told Gladbrook, "Even if we find a donor whose blood is in the same category as that of the princess's, to counteract the bleeding I will need gallons of compatible blood: indeed, *all* the donor's blood. In future years, I will be, I hope, able to isolate a reagent to cause the blood to clot. But at present, no. I need pure blood and in sufficient quantity so that any donor would not survive."

"Ah," the advisor had said. "Then we are presented with a difficult decision."

Adams had required a moment to grasp what the man was saying. "No. No! We are presented with no decision at all. I am a man of medicine. I cannot do what you are asking."

"This is to save the life of a royal and, perhaps, to preserve the Crown itself."

"That does not matter. I have my oath. I cannot take one life, even if to save another. That's the province of God."

Gladbrook had sat back in his chair, lit a cigar and said, "Let me pose you this, Doctor. Say two patients are brought to your surgery simultaneously, both *in extremis*. There is only you attending. You have the time and medicine to save only one. By choosing the cooper over the baker, the lady over the lord, the hansom driver over the charwoman, are you not killing the other?"

"That's a fatuous argument."

"I think not, Doctor. Every decision we make in life could have lethal consequences. Soldiers on the battlefield know this. Fishermen. Train engineers. Midwives. You as a man of medicine know this as well."

"Still, I cannot do it. I am sorry. And the Queen would never condone it."

Gladbrook had leaned forward and said fervently, "Her Majesty will never know. Nor anyone else, save for a few it is necessary to inform."

Adams had blustered, "Well, it is impossible. We'll speak no more of it."

"Then, Doctor," Gladbrook had said, in a low and chillingly calm voice, "I'll find another surgeon, fill his purse with sovereigns and tell him to cut away and pump the girl full of another's blood."

"No one other than I can perform this procedure."

"Nonetheless, I assure you, I *will* find someone else if you refuse to help us."

Adams, horrified at the thought of what Gladbrook was proposing, had fallen silent.

The man had gripped his arm. "Please, sir. We need you, the Palace needs you."

Adams had been silent for a moment, and then had whispered, "But who will the donor be?"

Gladbrook had considered this question for a moment. Then his eyes had narrowed. "My illustration a moment ago? The cooper or the baker, the lord or lady? Now I would posit that the patients you had to choose between were . . . a princess and a whore."

Adams closed his eyes and uttered a simple prayer: God forgive me.

The doctor had then hurried to an infirmary in the East End, run by nuns, who tended to, among others, many prostitutes in the area. Adams, with a vial of the princess's blood in a satchel, had set up at a table in the infirmary and taken samples of the ladies' blood to check for compatibility—provided, of course, that they showed no symptoms of the pox.

Some categories of blood, the doctor had found, were common. Some were rare. As if God were excoriating those involved in the matter, Princess Alix's blood fell into an exceedingly rare category and for a time Adams despaired of finding a donor whose blood was compatible. But finally a match was made.

Mary Ann Nichols.

Jacques was released from prison, given his chore and set loose. He tracked Mary Ann, murdered the woman, drained her blood into jars and, at Adams's instruction, savaged the body and spread the viscera about so that the authorities would not notice that there was a paucity of blood on the ground.

That had been, for Adams, the worst day of his life, mitigated though it was by the fact that within hours of the treatment the princess's bleeding stopped and she began her trek to recovery.

The "matter of blood" should have ended there—a bittersweet accomplishment that he would spend the rest of his life trying to forget. But it did not. Because Jacques LaFleur had decided to become Jack the Ripper and postpone his retirement, so that he might bask in the perverse glory afforded him by the hyenas of the Fleet Street reporters.

Now, sitting in the grand Osborne House, the doctor closed his eyes and, once again, begged God's forgiveness. Adams was quite aware that He chose not to respond.

A moment later the doctor was aware of footsteps approaching. He now set down his teacup, from which he had not taken a single sip, and rose.

"Dr Adams!" a girl's voice called.

His found himself looking into the bright eyes of a pretty teenage girl dressed in a simple white frock.

"Your Highness." The doctor bowed, as he greeted her.

"Doctor," she chided in a tone of good nature, "I always insist you call me Alix."

Adams smiled. "And *I* always hide behind courtly protocol. It is hardly in my nature, Your Highness, to break with a thousand-year tradition."

He greeted the princess's lady in waiting, a solid girl, not much older, with raven-black hair. She curtseyed demurely.

He then said, "Now to the point, Your Highness. Please tell me how you are feeling."

She described herself as quite healthy, no lightheadedness, no other symptoms. The princess had not worn stockings and she lifted her hem to reveal the site of her wound, which had healed completely. Even the scar was minimal.

He felt her forehead, listened to her heart and examined her eyes.

"Have you had any other incidents resulting in cuts or abrasions?"

"No. I've been so very careful, as you have insisted."

Adams still did not know if the transfusion had cured the

hemophilia or merely stanched the blood flow in that one instance and the girl's own, flawed blood was once again flowing through her veins. The scientist in him would have liked to know more. But this was not a patient to experiment upon.

He put his instruments back into his kit. "I pronounce you healthy as a filly at Ascot."

"You are a miracle worker, Doctor. My grandmother has told me you are to be invited for an audience. She wishes to thank you in person."

Adams had heard the same. He was not looking forward to receiving whatever commendation Her Majesty would confer upon him; that would exponentially increase his guilt. He dare not, however, refuse to attend.

"I shall be honored."

The princess added, "And you will stay for supper this evening? Oh, I do hope so. Father is here."

"I will pay my respects to the Grand Duke, but I am afraid I must be getting back to London. I have patients awaiting my attendance."

"Even on Sunday?"

"Illness observes no holy day."

"Of course, I understand, though I shall be disappointed."

"It has been a pleasure treating you, Your Highness, but I do hope I never have the chance to see you again . . . in a *professional* capacity."

The girl laughed. Then her rosy lips curled to a pout. "But, Doctor, you must understand that I shan't let you leave until you do my bidding."

He bowed and kissed her hand. "You are quite the charming—and formidable—young woman . . . *Alix*." The girl's face bloomed at the use of the name.

The doctor added, "I have no doubt that you will someday have the world at your command."

Epilogue

The London Daily Mirror, 26 November 1894

PRINCESS ALIX AND TSAR NICHOLAS OF RUSSIA WED

NUPTIALS BRING HOPE TO AN EMPIRE IN MOURNING

HER MAJESTY'S GRANDDAUGHTER
HENCEFORTH TO BE KNOWN AS
ALEXANDRA FEODOROVNA ROMANOVA

It was a joyous occasion today at the Winter Palace in St Petersburg as newly crowned Tsar Nicholas II, Nikolai Alexandrovich Romanov, and Princess Alix Viktoria Helene Luise Beatrix the beloved granddaughter of Her Royal Majesty Queen Victoria, were wed before the Palace priest at just before one o'clock this afternoon.

The wedding did much to dim the sorrow that has pervaded Russia, and the world, since the tragic and untimely death of Nicholas's father, Tsar Alexander III, at the age of forty-nine.

It was the Tsar's decision to move forward the ceremony, originally scheduled for the spring of next year, to today, which is his mother's, the Empress Dowager's, birthday.

Following the marriage, our beloved princess is to be known as Alexandra Feodorovna Romanova, Empress Consort of all the Russias.

As the wedding was celebrated during the official period of mourning following Tsar Alexander's death, there was no reception and the married couple forwent a honeymoon.

Countrymen throughout the realm rejoice in this holy union, tightening as it does the bond between these two glorious empires, and wish the couple a long and fruitful life together.

Crowned heads from throughout the United Kingdom and the Continent were present at the union, among them Her Royal Highness the Queen of the United Kingdom and Empress of India; the Prince and Princess of Wales; the Duke and Duchess of York; the Empress Dowager of All the Russias, Grand Duchess Xenia Alexandrovna, Grand Duke Alexander Mikhailovich and many other distinguished guests.

An Acceptable Sacrifice

I have always imagined that Paradise will be a kind of library.

Jorge Luis Borges

Wednesday

They'd met last night for the first time and now, mid-morning, they were finally starting to let go a bit, to relax, to trust each other. *Almost* to trust each other.

Such is the way it works when you're partnered with a stranger on a mission to kill.

"Is it always this hot?" P.Z. Evans asked, squinting painfully against the fierce glare. The dense lenses of his Ray-Bans were useless.

"No."

"Thank God."

"Usually is *hotter*," Alejo Díaz replied, his English enriched by a luscious accent.

"You're shitting me."

The month was May and the temperature was around ninety-seven. They were in Zaragoza Plaza, the picturesque square dominated by a statue of two stern men Evans had learned were generals. A cathedral too.

And then there was the sun . . . like burning gasoline.

Evans had flown to Hermosillo from outside DC, where he lived when he wasn't on the road. In the nation's capital—the nation to the north, that is—the temperature had been a pleasant seventy-five.

"Summer can be warm," Díaz admitted.

"Warm?" Evans echoed wryly.

"But then . . . You go to Arizona?"

"I played golf in Scottsdale once."

"Well, Scottsdale is hundreds of miles *north* of here. Think about that. We are in the middle of a desert. It has to be hot. What you expect?"

"I only played six rounds," Evans said.

"What?"

"In Arizona. For me to only play six rounds . . . I thought I'd die. And we started at seven in the morning. You golf?"

"Me? You crazy? Too hot here." Díaz smiled.

Evans was sipping a Coke from a bottle whose neck he'd religiously cleaned with a Handi Wipe before drinking. Supposedly Hermosillo, the capital of Sonora, was the only city in Mexico that treated its water, which meant that the ice the bottles nestled in was probably safe.

Probably.

He wiped the neck and mouth again. Wished he'd brought a miniature of Jack Daniels to use as purifier. Handi Wipe tasted like crap.

Díaz was drinking coffee, to which he'd added three or four sugars. Hot coffee, not iced. Evans couldn't get his head around that. A Starbucks addict at home and a coffee drinker in any number of the third-world places he traveled to (you didn't get dysentery from boiled water), he hadn't touched the stuff in Hermosillo. He didn't care if he never had a hot beverage again. Sweat trickled under his arms and down his temple and in his crotch. He believed his ears were sweating.

The men looked around them, at the students on the way to school, the businessmen and -women meandering to their offices or meetings. No shoppers; it was too early for that, but there were some mothers about, pushing carriages. The men not in suits were wearing blue jeans and boots and embroidered shirts. The cowboy culture, Evans had learned, was popular in Sonora. Pickup trucks were everywhere, as numerous as old American cars.

These two men resembled each other vaguely. Thirties, compact, athletic, with round faces—Díaz's pocked but not detracting from his craggy good looks, reflecting some Pima Indian in his ancestry. Dark hair both. Evans's face was smoother and paler, of course, and a little off kilter, eyes not quite plumb. Handsome too, though, in a way that might appeal to risk-taking women.

They were in jeans, running shoes and short-sleeved shirts, untucked, which would have concealed their weapons but they weren't carrying today.

So far there was no reason for anyone to wish them harm.

That would change.

Some tourists walked by. Hermosillo was a way station for people traveling from the US to the west coast of Sonora. Lots of people driving, lots of buses.

Buses . . .

Evans lowered his voice, though there was no one near. "You talked to your contact this morning, Al?"

Evans had tried out shortening the Mexican agent's name when they first met—to see how he'd react, if he'd be pissed, defensive, hostile. But the man had laughed. "You can call me Al," he'd said, the line from a Paul Simon song. So the test became a joke and Evans had decided then that he could like this guy. The humor also added to the infrastructure of trust. A lot of people working undercover think that saying "fuck" and making jokes about women creates trust. No. It's humor.

"*Sí*. And from what he say . . . I think our job, it will not be easy." He took the lid off his coffee and blew to cool it, which Evans thought was hilarious. "His security, very tight. Always his security man, a good one, José, is with him. And word is they know something's planned."

"What?" Evans's face curled up tight. "A leak?"

And *this*, Díaz seemed to find funny, "Oh, is always a leak. Every egg in Mexico has a crack. They won't know about us exactly but he has heard somebody is in town to kill him. Oh, *sí*, he has heard."

The "he" they were speaking of was Alonso María Carillo, better known as Cuchillo—in Spanish: "Knife." There was some debate about where the nickname came from. It probably wasn't because he used that weapon to kill rivals—he'd never been arrested for a violent crime . . . or *any* crime, for that matter. More likely the name was bestowed because he was brilliant. *Cuchillo*, as in sharp as a. He was supposedly the man behind one of the cartels in Sonora, the Mexican state that, along with neighboring Sinaloa, was home to the major drug gangs. But, though it was small, the Hermosillo Cartel was one of the most deadly, responsible for a thousand or more deaths . . . and the production of many tons of drugs—not only cocaine but insidious meth, which was the hot new profit center in the narcotics trade.

And yet Cuchillo was wily enough to avoid prosecution. The cartel was run by other men—who were, the *Federales* were sure, figureheads. To the world, Cuchillo was an innovative businessman and philanthropist. Educated at UCLA, a degree in business and one in English literature. He'd made his fortune, it appeared, through legitimate companies that were known for being good to workers and were environmentally and financially responsible.

So due process wasn't an option to bring him to justice. Hence the joint operation of Alejo Díaz and P.Z. Evans—an operation that didn't exist, by the way, if you happened to bring up the topic to anyone in Washington, DC, or Mexico City.

"So," Evans said, "he suspects someone is after him. That means we'll need a diversion, you know. Misdirection. Keep him focused on that, so he doesn't figure out what we're really up to."

"Yes, yes, that is right. At least one diversion. Maybe two. But we have another problem: we can't get him into the open."

"Why not?"

"My contact say he's staying in the compound for the next week. Maybe more. Until he think it's safe."

"Shit," Evans muttered.

Their mission was enwrapped with a tight deadline. Intelligence had been received that Cuchillo was planning an attack on a tourist bus. The vehicle would be stopped, the doors wired shut and then the bus set on fire. The attack would occur on Friday, two days from now, the anniversary of the day the Mexican president had announced his most recent war on the cartels. But there the report ended—as had, presumably, the life of the informant. It was therefore impossible to tell which bus would be targeted; there were hundreds of them daily driving many different routes and run by dozens of companies, most of whom didn't want to scare off passengers by suspending service or cooperating with law enforcement. (In his groundwork for the mission, Evans had researched the bus operators and noted one thing their ads all had in common: they began with variations on *Mexico Is Safe!!*)

Even without knowing the specific bus, however, Díaz and Evans had found a way to stop the attack. The biggest cartels in Sinaloa and Sonora were pulling back from violence. It was very bad publicity—not to mention dangerous to one's health—to kill tourists, even accidentally. An *intentional* attack on innocents, especially if Americans happened to be involved, could make the drug barons' lives pure hell. No rivals or anyone within his organization would challenge Cuchillo directly but the agents had learned that if he, say, met with an accident his lieutenants would not follow through with the attack.

However, if Cuchillo would be hiding in his compound until after the bus burned down to a scorched shell, then Díaz's contact was right; their job would not be easy. Drone surveillance had revealed that the house was on five acres, surrounded by a tall wall crowned with electric wire, the yard filled with sensors and scanned by cameras. Sniping wouldn't work because all the buildings—the large house, the separate library and detached garage—had thick bulletproof windows. And the walkways between those structures were out of sight of any vantage points where a shooter could set up.

As they sat bathed in the searing sun, Evans wondered if your mind slowed down the hotter it got. Oatmeal came to mind, steaming sludge.

He wiped his forehead, sipped Coke and asked for more details about Cuchillo's professional and personal life. Díaz had quite a bit of information; the man had been under investigation for the past year. Nodding, Evans took it all in. He'd been a good tactician in the Special Forces; he was a good tactician in his present job. He drained the Coke. His third of the day.

Nine fucking forty-five in the morning.

"Tell me about his weaknesses."

"Cuchillo? He *has* no weaknesses."

"Whatta you mean? Everybody has weaknesses. Drugs, women, men? Liquor? Gambling?"

Vulnerability was a very effective tool of the trade in Evans's business, as useful as bullets and plastic explosives. Usually, in fact, more so.

Díaz added yet one more sugar to his cup, though there was only a small amount of coffee remaining. He stirred elaborately. Figure eight. He sipped and then looked up. "There is maybe one thing."

"What?"

"Books," the Mexican agent said. "Books might be his weakness."

. . .

The weather in Washington, DC, was pleasant, this May evening, and so he picked a Starbucks with an outdoor patio . . . because, why not?

This was in a yuppie area of the district, if yuppies still existed. Peter Billings's father had been a yuppie. Shit, that was a long time ago.

Billings was drinking regular coffee, black, and no extra shots or foamed milk or fancy additives, which he secretly believed that people asked for sometimes simply because they liked the sound of ordering them.

He'd also bought a scone, which was loaded with calories, but he didn't care. Besides, he'd only eat half of it. At home in Bethesda his wife would feed him a Lean Cuisine later.

Billings liked Starbucks because you could count on being invisible. Business people typing résumés they didn't want their bosses to see, husbands and wives typing emails to friends of the opposite sex they ambivalently hoped might become lovers.

And government operatives meeting about issues that were, shall we say, sensitive.

Starbucks was also good because the steam machine made a shitload of noise and covered up the conversation if you were inside and the traffic covered up the conversation if you were outside. At least here on the streets of the District.

He ate some scone and launched the crumbs off his dark blue suit and light blue tie.

A moment later a man sat down across from him. He had a Starbuck's coffee too, but it'd been doctored up big time—almond or hazelnut, whipped cream, sprinkles. The man was weaselly, Billings reflected. When you're in your forties and somebody looks at you and the word weasel is the first thing that comes to mind, you might want to start thinking about image. Gain some weight.

Have a scone.

Billings now said to Harris, "Evening."

Harris nodded then licked the whipped cream from the top of his coffee carton.

Billings found it repulsive, the darting, weaselly tongue. "We're at the go/no-go point."

"Right."

"Your man down south."

"Adam."

His real name was Evans, but Adam was as good a code as any for Harris's contracting agent in Hermosillo, presently dogging Alonso María Carillo, AKA Cuchillo. Harris, of course, wasn't going to name him. Loud traffic on the streets of DC and cappuccino machines masks, not obliterates, and both Harris and Billings knew there were sound engineers who could extract incriminating words from cacophony with the precision of a hummingbird sipping nectar in a hover.

"Communication is good?" A near whisper by Billings.

No response. Of course communication would be good. Harris and his people were the best. No need for a nod either.

Billings wanted to take a bite of scone but was, for some reason, reluctant to do so in front of a man who'd killed at least a dozen people, or so the unwritten resume went. Billings had killed a number of people *indirectly* but, one on one? Zero. His voice now dropped lower yet. "Has he been in contact with the PIQ?"

Person in Question.

Cuchillo.

"No. He's doing the prep work. From a distance."

"So he hasn't seen, for instance, weapons or product at the compound?"

"No. They're staying clear. Both Adam and his counterpart from the *Distrito Federal*." Harris continued, "All the surveillance is by drone."

Which Billings had seen. And it wasn't helpful.

They fell silent as a couple at a table nearby stood and gathered their shopping bags.

Billings told himself to be a bit subtler with his questions. Harris was on the cusp of becoming curious. And that would not be good. Billings was not prepared to share what had been troubling him for the past several hours, since the new intelligence assessment came in: that he and his department might have subcontracted out a job to assassinate the wrong man.

There was now some doubt that Cuchillo was in fact head of the Hermosillo Cartel.

The intercepts Billings's people had interpreted as referring to drug shipments by the cartel in fact referred to legitimate products from Cuchillo's manufacturing factories, destined for US companies. A huge deposit into one of his Cayman accounts was perfectly legal—not a laundering scam, as originally thought—and was from the sale of a ranch he had owned in Texas. And the death of a nearby drug supplier they were sure was a hit ordered by Cuchillo turned out to be a real traffic accident involving a drunk driver. Much of the other data on which they'd based the terminate order remained ambiguous.

Billings had hoped that Adam, on the ground in Sonora, might have seen something to confirm their belief that Cuchillo ran the cartel and was going to push the button—figuratively—that destroyed a bus and its passengers.

But apparently not.

Harris licked the whipped cream again. Caught a few sprinkles in the process.

Billings looked him over once more. Yes, weaselly, but this wasn't necessarily an insult. After all, a sneaky weasel and a noble wolf weren't a lot different, at least not when they were sniffing after prey.

Harris asked bluntly, "So, do I tell Adam to go forward?"

Billings took a bite of scone. He had the lives of the passengers of the bus to save . . . and he had his career to think of too. He considered the question as he brushed crumbs. He'd studied law at the University of Chicago, where the theory of cost-benefit analysis had largely been developed. The idea was this: you balanced the cost of preventing a mishap versus the odds of it occurring and the severity of the consequences if it does.

In the Cuchillo assassination Billings had considered two options. Scenario One: Adam kills Cuchillo. If he's not the head of the cartel and is innocent, then the bus attack happens, because somebody else is behind it. If he's guilty, then the bus incident *doesn't* happen and there'd be no bus incidents in the future. Scenario Two: Adam stands down. Now, if Cuchillo's innocent, the bus incident happens. If he's guilty, the bus incident happens and there'll be more incidents like it in the future.

In other words, the hard and cold numbers favored going forward, even if Cuchillo was innocent.

But the obvious downside was that Billings could be crucified if that was the case . . . and if he and Harris and Adam were discovered.

An obvious solution occurred to him.

Oh, this was good. He finished the scone. "Yeah, Adam's green-lighted. But there's just one thing."

"What's that?"

"Tell him however he does it, all the evidence has to be obliterated. Completely. Nothing can trace the incident back here. Nothing at all. Physical evidence, digital evidence . . . People. Zip."

And looking very much like a cross-breed, a weasel-wolf, Harris nodded and sucked up the last of the whipped cream. "I have no problem with that whatsoever."

• • •

Díaz and Evans were back in the apartment in a nice section of Hermosillo, an apartment that was paid for by a company owned by a company owned by a company whose headquarters was a post office box in Northern Virginia. Evans was providing not only the technical expertise but most of the money as well. It was the least he could do, he'd joked, considering that it was America that supplied most of the weapons to the cartels; in Mexico it is virtually impossible to buy or possess weapons legally.

The time was now nearly 5 p.m. and Evans was reading an encrypted email from the US that he'd just received.

He looked up. "That's it. We're green-lighted."

Díaz smiled. "Good. I want that son of a bitch to go to hell."

And they got back to work, poring over data-mined information about Cuchillo's life: his businesses and associates and employees, household staff, his friends and mistresses, the restaurants and bars where he spent many evenings, what he bought, what he downloaded, what computer programs he used, what he enjoyed listening to, what he ate and drank. The information was voluminous; security forces here and in the US had been compiling it for months.

And, yes, much of this information had to do with books.

Weaknesses . . .

"Listen to this, Al. Last year he bought more than a million dollars' worth of books."

"You mean pesos."

"I mean dollars. Hey, you turn the AC down?"

"How can you even do that? Spend that much? You mean, down like the temperature goes down, or down like you make the air conditioner work less."

Evans had noticed that the late afternoon heat was flowing into the apartment like a slow, oppressive tide. "Temperature down."

Díaz warned, "Air conditioning, it's not so healthy."

"Cold temperature doesn't give you a cold," Evans said pedantically.

"I know that. I mean, the mold."

"What?"

"Mold in the ducts. Dangerous."

Oh. Evans conceded the point. He actually had been coughing a lot since he'd arrived. He got another Coke, wiped the neck and sipped. He spit Handi Wipe. He coughed. He left the AC where it was.

"You get used to the heat."

Evans scoffed. "That's not possible. In Mexico do you have words for winter, spring and fall?"

"Ha, funny."

They returned to the data-mined info. Not only was the credit card data available but insurance information about many of the books was often included. Some of the books were one of a kind, worth tens of thousands of dollars. They seemed to all be first editions.

"And look," Díaz said, looking over the documents. "He never sells them. He only buys."

It was true, Evans realized. There were no sales documents, no tax declarations of capital gains by selling. He kept everything.

He'd want them around him all the time, he'd covet them, he'd need.

Weakness . . .

Many people in the drug cartels were addicted to their own product; Cuchillo, it seemed, was not. Still, he had an addiction.

But how to exploit it?

Evans considered the list. Ideas were forming, as they always did. "Look at this. Last week he ordered a book inscribed by Dickens, *The Old Curiosity Shop*. The price is sixty thousand. Yeah, dollars."

"For a book?" the Mexican agent asked, looking astonished.

"And it's *used*," Evans pointed out. "It's supposed to be coming in, in a day or two." He thought for some moments. Finally he nodded. "Here's an idea. I think it could work . . . We'll contact this man—" He found a name on the sheet of data-mined print-outs. "Señor Davila. He seems to be Cuchillo's main book dealer. What we'll do is tell him we suspect him of money laundering."

"He probably is."

"And he'd pee his pants, thinking if we announce it, Cuchillo will . . ." Evans drew his index finger across his throat.

"Do you do that in America?"

"What?"

"You know. That thing, your finger, your throat? I only saw that in bad movies. Laurel and Hardy."

Evans asked, "Who?"

Alejo Díaz shrugged and seemed disappointed that he'd never heard of them.

Evans continued, "So Davila will do whatever we want."

"Which will be to call Cuchillo and tell him his Dickens book arrived early. Oh, and the seller wants cash only."

"Good. I like that. So somebody will have to meet Cuchillo in person—to collect the cash."

"And I'll come to his house to deliver the book and get the

money. His security man probably won't want that but Cuchillo will insist to take delivery. Because he's—"

"Addicted."

The Mexican agent added, "I'll have to meet him, not you. Your Spanish, it is terrible. Why did they send you here on assignment?"

The reason for sending P.Z. Evans to a conflict zone was not because of his language skills. "I like the soft drinks. Mexican Coke is better than our Coke. For real." He opened another one. Did the neck-cleaning thing.

Díaz said, "We'll need to get the book, though. That Dickens." Nodding at the list.

Evans said, "I'll make some calls to my people in the States, see if they can track one down."

Díaz asked, "Okay, so I'm inside. What do I do then? If I shoot him, they shoot me."

"Effective," Evans pointed out.

"But not the successful plans you're known for, P.Z."

"True. No, what you're going to do is plant a bomb."

"A bomb?" Díaz said uneasily. "I don't like them so much."

Evans gestured to his computer, referring to the email he'd just received. "Instructions are nothing's supposed to remain. Nothing to trace back to our bosses. Has to be a bomb. And one that produces a big honking fire."

Díaz added, "Always collateral damage."

The American agent shrugged. "Cuchillo doesn't have a wife. He doesn't have any children. Lives pretty much alone. Anybody around him is probably as guilty as he is." Evans tapped a drone picture of the compound. "Anything and anyone inside?" A shrug. "They're just acceptable sacrifices."

• • •

He liked his nickname.

Alonso María Carillo was honored that people thought enough of him to give him a name that sounded like it was attached to some Mafioso out of a movie. Like Joey "the Knife" Vitelli.

"Cuchillo"—like a blade, like a dagger: how he loved that! And it was ironic because he wasn't a thug, wasn't like Tony Soprano at all. He was solid physically and he was tough, yes, but in Mexico a businessman must be tough. Still, his voice was soft and, well, inquisitive-sounding. Almost innocent. His manner unassuming. His temper even.

He was in the office of his home not far from the upscale Hidalgo Plaza area of the city. Though the compound was surrounded by high walls, and sported a number of trees, from this spacious room he had a view of Cerro de la Compana, the city's grandest mountain—if a thousand-foot jut of rock can be described thus.

The hour was quitting time—he'd been working here since six that morning. No breaks. He put the documents aside and went online to download some apps for his new iPhone, which he would synchronize to his iPad. He loved gadgets—both in his personal life and in business he always stayed current with the latest technology. (Since his companies had sales reps throughout Mexico, and he needed to stay in constant touch with them, he used the Cloud and thought it was the best invention of the last ten years.)

Rising from his desk, declaring it the end of the day, he happened to regard himself in a mirror nearby. Not so bad for an old man.

Cuchillo was about five nine and stocky and resembled Emilio Fernández, Mexico's greatest actor and director, in the businessman's opinion. Though he was in scores of films, and directed a Palme d'Or winner, Cuchillo liked him best as the despicable Mapache in *The Wild Bunch* from the sixties, one of the more authentic films about early twentieth-century Mexico.

Looking over his face, thick black hair, keen brown eyes. Cuchillo thought again, No, not so bad . . . The women still appreciated him. Sure, he paid some of them—one way or another—but he also had a connection with them. He could converse. He listened. He also made love for hours. Not a lot of fifty-seven-year-olds could do that.

"You old devil," he whispered.

Then he gave a wry grin at his own vanity and left the office. He told his maid he'd be staying at home for dinner.

And he walked into his most favorite place on earth, his library. The building was large: sixty feet by forty, and very cool, as well as carefully humidity-controlled (which was ironic in Hermosillo, in the heart of the Sonoran desert, where there were two or three rainy days a year). Gauze curtains kept the sun from bleaching the jackets and leather bindings of the books.

The ceilings were thirty feet off the ground and the entire space was open, lined with tall shelves on the ground floor and encircled with levels above, which one could reach by climbing an iron spiral staircase to narrow walkways. In the center were three parallel shelves ten feet high. At the front of the room was a library table, surrounded by comfortable chairs and an over-stuffed armchair and a floor lamp with a warm yellow bulb. A small bar featured the best brandy and single-malt Scotches. Cuchillo enjoyed Cuban cigars too. But never here, of course.

The building was home to twenty-two thousand titles, nearly all of them first editions. Many, the only ones in existence.

On a night like this, after a long day working by himself, Cuchillo would normally have gone out into the relatively cool evening and eaten at Sonora Steak and then gone to Ruby's bar with his friends and—of course, his security. But the rumors of this impending attack were too real to ignore and he'd have to stay within the compound until more was learned about the threat.

Ah, what a country we live in, he reflected. The most philanthropic businessman and the most hardworking farmer and the worst drug baron all are treated equally . . . treated to fear.

Someday it will be different.

But at least Cuchillo had no problem staying home tonight, in his beloved library. He called his housekeeper and had her prepare dinner, a simple linguine primavera, made with organic vegetables and herbs out of his own garden. A California cabernet, too, and ice water.

He turned on a small high-definition TV, the news. There were several stories about the ceremony planned for Friday in the *Distrito Federal*—Mexico City—commemorating the latest war against the cartels. The event would include speeches by the country's president and an American official from the DEA. Other stories too: inflation was rising. A plane crashed. More drug killings in Chihuahua. He shook his head.

In a half hour the food arrived and he sat down at the table, removed his tie—he dressed for work, even when staying home—and stuffed a napkin into his collar. As he ate, his mind wandered to the Dickens that his book dealer Señor Davila would be delivering tomorrow. He was delighted that it had arrived early, but pleased too that he was getting it for a lower price than originally agreed. The seller whom Davila had found apparently needed cash and would reduce the price by five thousand if Cuchillo paid in US dollars, which he immediately agreed to do. Davila had said he would reduce his percentage of the finder's fee accordingly, but Cuchillo had insisted that he receive the full amount. Davila had always been good to him.

There was a knock on the door and his security chief, José, a tall, solid bald man, entered.

He could tell at once: bad news.

"I heard from a contact in the *Federales*, sir. There is intelligence about this bus attack on Friday? The tourist bus? The reports are linking you to it."

"No!"

"I'm afraid so."

"Dammit," he muttered. Cuchillo had spoken only a few obscenities in his life; this was usually the worst his language got. "*Me*? This is absurd. This is completely wrong! They blame me for everything!"

"I'm sorry, sir."

Cuchillo calmed and considered the problem. "Call the bus lines, call the security people, call whoever you have to. Do what you can to make sure passengers are safe in Sonora. You understand, I want to be certain that no one is hurt here. They will blame me if anything happens."

"I'll do what I can, sir, but—"

His boss said patiently, "I understand you can't control the entire state. But use our resources to do whatever you can."

"Yessir, I will."

The man hurried off.

Cuchillo finally shrugged off the anger, finished dinner and, sipping his wine, walked up and down the aisles enjoying the sight of his many titles.

Twenty-two thousand . . .

He returned to his office and worked some more on the project that had obsessed him for the past few months: opening another auto-parts fabrication plant outside of town. There was a huge US automobile manufacturer here in Hermosillo and Cuchillo had made much of his fortune by supplying parts to the company. His new factory would employ another four hundred local workers. Though he benefitted from their foolishness, he couldn't understand the Americans' sending manufacturing *away* from their country. He would never do that. Business—no, all of life—was about loyalty.

At 10 p.m., he decided to retire early. He washed and walked into his large bedroom, thinking again of *The Old Curiosity Shop* he would receive tomorrow. This buoyed his spirits. He dressed in pajamas and glanced at his bedside table.

What should he read now, he wondered, to lull him to sleep?

He decided he would continue with *War and Peace*, a title that, he thought wryly, perfectly described a businessman's life in Mexico.

. . .

In the living room of the apartment with the complicated ownership, P.Z. Evans was hunched over his improvised workbench, carefully constructing the bomb.

The care wasn't necessary because he risked getting turned into red vapor, not yet, in any event; it was simply that the circuits and wiring were very small and he had big hands. In the old days he would have been soldering the connections. But now improvised explosive devices were plug and play. He was pressing the circuits into sheets of especially powerful plastic explosive, which he'd packed into the leather cover after slicing it open with a surgeon's scalpel.

It was 11 p.m. and the agents had not had a moment's respite today. They'd spent the past twelve hours acquiring the key items for the project, like the surgeon's instruments, electronics and a leather-bound edition of the play *The Robbers* by Friedrich Schiller, which their new partner—book dealer Señor Davila—had suggested because Cuchillo liked the German author.

Through a jeweler's loupe over his right eye, Evans examined his handiwork and made some small adjustments.

Outside their door they could hear infectious *norteño* music in a nearby square. An accordion was prominent. The windows were open because the evening air teased that it was heading toward the bearable, and the AC was off. Evans had convinced himself he had a mold-induced cough.

Alejo Díaz sat nearby, not saying anything and seemingly uneasy. This was not because of the bomb, but because he'd apparently found the task of becoming an expert on book collecting and Charles Dickens daunting, to say the least.

Still, Díaz would occasionally look up from Joseph Connolly's *Collecting Modern First Editions*, his eyes on the bomb. Evans thought about diving to the floor, shouting, "Oh, shit! Five . . . four . . . three . . ." But while the Mexican agent had a sense of humor, that might be over the line.

A half hour later he was gluing the leather into place. "Okay, that's it. Done."

Díaz eyed his handicraft. "Is small."

"Bombs are, yes. That's what makes them so nice."

"It will get the job done?"

A brief laugh. "Oh, yeah."

"Nice," Díaz repeated uneasily.

Evans's phone buzzed with an encrypted text. He read it.

"Bait's here."

A moment later there was a knock on the door and, even though the text he'd just received had included all the proper codes, both men drew their weapons.

But the delivery man was just who he purported to be—a man attached to the Economic Development Council for the US consulate in northern Mexico. Evans had worked with him before. With a nod the man handed Evans a small package and turned and left.

Evans opened it and extracted the copy of Charles Dickens's *The Old Curiosity Shop*. Six hours ago it had been sitting in a famed book dealer's store on Warren Street in New York City. It had been bought with cash by the man who had just delivered it, and its journey to Sonora had been via chartered jet.

Killing bad guys is not only dangerous, it's expensive.

The American wrapped the book back up.

Díaz asked, "So, what are the next steps?"

"Well, you—you just keep on reading." A nod toward the book in his hands. "And when you're through with that, you might want to brush up on the history of English literature in general. You never know what subject might come up."

Díaz rolled his eyes and shifted in his chair, stretching. "And while I'm stuck in school, what are you going to do?"

"I'm going out and getting drunk."

"That is so not fair," Díaz pointed out.

"And it's even less fair considering I'm thinking I may get laid too."

Thursday

The latter part of his plans the night before did not happen, though Evans had come close.

But Carmella, the gorgeous young woman he met at a nearby bar, was a little too eager, which set off warning bells that she had designs to land a good-looking and apparently employed American husband.

In any event, tequila had intervened big time and the dance of your-place-or-mine never occurred.

It was now ten in the morning and, natch, hot as searing iron. No AC, but Evans's cough was gone.

Díaz examined his partner. "You look awful. Hey, you know that many of Charles Dickens's most popular novels were published first serially in magazines and newspapers and that he wrote in a style influenced by Gothic popular novels of the Victorian era, but with a whimsical touch?"

"You're fucked if you go in talking like that."

"I going to read one of his books. Is Dickens translated into Spanish?"

"I think so. I don't know."

Evans opened an attaché case he'd bought yesterday and had rigged with a false compartment. Into this narrow space he added the Schiller he'd doctored last night and sealed it. Then he added receipts, price guides, scraps of paper—everything that a book dealer would carry with him to a meeting with a collector. The Dickens, too, which was packed in bubble wrap. Evans then tested the communications app on the iPad that Díaz would have with him—it would appear to be in sleep mode, but a hypersensitive microphone would be picking up all the conversation between Cuchillo and Díaz. The system worked fine.

"Okay." Evans then checked his 9mm Beretta. He slipped it into his waistband. "Diversion's ready, device is ready. Sacrificial lamb is ready."

"Fuck you."

"Let's do it."

They walked down to the parking lot. Evans went to a huge old Mercury—yes, a real Mercury, in sun-faded Mercury brown, with an untraceable registration. Díaz's car was a midnight blue Lincoln registered to Davila Collectable Books, which Señor Davila had quickly, almost tearfully, agreed to let them borrow.

According to the unwritten rules of times like these, the start of a mission, when either or both might be dead within the hour, they said nothing of luck, hope, or the pleasure of working together. Much less did they shake hands.

"See you later."

"*Sí.*"

They climbed in, fired up the engines and hurried out of the lot.

• • •

As he drove to Cuchillo's compound Alejo Díaz could not help but think of the bus.

The people tomorrow, the tourists, who would be trapped and burned to death by this butcher. He recalled P.Z. Evans's words yesterday and reflected that these people were also—to Cuchillo—acceptable sacrifices.

Díaz was suddenly swept with fury at what people like him were doing to his country. Yes, the place was hot and dusty and the economy staggered and it dwelt forever in the shadow of that behemoth to the north—the country that Mexicans both loved and hated.

But this land is our home, he thought. And home, however flawed, deserves respect.

People like Alonso María Carillo treated Mexico with nothing but contempt.

Of course, Díaz would have to keep his revulsion deeply hidden when he met Cuchillo. He was just a shopkeeper's assistant; the drug lord was just another rich businessman with a love of books.

If he screwed that up, then many people—himself included—were going to die.

Then he was at the compound. He was admitted through a gate that swung open slowly and he parked near the modest front door. A swarthy, squat man who clearly was carrying a pistol greeted him pleasantly and asked him to step to a table in the entryway. Another guard gently but thoroughly frisked him.

Then the briefcase was searched.

Díaz regarded the operation with surprising detachment, he decided, considering he might be one minute away from being shot.

The detachment vanished and his heart thudded fiercely when the man frowned and dug into the case.

Jesus . . .

The man gazed at Díaz with wide eyes. Then he grinned. "Is this the new iPad?" He pulled it out and displayed it to the other guard.

His breathing stuttering in and out, Díaz nodded and wondered if his question had burst Evans's eardrum.

"Four-G?"

"If there's a server."

"How many gig?"

"Thirty-two," the Mexican agent managed to say.

"My son has that too. His is nearly filled. Music videos." The man replaced it and handed the briefcase back. The Schiller novel remained undiscovered.

Struggling to control his breathing, Díaz said, "I don't have many videos. I use it mostly for work."

A few minutes later he was led into the living room. He declined water or any other beverage. Alone, the Mexican agent sat with the briefcase on his lap. He opened it again and smoothly freed the Schiller and slipped it into his waistband, absently thinking about the explosive two inches from his penis. The open lid obscured prying eyes or cameras if there were any. He extracted the Dickens and closed the case.

A moment later a shadow spread on the floor and Díaz looked up to see Cuchillo walking steadily forward on quiet feet.

The Knife.

The stocky man strode forward, smiling. He seemed pleasant enough, if a bit distracted.

"Señor Abrossa," he said   the cover name Davila had given when he'd called yesterday. Díaz now presented a business card they'd just had printed up. "Good day. Delighted to meet you."

"And I'm pleased to meet such an illustrious client of Señor Davila."

"And how is he? I thought he might come himself."

"He sends his regards. He's getting ready for the auction of eighteenth-century bibles."

"Yes, yes, that's right. One of the few books I *don't* collect. Which is a shame. I understand that the plot is very compelling."

Díaz laughed. "The characters too. Especially the protagonist."

Cuchillo joined with a chuckle. "Ah, the Dickens."

Taking it reverently, the man unwrapped the bubble plastic and examined the volume and signature and flipped through the pages. "It is thrilling to know that Dickens himself held this very book."

Cuchillo was lost in the book, a gaze of admiration and respect. Not lust or possessiveness.

And in the silence, Díaz looked around and noted that this house was filled with much art and sculpture. All tasteful and subdued. This was not the house of a gaudy drug lord. He had been inside those. Filled with excess—and usually brimming with beautiful and marginally clad women, overflowing bars and obvious drug stations.

It was then that a sudden and difficult thought came to Díaz. Was it at all possible that they'd made a mistake? Was this subdued, cultured man *not* the vicious dog he was rumored to be? After all, there'd never been any hard proof that Cuchillo was the drug lord many believed him to be. Just because a person was rich and tough didn't mean he was a criminal.

Where exactly had the intelligence assigning guilt come from? How reliable was it?

He realized Cuchillo was looking at him with curiosity. "Now, Señor Abrossa, are you *sure* you're the book dealer I've been led to believe?"

Using all his willpower, Díaz kept a smile on his face and dipped a brow in curiosity.

The man laughed hard. "You've forgotten to ask for the money."

"Ah, sometimes I get so caught up in the books themselves that, you're right, I *do* forget it's a business. I personally would give books away to people who appreciate them."

"I most certainly *won't* tell your employer you said that." He reached into his pocket and extracted a thick envelope. "There is the fifty-five thousand. US." Díaz handed him the receipt on Davila's letterhead and signed "*V. Abrossa.*"

"Thank you . . ." Cuchillo raised a querying eyebrow.

"Victor." Díaz put the money in the attaché case and closed it. He looked around. "Your home, it is very lovely. I've always wondered about the houses in this neighborhood."

"Thank you. Would you like to see the place?"

"Please. And your collection, too, if possible."

"Of course."

Cuchillo then led him on a tour of the house, which was like the living room—all filled with understated elegance. Pictures of youngsters—his nieces and nephews who lived in Mexico City and Chihuahua, he explained. He seemed proud of them.

Díaz couldn't help wondering again: was this a mistake?

"Now, come to my library. As a book-lover, I hope you will be impressed."

They walked through the kitchen, where Cuchillo paused and asked the housekeeper how her ailing mother was doing. He nodded as she answered. He told her to take any time off she needed. His eyes were narrow with genuine sympathy.

A mistake? . . .

They walked out the back door and through the shade of twin brick walls, the ones protecting him from sniper shots, and then into the library.

Even as a nonbook-lover, Díaz was impressed. *More* than impressed.

The place astonished him. He knew the exterior size from the drone images, but he hadn't imagined it would be filled as completely as it was. Everywhere, books. It seemed the walls were made of them, like rich tiles in all different sizes and colors and textures.

"I don't know what to say, sir."

They walked slowly through the cool room and Cuchillo talked about some of the highlights in the collection. "My superstars," he said. He pointed out some as they walked.

The Hound of the Baskervilles by Conan Doyle, *Seven Pillars of Wisdom* by T.E. Lawrence, *The Great Gatsby* by F. Scott Fitzgerald, *The Tale of Peter Rabbit* by Beatrix Potter, *Brighton Rock* by Graham Greene, *The Maltese Falcon* by Dashiell Hammett, *Night and Day* by Virginia Woolf , *The Hobbit* by J.R.R. Tolkien, *The Sound and the Fury* by William Faulkner, *A Portrait of the Artist as a Young Man* by James Joyce, *A La Recherche Du Temps Perdu* by Marcel Proust, *The Wonderful Wizard of Oz* by Frank Baum, *Harry Potter and the Philosopher's Stone* by J.K. Rowling, *The Bridge* by Hart Crane, *The Catcher in the Rye* by J.D. Salinger, *The Thirty-Nine Steps* by John Buchan, *The Murder on the Links* by Agatha Christie, *Casino Royale* by Ian Fleming.

"And our nation's writers too, of course—that whole wall there. I love all books, but it's important for us in Mexico to be aware of *our* people's voice." He strode forward and displayed a few. "Salvador Novo, José Gorostiza, Xavier Villaurrutia and the incomparable Octavio Paz. Whom you're read, of course."

"Of course," Díaz said, praying that Cuchillo would not ask for the name of one of Paz's books, much less a plot or protagonist.

Díaz noted a book near the man's plush armchair. It was in a display case, James Joyce's *Ulysses*. He happened to have read about the title last night on a rare book website. "Is that the original 1922 edition?"

"Yes, that's right."

"It's worth about a hundred and fifty thousand dollars."

Cuchillo smiled. "No. It's worth nothing."

"Nothing?"

His arm swept in a slow circle, indicating the room. "This entire *collection* is worth nothing."

"How do you mean, sir?"

"Something has value only to the extent the owner is willing to sell. I would never sell a single volume. Most book collectors feel this way, more so than paintings or cars or sculpture."

The businessman picked up *The Maltese Falcon*. "You are perhaps surprised I have in my collection spy and detective stories?"

The agent recited a fact he'd read. "Of course, popular commercial fiction is usually *more* valuable than literature." He hoped he'd got this straight.

He must have. Cuchillo was nodding. "But I enjoy them for their substance as well as their collectability."

This was interesting. The agent said, "I suppose crime is an art form in a way."

Cuchillo's head cocked and he seemed confused. Díaz's heart beat faster.

The collector said, "I don't mean that. I mean that crime and popular novelists are often better craftspeople than so-called literary writers. The readers know this; they appreciate good storytelling over pretentious artifice. Take that book I just bought, *The Old Curiosity Shop*. When it first came out, serialized in weekly parts, people in New York and Boston would wait on the docks when the latest installment was due to arrive from England. They'd shout to the sailors, 'Tell us, is Little Nell dead?'" He glanced at the display case. "I suspect not so many people did that for *Ulysses*. Don't you agree?"

"I do, sir, yes." Then he frowned. "But wasn't *Curiosity Shop* serialized in *monthly* parts?"

After a moment Cuchillo smiled. "Ah, right you are. I don't collect periodicals, so I'm always getting that confused."

Was this a test, or a legitimate error?

Díaz could not tell.

He glanced past Cuchillo and pointed to a shelf. "Is that a Mark Twain?"

When the man turned Díaz quickly withdrew the doctored

Schiller and slipped it onto a shelf just above *Ulysses*, near the drug baron's armchair.

He lowered his arm just as Cuchillo turned back. "No, not there. But I have several. You've read *Huckleberry Finn*?"

"No. I just know it as a collector's item."

"Some people consider it the greatest *American* novel. That is true, but I qualify it by adding *North American*. It has lessons for *us* as well." A shake of the head. "And the Lord knows we need some lessons in this poor country of ours."

They returned to the living room and Díaz dug the iPad from the case. "Let me show you some new titles that Señor Davila has just gotten in." He supposed P.Z. Evans was relieved to hear his voice and learn that he had not been discovered and spirited off to a grave in the graceless Sonora desert.

He called up Safari and went to the website. "Now, we have—"

But his phony sales pitch was interrupted when a huge bang startled them all. A bullet had struck and spattered against the resistant glass of a window nearby.

Then more.

"My God! What's that?" Díaz called.

"Get out of the room, away from the windows! Now!" José, the security man, gestured them toward the doorways leading out of the living room.

"They're bulletproof," Cuchillo protested.

"But they could try armor piercing when they realize! Move, sir!"

Everyone scattered.

• • •

P.Z. Evans didn't get a chance to shoot his gun very often.

Although he and Díaz had earlier commented about Cuchillo meeting with an "accident" in a euphemistic way, in fact staging natural deaths was the preferred way to eliminate people. While the police would often *suspect* that the death of a terrorist or a criminal was not happenstance, a good craftsman could create a credible scenario that was satisfactory to avoid further investigation. A fall down stairs, a car crash, a pool drowning.

But nothing was as much fun as pulling out your long-barreled Italian pistol and blasting away.

He was about fifty yards from the compound, standing on a Dumpster behind a luxury apartment complex. There wasn't a support for the gun, but he was strong—shooters have to have good muscles—and he easily hit the window he was aiming for. He had a decent view through the glass and for his first shot aimed where nobody was standing—just in case this window happened not to be bulletproof. But the slugs smacked harmlessly into the strong glass.

And kept firing.

He emptied one mag, reloaded and leapt off the Dumpster, sprinting to the car, just as the side gate opened and Cuchillo's security people carefully looked out. Evans fired once into the wall to keep them down and then drove around the block to the other side of the compound.

No Dumpsters here, but he climbed on top of the roof of the car and fired three rounds into the window of Cuchillo's bedroom.

Then he hopped down and climbed into the driver's seat. A moment later he was skidding away.

Windows up, AC on full. If there was mold in car's vents he'd just take his chances. He was sweating like he'd spent an hour in the sauna.

• • •

Inside the house, after the shooter had vanished and calm—relative calm—was restored, Cuchillo did something that astonished Alejo Díaz.

He ordered his security chief to call the police.

This hardly seemed like the sort of thing that a drug baron would do. You'd think he'd want as little attention—and as little contact with the authorities—as possible.

But when a Hermosillo police captain, along with four uniformed officers, arrived twenty minutes later, Cuchillo was grim and angry. "Once again, I've been targeted! People can't accept that I'm just a businessman. They assume because I'm successful that I'm a criminal and therefore I deserve to be shot. It's unfair! You work hard, you're responsible, you give back to your country and your city . . . and still people believe the worst of you!"

The police conducted a brief investigation, but the shooter was, of course, long gone. And no one had seen anything— everyone inside had fled to the den, bedroom or bathroom, as the security chief had instructed. Díaz's response: "I'm afraid I didn't see much, anything really. I was on the floor, hiding." He shrugged, as if faintly embarrassed by his cowardice.

The officer nodded and jotted his words down. He didn't believe him, but nor did he challenge Díaz to be more thorough; in Mexico one was used to witnesses who "didn't see much, anything really."

The police left and Cuchillo, no longer angry but once more distracted, said goodbye to Díaz.

"I'm not much in the mood to consider Señor Davila's books now," he said, with a nod to the iPad. He would check the website later.

"Of course. And thank you, sir."

"It's nothing."

Díaz left, feeling even more conflicted than ever.

You work hard, you're responsible, you give back to your country and your city . . . and still people believe the worst of you . . .

My God, was he a murderous drug baron or a generous businessman?

And whether Cuchillo was guilty or innocent, Díaz realized he was stabbed by guilt at the thought that he'd just planted a bomb that would take the life of a man at his most vulnerable, doing something he loved and found comfort in: reading a book.

. . .

An hour later Cuchillo was sitting in his den, blinds closed over the bulletproof windows. And despite the attack, he was feeling relieved.

Actually, *because* of the attack, he was feeling relieved.

He had thought that the rumors they'd heard for the past few days, the snippets of intelligence, were referring to some kind of brilliant, insidious plan to murder him, a plan that he couldn't anticipate. But it had turned out to be a simple shooting, which had been foiled by the bulletproof glass; the assassin was surely headed out of the area.

José knocked and entered. "Sir, I think we have a lead about the attack. I heard from Carmella at Ruby's. She spent much of last evening with an American, a businessman, he claimed. He got drunk and said some things that seemed odd to her. She heard of the shooting and called me."

"Carmella," Cuchillo said, grinning. She was a beautiful if slightly unbalanced young woman who could get by on her looks for the time being, but if she didn't hook a husband soon she'd be in trouble.

Not that Cuchillo was in any hurry for that to happen; he'd slept with her occasionally. She was very, very talented.

"And what about this American?"

"He was asking her about this neighborhood. The houses in it. If there were any hotels nearby, even though earlier he'd said he was staying near the bar."

While there were sights to see in the sprawling city of

Hermosillo, Cuchillo's compound was in a nondescript residential area. Nothing here would draw either businessmen or tourists.

"Hotel," Cuchillo mused. "For a vantage point for shooting?"

"That's what I wondered. Now, I've gotten his credit card information from the bar and data-mined it. I'm waiting for more information but we know for a fact it's an assumed identity."

"So he's an operative. But who's he working for? A drug cartel from *north* of the border? A hit man from Texas hired by the Sinaloans? . . . The American government?"

"I hope to know more soon, sir."

"Thank you."

Cuchillo rose and, carrying the Dickens, started for the library. He stopped. "José?"

"Sir?"

"I want to change our plans with the bus."

"Yessir?"

"I know I said I wanted safe haven for all bus passengers in Sonora on Friday, that nothing should happen to the passengers here."

"Right, I told the men to wait to attack until it crossed the border into Sinaloa."

"But now, I want the opposite. I wish the attack to happen in *our* state."

"That's right. Whoever is behind this attack *must* know that I won't be intimidated. Any attempts on my life will be met with retribution. And I want to find a bus that is fully packed with passengers."

"Yessir."

Cuchillo looked at his security man carefully. "You don't think I should be doing this, do you?" He encouraged those working for him to make their opinions known, even—especially—differing opinions.

"Frankly, sir, not a tourist bus, no. Not civilians. I think it works to our disadvantage."

"I disagree," Cuchillo said calmly. "We need to take a strong stand."

"Of course, sir, if that's what you want."

"Yes, it is." But a moment later he frowned. "But wait. There's something to what you say."

The security man looked his boss's way.

"When your men attack the bus, get the women and children off before you set it on fire. Only burn the adults to death."

"Yessir."

Cuchillo considered his decision a weakness. But José had a point. The new reality was that, yes, sometimes you *did* need to take public relations into account.

• • •

At 8 p.m. that evening Cuchillo received a call in his library.

He was pleased at what he learned. One of his lieutenants explained that a shooting team was in place and would assault a large bus as it headed along Highway 26 west toward Bahia de Kino tomorrow morning.

They would stop the vehicle, leave the men on board, then wire shut the door and douse the bus in petrol and shoot anybody who tried to leap from the windows.

The communications man on the shooting team would call the press to make sure they arrived for video and photos before the fire was out.

Cuchillo thanked the man and disconnected, thinking of how much he was looking forward to seeing those news accounts.

He hoped the man who had shot at him would be watching the news too, and would feel responsible for the pain the victims would experience.

Glancing up from his armchair, he happened to notice that a book was out of order.

It was on the shelf above the case containing the *Ulysses*.

He rose and noted the leather spine. *The Robbers*. How had a Schiller gotten here? He disliked disorder of any kind, particularly in his book collection. One of the maids, perhaps.

Just as he plucked the volume from the shelf, the door burst open.

"Sir!"

"What?" He turned quickly to José.

"I think there's a bomb here! That man with the book dealer, Davila, he's fake. He was working with the American!"

Cuchillo's eyes first went to the Dickens, but, no, he'd flipped through the entire volume and there'd been no explosives inside. The assassins had simply used that as bait to gain access to his compound.

Then he looked down at what he held in his hand. The Schiller.

"What is it, sir?"

"This book . . . It wasn't here earlier. Victor Abrossa! He planted it when I gave him the tour." Cuchillo realized that, yes, the book was heavier than a comparable book of this size.

"Set it down! Run!"

"No! The books!" He glanced around at the library.

Twenty-two thousand volumes . . .

"It could blow up at any moment."

Cuchillo started to set it down, then hesitated. "I can't do it! You get back, José!" Then still holding the bomb, he ran outside, the security guard remaining loyally beside him. Once they were into the garden, Cuchillo flung the Schiller as far as he could. The men dropped to the ground behind one of the brick walls.

There was no explosion.

When Cuchillo looked he saw that the book had opened. The

contents—electronics and a wad of clay-colored explosive—had tumbled out.

"Jesus, Jesus."

"Please, sir. Inside now!"

They hurried into his home and got the staff away from the side of the house where the box lay in the garden. José called the man they used for making their *own* bombs. He would race to the house and disarm or otherwise dispose of the device.

Cuchillo poured a large Scotch. "How did you find this out?"

"I got the data-mined information on the American in the bar, the one who was drinking with Carmella. I found records that he was making calls to the book dealer. And he used his credit card to buy electronic parts at a supplier in town—the sort of circuits that are used in IEDs."

"Yes, yes. I see. They threatened Davila to help them. Or paid the bastard. You know, I suspected that man, Abrossa. I suspected him for a moment. Then I decided, no, he was legitimate."

Because I wanted the Dickens so much.

"I appreciate what you did, José. That was a good job. Would you like a drink too?"

"No, thank you, sir."

Still calm, Cuchillo wrinkled his brow. "Considering how the American tried to kill us—and nearly destroyed a priceless collection of books—how would you feel if we instructed our people on Highway 26 *not* to get the women and children off before setting fire to the bus?"

José smiled. "I think that's an excellent suggestion, sir. I'll call the men."

• • •

Several hours later the bomb had been slipped into a steel disposal container and taken away. Cuchillo, the engineer explained, had unwittingly disarmed it himself. The panicked throw had dislodged the wires from the detonator, rendering it safe.

Cuchillo had enjoyed watching the bomb-disposal robot—the same way he liked being in his parts manufacturing operation and his drug synthesizing facilities. He enjoyed watching technology at work. He had always wanted the *Codex Leicester*—the Da Vinci manuscript that contained the inventor's musings on mechanics and science. Bill Gates had paid thirty million dollars for it some years ago. Cuchillo could easily afford that, but the book was not presently for sale. Besides, such a purchase would draw too much attention to him, and a man who has tortured hundreds to death and—in the spirit of mercy—painlessly shot perhaps a thousand, does not want too many eyes turned in his direction.

Cuchillo spent the rest of the night on the phone with associates, trying to find more details of the two assassins, and any associates they might have, but there was no other information. He'd learn more tomorrow. It was nearly midnight when finally he sat down to a modest dinner of grilled chicken and beans with tomatillo sauce.

As he ate, and sipped a very nice cabernet, he found himself relaxed and curiously content, despite the horror of what might have happened today. Neither he nor any of his people had been injured in the attack. His twenty-two thousand volumes were safe.

And he had some enjoyable projects on the horizon: killing Davila, of course. And he'd find the name of the person masquerading as Abrossa, his assistant, and the shooter who'd fired the shots—a clumsy diversionary tactic, he now realized. Probably the American. Those two would not die as quickly as the book dealer. They had destroyed an original Friedrich Schiller (albeit a third printing with water damage on the spine). Cuchillo would stay true to his name and would use a knife on them himself—in his special interrogation room in the basement below his library.

But best of all: he had the burning bus and its scores of screaming passengers to look forward to.

Friday

At 1 a.m. Cuchillo washed for bed and climbed between the smooth sheets, not silk but luxurious and expensive cotton.

He would read something calming to lull him to sleep tonight. Not *War and Peace*. Perhaps some poetry.

He picked up his iPad from the bedside table, flipped open the cover and tapped the icon to bring up his e-reader app. Cuchillo, of course, generally preferred traditional books for the most part. But he was a man of the twenty-first century and found e-books were often more convenient and easier to read than their paper forebears. His iPad library contained nearly a thousand titles.

As he looked at the tablet, though, he realized he must have hit the wrong app icon—the forward camera had opened and he found he was staring at himself.

Cuchillo didn't close the camera right away, however. He took a moment to regard the image. And laughed and whispered the phrase he'd used to describe himself earlier, "Not so bad, you old devil."

• • •

Five hundred yards from Cuchillo's compound, Alejo Díaz and P.Z. Evans were sitting in the front seat of the big Mercury. They were leaning forward, staring at the screen of Evans's impressive laptop computer.

What they were observing was the same image that Cuchillo happened to be basking in—his own wide-angle face—which was being beamed from his iPad's camera to the laptop via a surveillance app Evans had loaded. They could hear the man's softer voice too.

You old devil . . .

"He's in bed, alone," Evans said. "Good enough for me." Then he glanced at Díaz. "He's all yours."

"*Sí?*" asked the Mexican agent.

"Yep."

"*Gracias.*"

"*Nada.*"

And without any dramatic flair, Díaz pressed a button on what looked like a garage door opener.

In Cuchillo's bedroom, the iPad's leather case, which Evans had stuffed with the potent incendiary explosive last night, detonated. The explosion was far larger than the American agent had expected. Even the bulletproof windows blew to splinters and a gaseous cloud of flame shot into the night.

They waited until it was clear the bedroom was engulfed in flame—and all the evidence of the attack was burning to vapors, as they'd been instructed to do by Washington—and then Díaz started the car and drove slowly through the night.

After ten minutes of silence, looking over their shoulders for police or other pursuers, Díaz said, "Have to say, *amigo*, you came up with a good plan."

Evans didn't gloat—or shy with false modesty either. It *was* a good plan. Data mining had revealed a lot about Cuchillo (this was often true in the case of targets like him—wealthy and, accordingly, big spenders). Evans and Díaz had noted not only his purchases of collectable books, but his high-tech acquisitions too: an iPad, an e-reader app and a number of e-books, as well as a leather case for the Apple device.

Armed with this information, Evans duplicated the iPad and filled the case with the deadly explosive. *This* was the actual weapon that Díaz smuggled into the compound and swapped with Cuchillo's iPad, whose location they could pinpoint thanks to the finder service Evans had hacked into. With Díaz inside, holding the iPad to show Cuchillo Davila's latest inventory of books, Evans had fired into the windows, scattering everyone and giving his partner a chance to slip into the bedroom and switch the devices. He'd fired into that room's windows too, just in case Díaz had not been alone there.

The bullets would also serve a second purpose—to let Cuchillo and his security people believe the shooting was the assault they'd heard about and lessen their suspicion that another attack was coming.

Lessen, but not eliminate. The Knife was too sharp for that.

And so they needed a second misdirection. Evans let slip fake information about himself—to Carmella, the beautiful woman who was part of Cuchillo's entourage at Ruby's bar (phone records revealed he called her once or twice a month). Evans also fed phony data-mined facts that suggested he and Díaz might have snuck a bomb into the library. He'd hollowed out a copy of Schiller's *The Robbers*—sorry, Fred—and filled it with real explosives and a circuit, but failed to connect the detonators.

Cuchillo would know his library so well it wouldn't take much to find this out-of-place volume, which Díaz had intentionally planted askew.

After finding this device, they would surely think no more threats existed and not suspect the deadly iPad on Cuchillo's bedside table.

Díaz now called José, the security chief for the late drug baron, and explained—in a loud voice due to the chief's sudden hearing loss—that if any bus attacks occurred he would end up in jail accompanied by the rumor that he had sold his boss out. As unpopular as Cuchillo had been among the competing cartel figures, nothing was more unpopular in a Mexican prison than a snitch.

Any doubt that Cuchillo was indeed behind the bus arson plan was put to rest when they heard his instructions to José earlier via the bug that Díaz had planted during his delivery of the Dickens.

José desperately assured them that there would be no attacks. Díaz had to say goodbye three times before the man heard him.

A good plan. If a bit complicated. It would have been much easier, of course, simply to get a real bomb into the library and detonate it when a drone surveillance revealed Cuchillo inside.

That idea, however, hadn't even been on the table. They would never have destroyed the library. Aside from the moral issue—and P.Z. Evans *did* have his standards—there was the little matter of how such a conflagration would play in the press if word got out about the identity of the two agents who'd orchestrated it and who their employers were.

You can kill drug barons and their henchmen with impunity; twenty thousand destroyed classics were *not* acceptable sacrifices. That was the sort of blot from which careers do not recover.

In a half hour they were back at the hotel and watching the news, which confirmed that indeed Alonso María Carillo, known as Cuchillo, the head of the Hermosillo Cartel, was dead. No one else had been injured in the attack, which was blamed on a rival cartel, probably from Sinaloa.

He shut the set off. They decided to get a little dinner and a lot of tequila—though definitely not at Sonora Steak or Ruby's bar. They'd go somewhere across town. They'd probably be safe; the Hermosillo Cartel had been neutralized. Still, both men had their weapons underneath their untucked shirts. And extra magazines in their left pockets.

As they walked to the big old Mercury, Díaz said, "You should have seen all those books in the library. I never saw so many books in my life."

"Uhn," Evans said.

"What does that mean, that sound? You don't *like* books?"

"I like books."

The Mexican agent gave a fast laugh. "You no sound like you do. You read at all?"

"Of course I read."

"So, what do you read? Tell me."

Evans climbed into the passenger seat and counted three pickup trucks passing by before he answered. "Okay, you want to know? The sports section. That's all I read."

Díaz started the car. "*Sí*, me too."

Evans said, "Could we get that AC going, Al? Does it *ever* cool off in this goddamn town?"

The Adventure of the Laughing Fisherman

Sometimes it's overwhelming: the burden of knowing that the man you most admire isn't real.

Then the depression that you've fought all your life creeps in, the anxiety. The borders of your life contract, stifling, suffocating.

And so slim Paul Winslow, twenty-eight, was presently walking into the neat, unadorned office of his on-again, off-again therapist, Dr Levine, on the Upper West Side of Manhattan.

"Hello, Paul, come on in. Sit down."

Dr Levine was one of those shrinks who offer basic armchairs, not couches, for their patients. He spoke frequently during the sessions, wasn't afraid to offer advice and ask, "How do you feel about that?" only when it was important to know how his patients felt. Which was pretty rare.

He never used the verb "explore."

Paul had read Freud's *Psychopathology of Everyday Life* (not bad, though a bit repetitive) and the works of Jung and Horney and some of the other biggies. He knew that a lot of what brain docs told you was a crock. But Dr Levine was a good man.

"I did the best I could," Paul now explained to him. "Everything was going along okay, pretty much okay, but over the past couple of months it got worse and I couldn't shake it, you know, the sadness. I guess I need a tune-up," Paul added, smiling ruefully. Even at the worst times, his humor never wholly deserted him.

A laugh from the mouth of the clean-shaven, trim physician, who wore slacks and a shirt during the appointments. His glasses were unstylish wire rims, but that seemed to fit his casual style and friendly demeanor.

Paul had not been here for nearly eight months and the doctor now glanced through his patient's file to refresh his memory. The folder was thick. Paul had seen Dr Levine off and on for the past five years and had been to other shrinks before that. Diagnosed from a young age with bipolar and anxiety disorders, Paul had worked hard to control his maladies. He didn't self-medicate with illegal drugs or liquor. He'd seen therapists, attended workshops, taken medicine—though not regularly and only those run-of-the-mill antidepressants ingested by the ton in the New York metropolitan area. He'd never been institutionalized, never had any breaks with reality.

Still, the condition—which his mother also suffered from— had sidelined him. Never one to get along well with others, Paul was impatient, had little respect for authority, could be acerbic and never hesitated to verbally eviscerate the prejudiced and the stupid.

Oh, he was brilliant, with an IQ residing well up in the high digits. He'd zipped through university in three years, grad school in one. But then came the brick wall: the real world. Teaching at community colleges hadn't worked out (you don't necessarily have to get along with fellow professors, but a modicum of tolerance for your students' foibles is a requirement). A job editing for scientific publishers had been equally disastrous (the same problem with his bosses and authors). Recently he'd taken up freelance copy-editing for one of his former employers, and this solitary job more or less suited, at least for the time being.

Not that money was important; his parents, both bankers, were well off and, sympathetic to their son's condition, had established a trust fund for him, which supported him nicely. Given these resources, he was free to live a simple, stress-free life, working part time, playing chess at a club in the Village, dating occasionally (though without much enthusiasm) and doing plenty of what he loved most: reading.

Paul Winslow didn't care much for real people but he loved the characters in fiction. He always had.

Lou Ford and Anna Wulf and Sam Spade and Clyde Griffiths and Frank Chambers and Mike Hammer and Pierre Bezukhov and Huck Finn—these and a hundred others made up Paul's circle of intimates. Harry Potter was a good friend; Frodo Baggins, a better one.

As for vampires and zombies . . . well, better not to get Paul started.

Yet no fiction, high-brow or -low, captivated him like the short stories and novels of one writer in particular: Arthur Conan Doyle, the creator of Sherlock Holmes.

Upon first reading him, some years ago, he knew instantly that he'd found his hero—a man who reflected his personality, his outlook, his soul.

His passion extended beyond the printed page. He collected Victorian memorabilia and artwork. Sitting prominently on the wall in his living room was a very fine reproduction of Sidney Paget's pen-and-ink drawing of archenemies Holmes and Professor Moriarty grappling on a narrow ledge above Reichenbach Falls, a scene from the short story "The Final Problem," in which Moriarty dies and Holmes appears to. Paul owned all the various filmed versions of the Holmes adventures, though he believed the old BBC version with Jeremy Brett was the only one that got it right.

Yet in recent months Paul had found that spending time in the world of the printed page was growing less and less comforting. And as the allure of the books wore off, the depression and anxiety seeped in to fill its place.

Now, sitting back in Dr Levine's bright office—shrink contempo, Paul had once described it—he ran a hand through his unruly black curly hair, which he often forgot to comb. He explained that the high he got from reading the books and stories had faded dramatically.

"It hit me today that, well, it's lame, totally lame, having a hero who's fictional. I've been so, I don't know, *confined* within the covers of the books, I'm missing out on . . . everything." He exhaled slowly through puffed cheeks. "And I thought maybe it's too late. The best part of my life is over."

Paul didn't mind the doctor's smile. "Paul, you're a young man. You've made huge strides. You have your whole life ahead of you."

"But how stupid is that, having this hero who's made up? I mean, they're only books."

"Don't dismiss the legitimate emotional attraction between readers and literature," the doctor said.

Paul shrugged in concession, "Well, I know when it looked like Sherlock Holmes died in 'The Final Problem,' Doyle was so hounded that he had to write a story that brought Holmes back."

"Exactly. People love their characters. But apart from the valid role that fiction plays in our lives, in your case I think your diminished response to Sherlock Holmes stories is a huge step forward." The doctor seemed unusually enthusiastic.

"It is?"

"It's a sign that you're willing—and *prepared*—to step from a fictional existence to a real one."

This was intriguing. Paul found his heart beating a bit faster.

"Your goal in coming to see me and the other therapists in the past has always been to lead a less solitary, more social existence.

Find a job, a partner, possibly have a family. And this is a perfect opportunity."

"How?"

"The Sherlock Holmes stories resonated with you for several reasons. I think primarily because of your talents: your intelligence, your natural skills at analysis, your powers of deduction—just like his."

"My mind does kind of work that way."

Dr Levine said, "I remember the first time you came to see me. You asked about my wife and son—how was he doing in kindergarten? But I didn't wear a wedding ring and had no pictures of family here. I never mentioned them, and I don't put any personal information on the internet. I assumed at the time you were just guessing—you were right, by the way—but now I suspect you deduced those facts about me, right?"

Paul cocked his head. "That's right."

"How?"

"Well, as for the fact you had a child and his age, there was a tiny jelly or jam fingerprint on the side of your slacks—about the height of a four- or five-year-old hugging Daddy at breakfast. And you never have appointments before eleven a.m., which told me that you probably were the spouse who took your child to school; if he'd been in first grade or older you would have gotten him to school much earlier and could see patients at nine or ten. You did the school run, I was assuming, because you have more flexible hours than your wife, working for yourself. I was sure she had a full-time job. This *is* Manhattan, of course—two incomes are the rule.

"Now, why a son? I thought the odds were that a girl of that age would be more careful about wiping her fingers before hugging you. Why an only child? Your office and this building are pretty modest, you know. I guessed you weren't a millionaire. That and your age told me it was more likely than not you had only one child. As to the wife, I suspected that even if you had had marital problems, as a therapist you'd work hard to keep the marriage together, so divorce was very unlikely. There was the widower factor, but the odds seemed against that."

Dr Levine shook his head, laughing. "Sherlock Holmes would be proud of you, Paul. Tell me, that comes naturally to you?"

"Real natural. It's kind of a game I play. A hobby. When I'm out, I deduce things about people."

"I think you should consider using these skills of yours in the real world."

"How do you mean?"

"I've always thought you were misplaced in academia and publishing. I think you should find a job where you can put those skills to work."

"Like what?"

"Maybe the law. Or . . . Well, how's this: you studied math and science."

"That's right."

"Maybe forensics would be a good choice. Not going to the police academy but maybe working for a private firm. Consulting . . . Like Sherlock Holmes did.'"

"I've thought about that," Paul said uncertainly. "But do you think I'm ready? I mean, ready to get out in the real world?"

The doctor didn't hesitate. "I absolutely do."

• • •

Several days later Paul was doing what he often did at 10 a.m. on a weekday: having a coffee at Starbucks near his apartment on the Upper West Side and scrolling through his laptop.

He was considering what Dr Levine had told him and was trying to find some way to use his skills in a practical way. He wasn't having much luck. Private forensic analysis was mostly corporate in nature, or expert witnesses for commercial and personal injury litigation. And you needed specific advanced degrees.

No, not for him.

Occasionally he would look around and make deductions about people sitting near him—a woman had broken up with a boyfriend, one man was an artistic painter, another was very likely a petty criminal.

Yes, this was a talent.

Just how to put it to use?

It was as he was pondering this that he happened to overhear one patron, looking down at her Mac screen, turn to her friend and say, "Oh, my God. They found another one!"

"What?" her companion asked.

"Another, you know, stabbing victim. In the park. It happened last night. They just found the body." She waved at the screen. "It's in the *Times*."

"Jesus. Who was it?"

"Doesn't say, doesn't give her name, I mean." The blond, hair pulled back, ponytail, read. "Twenty-nine, financial advisor. They shouldn't say what she does without giving her name. Now everybody who knows somebody like that's going to worry."

Paul realized this would be the man—*surely* a man, according to a typical criminal profile—who had been dubbed the "East Side Slasher." Over the course of several months he'd killed two, now three, women. The killer took trophies. With the first two victims, at least, he cut off the left index finger. Post-mortem, after he'd slashed their jugulars. There'd been no obvious sexual overtones to the crimes. Police could find no motives.

"Where?" Paul asked the Starbucks blond.

"What?" She turned, frowning.

"Where did they find the body?" he repeated impatiently.

She looked put out, offended at his apparent nosiness.

Paul lifted his eyebrows. "It's not eavesdropping when the person you're listening to makes a statement loud enough for the whole place to hear. Now. *Where* is the body?"

A gasp. She whispered, "Near Turtle Pond."

"How near?" Paul persisted.

She glanced at her laptop screen. "It doesn't say." Then she turned away in a huff.

Paul rose quickly, feeling his pulse start to pound. He tossed out his half-finished coffee and headed for the door. He gave a faint laugh, thinking to himself: the game's afoot.

• • •

"Sir, what're you doing?"

Crouching on the ground, Paul glanced up at a heavy-set man, white, pale white, with slicked-back, thinning hair. Paul rose slowly. "I'm sorry?"

"Could I see some identification?"

"I guess, sure. Could I?" Paul held the man's stare evenly.

The man frowned then coolly displayed his NYPD detective's shield. His name was Albert Carrera.

Paul handed over his driver's license.

"You live in the area?"

"It's on my license."

"Doesn't mean it's current," the detective responded, handing the card back.

He'd renewed two months ago. He said, "It is. West Eighty-Second. Near Broadway."

They were just north of the traverse road in Central Park, near the pond where the Starbucks woman had told him the body had been found. The area was filled with trees and bushes and rock formations. Grass fields, trisected by paths bordered with mini shoulders of dirt—which is what Paul had been examining.

Yellow police tape fluttered, but the body and crime scene people were gone.

A few spectators milled nearby, taking mobile phone pictures or just staring, waiting to glimpse some fancy *CSI* gadgets perhaps. Though not everyone was playing voyeur. Two nannies pushed perambulators and chatted. One worker in dungarees was taking a break, sipping coffee and reading the sports section. Two college-age girls Rollerbladed past. All seemed oblivious to the carnage that had occurred only fifty feet away.

The detective asked, "How long have you been here, Mr Winslow?"

"I heard about the murder about a half hour ago and I came over. I've never seen a crime scene before. I was curious."

"Did you happen to be in the park at around midnight?"

"Was that the time of death?"

The detective persisted, "Sir? Midnight?"

"No."

"Have you seen anyone in the park recently, wearing a Yankees jacket and red shoes?"

"Is that what the killer was wearing last night? . . . Sorry. No, I haven't. But is that what he was wearing?"

The detective seemed to debate answering. Finally, he said, "A witness from a street-sweeping crew reported seeing somebody walk out of bushes there"—he pointed—"about twelve thirty this morning in the jacket and red shoes."

Paul squinted. "There?"

The detective sighed. "Yeah, there."

"And the witness was in his street-sweeping truck?"

"Yeah."

"Then he's wrong," Paul said dismissingly.

"I'm sorry?"

"Look." Paul nodded, walking to the traverse. "His truck was over there, right?"

The detective joined him. "Sir, I'm going to have to ask you to—"

"That streetlight would've been right in his face and I'd be very surprised if he'd have been able to see writing on the jacket. As for the shoes, I'd say they were blue, not red."

"What?"

"He would have seen them for only a second or two as he drove past. An instant later his mind would have registered them as red—because of the after image. That means they were really blue, the opposite color. How the physiology of the eye works. And, by the way, they weren't shoes at all. He was wearing coverings of some kind. Booties, like surgeons wear. Those are usually blue."

"Covering? What're you talking about?" Carrera was penduluming between interested and irritated.

"Look at this." Paul returned to the patch of dirt he'd been crouching over. "See these footprints? Somebody walked from the body through the grass, then onto the dirt here. He stopped—you can see that here—and then he stood in a pattern that suggests he pulled something off his shoes. The same size prints start up again, but they're much more distinct. So your suspect wore booties to keep you from finding out the brand of shoe he was wearing. But he made a mistake. He figured it was safe to take them off once he was away from the body. A good idea, except he should have waited and gone another thirty, forty yards."

Carrera was staring down. Then he jotted notes.

Paul added, "And as for the brand? I guess your crime scene people have databases."

"Yessir. Thanks for that. We'll check it out." The detective's voice was gruff but he seemed appreciative, if reluctantly so. He pulled out his mobile and made a call.

"Oh, Detective," Paul interrupted, "remember that just because the shoe's big—it looks like a twelve—doesn't mean his *foot* is that size. It's a lot less painful to wear two sizes too large than two sizes smaller, if you want to fool somebody about your stature."

After Carrera had ordered the crime scene techs to come back and disconnected, Paul said, "Oh, one other thing, Detective?"

"Yessir?"

"See that bud there?

"That flower?" The detective gazed downward.

"Right. It's from a knapweed. The only place in the park where it grows is in the Shakespeare Garden."

"How do you know that?"

"I observe things," Paul said dismissively. "Now. There's a small rock formation. It'd be a good place to hide and I'll bet that's where he lay in wait for the victim."

"Why?"

"It's not unreasonable to speculate that his cuff scooped up the bud while he was crouched down. When he lifted his foot to pull off the booties here, the bud fell out."

"But that's two hundred yards away, the garden."

"Which means you haven't searched it."

Carrera stiffened, but then admitted, "No."

"I'd have your people search the garden for trace evidence—or whatever your forensic people look for nowadays. You see so much on TV. You never know what's real or not."

After he'd finished jotting notes, Carrera asked, "Are you in law enforcement?"

"No, I just read a lot of murder mysteries."

"Uh-huh. You have a card?"

"No. But I'll give you my number."

Carrera handed him one of his own cards and Paul wrote the number down then handed it back. He looked up into the man's eyes; the cop was about six inches taller. "You think this is suspicious, I'm sure. I also wrote down the name of the chess club where I play, in Greenwich Village. I was there last night until midnight. And I'd guess the CCTV cameras in the subway—I took the Number One train to Seventy-Second—would show me getting off around one thirty. And then went to Alonzo's deli. I know the counterman. He can identify me."

"Yessir." Carrera tried to sound like he hadn't suspected Paul, but in fact even the slow Scotland Yard investigator, Lestrade, in the Sherlock Holmes books would have him checked out.

Still, at the moment, Carrera actually offered what seemed to be a warm handshake. "Thanks for your help, Mr Winslow. We don't always find such cooperative citizens. And helpful ones too."

"My pleasure."

Carrera pulled on gloves and put the bud in a plastic evidence bag. He then walked toward the Shakespeare Garden.

As Paul turned back to examine the scene again a voice behind him asked, "Excuse me?"

He turned to see a balding man, stocky and tall, in tan slacks and a Polo jacket. Topsiders. He looked like a Connecticut businessman in the city on the weekend. He was holding a digital recorder.

"I'm Franklyn Moss. I'm a reporter for the *Daily Feed*."

"Is that an agricultural newspaper?" Paul asked.

Moss blinked. "Blog. Feed. Like new feed." He paused, and his face changed. "Oh, that was a joke."

Paul gave no response.

Moss asked, "Can I ask your name?"

"I don't know. What do you want?" He looked at the recorder. Something about the man's eager eyes, too eager, made him uneasy.

"I saw you talking to that detective, Carrera. He's not real cooperative. Kind of a prick. Between you and I."

You and *me*, Paul silently corrected the journalist, who, he thought, should have known better. "Well, he was just asking me if I'd seen anything—about the murder, you know. They call that canvassing, I think."

"So, did you?"

"No. I just live near here."

Moss looked around in frustration. "Not much good stuff, this one. Everything was gone before we heard about it."

"Good stuff? You mean the body?"

"Yeah. I wanted to get some pix. But no luck this time." Moss stared at the shadowy ring of bushes where the woman had died. "He rape this one? Cut off anything other than the finger?"

"I don't know. The detective—"

"Didn't say."

"Right."

"They always play it so close to the damn chest. Prick, I was saying. You mind if I interview you?"

"I don't really have anything to say."

"Most people don't. Who cares? Gotta fill the stories with something. If you want your fifteen minutes of fame, gimme a call. Here's my card." He handed one over. Paul glanced at and then pocketed it. "I'm writing a sidebar on what people think about somebody getting killed like this."

Paul cocked his head. "I'll bet the general consensus is they're against it."

• • •

All the next day, Paul had been in and out of the apartment constantly, visiting the crime scenes of the Upper East Side Slasher, getting as close as he could to the cordoned-off sites, observing, taking notes. Then returning and, as he was doing now, sitting at his computer, continuing his research and thinking hard about how to put into practical use everything he'd learned from his immersion in the Sherlock Holmes books.

His doorbell rang.

"Yes?" he asked into the intercom.

"Yeah, hi. Paul Winslow?"

"Yes."

"It's Detective Carrera. We met yesterday. In Central Park?"

Hm.

"Come on up." He hit the unlock button.

A moment later there came a knock on the apartment door. Paul admitted the detective. Breathing heavily from the two-story walk up the steep stairs—he apparently hadn't waited for the elevator—the man looked around the apartment. Maybe his cop training precluded him from saying, "Nice digs," or whatever a visitor normally said, but Paul could tell he was impressed at the small but elegant place.

Paul's trust fund was really quite substantial.

"So," Paul said. "Did you check me out? I'm guessing you did, 'cause you don't have your handcuffs out."

Carrera, who was carrying a thick, dark brown folder, started to deny it but then laughed. "You weren't much of a suspect."

"Perps *do* come back to the scene of the crime, though."

"Yeah, but only the stupid ones give the cops advice . . . and good advice, in your case. The shoe was a Ferragamo, size twelve—you've got a good eye. So our perp's pretty well off."

"And you checked the indentation?"

"It was pretty deep. He's a big man, so shoe's probably the right fit."

"How old was the shoe?"

"They couldn't tell wear patterns on the soles."

"Too bad."

"And you were right about the jacket. The street cleaner didn't really see the logo. He was speculating—because it was black and had the cut of a Yankees jacket his kid owns. Trying to be helpful. Happens with witnesses a lot."

"Remember the back lighting. It might not have been black at all. It could have been any dark color. Can I get you anything?"

"Uhm, well, water, yeah. Thanks."

"I'm having milk. I love milk. I drink a glass a day, sometimes two. You want some milk?"

"Water's fine."

Paul got a glass of milk for himself and a bottle of Danone for the detective.

He returned to find the man sitting on the couch, studying the shelves. "Man, you got a lot of books. And that whole wall there: true crime. And forensics."

"It's fascinating. Like solving puzzles."

Carrera turned away and said, "Mr Winslow?"

"Paul."

"Okay, and I'm Al. Paul, have you heard that sometimes police departments use civilians when there's a tough investigation going. Like psychics."

"I've heard that. I don't believe in psychics. I'm a rationalist."

"I don't either. But sometimes I *do* use consultants. Specialists. Like on computer work, we'll use a hacker. Or if there's been an art theft, we'll bring in somebody from a museum to help us."

"And you want *me* to be a consultant?" Paul asked, feeling his heart pounding hard.

"I was impressed, what you told me in the park. I've brought some files from the UNSUB Two Eight Seven homicides—that's what we call the perp."

"Police don't really use the word 'Slasher' much, I'd guess."

Carrera laughed. "Not too, you know, professional." He sipped water. "So. Any chance you could take a look at these files and tell us what you think?"

"You bet I will." He held his hand out eagerly for the folder.

• • •

George Lassiter was upset.

The forty-year-old Manhattanite, whose nickname in the press was the sensational but admittedly accurate "Upper East Side Slasher," had a problem.

No one was more meticulous than he when it came to planning out and committing the crimes that soothed him, that drenched the fire in his heart. In fact, part of the relaxation derived from the planning. (The actual killing—the *execution*, he sometimes joked—could be a letdown, compared with the meticulous plotting, if, say, the victim didn't scream or fight as much as he'd hoped.)

Taking scrupulous care to select the right kill zone, to leave minimal or confusing evidence, to learn all he could about the victim so there'd be no surprises when he attacked . . . this was the way he approached all his crimes.

But apparently he'd screwed up in the latest Central Park murder a few nights ago.

The solidly built Lassiter, dressed in slacks and a black sweater, was now outside an apartment on Eighty-Second Street, on the Upper West Side of Manhattan. Lassiter had returned to the crime scene the next morning, to see how far the police were getting in the investigation, when he'd noted a skinny young man talking to Albert Carrera, whom Lassiter had identified as the lead detective on the case. The man seemed to be giving advice, which Carrera was obviously impressed with.

That wasn't good.

After the civilian had left the crime scene, Lassiter had followed him to his apartment. He'd waited a half hour for someone to exit the building and, when an elderly woman walked down the stairs, Lassiter had approached her with a big smile. He'd described the man and had asked his name, saying he looked like somebody Lassiter had been in the army with. The neighbor had said that the man she believed he was referring to was Paul Winslow.

Lassiter had shaken his head and said that, no, it wasn't him. Then he'd thanked her and headed off.

Once home, he'd researched Paul Winslow at the address he'd tracked him to. Very little came up. No Facebook page, Instagram, MySpace, Twitter, Flickr, LinkedIn . . . no social media at all. A criminal background check came back negative, too. At the least, it was pretty clear the young man wasn't a professional law enforcer, just a private meddler.

Which didn't mean he wasn't dangerous.

He might even have seen Lassiter step out of the hiding place in the Shakespeare Garden and grab Ms Rachel Garner around the neck, throttling her to unconsciousness and then carrying her into the park. For the knife work.

Or seen him slip away from the scene around midnight after he was through. That was more likely; after all, Lassiter had seen Winslow staring at the very spot where he'd vanished from the bloody murder site.

Why hadn't he called the police then? Well, possibly he'd spent the night debating the pros and cons of getting involved.

It was Winslow's apartment Lassiter was surreptitiously checking out at the moment. His intention had been to follow the young man again and find out where he worked, perhaps learning more about him.

But then, lo and behold, who came knocking at Winslow's front door, carrying a big fat file folder?

Detective Carrera, in need of a tan and a workout regimen.

What to do, what to do?

Several thoughts came to mind. But, as always, Lassiter didn't leap to any conclusions right away.

Think, plan. And think some more.

Only then could you act safely and the murder be successful.

. . .

"We did find something," Al Carrera was saying as he spread the contents of the case file out before them on Paul Winslow's coffee table. "In the rocks, where you said the UNSUB waited—Shakespeare Garden."

"What was it?"

"Indentations that match the bootie prints. And a tiny bit of wrapper, food wrapper. Forensics found it was from one of those energy bars that campers and hikers eat. From the paper and ink analysis we found it was a Sports Plus bar—their four-ounce, peanut butter and raisin one. Probably the perp's because of the dew content analysis. That told us it'd been dropped on the ground about midnight."

"Your people are good," Paul said. He was impressed. Sherlock Holmes had his own laboratory. Author Conan Doyle, a doctor and man of science himself, had been quite prescient when it came to forensics.

The detective lifted an envelope, eight and a half by eleven. "These're the pictures of the crime scenes—and the victims. But I have to warn you. They're a little disturbing."

"I don't know that I've even seen a picture of real body. I mean, on the news I have, but not up close." He stared at the envelope, hesitated. Finally he nodded. "Okay, go ahead."

Carrera spread the photos out.

Paul was surprised to find they were in color—vivid color. He supposed he shouldn't have been. Why would police photographers use black and white, when nobody else did nowadays?

As he stared at the unfiltered, bloody images, Paul felt squeamish. But he thought back to the Sherlock Holmes stories and reminded himself to be as detached and professional as his hero.

He bent forward and concentrated.

Finally he offered, "Some observations." He put a hand to his chin. "He's really strong. You can see the bruises on their necks.

See. Here? And here?" He pointed. "He didn't have to reposition his hands. He just gripped and squeezed and they went unconscious—not dead, mind you. The amount of blood loss tells us they were stabbed while still alive. Let's see, let's see . . ." A shuffling of photos, Winslow's head bent down. "All right, he's right-handed. A lefty pretending to be right-handed wouldn't have gotten the cuts to the soft tissue so even."

"Good."

"Also he's cautious, very aware and observant. Look at his footprints in the dirt at all three scenes. He's constantly standing up and walking to the perimeter and looking for threats. Smart."

Carrera wrote.

Paul tapped the picture that showed the perp's bloody hand print on the ground, perhaps as he pushed himself up to a standing position. "Look at the thumb. Interesting."

"What?"

"It's not spread out very far—which you'd think it would be if he was using the hand for leverage to rise."

"I see it."

"That might mean that he spends a lot of time on a computer."

"Why?"

"People who regularly type tend to keep their thumbs close in, to hit the spacebar."

Carrera's eyebrow rose and he jotted this down too.

Paul gave a faint smile. "He's a fisherman. Well, amateur fisherman."

"What?" The arched brow again.

"I'm fairly certain. See those marks on the victims' wrists?"

"Ligature marks."

Paul squinted as he shuffled through the pictures. "They're about the thickness of fishing line. And see how he made those incisions *before* he removed the victims' fingers. That's how you skin fish." He paused, as if remembering something. "And, yes, the power bar—just the sort of food a fisherman would take with him for lunch or a mid-morning snack."

Paul sat back and glanced at Carrera, who was writing feverishly. The young man said, "If he *is* a fisherman, which I'm pretty sure he is, he probably has a lake house somewhere in the Tri-State area. We know he's got money. He's not fishing with the locals in the East River. He'll go out to the country in his BMW. Wait," Paul said quickly with a smile, noting Carrera had started to write this down. "The Beemer's just a guess. But I'm sure his car's a nice one. We know he's upper income—his Italian shoes. And the arrogance of the crimes suggests that he'd have an ostentatious car. Mercedes, BMW, Porsche."

After he finished writing, Carrera asked, "Is there any reason he'd take the index finger?"

Paul said, "Oh, I think it's an insult."

"Insult. To who?"

"Well, to you. The police. He's contemptuous of authority. He's saying someone could point directly to the killer and you'd still miss it. He's laughing at you."

Carrera shook his head at this. "Son of a bitch."

Paul looked over the pictures once more. "The laughing fisherman," he mused, thinking that would have made a good title for a Sherlock Holmes story: "The Adventure of the Laughing Fisherman."

Then Paul cocked his head. "Fish . . ."

"What?" Carrera was looking at Paul's focused eyes, as the young man strode to his computer and began typing. After a moment of browsing he said, "There's fishing in Central Park—the Lake, the Pond and Harlem Meer. Yes! I'll bet that's where your perp goes fishing . . . for his victims." He glanced at Carrera eagerly. "Let's go take a look, maybe see if we can find another wrapper or some other evidence. We could set up surveillance."

"It's not authorized for a civilian to go on field operations."

"I'll just tag along. To observe. Offer suggestions."

Carrera debated. "Okay. But if you see anyone or anything that looks suspicious, I take over. You step way back. I mean it."

"Fine with me."

Paul collected his jacket from the den and returned to the living room. Pulling it on, he frowned. "There's something else that just occurred to me. I'll bet he knows about you."

"Me? Personally?"

"You and the other investigators."

"How?"

"I'm thinking he's been to the crime scenes, checking out the investigation. That means you could be in danger. All of you. You should let everyone on your team know." He added gravely, "Sooner rather than later."

Carrera sent a text. "My partner. He'll tell everybody to keep an eye out. You should be careful too, Paul."

"Me? Like you said, I'm just a civilian. I'm sure I don't have anything to worry about."

• • •

Paul Winslow's apartment was pitifully easy to break into.

After George Lassiter had seen Winslow and Carrera leave, he'd slipped around the back and jimmied the building's basement door. Then up a few flights of stairs to the apartment itself. The lock-pick gun had done the job in five seconds, and he'd stepped inside, pleased to note that the apartment, though pretty swanky, wasn't protected by an alarm system.

Piece of cake.

He now stood in the bay window of the dim living room, scanning the street. He was wearing latex gloves and a stocking cap. Lassiter had been impressed with the fancy apartment, and the opulence would work to his advantage. Having so many nice things in an unalarmed house? Why, that simply invited the place to be burgled. He'd decided that, yes, he had to get rid of this meddling Winslow, but he couldn't be a victim of the Upper East Side Slasher, because then Carrera and the other investigators would know immediately that Winslow's advice—which might lead to Lassiter—was accurate. No, the crime would be your basic break-in, the burglar surprised when Winslow returned home.

His plan was that if Carrera returned with Winslow, he'd slip out the back and wait another day. But if the young man returned alone, Lassiter would throw him to the floor and pistol whip him. Blind him, shatter his jaw. Put him in the hospital for months and render him useless as a witness. Murder ups the ante exponentially in a crime. Police, frankly, don't care so much about a beating, however serious.

Jesus, look at all the books . . . Lassiter almost felt bad, thinking that blinding Winslow would pretty much finish his days as a reader.

But it's your own fault, Mr Meddling Winslow.

He took up a position where he could see the street in front of the building.

And he waited—with edgy, yet pleasant, anticipation.

A half hour later, Lassiter tensed. Yes, there was Winslow returning from the direction of Central Park. Alone! He didn't come straight to the front door but stepped into the quick mart next door. Lassiter drew his gun and hid behind the apartment door.

Three minutes passed, then four. He was awaiting the key in the latch, but instead jumped, heart thumping, at the sound of the door's buzzer, right near his ear.

Lassiter cautiously peered through the door's eyehole. He was looking at a fisheye image of a pizza delivery kid, holding a box.

He nearly laughed. But then wondered, Wait, how had the guy gotten through the front security door without hitting the intercom from outside?

Oh, shit. Because Winslow had given him the key and told him to ring the buzzer, to draw Lassiter's attention to the front door. Which meant—

A gun muzzle touched the back of Lassiter's neck, cold. Painfully cold.

"Settle down there, Lassiter," Winslow said in a calm voice. "Drop the gun, put your hands behind your back. I'm in the mood to shoot somebody. And you're my only option."

Lassiter sighed. He let his pistol bounce noisily on the wood floor.

In an instant, expertly, Winslow had cuffed his hands and picked up the gun. Lassiter turned and grimaced. Winslow, it turned out, didn't have a weapon, after all. He'd been bluffing, using a piece of pipe.

Winslow nodded to the door and said, "The pizza guy? I gave him the key outside and told him to let himself in the building. If you were wondering. But you probably figured."

The buzzer rang again and Winslow eased Lassiter onto the floor.

"Don't move. All right?" The young man checked the gun to see that it was loaded and ready to fire, which it was. Appearing satisfied, Winslow aimed the gun at Lassiter's head.

Lassiter flinched. "Yes. Right. I won't."

Winslow slipped the gun away, opened the door and took the pizza, leaving a generous tip."

"Hey, thanks man."

The door closed. They were alone again.

Lassiter muttered, How did you . . .?"

"Fire escape. I'm surprised you didn't keep that covered too. It's the first thing I myself would have done."

• • •

Paul didn't care much for pizza. Or for any food, really. He'd only placed the order to distract Lassiter and give him the chance to sneak into the building and get behind the killer. He did, however, have a thirst. "I could use a glass of milk. You?"

"Milk?" Lassiter frowned.

"Or water? That's about all I can offer you. I don't have any liquor or soda. They're not good for you."

Lassiter didn't respond. Paul walked into the kitchen and poured himself a glass of milk. He returned and helped Lassiter onto a chair. Then he too sat and sipped from the tall glass, reflecting on how different he felt, how confident, compared with just two days ago. The depression was gone completely, the anxiety too.

Thank you, Dr Levine.

Paul regarded the glass. "Did you know milk has a terroir too, just like wine? You can tell, by analysis of the milk, what the cows were eating during the lactation period: the substances in the soil, chemical residues, even insect activity. Why do you wrap your trophies in silk? The fingers? That's one thing I couldn't deduce."

Lassiter gasped and his eyes, wide, cut into Paul's like a torch.

"I know it wasn't on the news. The police don't even know that." He explained, "There was a single bloody thread at one of the scenes. It couldn't have come from a silk garment you were wearing. That would have been too ostentatious and obvious for a man on a killing mission. And none of the victims' clothing or accessories were silk. Silk is used for cold-weather undergarments, yes, but you wouldn't have worn anything like that in these temperatures; very bad idea to sweat at a crime scene. Weren't the days better for people like you when there was no DNA analysis?"

Did a moan issue from Lassiter's throat? Paul couldn't be sure. He smiled. "Well, I'm not too concerned about the silk. Merely curious. Not relevant to our purposes here. The more vital question you have surely is how I found *you*. Understandable. The short answer is that I learned from the newspaper accounts of the murders that you're an organized offender. I deduced you plot everything out ahead of time. And you plan the sites of the killings and the escape routes meticulously."

Lassiter said nothing.

"Someone like that would also want to know about the people tracking him down. I decided you'd be at the scene the morning after the killing. I observed everyone who was there. I was suspicious of the man sipping coffee and reading the sports section of the *Post*. I was pretty sure it was you. I'd known that the clue about the Ferragamo shoe was fake—why take off the booties in the dirt when you could have walked three feet further onto the asphalt and pulled them off there, not leaving any impressions for the police. That meant you weren't rich at all but middle class—the shoes were to misdirect the cops. I knew you were strong and solidly built. All those describe your typical *Post* reader pretty well.

"When I left the scene I was aware that you'd followed me back here. As soon as I got inside I grabbed a hat and new jacket and sunglasses and went down the fire escape. And I started following *you*—right back to your apartment in Queens. A few internet searches and I got your identity."

Paul enjoyed a long sip of milk. "An average cow in the US produces nearly twenty thousand pounds of milk a year. I find that amazing." He regarded the unfortunate man for a moment. "I'm a great fan of the Sherlock Holmes stories." He nodded around the room at his shelves. "As you can probably see."

"So that's why the police aren't here," his prisoner muttered. "You're going to play the big hero, like Sherlock Holmes, showing up the police with your brilliance. Who're you going to turn me over to? The mayor? The police commissioner?"

"Not at all." Paul added, "What I want is to *employ* you. As my assistant."

"*Assistant?*"

"I want you to work for me. Be my sidekick. Though that's a word I've never cared for, I must say."

Lassiter gave a sour laugh. "This's all pretty messed up. You think you're some kind of Sherlock Holmes and you want me to be your Watson?"

Paul grimaced. "No, no, no. My hero in the stories"—he waved at his shelves—"isn't *Holmes*. It's *Moriarty*. Professor James Moriarty."

"But wasn't he, what do they say? Holmes's nemesis."

Paul quoted from memory, "'In calling Moriarty a criminal you are uttering libel in the eyes of the law—and there lie the glory and the wonder of it! The greatest schemer of all time, the organizer of every deviltry, the controlling brain of the under-world, a brain which might have made or marred the destiny of nations—that's the man!'"

He continued, "Holmes was brilliant, yes, but he had no grand design, no drive. He was passive. Moriarty, on the other hand, was ambition personified. Always making plans for plots and conspiracies. He's been my hero ever since I first read about him." Paul gazed affectionately at the books on his shelves that contained the stories involving Moriarty. "I studied math and science because of him. I became a professor, just like my hero."

He thought back to his session with Dr Levine not long ago.

The Sherlock Holmes stories resonated with you for several reasons. I think primarily because of your talents: your intelligence, your natural skills at analysis, your powers of deduction—just like his . . .

Dr Levine had assumed Paul worshipped Holmes, and the patient didn't think it wise to correct him; therapists presumably take rather seriously a patient's role modeling of perpetrators like Moriarty, even if fictional.

"Moriarty appeared in only two stories as a character, was

mentioned in just five others. But the shadow of his evil runs throughout the entire series and you get the impression that Holmes was always aware that a villain even smarter and more resourceful than he, was always hovering nearby." Paul shrugged. "So. I've decided to become a modern-day Moriarty. And that means having an assistant just like my hero did."

"Like Watson?"

"No. Moriarty's sidekick was Colonel Sebastian Moran, a retired military man who specialized in murder. Exactly what I need. I wondered whom to pick. I don't exactly hang out in criminal circles. So I began studying recent crimes in the city and read about the Upper East Side Slasher. You had the most promise. Oh, you made some mistakes, but I thought I could help you overcome your flaws—like returning to visit the scene of the crime, not planting enough fake evidence to shift the blame, attacking victims who were very similar, which establishes patterns and makes profiling easier. And for heaven's sake, eating a power bar while you waited for your victim? Please. You're capable of better, Lassiter."

The man was silent. His expression said he acknowledged Paul to be correct.

"But first I needed to save you from the police. I helped Detective Carrera come up with a profile of the perp that was very specific, very credible . . . and described someone completely different from you."

"Maybe, but they're out there looking for me."

"Oh, they are?" Paul asked wryly.

"What do you mean?"

He found the cable box remote. He fiddled with it for a moment. "You know, in the past we'd have to wait until the top of the hour to see the news. Now they've got that twenty-four/seven cycle. Tedious usually but helpful now."

The TV came to life.

Actually it was a Geico commercial.

"Can't do much about those," Paul said with a grimacing nod at the screen. "Though they *can* be funny."

A moment later an anchorwoman appeared. "If you're just joining us—"

"Which we are," Paul chimed in.

"NYPD officials have reported that the so-called Upper East Side Slasher, allegedly responsible for the murders of three women in Manhattan and, earlier tonight, of Detective Albert Carrera of the NYPD, has been arrested. He's been identified as Franklyn Moss, a journalist and blogger."

"Jesus! What?"

Paul shushed Lassiter.

"Detective Carrera was found stabbed to death about five p.m. near the Harlem Meer fishing area in Central Park. An anonymous tip—"

"*Moi*," Paul said.

"—led authorities to Moss's apartment in Brooklyn, where police found evidence implicating him in the murder of Detective Carrera and the other victims. He is being held without bond in the Manhattan Detention Center."

Paul shut the set off.

He turned and was amused to see that Lassiter's expression was one of pure bewilderment. "I think we don't need these anymore." Paul rose and unhooked the handcuffs. Lassiter shook his hands and rubbed his wrists. "Just to let you know, though, my lawyer has plenty of evidence implicating *you* in the crimes, so don't do anything foolish."

"No, I'm cool."

"Good. Now when I decided I wanted you as an assistant I had to make sure somebody else took the fall for the killings. Whom to pick? I've never liked reporters very much, and I found Franklyn Moss particularly irritating. So I data-mined him. I learned he was quite the fisherman, so I fed Carrera this mumbo jumbo that that was the killer's hobby.

"Earlier today I convinced Carrera we should go to Central Park, one of the fishing preserves there, to look for clues. When we were alone at the Meer I slit his throat and sawed off his index finger. That's a lot of work, by the way. Couldn't you have picked the pinkie? Never mind. Then I went to Moss's apartment and hid the knife and finger in his garage, along with some physical evidence from the other scenes, a pair of Ferragamos I bought yesterday and a packet of those energy bars you like. I left some of Carrera's blood on the doorstep so the police would have probable cause to get a warrant."

Paul enjoyed another long sip of milk. Lassiter was taking this all in carefully, he could see.

"The evidence's circumstantial, but compelling." Paul counted off on his fingers as he spoke: "Moss drives a Mercedes, which I told Carrera was the kind of car the killer would drive because I'd seen Moss in it earlier. Public records show Moss has a lake house in Westchester—which I also told Carrera. And I suggested that the ligature marks were from fishing line, which Moss has plenty of in his garage and basement . . . You used bell wire, right?"

"Uhm, yes," Lassiter said.

Paul continued: "Anyway, I also fed the detective this nonsense that the killer probably spent a lot of time keyboarding at a computer—like a blogger would do. So our friend Moss is going away forever. You're clean."

Lassiter frowned. "But wouldn't Carrera have told other officers that *you* gave him the profile? That'd make you a suspect."

"Good point, Lassiter. But I knew he wouldn't. Why bring the file to me here in my house to review rather than invite me downtown to examine it? And why did he come alone, not with his partners? No, he asked my advice *privately* so he could steal my ideas and take credit for them." Paul ran his hand through his hair and regarded the killer with a coy smile. "Now, tell me about the assignment—about the person who hired you. I'm really curious about that."

"Assignment?" Lassiter made an attempt to look perplexed, but the feigned innocence didn't work.

"Please, Lassiter. You're not a serial killer. I wouldn't want you as an assistant if you were. No, serial killers're far too capricious. Too driven by emotion." Paul said the last word as if it were a bit of foul food. "No, you came up with the plan for the multiple murders to cover up your real crime. You'd been hired to murder a particular individual—one of the three victims."

Lassiter's mouth was actually gaping open. He slowly pressed his lips back together.

Paul continued: "It was so obvious. There was no sexual component to the killings, which there always is in serial murders. And there's no psychopathological archetype for taking an index finger trophy—you improvised because you thought it would look suitably spooky. Now, which of the three was the woman you were hired to kill?"

The man gave a why-bother shrug. "Rachel Garner. The last one. She was going to blow the whistle on her boss. He runs a hedge fund that's waist deep in money laundering."

"Or—alternative spelling—'waste deep,' If it needs *laundering*." Paul couldn't help the play on words. He chuckled. "Yeah. I thought it was something like that."

Lassiter said, "I'd met the guy in the army. He knew I did a few dirty tricks, and he called me up."

"So, it was a one-time job?"

"Right."

"Good. So you can come work for me."

Lassiter debated.

Paul leaned forward. "Ah, there's a lot of carnage out there to perpetrate. Lots of foolish men and women on Wall Street who need to be relieved of some of their gains, ill- or well-gotten. There're illegal arms sales waiting to be made, and cheating politicians to extort and humans to traffic and terrorists who may hold intellectually indefensible views but who have very large bank accounts and are willing to write checks to people like us, who can provide what they need."

Paul's eyes narrowed. "And, you know, Lassiter, sometimes you just need to slice a throat or two for the fun of it."

Lassiter's eyes were fixed on the carpet. After a long moment he whispered, "The silk?"

"Yes?"

"My mother would stuff a silk handkerchief in my mouth when she beat me. To mute the screams, you know."

"Ah, I see," Paul replied softly. "I'm sorry. But I can guarantee you plenty of opportunities to get even for that tragedy, Lassiter." He eyed the other man. "So. Do you want the job?"

The killer looked down, debating for merely a few seconds. Then he looked up at Paul and smiled broadly. "I do, Professor. I sure do." The two men shook hands.

A Significant Find

Monday, April 11, 11 a.m.

"A crisis of conscience. Pure and simple. What are we going to do?" He poured red wine into her glass. Both sipped.

They were sitting in mismatched armchairs, before an ancient fireplace of stacked stone in the deserted lounge. The inn, probably two hundred years old, was clearly not a tourist destination, at least not in this season; it was a chilly spring in the countryside of southern France.

He tasted the wine again and turned his gaze from the label of the bottle to the woman's intense blue eyes, which were cast down at the wormwood floor. Her face was as beautiful as when they'd met, though a bit more worn, as ten years had passed, many of which had been spent outside under less than kind conditions; hats and SPF 30 could only give you so much protection.

"I'm not sure. I'm really at a loss," Della Fanning said in answer to her husband's question. She brushed her dark blond hair from her eyes.

Roger, fifteen years older, was considerably more weathered than she, though, he believed (on a good day), the toll from the out-of-doors gave him character, bestowing a ruggedness on his face. His thick hair, cut short, was largely the brown of his youth, dotted with strands lightened blond by the sun and gray from his age.

He stretched and felt a bone pop. It had been a busy, exhausting day. "There are two sides to it. You know, one says do the right thing. But it's not as easy as that."

She offered, "And sometimes you have to choose what looks like the wrong thing, if it's for the greater good."

He asked, "So. Do you think that's what we should do?"

They were interrupted by the innkeeper who stuck his head in the door and, smiling, asked in French if they wanted anything else. He glanced at the clock: 11 p.m.

Roger and Della were fluent and he answered, no, but thanks. Della added, "*Bonne nuit.*"

Roger waited until the man was gone and then mused, "Doing the right thing." He shook his head and sipped more of the mild wine, *un vin du Provence.*

Yes, this was a complicated dilemma. It had occupied his thoughts, and, he was sure, Della's as well, for the better part of the past day.

Though the genesis of the conflict was far older: seventeen thousand years, give or take.

Sunday, April 10, One Day Earlier, 2 p.m.

It was the last day of the conferences, a five-day event devoted to the astonishing cave paintings of Lascaux.

These were one of the greatest archeologic finds in history: nine hundred colorful paintings, primarily animals, outlines of hands and symbols, created by tribes during the Upper Paleolithic era—the late Stone Age. The caverns were located near Montignac in the Dordogne region of southwestern France.

The conference was one of several over the past few years attended by archeologists like Roger and Della Fanning, as well as anthropologists and environmental scientists and French Interior Ministry officials, who were troubled by the accelerating degradation of the caves, which were presently closed—to all but a few researchers. Humidity, mold and bacteria were taking their toll, in some cases so severely that the paintings had all but disappeared. This gathering was meant to try to find solutions to the ecological problems plaguing the caves, as well as to offer recent insights from the scholarly analysis of the artwork and to give attendees the chance to present papers on recent developments in the exploration of "decorated caves," as they were called, in this region and elsewhere.

Presently, with Della in a session on attempts to attack a new strain of mold threatening portions of the caves, and Roger found himself on a break between sessions, sipping coffee beside a man who fit the archeologist stereotype to a tee (no one Roger had ever known in the field looked and acted like Indiana Jones from the adventure films). The nerdy fellow was skinny, his head covered with a floppy, olive-drab hat. He wore thick glasses and a rumpled tan suit. On his wrist was a battered Timex with a large chipped dial, the sort an archeologist from the 1930s might sport.

They introduced themselves.

"Trevor Hall," he said, shaking hands.

"Roger Fanning."

Hall lifted an eyebrow at the name, apparently impressed. He explained he'd read the archeology blog Roger and Della posted, which devoted much space to the plight of the Lascaux caves. Hall complimented them on raising awareness of the problems facing the site and on encouraging donations. The man was from Seattle. He'd come here to attend the conference and spend some weeks hunting for other, undiscovered decorated caves—a popular pastime of both professional and amateur archeologists.

His eyes grew wistful. "I thought I had a good lead. But, nope. And I've been so excited . . . I *was* so excited."

This happened a lot in the field, like fishermen talking about the one that got away.

Hall continued, "I was hiking in the valley up the road and I met this farm boy who told me he'd overheard somebody talking about a small cavern near Loup that might've had some paintings in it."

Many decorated caves were found this way—by locals hiking or bicycling through the countryside. The Lascaux caves were discovered, in 1940, by four French students and, the story went, a dog named Robot.

"Loup?"

"That's right. It's a small town about fifteen miles from here. He didn't know anything more and couldn't remember who'd mentioned it. I've spent the last week searching every acre around the damn town. Nothing." He had to leave this afternoon; the hunt was over. "No Carter moments for me," he said with a sour smile. "Never had one. Maybe I never will. Oh, well."

Referring to Howard Carter, the archeologist who, in 1922, discovered the tomb of King Tutankhamen in Egypt, perhaps the most famous archeological find in history.

Roger had never heard that phrase before: "A Carter Moment." But he and Della certainly knew the concept well—making a discovery that captured the world's imagination and put you, as an explorer, on the map.

They referred to such a coup in a rather more understated way: making "a significant find."

The conference had resumed and Roger returned to his seat, half-heartedly listening to the presentations. He was distracted. One word kept circling through his mind: Loup, Loup, Loup.

• • •

Della and Roger Fanning had come to the field of archeology from different routes.

Roger had been involved in archeology all his life. The son of an academic (Roger Sr specialized in Middle Eastern Studies), the boy would often spend time with his parents when Dad was on digs in Jordan, Yemen and the Emirates. It was natural that he would follow a similar path, though as he grew up he found he preferred the rather easier lifestyle an archeologist experiences in Europe to the arduous—and often dangerous—world of the Middle East.

He got a job as a professor at his father's alma mater, Grosvenor College in central Ohio, and spent three or four months a year in the field, specializing in archeologic sites in France, Germany and Italy.

It was there that he met Della, ten years ago. The woman was in an unhappy marriage and had an unsatisfying job in public relations. She had returned to school to get her MBA. But, on a whim, decided to take Professor Fanning's Introduction to Anthropology. Della loved the field, changed majors and went on to get her masters in the subject.

After graduating, she left her old life behind, enduring a messy divorce and quitting her dull office job. She and Roger soon married; their honeymoon was spent in a tent, at a newly discovered pre-historic site near Arles amphitheater, in France.

Childless—hard with all the travel—they devoted their life to archeology and caught the attention of the academic community, publishing important papers and making some solid discoveries. They were popular at the conferences, being charming and witty . . . and it didn't hurt that they had nearly model-quality looks.

Still, that significant find continued to elude them.

This was a constant disappointment, a vexing tarnish on their reputation. The failure also hurt their bottom line. Unlike academia in, say, medicine or physics or computer science, archeology didn't offer any hope for corporate income from consulting or patents. But if you discovered something big, something that made the press, your university might double your salary—afraid you'd go elsewhere—and your lecture fees would skyrocket. If you could put sentences together—and both Della and Anthony were solid writers—you had the chance of publishing a best-selling book (and if you were as good-looking as the Fannings, TV shows were a possibility).

Roger waited to meet Della—her final session concluded—in the small park outside the conference hotel and he kept wondering: was this their opportunity?

As soon as she joined him he told Della about the man.

"Hm," she said, smiling. "Hidden treasure. He has no idea who told this boy about the cave?"

"No, he would've tracked him down if he could. The poor guy's spent a week slogging through the countryside."

Roger reached into his backpack, found the guidebook about the region and flipped to the map. She scooted close. He scanned until he found Loup, a small town in the middle of farmland. "There."

"That's not cave geology," she said, brows furrowed.

"No, it's not."

Caves form because of volcanic, seismic, or erosive activity—usually from water. The caves in this region fell invariably into this last category. Certainly a river carving out caverns might have dried up eons ago, but the odds were those large enough to support habitation would be closer to a large water source, and there was none anywhere near Loup.

Roger began looking further afield, following the Dordogne River, a long and wide waterway that ran for hundreds of miles, a likely source of other caves, but archeologists for hundreds of years had scoured the river's banks. Roger concentrated his search on smaller tributaries, and those near where they were now.

He cocked his head and squinted. "My God, look." He took a mechanical pencil and circled what he was staring at. It was a minuscule blue line, representing a creek, running from some rocky hills to another tributary that ran eventually into the Dordogne.

And the creek had a name.

Le Loue.

Pronounced in French exactly the same as Loup.

"*That's* what the boy told Hall."

Della said, "It's only about fifteen miles from here."

They stared into each other's eyes. Roger said, "What do you say about a day in the country tomorrow?"

"I can't think of anything I'd rather do."

• • •

They took a taxi from the hotel to a small village near Loue Creek.

They found a scruffy but quaint inn, squatting in a lot filled with enthusiastic grass and weeds, close to the narrow road. Its name was *L'Écureuil Roux.*

The Red Squirrel.

Sounded more like a British pub than a French country inn.

Roger asked for a room and the manager hemmed and hawed, though it was clear the place was virtually empty. He grudgingly took their credit card after saying that he preferred cash and cocked his head, gazing in anticipation. They took their bags to the room and returned to the lobby with their trekking backpacks. They asked borrow two bicycles for a ride into the country. Roger had seen several bikes sitting in the tall grass behind the garage.

Twenty euros later—the rental fee, excessive, he thought—and he and Della were cycling in the direction of Loue Creek.

The lazy stream was situated in a shallow valley of rock cliff faces on one side and grasses, flowering trees and lavender on the other. The road was on the rocky side and they biked along the shoulder, seeing hardly a single person. A few old Peugeots and Toyotas cruised past, oblivious to the bikers. They stopped at every rock outcropping that might support a cave, but the only possibilities were mere fissures in the limestone, too narrow to fit through.

Della braked to a stop and looked around the rolling scenery. "Sun'll be down soon."

They were some miles from the hotel. But Roger was still feeling the excitement of the hunt. "Just one more. Over there." He pointed to a large crescent of stone that jutted off the road, thirty feet above the creek, covered with rocks, boulders and gravel. Leaving the bikes at the top, they made their way to the base of the cliff face. At first, Roger was skeptical, thinking that the place was too near both the road and the waterway; surely a hiker or a boater would have discovered a cave long ago. But he saw at once that covering a view of the base of the outcropping was a thick tangle of brush and branches. They donned leather gloves and started to clear it away.

"Look!" he said, staring at what they'd revealed: a tunnel, three by four feet around, extending about a yard into the rocky interior, which was blocked by a pile of gravel and dirt. Roger crawled forward on his hands and knees and cleared away enough debris to open an eight-inch gap at the top.

And to his excitement he found himself looking at: deep blackness, from which issued damp, musty air.

A cave.

"Oh, honey!" Della joined him, getting as close as she could into the narrow opening. She handed him a flashlight and he clicked it on, then aimed the beam into the opening.

"My God. Yes!"

You couldn't see much of the cave from this angle through the tiny opening, but there was no doubt that Roger was looking at a portion of a cave painting. A horse, he believed.

"Take a look."

They changed position, and she too examined the walls. "Oh, Roger. I can't believe it!" She scooted higher on the pile of gravel. "I can't see in any further." She played the light on the sliver of the painting.

They backed out and studied the obstructing pile of stone and gravel. He said, "I'd guess an hour or so to clear enough so we can get inside. It's too late to do anything more now. We'll come back in the morning."

He put his arms around her, kissed her hard.

A significant find . . .

At last.

Though, of course, there was one more matter to be addressed.

Monday, April 11, Present Day, 10 a.m.

"It's a crisis of conscience. Pure and simple. What are we going to do?"

"I'm not sure. I'm really at a loss," Della was saying.

Now, Monday night, they were in the lounge of the inn, debating.

Stretching till a bone popped, he said, "There are two sides to it. You know, one says do the right thing. But it's not as easy as that."

"And sometimes you have to choose what looks like the wrong thing, if it's for the greater good."

"Do you think that's what we should do?"

They were interrupted by the innkeeper, a smirky, condescending smile on his face. "Is there something else you'd like? Another bottle of wine? Whisky? Food?"

The shifty guy, always trying to make an extra buck.

"*Non, merci.*"

The man pouted and didn't leave until Della said, "*Bonne nuit.*"

Roger waited until the man was gone and then mused, "Doing the right thing."

As with many dilemmas, their crisis of conscience was quite simple: whether or not to give Trevor Hall credit.

For his Carter Moment, his significant find.

Roger remembered the man's morose expression when he said that he hadn't had any great discoveries.

Maybe I never will. Oh, well . . .

Then her voice grew soft. "We haven't even published for a year, honey."

It *had* been a dry spell for their career recently. And the trips to Europe for digs and conferences were paid for largely by the couple themselves; the travel expenses provided for the university were minuscule. They'd just moved into a larger house, and the mortgage payments were quite the burden.

The discovery of a new decorated cave would make a huge difference in their lives.

After a moment she asked softly, "Would Hall even know?" She shook her head. "Sorry. I shouldn't have said that."

Roger shrugged. "I introduced myself. He'd find out."

Crises of conscience can rarely be sidestepped.

They fell silent, the room filling with ambient noise—a creak from upstairs, an owl in the distance, the staccato snap of the licking flames.

Roger explained his thoughts: this was the real world. If Hall had the mettle to stick it out, he probably would have found the cave. If he'd thought more cleverly—like he and Della did—he would have found the cave.

She added, "And he didn't need to give you any information. If he was that concerned about getting credit he could have kept quiet and come back again."

"True. You're right. And, dammit, if it wasn't for us, there'd never *be* a discovery in the first place."

And yet Hall's face had seemed so wistful.

Include him or not?

Crisis of conscience . . .

And as with most such predicaments, the solution was easy and comforting.

Kick the can down the road.

"Let's decide after we know more."

"Perfect."

Into his backpack, Roger placed the folding shovel, gloves, the camera, flashlights, a sketchpad and pens, and energy bars and bottles of water. Della packed much the same, though not the shovel.

In ten minutes they were bicycling down the road, under an overcast sky. Soon they arrived at the cave.

Roger half-expected to find it jammed with other archeologists, or at least guarded by Trevor Hall. But, no, the place was deserted.

They left the bikes at the top of the outcropping, wove through the piles of loose stone and gravel and made their way down the steep hill and into the tunnel entrance they'd discovered earlier.

Using the short camping shovel, Roger cleared enough debris to allow them access.

Breathing fast from the exertion—and the excitement—he turned to his wife. "Ready?"

"Let's do it."

With some effort, they slipped through the gap and into the cave.

It was about thirty feet long, twenty wide and ten high. The floor was flat—limestone, as most of them here—without standing water or pits. The ceiling was intact. These were instinctive observations—for safety—and once satisfied the place was structurally sound, they turned to the wall on which was the fragment of image Roger had seen yesterday. It contained dozens of paintings.

"Oh, my God," Della whispered.

Roger was unable to speak.

He had never seen any cave paintings this brilliant and well defined. It was as if the chamber had been hermetically sealed since their creation and no moisture or gases had entered to bleach or damage the art.

She gripped his arm.

The style was clearly Paleolithic, similar to that of the paintings at Lascaux: the figures were rendered in dark outline and filled in with red, beige and sienna colorings. There were a number of animals, mostly cattle and a few horses. Curiously, though the diet of the tribes in this region was primarily reindeer—various piles of bones told this story—there were no depictions of this creature, either at Lascaux or here.

What was most astonishing, however, were not the animals but a series of paintings of humans in the middle of the wall.

This took Roger's breath away.

Della could only stare in shock.

Human figures were rare in Lascaux and other Upper Paleolithic caverns in this area, and when they did appear, they were rendered as stick figures. Anthropologists believed that this was due to some taboos or primitive religious proscriptions against representing humans.

But here the pictures of people were as carefully done as the animals: outlined and then filled in. These would be Homo Sapiens, anatomically similar to humans today (as opposed to Neanderthal and Homo Erectus, human-like species that died out before the cave-painting years of the Upper Paleolithic era). The artist (probably male, though not necessarily) was primitive stylistically but had made an attempt at perspective and three-dimensional representation. The figures had crudely drawn facial features and wore clothing that was baggy and brown-hides presumably.

Roger whispered, "This might be the first attempts to authentically represent humans."

"Maybe we've found a new tribe altogether."

He nodded. "Drawing humans like this means maybe they'd discarded at least one primitive taboo. God, we could be looking at a radical step forward in behavioral modernity."

This was the developmental state that set Homo Sapiens apart from earlier and nonhuman species: the ability to think abstractly, create art, make and execute plans and engage in symbolic acts. These paintings suggested that perhaps behavior modernity might have been achieved earlier than believed, among some tribes at least.

"This is it," Roger said, choked with emotion.

"Significant," he reflected did not even begin to describe the find.

They looked at each other and she nodded. "We tell him? Trevor Hall."

Roger whispered, "We should But . . ."

She grinned as well.

Do the right thing.

The crisis of conscience.

"He'll never know," Roger said.

And his wife: "He could have followed up. He did choose not to."

"Lazy."

She was nodding.

Roger felt in his gut a swelling relief.

He kissed her forehead. "I find. Our significant find."

"Roger?" She swept her flashlight beam over the mottled gray wall. The image she was pointing at was in the center, where the humans and animals were depicted together. She indicated a man standing beside a dozen cattle. At his feet was a crude image of a black cat. The Upper Paleolithic era had its share of lions and leopards and other big cats in this region. The animals we know as house cats existed but were far more common in Northern Africa than in Europe.

"And, my God, Roger . . . Look at the cattle!"

He understood, and whispered, "They're domesticated."

Domestication of what we call farm animals—raising and slaughtering them, rather than hunting—was just beginning around this era. But nearly all the Lascaux and other cave paintings around this time in pre-history depicted animals being hunted; these were clustered in what seemed to be a herd. The man, near whom the cat was standing, seemed to be looking over the creatures. He had a full beard and was balding.

"A cowherd?"

"It might be. Astonishing to find organized animal farming that long ago. This is a first too."

"And look to the right," Roger said.

Della played her beam over the images adjacent to the cowherd. It depicted him once again but this time standing with a woman, with long straight hair. The cat was at their feet. A depiction of what might be a domestic union.

"Look, Roger—the paintings seem to be sequential. They're telling a story, like panels of a cartoon."

More evidence of advanced behavioral modernity in a surprisingly early era.

They turned to the next painting in the sequence.

This showed the woman from the second panel, with the long hair, now standing beside a third figure—a clean-shaven man. The balding, bearded man stood by himself, some distance away, the cat still at his feet.

Roger and Della moved further to the right and looked at the final painting in the center panel. It showed the balding man, along with the cat, standing on a small hill, alone.

"Something's odd," Della said. Frowning, she walked close and touched the picture.

"Honey!" Roger whispered urgently. You should never touch anything painted at an archeologic site with unprotected fingers; oils can ruin the fragile works. This was one of the first rules of archeology.

Her face alarmed, she turned to her husband. "What do you think these were painted with?"

"Charcoal, pigments?

"No, take a close look."

Roger walked up and removed from the backpack a folding magnifying glass. He leaned close and examined the image of the bearded man and hillock of earth he stood on. He shook his head and sighed. "Goddamnit."

"A hoax," she said.

He nodded. "It's acrylic. Probably done in the last year or so."

"Somebody's having a laugh."

There was a long history of fake archeologic finds—the Cardiff giant, the Michigan relics, the Piltdown Man. Some were done for profit, some to boost an explorer's prestige, some simple pranks.

"So close," Roger said, sighing.

Della shook her head and laughed, gazing at the picture. "Funny. We used to have a black cat."

"Really?" Roger asked absently. He was getting the camera out to take pictures. He'd send them to Hall and report what the find had turned out to be.

"Fred, my ex, and I did, around the time I went back to school."

"Cat, hum? What happened to it?" Roger asked absently.

"Her. Fred got her in the divorce. Fine with me."

Roger knew Della felt guilty about running off with the professor she'd had an affair with. Taking her ex's cat would be pretty low.

Her face tightened into a frown. "And you know? The cattle?" Nodding at the herd painting on the wall. "Fred and I lived near that dairy farm." Her breath was coming fast. "And he was balding and had a beard . . . Roger, this is odd." She gripped his arm. "What did Trevor Hall look like?"

"Slim, fifties. No beard." But Roger thought instantly: razor.

"Bald?" she asked.

"Hat."

"You never met Freddy, my ex. But you saw pictures."

"Years ago, maybe."

Della asked, "Did Hall wear an old watch?"

"Yes, a Timex, I think. Gold-colored."

She gaped. "It was his father's. He never took it off!"

So her ex pretended to be this Trevor Hall? Impossible.

But, then again.

Roger looked at the paintings. The sequence: Freddy by himself, Freddy with Della, Freddy nearby when Roger and Della were together.

"Shit. Think about it. He sets this all up. He leads us here, knowing we'll report the find. And then it turns out to be counterfeit. We end up with egg on our face. Son of a bitch."

"After all these years? It was a decade ago."

"You didn't know him. He was crazy. Sometimes he scared—" Her voice ended in a gasp.

She was looking at the last panel of the paintings.

The balding character—they had to assume it was Freddy—was standing on top of a hill.

But not a natural formation.

There were skulls and bones underground.

It was a burial mound.

"Oh, Jesus. Get out! Now!"

But before they took one step forward, there came a rumble from overhead.

No, no!

It would be, Roger knew in despair, a truck or tractor fitted with a bulldozer blade, Freddy behind the wheel, shoving the boulders and gravel atop the outcropping to the edge. Just seconds later the downpour streamed into the tunnel, sending clouds of dust into the cave and cutting off the light from outside.

Roger and Della began to choke.

There was a pause then more debris crashed down, as Freddy backed up and eased to the edge once more, continuing to seal them in the tomb.

"No! Freddy! No!"

But no shouting, no screaming, however loud, could penetrate stone and earth.

"Phone!" Della cried.

They both grabbed their mobiles and tried to call. But there was no signal.

Of course not. Freddy had planned it all out. He would have been thinking of this for years, probably from the day he'd learned of the affair. He would have seen months ago on their blog that Roger and Della would be attending the conference at Lascaux and started his plans. He'd found the perfect cave, trucked stone and gravel to the hill above it, studied the original paintings and

mimicked them in his drawings here. He then signed up for the
conference under the name Trevor Hall and waited until he could
get to Roger alone and plant the seed of the hidden cave.

"Honey," she said in a raw, panicked voice that echoed through
the small chamber.

"It's okay." He shone a beam on the entrance. "It's mostly
gravel, I think. We can dig our way out. It'll take some time. But
we can do it."

They propped the flashlights up, pointed toward the pile of
rock, and began to grab the larger pieces and fling them aside
and dig away at the gravel with the small shovel.

They got about two feet forward when Roger felt himself
growing dizzy from lack of oxygen.

"I don't think . . ." Della began.

"It's okay. We're making good progress." He began choking as
he inhaled the dusty, thinning air. Not enough, not enough . . .
It was like drinking salty water when you were thirsty. "We'll just
take a break. Need some rest. Just for . . . just . . . for a bit."

He lay back against the wall. Della dropped the rock she held
and crawled to him, flopping to the floor, resting her head against
his shoulder, gasping.

One flashlight faded to yellow and went out.

A moment later he felt his wife go limp.

Good, good, Roger thought, his thoughts growing fuzzy.
Conserving her strength.

He said, "We'll just take . . . a . . . little . . . rest."

Did he say that before?

He couldn't remember.

"Just five . . . minutes. We'll just rest a little. We're as good as
out already. Just . . . some . . ."

His head lolled back against the rock.

Roger stared at the remaining flashlight, the beam turning to
yellow, then dimming, amber. Like the sun growing low in the

Valley of the Kings in Egypt, where Howard Carter had found Tutankhamen's tomb.

Just a few more minutes' rest, and we'll get back to work. It's going to be fine.

He said this to Della. Or maybe he didn't.

The light went out and blackness filled the cave.

Where the Evidence Lies

A Lincoln Rhyme Story

Tuesday

"Mayday, mayday. This is TrailJet Eight Five Eight Four, to San Juan Center. Do you read me?"

"Go ahead, Eight Five Eight Four. We read you, sir."

"Descending through nine thousand feet. About one hundred miles north of airport. I'm declaring an emergency."

"Roger, Five Eight Eight Four. We have you."

"Closest airport, San Juan?"

"For your aircraft, Eight Five Eight Four, It'll have to be Muñoz Marín airport. Turn to heading One eight seven."

"One eight seven, San Juan Center."

"Descend and maintain seven thousand, Eight Five Eight Four."

"I'm through seven. Six thousand five hundred. Rapid decent."

"Altitude at your discretion, Eight Five Eight Four. What's the nature of your emergency?"

"Power loss. Heard a bang in the rear. Big one. Tail or engines. I

don't know. No fire indicator. EPR dropping critically. Both engines. Distance from airport?"

"You're eighty-three miles. Maintain heading of one eight seven."

"Jesus . . . Descending through four thousand four hundred. Three thousand seven hundred. I'm not going to make it."

"Eight Five Eight Four. We're alerting Coast Guard air-sea rescue. They're getting your position. Can you execute a water landing?"

"I'll try. Descending through fifteen hundred. Nine hundred. I—"

"Eight Five Eight Four? Do you copy? . . . Do you copy?"

• • •

Eastern Dade Airport, in Miami, Florida, was a small facility near the Atlantic Ocean. It featured a runway about three thousand feet long, big enough for small jets, though the majority of the two dozen planes parked on the tarmac were one- and two-engine prop.

There was definitely some Everglades ambiance in the area—mangroves, royal palm, cabbage palm, live oak, gumbo limbo and West Indian mahogany, as well as orchids, bromeliads and ferns. Lincoln Rhyme, presently in this part of Florida to lecture to the county police about forensics, had spotted an alligator.

"Look, well," he said to Amelia Sachs, his partner—in both the professional and personal senses. She'd leaned over his wheelchair in the accessible van (Rhyme was a quadriplegic, largely paralyzed from the neck down) and gazed at the shallow canal just inside the airport's chain-link fence, in which a bored-looking gator sat in the humid heat, seemingly too tired to even think about chomping down whatever bored-looking gators ate.

Rhyme's caregiver, slim but strong and decidedly handsome Thom Reston, drove the van in a slow circle around this part of the field and then paused, as directed by Rhyme. "Okay, keep going."

The man drove on.

Sachs, a tall, redheaded former fashion model, said, "There's a rumor they have them in the sewers of New York, you know. Parents buy them for kids and then flush them. I never saw any. Not that I was looking."

"Really?" Rhyme said. The details of the flora and fauna of this part of the state grew less interesting; he was more intrigued about where they were headed presently. His eyes took in the airfield once more.

Rhyme was here because a detective with the local Sheriff's Department had approached him after one of his lectures and asked for some help. Preston Gillette was a trim forty-five-year-old with impressive posture, a hairstyle that an army major would have loved and a face that seemed incapable of smiling.

Despite that quality, though, he'd revealed a droll sense of humor by asking Rhyme which he'd prefer as a thank-you for the lecture: a coupon to the local Red Lobster or an incident report on a local businessman who'd just died in what might or might not be an aircraft sabotage incident.

Rhyme had eased his head, covered in thick dark hair, against the backstop of his chair, eyes skyward, in thought. He had replied, "Hm. Murdered crustacean or murdered human. I'll pick the latter. You up for that, Sachs?"

"Sure. Nothing pressing back in New York." She was an NYPD detective. He was a former captain with the same organization and frequently consulted on particularly difficult cases—like Sherlock Holmes did for Scotland Yard, someone had once said. Rhyme took that on faith; he was only marginally familiar with any fictional character and their adventures.

The lecture at the Dade County East Sheriff's Office was finished anyway and so Rhyme agreed to stay for an extra day or two and help out on the Stephen Nash investigation.

Why not? He'd enjoyed the trip here and had found for the

first time something called stone crabs. Quite the delicacy. And the rum in Florida seemed better than the rum anywhere else but the Bahamas. Imagination perhaps, but he'd enjoyed the taste testing—with the servings undoctored by any fruity or sweet addition; water, in liquid or frozen states, was the only adulteration allowed in liquor.

Rhyme had concluded his examination of the perimeter of the field, and Thom now piloted the accessible van into the airport itself and aimed for the unmarked police car at the far end of the field.

Gillette had explained that the crash might have been caused by an IED planted in the craft—probably here before it took off. Security where the flight originated, Orlando, where Nash lived, was tighter and included bomb sniffing dogs. Not the case here.

Of course, the mishap might have been an accident.

But the FAA and National Transportation Safety Board would not be issuing reports for weeks at the earliest, and Gillette wanted to move forward immediately so that evidence of a crime could be preserved and witnesses identified.

They drove to the cruiser, in front of the one hangar on this side of the airport, on the far eastern edge. It was a fifty-by-fifty-foot structure, windowless and doorless at the rear—facing the water. The side facing the runway and tarmac was open. There appeared no doors one could close.

Thom parked near the squad car, and Rhyme descended via the ramp to the tarmac. A fierce storm had hit the area yesterday; it had passed and the sky was clear but the wind still buffeted the law enforcers and the aide. Rhyme pushed his sunglasses onto his face more firmly with his one working appendage—his right arm.

Gillette stepped forward and shook Sachs's and Thom's hand. Nodded to Rhyme.

"Thank you again, Mr Rhyme. Detective Sachs."

"'Lincoln' and 'Amelia' are fine," she said.

Gillette turned toward the tarmac, where a twenty-by-thirty-foot rectangle was cordoned off with yellow tape, weighted down with wheel chocks. "That's where the plane was."

"What was the aircraft?"

"TrailJet, twin engine. Powerplants mounted in the rear. New breed of personal jets. It's small, seats four."

"Hm." Sachs seemed intrigued. She was a driver of fast cars—well, that was true, Rhyme reflected after the thought, but more accurately: she was a race-car driver in *any* vehicle. She simply preferred the fast ones. The idea of a jet that was probably not much larger than her muscle car? Maybe she was pondering getting her pilot's license.

"Nobody else on board?" he asked.

"No. For those planes you don't need a co-pilot. The autopilot's so good; they do most of the work. They can even land themselves."

Sachs was frowning. "Did he have a family?" She was always far more concerned about the personal impact of crimes than Rhyme, whose focus on science sometimes led people to cast him as a cold fish. He didn't mind. He never objected to the truth.

"No. Divorced, no children. Nash was sort of your classic well-heeled bachelor. He even jetted to Miami and Key West for dates. When your quote 'wheels' burn a hundred and fifty gallons of gas an hour, that's a pretty expensive night out."

He added that this portion of the field was owned by Southern Flight Services, a fixed-base operator, the term used to describe a company that provided ground services to private pilots.

Rhyme was familiar with such facilities from a prior case, and noted that this was a shoestring FBO. There was only one jet and two twin-engine prop planes parked in front of the hangar now. They were covered with tarps and leaf-strewn from the storm.

"So it wasn't in the hangar."

"No. Nash basically just needed a place to park for a couple of hours before he went on to a meeting in San Juan."

A grimace. The storm would have destroyed any evidence of anybody trying to plant a bomb on the airplane—tread or shoe marks would have been the best source of information. But trace evidence too that the perp might have shed.

The storm, which Rhyme remembered clearly, had not exactly been a hurricane but the winds had been close to sixty miles an hour and the rain had been torrential.

Still, this was a secondary crime scene. The more important one was the plane itself. However powerful the improvised explosive device had been, it would have left bits of trace on the wreckage. There would be fingerprints, possibly, chemical residue profiling, even a bomb maker's signature—a unique construction pattern that ties a bomb to its builder. Sometimes the perps even intentionally leave a calling card of some kind; of all the criminals Rhyme had been up against, bombmakers had perhaps the biggest egos.

Rhyme explained this now.

"Ah, well, that's the problem, Mr . . . That's the problem, Lincoln. The plane didn't break up. Whatever the explosion was it didn't blow it up, just affected the engines. The EPR—engine pressure ration—was dropping. That's sort of the tachometer for jets. He crash landed but it sank almost immediately."

"Well, that's okay. Water won't destroy all the evidence." He frowned. "Unless you don't know where it is."

"Oh, we do."

"Good."

"Not really. It's at the bottom of the Puerto Rican Trench."

"I don't know what that is."

"The deepest part of the Atlantic Ocean. About twenty-eight thousand feet under water. More than twice as deep as the *Titanic*.

There's no way we're getting the plane to the surface. And there's no way to get to where the evidence lies."

. . .

They had moved into the hangar to get out of the wind.

Rhyme said to Gillette, "I'm not sure how I can help you, Detective. You're asking my advice on a case where there's no evidence. That's my expertise."

"I heard your lectures, Lincoln. You've got a mind that's, well, like nothing I've ever seen. I was hoping you could just give us your insights."

Sachs gave a smile. "You like your challenges, Rhyme. Doesn't get any more challenging than this."

True, he was thinking.

He shrugged, one of the few physical gestures he was capable of. "All right, we'll give it a shot. Now, any witnesses to the crash itself?"

"A container ship, not too far away. They saw it come in and crash-land and go under before the pilot could get out. They changed course and steamed over to the spot. But there was nothing there except a little oil."

"Ah, oil." It would have been helpful, but had surely been dispersed by now. "Any debris?"

"Not that they could see. And the currents there? If there *was* anything, it's long gone."

"Do you have the last transmission?"

"I do. On my computer. I'll get it."

He went out to his car and returned a minute later. He called up an audio file of the exchange between Nash and air traffic control.

Those in the hangar remained silent as they listened to the tragedy unfolding.

"Okay. Well, I think a preliminary question is: why don't you think it was an accident? Nash didn't mention a bomb. He just said a bang."

"Sure, it could've been. I'm leaning that way. But I'm suspicious by nature. And looked into Nash's life last night. He had enemies."

At this Sachs's eyes narrowed. She was far more interested in motive and dark psychology than he, and she asked who they were in particular.

"Well, there was an ex. Sally Nash. Divorced two years and under a restraining order. And that name is part of the clue—she's still Nash. Never let go."

Sachs asked, "He had an affair? He dumped her?"

"No, ma'am. The other way around. She cheated on him and when he found out he filed for divorce. Didn't ask for money or anything, but wanted out. Still, she was incensed that he'd wanted to split up. Go figure."

"Any threats?"

"From time to time. Never amounted to much. He lived in Orlando, so he had Orange County deputies go out there and remind her of the restraining order. More than once. She didn't take it well."

Rhyme said, "Okay, angry ex. Who else?"

"Nash was in a dispute with his business partner, who, it turned out, was talking to competitors. At least, those were the facts in court."

"Angry ex-business partner. And it went to trial. Interesting. Any threats?"

"Apparently not."

"What was his business, Nash's?" Sachs asked.

Gillette chuckled. "I really couldn't tell you. He owned companies that made components that went into other components. Apparently he was pretty good at coming up with parts like that. Nothing sexy. But he made a ton of money."

"Anyone else?" she asked.

"He'd had problems with a stalker. A woman he dated. She was accounted for when the bomb was planted but . . . well, it was a bomb. That's what somebody'd hire a pro for."

Gillette continued, "And Nash was serving on a grand jury and so we wondered if that exposed him to threats. But they were pretty mundane cases. Mugging, larceny, simple assaults, some drug cases. Lot of them. But low level. Real low. Not the sort of thing a defendant would want to take out a grand juror over."

"No obvious motive," Sachs said. "And it's not the world of cartels and the mob, who'd have easy access to bombmakers. True, you can find just about anything on the internet nowadays, but it sounds like the most likely explanation is mechanical failure."

"Should say we're exploring that with the manufacturer. They're going to run some simulations. They weren't optimistic about finding anything, not without the black box."

Rhyme then asked, "And you're pretty sure it would've been planted here, not Orlando. Because of security."

"Right. Here—well, like I said, cameras and barbed wire and deputies make the rounds occasionally but that's it. And this part of the field's pretty deserted. As you can see."

"Let's go through the possibilities."

He wheeled to the front of the hangar and looked out over the tarmac, the chain-link fence, the buildings on the other side of the highway.

Gillette explained that in the short time Nash's jet had been parked here there had been only four people nearby. Three employees of the FBO and the deputy making his semi-daily security check, though the man checked the buildings and gates only, not the aircraft. Besides, Gillette knew the law enforcer personally and could vouch for the man.

"Videos?" Rhyme said, nodding at a camera on a tall pole in front of the hangar. Another was nearby.

But the detective reported that he'd looked. The footage revealed only the plane taxiing toward the FBO, then it went out of sight. Then it appeared again as he was leaving to take off.

"What was the timing of the events?" Sachs asked.

"The employees arrived here between seven and eight."

"Who are they?"

The manager, two mechanics." He nodded to two men in coveralls working on a prop plane in the hangar—working *and* occasionally eyeing the visitors.

"So," Rhyme said. "Nash lands when?"

It was eight ten, Gillette explained. "A cab pulled up about eight twenty. He got in. They drove six miles to a lawyer Nash uses here. Some business deal. They met for about an hour. Another cab brought him back and dropped him off. The cabbies never got out of the cars. Nash took off a half hour later."

"How hard would it be to turn a video camera toward the tarmac, hm?" Sachs muttered. She added, "Tell me about the employees."

The detective pulled out a notebook. "Same staff here today was here yesterday. The manager of the FBO is Anita Ruiz. Forty-two, married. Joey Wilson is a mechanic and runs the re-fueling truck. Twenty-eight. Single. Busted twice for pot, but years ago and it was possession only. Nominal amount. And Mark Clinton is a mechanic. He's fifty, divorced. Veteran in Iraq. There're other mechanics but they weren't working this week. Been a slow time, apparently. Aside from the grass, none of them have any convics. And none of them have any connection with Nash. Other than the few times he flies through here on his way to San Juan."

Rhyme said, "It'd be too obvious anyway. Nash happens to fly through here and pick up a bomb at the exact time as somebody who's got a gripe against him is working? No, if any of them planted the IED, it was because they got paid to do it. Or extorted into it."

"And," Sachs added, "they'd all know airplanes and know exactly where to put a bomb to do the most damage."

"We're absolutely sure that security was tight enough so that nobody else could've gotten in?" Rhyme was recalling the perimeter cameras on the fences and the razor wire.

"That's right."

Rhyme gazed around the field again.

"How do you want to proceed, sir?"

He was silent for a moment. He glanced at Sachs, who appeared lost in thought. Then she said, "We could make them think we suspect the deputy. Treat them solely as witnesses. And then see if they try to shift any blame to him. Since we know he's innocent, that'll be a red flag."

Rhyme liked it.

He wasn't sure, though, about her amused gaze his way.

"What?"

"I think you should take it, Rhyme."

"Me? *Witnesses*?"

"There's no evidence. What else are you going to do? Come on, I think it's time to see how the other half lives."

• • •

Anita Ruiz was a businesslike woman, stocky, wearing a close-fitting, high-necked navy-blue dress. She had short dark hair, a dark complexion and wore bright red lipstick.

She sat across from Rhyme at a desk and seemed uneasy but no more uneasy than you'd expect under these circumstances—especially considering Rhyme's condition. The wheelchair, a complex motorized model, was an attention-getter. Her eyes made a circuit—from his uncooperative legs to a face he'd been told was handsome and, in fact, resembled that of a particular—and popular—film actor, right down to a prominent nose.

He was running this more or less solo. Gillette was present but Sachs and Thom had motored off to an office building, convenience store and fast-food place across the road that Gillette reported had not been canvassed yet.

Thanks loads, Sachs, Rhyme thought. His attention once more returned fully to Ruiz.

She frowned when he said he was only interested in the movements of the deputy making the security rounds, Jim Cable, when the plane was on the ground here.

"Deputy Cable? He's such a nice man. Do you think he had anything to do with . . . what happened?" She looked down at the digital recorder.

"We're just getting facts. He's not a suspect."

It was clear that she did not believe him.

Just as Rhyme had hoped. He continued, "Did you see him around the wings or engines of the airplane at any time?"

"I'm sorry, Officer . . . Mr Rhyme. I was in my office the whole time and you can't see the tarmac from where I was."

"The whole time?" He asked this because she'd used the words, which raised suspicions in his mind.

Should it?

Damn interviewing . . . He wanted test tubes and mass spectrometers.

Ruiz added quickly, as if Rhyme had known the truth, "Now that I think about it, I did go outside once. But I just went to my car. That's the other direction from the aircraft. It was behind me so, even if the deputy was there, I didn't see him."

He asked other questions about Cable and if she'd seen anyone from the airport staff, even if not particularly close. Had she seen *anything* else that aroused her suspicions? The responses, all negative, were short—she didn't ramble or volunteer information.

Rhyme had a friend, Kathryn Dance, who was an agent with

the California Bureau of Investigation. She specialized in using kinesics—body language analysis—in interrogating suspects and interviewing witnesses, and he'd formed a grudging respect for the art by watching her in action. One thing he'd learned was when suspects rambled and offered irrelevant or excessive details it was more likely that they were being deceptive.

His reaction to Ruiz was that she was probably telling the truth and, accordingly, fell low in the hierarchy of guilt.

After she left, Detective Gillette brought mechanic Mark Clinton into the hangar. The lean man, beard slightly yellow from chewing tobacco, looked everywhere but at Rhyme as he sat down.

Rhyme began with some preliminaries. Had he known Nash, did he know anybody who wanted to harm him?

He answered negative to those. And gave brief answers to other questions about Nash and the aircraft. He swallowed frequently, but that wasn't necessarily the sign of being deceptive, simply nerves—though nerves *could* be symptoms of deception, he'd learned from Kathryn Dance.

Finally, Rhyme steered the questioning around to Cable. Did he know the deputy?

"No, sir, not other than to say hello, good morning, or whatever."

Had he seen the deputy near the airplane?

Frowning, taking in the implication of the question. He hesitated then asked, "When would that have been?"

Odd question. The obvious answer: "Whenever the jet was here. Eight fifteen to ten thirty or so."

"Oh, I was working in here then on the Cherokee but I didn't see anything. I mean, I couldn't. There was too much glare when I looked out of the hangar door."

He asked a few more questions about Cable and what Clinton knew about him. He asked, "Did you ever hear that he had a gambling problem?"

The man simply shook his head, as if an addiction like this didn't even register on Clinton's radar, if it was true.

A few minutes later, using his good arm, Rhyme reached forward and paused the recorder. "All right. Thanks." He looked up and caught Detective Gillette's eye.

The mechanic stood and followed the deputy out of the hangar. Gillette returned a few minutes later with a heavy-set man in a uniform and a baseball cap, from which sprouted masses of curly brown hair, flecked with gray.

Joey Wilson responded to Rhyme's preliminary questions—again about any known enemies of Nash—with an attitude of trying to be helpful. But he hardly knew the man. Nash flew in occasionally for meetings or refueling. Once, he needed a fuse. They'd spoken no more than a couple dozen words.

Rhyme asked if he'd seen Cable near the airplane yesterday.

"Jim Cable?" A frown, as Wilson perhaps wondered why Rhyme was curious about him. "Uhm, I think I did."

"Where, exactly?"

"I don't know, not for certain. I was headed to the lunchroom. For some breakfast. But Jim, I think, he was kind of near the starboard wing. I don't know for one hundred percent sure, because I wasn't topping him off so I wasn't near the plane myself."

"No gas?"

Wilson looked up from the floor. "No, see, he wasn't scheduled for gas. That jet of his can go two thousand miles on a tank. The more you carry, the more gas, I mean, the heavier it is and the worse the mileage. Best to fly with as little juice as you can. I remember one guy one time was flying a Cessna Citation—now, that is a fine airplane. You ever been in one? Well, I guess you couldn't . . ." He blushed. "Well, I mean you could, but . . . Well, it's a superb piece of aviation machinery and he lands, he comes in and he has about eighty gallons left, which is really a no-no. That'll get you maybe sixty miles. He was trying to save the money on fuel, you know, but guess what? He bought the airplane himself. Outright! I mean, this is what he told me, he wrote a check for it. Can you imagine. Seven figures! And he was skimping on gas? Stupid."

"You know anything about Deputy Cable's personal life?"

A blink. "No, sir. I don't. Nothing. Really. He just made the rounds. The quiet type. Mysterious."

"How do you mean?"

"Well, he was a mystery."

Rhyme waited. "Can you add anything specific?"

"No. Just, like, my impressions, you know."

No, he didn't know. Didn't have a goddamn idea. "Thanks for your help, Joey." Rhyme was pleased that he'd been able to tamp down his natural impatience and curmudgeonly nature long enough to play a nonforensic detective.

The man gave another look at the wheelchair and then headed off.

Gillette joined him.

Before he could run through the employees' performances specifically, though, his van pulled up outside. Sachs got out and, noting them in the office, walked through the hangar, brushing rain from her sleeves. "Got something, Rhyme." She was carrying her backpack and she now dug her laptop from it.

"A video of somebody with a moustache and black top hat filling a bowling ball bomb with gunpowder and sticking a fuse in it?"

Gillette blinked at the joke. Over the years the pair had developed a rapport that was, as far as Rhyme knew, unique among law enforcers.

"No such luck. No human wits. And most of the security cameras weren't aimed this way. But I caught one. From the closest office building. No idea if it's helpful, but it's all I could score."

As she booted it up, he told her that the scheme to see if the employees would try to implicate the Deputy Jim Cable was largely a bust. The only hint of a lead was that the refueler/mechanic Wilson had said he'd seen Cable near the plane, while he had not been. And the deputy was "mysterious," whatever that meant.

Sachs started the video she had copied from the security system of the office building across the road.

The camera was, of course, some distance away—several hundred feet—but there was a more or less unobstructed view of the FBO, though not Nash's jet.

They saw a dim image of swaying grass and branches in the foreground and behind them, the office door of the company.

Then Rhyme's head eased closer to the screen. "There. Look."

They were gazing at the door of the FBO opening and Anita Ruiz walking outside.

She turned and disappeared off camera.

"Ah."

"Interesting, Rhyme?" Sachs asked.

"Got her!"

He explained that she was walking to the left. Exactly the opposite of the way she said she turned. "So she was lying. She *did* walk toward the plane."

"Was she carrying anything?" Gillette asked.

Sachs ran it again.

It was hard to see, given the bad quality of the image. She might have been carrying a purse.

Or maybe a small package containing C4 explosive.

A lie . . .

Rhyme was beginning to think this interrogation business had something to it.

Gillette said, "It's probably not enough to bring her in."

Sachs offered, "You have a cooperative magistrate? Maybe we

could get a warrant to listen in to her conversations. Maybe poke around in her office."

"Sure, I'll put that together." He pulled out his cell phone.

Then Rhyme cocked his head. "Dammit."

"What, Rhyme?"

"Gnissapsert on."

"What?" Gillette asked, the phone pausing in his hand.

Then Sachs was nodding. She gave a sour laugh as she figured it out.

He told the detective, "Look at the upper-right-hand corner."

"That sign?"

"Right."

GNISSAPSERT ON

"Oh, it's backwards."

NO TRESPASSING

Gillette was chuckling.

Rhyme, though, was not amused. "That's why the image was so dim. It was a reflection."

Sachs said, "The camera must've been pointed at the window of one of the office buildings. The glass façade was like a mirror. It looked like Ruiz turned toward the plane. Actually she turned away from it. Just like she said. She was telling the truth."

"Almost as bad as witnesses—goddamn videos. Hell." He actually felt betrayed by the one forensic clue they'd unearthed.

"She's innocent," the detective said.

"Not innocent," Rhyme corrected. "We just didn't catch her up with that particular lie." He shrugged. "Though there's nothing else in her interview to implicate her."

"What about the mechanics?" Sachs asked.

"Mark Clinton? He was blinded by the glare, he said . . ." Rhyme's voice faded momentarily, "But wait. *Was* it sunny? There was that terrible storm yesterday. What about in the morning? I don't remember."

Gillette said, "Clear blue skies until about ten. Then the storm came in. Yes, he's telling the truth."

"Or maybe not."

"How do you mean, Lincoln?"

He looked around the hangar. Then said, "Which way does the hangar door face?"

Gillette said, "Son of a gun. Right. West."

Sachs: "At nine in the morning, nobody in here would see any sun at all. The light was coming from the opposite direction."

"Okay, so he was lying. Get him back in here."

A few minutes later Clinton was in the hangar office once more. Rhyme looked him over with a curious expression. He wasn't in the mood for subtlety. He was pissed he didn't have any evidence. He said bluntly, "You said you were blinded yesterday. You couldn't see the plane very well."

"Yessir. It was really glary."

"How could that be? The sun was behind you. You were looking west."

Clinton responded casually, as if he didn't even get he was being considered untrustworthy. "Yessir. It was."

"Well?"

"Oh. The sun was reflecting off Mr Nash's aircraft. The fuselage. It was silver, you know. Not white, like most of the private jets. It was really, really bright. Couldn't see a thing."

Rhyme cleared his throat. Silence for a moment. "All right. Thank you."

After he'd gone: "*Another* reflection issue. See why we can't trust our goddamn senses?"

Sachs laughed. Rhyme was not amused.

"Let's follow up with Wilson. He's the one who lied about the deputy. And he was rambling. Kathryn Dance said that's deception flag."

Gillette said, "I'll play bad cop."

The man strode out of the hanger and up to Wilson, doing something with the controls on his fuel truck. Rhyme saw the man stiffen. He'd spotted Gillette approaching in the side-view mirror—yet more reflections!—and walk fast to a battered Honda Accord, jump in and speed away.

"He's rabbiting," Sachs said. She instinctively glanced at the only wheels available to her here. Sachs was a master of high-speed chases but she wasn't going to be doing any Indy 500s in a wheelchair-accessible van.

Not that it mattered. Detective Gillette was apparently a pretty good wheelman himself. He was in the driver's seat of his cruiser in seconds and, with the lights and siren going, he sped the car forward. It skidded once, but he controlled the big Chrysler from skidding into the fuel truck and spun around it. Then he followed Wilson to the main gate, near the terminal, and, once through it, onto the highway.

• • •

A half hour later Detective Gillette led a handcuffed Joey Wilson into the hangar.

"Man, this is bullshit!"

He directed the mechanic to the chair he'd just been interrogated in and helped him sit. None too gently, Rhyme observed, thinking it must have been a harrowing, if short, chase.

"What's the story?" Rhyme asked.

"I don't know what you mean."

Leaning close, Gillette snapped. "Why'd you run?"

"I wasn't running. I just wanted to get home and close up my windows. Because I heard there was going to be another storm. I forgot about them this morning."

Rhyme gave an oh-please look. "Let's take that bullshit off the table. You were running. Which is as a good as confessing you lied to me. You did go to the plane."

He gaped.

"Oh, how did I make that connection?" Rhyme asked. He glanced at Gillette, who leaned close again. "That's what the fuck he does. This guy can figure out stuff you can't even imagine. I want to just book you. He said no."

Rhyme was nodding. "You volunteered that you hadn't gone to the plane, when I didn't ask. Since that—and seeing Cable at the aircraft—were the only two things of substance you told me, that said, you were lying about one or both. Probably both. So. There we are. You were at the plane, and you didn't see the deputy there."

Just then Gillette's phone hummed. He took the call and spoke for a few minutes and then hung up. He grinned as he looked over Wilson. "The crime scene people just went over your car."

"Oh, hell."

"And guess what they found?"

Rhyme said, "How good was the pot in his trunk?"

Both Gillette and Wilson gave a brief reaction of surprise. Gillette's cleared first. "I told you he was good," he said. "Some of the best they'd seen. And enough buds and leaves to tell me it was dealer quantity."

The young man was staring at Rhyme, who said to Gillette, "It occurred to me that the last thing he'd want to do is blow Nash up. He flies here regularly from Orlando. There's a mechanic or refueler up there who hides the stash in Nash's plane and then our friend Joey here swaps that out for the cash."

Wilson closed his eyes.

Gillette leaned close once again. "So. Some kind of network you FBO people have to ship drugs. You use small airports like this one. No dogs, hardly any security."

Sachs said, "And none of the people who fly the private planes know. That's what makes the plan work so well. If they cross borders, they don't get nervous talking to Customs."

Rhyme continued, "Where were the drugs and the money? And please tell me it was in the rear."

He looked at Gillette. "If it was, and we're lucky with the timing, the package the pot was in might've picked up some trace from the bomb—or the *bomber*. And it's sitting in his trunk right now."

A beat.

Gillette raged, "Not the time for quiet, son."

Wilson said quickly, "Front wheel well."

"Hell." Rhyme grimaced. "No transfer."

Gillette muttered, "And you were, what, trying to point the finger at Cable?"

"I guess." Another look down. "I just said that because if you found the drugs or money where the plane crashed, you'd think *he* was the one. I'm sorry. I wasn't thinking."

Gillette escorted him to his feet and took him to the Dade County East Sheriff's Department car that had accompanied them here. He was taken away.

Gillette said, "Well, this was the only place a bomb could've been planted and it looks like it wasn't. So I guess whatever happened, it probably was a mechanical. I thank you both, Lincoln and Amelia. Especially for coming out to help us on one of our oh-so-pleasant Florida days." A nod toward the darkening sky.

Rhyme extended his good hand and the men shook. Sachs too gripped Gillette's palm. Rhyme said, "Let's check in with New York, Sachs. Find out if there's anything that needs our attention. And, look at the time. I see it's close to cocktail hour."

Wednesday

But the case was not quite completely closed.

The next morning, Deputy Gillette, Sachs and Rhyme were reassembled on the tarmac, at Rhyme's request. Thom was nearby. He'd occasionally wipe sweat from Rhyme's forehead. Today was much clearer, sunny and bright, and not a breath of wind, but the temperature was already soaring.

Sachs was explaining to Gillette, "When I was canvassing yesterday at those buildings and the restaurants, where I got the video tape?"

"Remember."

"I gave my number to all the businesses there, told them if anybody remembered seeing anybody next to a jet parked on the tarmac by the Southern Flight Service's office, to let me know. I got a call this morning. Seems a tourist and his family were sitting at that Burger King, outside around the time Nash's plane was there." She pointed. "They heard the story of the investigation on the news last night and got my number. The father has some pictures."

Rhyme squinted as he studied the fast-food place. "He would have had a perfect view of the plane's tail end. Where the bomb was planted—or not planted."

Gillette asked, "Where is he, still in the area?"

"Family's at the Blue Heron Inn."

"Sure, I know it. Five miles from here. Let's go talk to him. You want to follow me?"

"Will do," said Thom.

"I'll call dispatch on the way. Have a forensic team meet us there. And bring along one of those programs they have to enhance photos."

"Forensic," Rhyme said, drawing a satisfied breath. "If I believed in clichés, I'd say, the fish is back in the water."

"That's not a cliché, Rhyme." Sachs offered. "It's not even an expression."

"It is now."

• • •

Dade County East Patrolman Jim Cable pulled off the highway and nosed his car—his personal Buick—into a stand of magnolia. Pulling on latex gloves, he reached into the glove box and removed a cold gun, a .38 special Smittie. He'd taken it off Billy or Rodrigo or Juan sometime, someplace over the past six months.

And he'd told the kid to get lost. Because a collar for little coke and firearms possession wasn't as good as getting a gun that couldn't be traced to Cable. A gun that could be used for a situation like this.

Cable loaded it with bullets fresh from the box—rounds were always untraceable, if you touched them only with gloves.

And then he headed into the marshy field behind the Blue Heron Inn and made his way toward cabin 43, which is where the tourist was staying, the tourist who'd videoed Nash's private jet the other day—and had very possibly gotten an image of Cable himself slipping the bomb into the right engine hydraulic access compartment.

At thirty-two Cable was too old to be a patrolman, looking through airport restrooms for illegals and chasing Billys and Rodrigos and Juans for little bags of drugs and big pistols. And, for Christ's sake, making security rounds of airports and shopping malls like a rent-a-cop. But he had a mouth and he had a problem with the bottle, so he hadn't moved up the way he should have, the way he deserved to.

But he wasn't going to have to worry about that anymore. He'd just made a cool hundred thousand bucks by slipping a little package into the back of Nash's plane, timed to blow up when the plane was over the deepest part of the Atlantic. Cable knew ordnance—he'd been a combat soldier until the fucking dishonorable—and had set up the device just right.

Things had seemed to go smoothly enough. But now the job had turned messy. This tourist and his family would have to be killed. The gun would be traced to the streets of Miami and Cable would scatter enough coke around the room to make it look like a drug-related robbery and homicide.

He hoped the tourist was in the room alone. On the other hand, if the guy was reluctant to tell him where the camera was, pointing a gun at your kid's head makes you talk really fast.

He didn't want to kill anybody else. But you did what you had to.

One hundred thousand cash . . .

New boat or mortgage?

Tough call.

No, it's not. Boat.

Then he was at the door of the bungalow where the Johnson family, from Nyack, New York, wherever the hell that was, was staying.

He looked around. Nobody. This cabin was the last in a row near the field he'd just come through. Pulling back the hammer on the gun until it clicked, he leaned forward and put his head close to the door, listening. TV was on. Cartoons. They were probably just finishing room-service breakfast, before heading to the beach.

So the kids were in the room. He grimaced. He'd have to take everybody out.

The good news, at least, was that if he wasn't going to leave any witnesses he didn't need to wear the ski mask. It itched like hell and the day was already close to ninety degrees.

• • •

Thom parked the van beside Gillette's unmarked in the front parking lot of the Blue Heron Inn.

It was what Rhyme expected of a near-the-beach resort in this part of Florida. The rear-facing rooms got a view of trees and power lines, the front got the highway and strip mall. An anemic pool, sandy parking lot, breakfast room with plate glass two days past a half-hearted Windexing.

EGGS ANYWAY
ASK ABOUT OUR SPECIALS.

Rhyme thought about commenting to Sachs that the "anyway" didn't mean what the writer intended about the options for breakfast and the capitalization of the pronoun carried a certain theological connotation. But he refrained. This was serious business.

Together they walked and wheeled toward the tourists' cabin.

"There's nobody here from the department yet," Sachs said.

Gillette looked around. There were no other police cars in view. "I'll give 'em a call. But first, let's talk to this tourist. I'm eager to see what he has to say."

They approached the front door of the cabin and Gillette knocked. "Dade County East Sheriff's Office."

The door opened, though no one appeared at first. Gillette stepped in, saying, "Hello?"

It was at that moment that a pistol, held by someone inside, appeared out of nowhere, the muzzle touching the side of the detective's head.

• • •

Archie Coughlin, the chief sheriff of Dade County East, read Preston Gillette his rights.

The massive fellow, tanned and sweating through his beige

uniform, had nearly deferred to Lincoln Rhyme in this regard, so impressed was he that the New Yorker had broken the case.

Rhyme pointed out, though, that he was no longer an official law enforcer. Amelia Sachs was active duty, of course, but not of this jurisdiction. And one never wanted to screw up when it came to Constitutional protections of suspects. Always a black mark when they got off on technicalities.

The jurisdictional matter was also true for the third member of the Big Apple team: Ron Pulaski, the young, blond NYPD patrol officer who often assisted Rhyme and Sachs. He had jetted in last night to participate in the sting.

Pulaski and Sachs and several local deputies were inside the cabin momentarily with Gillette's partner in crime—Jim Cable, the deputy who'd actually planted the bomb in Nash's aircraft when none of the employees of the FBO could see him. Rhyme was outside with Coughlin and the handcuffed Gillette and a half-dozen other deputies from the Sheriff's Department.

Now Sachs and Pulaski emerged from the cabin, followed by Cable, also in cuffs, his arms gripped by two grim-faced deputies. He was led off to the back of an unmarked car.

The two NYPD officers joined Rhyme, Coughlin and Gillette.

Sachs nodded in the direction of Cable. "Told us everything we needed."

"What?" Gillette raged. "He gave me up?"

Coughlin produced a toothpick and stuck it in his mouth.

Now *that*, Rhyme reflected, is a cliché. He wanted to catch Sachs's eye but she was concentrating on their suspect.

Coughlin asked, "You going to cooperate too, Gillette? I'll put in a good word with the DA."

Ignoring his boss—well, soon to be former—the deputy raged, "You!" A glare at Rhyme. "How'd you know?"

Rhyme, always pleased to explain—and to show off his reasoning—said, "What's the key to this case? I didn't have evidence, so I had to work with witnesses. Words. Expressions. And I told myself what if I were to treat them the same way that I treated evidence. Thinking of Monsieur Locard—there's always a transfer of trace between the criminal and scene. What if this witness stuff worked the same way . . . I'm boring you probably. But sorry. I find it quite interesting.

"I looked at everything that the principals in the case had said. Did anything rub off on the scene? And in your case, I thought it might have. You seemed to know a lot about the aircraft in question. Range, size, autopilot, seats, the phrase 'a mechanical.' Did it mean you'd definitely learned those terms researching how to blow up Nash's plane? No. Did it merit further investigation? Yes."

"So, an empirical test. A laboratory test, if you will. Just like with the gas chromatograph. We put together the Blue Heron scam—the witness with a photograph of the airplane. And we waited for the results—i.e., to see how you would do. Of course, if you simply showed up to collect the picture and log it into evidence, I would have been wrong. And I would have apologized, wouldn't I, Sachs?"

Her look said, No.

And she'd be right.

But that's not what had happened, not by a longshot.

It had been a perfect operation. Not a single gunshot, no injuries, a righteous collar. But more important, for Lincoln Rhyme, he now had access to trace, fingerprints, DNA and impression evidence that was not five miles under water.

Rhyme then looked the blustering man over. "But why did you ask me to help? It was foolish."

"Because you're famous," Gillette muttered. "And when you would conclude that the plane crash was an accident—which I thought you'd do—everybody'd believe it."

"So. You going to help us, Preston? You don't, Cable'll come off as the cooperating one."

"Prick, selling me out . . . Yeah, I'll give you a statement."

"It'll have to include who hired you."

"What can you give me?"

Coughlin made a call and removed the toothpick to talk. He had a conversation that Rhyme could not hear. Then disconnected. He looked toward Gillette. "You give whoever hired you and Cable, and the state'll waive capital murder."

Gillette was considering this.

"Or you call a lawyer and take your chances."

"All right, all right."

A half hour later, Gillette signed the handwritten statement.

It was, Rhyme was actually disappointed to learn, Nash's business partner. There was a subtle provision in the partnership agreement that if he died before a certain date the partner could buy out the shares at a very discounted rate.

Money. The dullest of motives.

Though certainly one of the most common.

The partner knew Cable from the army and Cable suggested both he and Gillette—who had put together various criminal projects in the Miami area—would take care of Nash for two hundred thousand dollars.

"You did the right thing, talking to us," Coughlin said, pocketing the statement. "Come on. Let's get you to the station."

As they walked past the squad car where Cable sat, Gillette glanced at him with a glare.

The younger deputy said, "Don't worry. We'll beat 'em."

Gillette stopped, frowning.

Cable continued, "Just don't say a word and we'll be okay. They don't have anything. No evidence, remember? It's all at the bottom of the ocean."

Gillette blurted, "Fuck, no." In a whisper: "But didn't you . . .? You gave me up!"

"Me. I didn't say a word! What're you talking about?"

Gillette spun around and glared at Sachs. "You said he gave you everything you needed."

She replied, "He did. His address, phone number and social. That was all we needed."

"You lied!"

Rhyme said, offended, "It was hardly a lie. You misinterpreted what she said."

Coughlin nodded toward the two officers beside Gillette. "Get 'em both downtown."

He then thanked Rhyme and Sachs and walked back to his own car.

The pair returned to the van, where Thom was getting the accessible ramp ready. She said, "So what did you think, Rhyme? Handling your first evidence-free case?"

He was thoughtful for a moment. "It worked out, there's no denying that. But on the whole I'll take trace evidence and DNA and fingerprints any day. People? They're way too much trouble."

A Woman of Mystery

Ah, yes, there she was in front of him.

Ms Number Five.

The woman he had to kill.

The man stood beside a streetlamp pole, peering at her from outside the café where she was sipping an Americano.

He was a slim man, though strong, and had suffered from some minor pox when young. His long, pale face was mottled. Today, a chill April, he was in a leather jacket and tight-fitting jeans. Boots too. Boots with tall heels. He himself was troubled by his short stature and so he preferred to elevate. His name was Crespi; there was a first name but he never used it.

Ms Number Five . . .

That is, fifth *victim*—well, soon to be—sitting obliviously near the Galleria Vittorio Emanuele II, Italy's oldest shopping mall, in central Milan. Enjoying her coffee and a pastry of some sort, Emily French was texting or reading email on her phone. She had, Crespi knew, a boyfriend, who was away at the moment; perhaps they were sharing intimate secrets.

Crespi didn't care. He wasn't jealous; he had no romantic interest in Emily, as lovely as she was. No, his obsession with the woman was a simple one: death. Simple, but intense: he would remain in his present, frantic state until she was no longer of this earth.

He glanced about. Since the galleria and the neighboring Duomo were tourist—and therefore terrorist—targets, a dozen city and state police, as well as Carabinieri, were present. They were watchful and the majority carried machine guns. Crespi was careful to avoid them.

His eyes scanned Emily once more. She was in her late twenties, with long black hair and straight-cut bangs. Her figure was trim and he knew she enjoyed jogging—which is not something most Milanese did. She was a New Yorker, who'd come here three months ago to work for an American company with a sales office in Milan. Fashion, of course. Crespi found the whole business distasteful—and he had the same feelings for Americans. (Zero sense of culture or creativity or humility.)

But this was not why Emily French would die.

Her demise would be for an entirely different reason.

Another look about him. The time was toward the end of the afternoon, 17:30 hours, and the streets were filled with locals and tourists meandering to a favorite bar for an aperitivo, or returning to homes or hotels. It was Sunday, and there were few offices open; but this part of Milan was a favorite for families, for lovers, for sightseers. The spring wind was chill but not so harsh as to keep people from the streets.

The crowds meant, of course, that Crespi had had no opportunity to get close to Emily and play his game with the kitchen knife in this area. No, the attack would have to be at her apartment, about a kilometer from here. The flat was on a quiet street, Via della Moscova, not far from the old zoo. He would wait until she was at the door and as soon as she unlocked it, strike.

Inhaling deeply, smelling the damp exhaust, the perfume from a beautiful young woman, dressed head to toe in leather, just passing him by. She'd been shopping at one of the posh stores on Via Manzoni: Armani or Prada. Stores used to be closed on Sunday, the day of worship. Not any longer. Crespi didn't approve—though he did have the retail outlets to thank for the opportunity to see the gorgeous creature parading past.

Ah, now it was time.

Emily French waved for the bill—a rude, American gesture.

But, to his disappointment, after she paid and left the café, she turned away from her home. She was going to visit friends for dinner, he guessed, or perhaps go to a concert or film.

Crespi sighed angrily. He pushed into the establishment she'd just left and rudely brushed aside several other patrons to take the table Emily had been sitting at.

"Say, what the hell're you doing?" a bulky Australian tourist snapped.

One look from Crespi, though, and the man fell silent. He and his family skulked off to find another table.

He ordered a cappuccino, then pulled out a paperback book and tried to read. Crespi was, however, distracted and edgy. He needed to kill, the way a drunk needs liquor, a baby needs milk.

But satisfaction, it seemed, would have to wait.

• • •

Detective Inspector Rinaldo Tosca sat back on his unsteady chair. He was in his office overlooking the Homicide Squad in Milan's main Questura. The police station was a boxy post-war structure—not fancy like the one in Naples—and scuffed and dingy, just like Tosca's office.

But the forty-five-year-old State Police officer paid no attention to the exhausted nature of his quarters, none whatsoever. He toyed with a pencil, weaving it through his fingers, and stared at four large pieces of paper taped to his wall. The first one had gone up two months ago. The pictures and words penned upon it had consumed him; now that it had three brethren beside it, Tosca was even more focused on what the sheets revealed. The contents filled virtually every waking moment of his life.

The heavy-set man had a fierce moustache and black hair, swept back. His legs were like hams. The massive muscles had developed in his youthful days as a beat policeman roaming the streets of the darker parts of Milan on foot. He covered more territory than any other policeman in his squad—perhaps in the whole of the State Police. He still walked ten kilometers a day, to and from work, and on the cases he was handling.

At the moment, though, he was stuck in his office.

He would have given anything to be pursuing the Sunday Killer out in the field.

But there were absolutely no leads to follow up on. None.

A call came in from the public prosecutor, who was running the case jointly with Tosca. The man, whose office was several blocks away, barked, "Journalists! They're popping up like moles in my garden. They won't let me alone."

They wouldn't leave Tosca alone either but he simply ignored them. The prosecutor had political ambition, it was rumored, and so he could not afford to alienate the press.

The prosecutor added, "Rinaldo, do you have anything at all? I must tell them *something*."

Tosca explained that the Sunday Killer homicide team—eighteen strong—was having little luck in making headway. "Once more, Prosecutor, the forensics that the Scientific Police have provided link the four murders. That is clear. But the evidence does not lead elsewhere—to who the perpetrator might be. He's scrupulous about the crime scenes. He's a craftsman."

"Craftsman," the prosecutor muttered. Then he said, "The

whole city is watching us, Rinaldo. And do I need to remind you that today is Sunday?"

The killer struck only on the day of rest. Not every Sunday, but four of them in the past two months. Tosca had used criminal databases and the psychopathologist experts to see if there was any significance to killing on Sunday. But since the victims were not connected to churches or otherwise religious in nature, they could come up with no insights.

The prosecutor wasn't pleased. He scoffed, "I'll stall the reporters, I suppose, though I'll need something soon. And," he muttered darkly, "the mayor and the interior minister keep calling. The killings—and our failure to catch this bastard—are making the news around the world. And that hardly presents the city in a very good light."

And are tarnishing my potential political career, the prosecutor might as well have added.

He disconnected abruptly.

With a sigh, Tosca set the phone down.

He stared at the four sheets of paper, each a crime scene chart on which he'd written down all the details of the murders—names and photos of the individuals, the locations of their deaths (all killed in their homes), the COD (a knife), possible suspects from their past (none), possible suspects from their present lives (none), and the other forensics and witness statements (damn little).

All they knew was the Sunday Killer was male, not particularly large, probably Italian. And, as Tosca had reminded the prosecutor, he seemed to know a great deal about crime scenes because he was careful to leave virtually no physical evidence.

The difficulty in the case was that, unlike every other murder he'd run, there was no obvious motive and no connection between the victims. Tosca now looked at the charts, each one devoted to a person murdered by the Sunday Killer: Percy Glyde was a fifty-six-year-old executive with an energy company posted to Milan from Scotland. Becky Winter, twenty-six, was an American graduate student at Bocconi University, the business school in Milan. Camile L'Espanaye, from Piemonte, was a forty-four-year-old ski instructor at Courmayeur during season and came to Milan in the spring and summer to manage a health club. A French woman, Lucy Ferrier, forty-eight, lived both here and in Nice, where she owned a company that put together venues for weddings and other formal get-togethers.

The fact that three of the four were not Italian raised eyebrows, of course, and it was well known that asylum seekers were occasionally targeted by the ultra-right elements and gangs, but the Sunday Killer's victims hardly fell into that category.

Tosca rose and paced slowly in front of the charts, navigating as best he could through the boxes and stacks of case files.

Why would someone want to kill you? he asked silently. No criminal records, no difficult romantic entanglements, no sexual scenarios at the crime scenes, no money or other valuables stolen.

Why?

That question lingered, frustratingly.

Until it was replaced by one more urgent, more troubling. The echo of the public prosecutor's words a moment ago.

And do I need to remind you that today is Sunday?

No, my dear Prosecutor. You do not.

• • •

Crespi had been waiting for hours, in an alley near Emily French's flat, hiding behind one of those big round refuse containers with the hoop on top. This one was blue and covered with graffiti.

He wondered if he should have followed Emily earlier in the evening . . . and grabbed her as she passed a construction site or deserted building. It was getting late. There were not many hours left of Sunday, and she *had* to die today; those were the rules and they could not be changed.

But he knew too that he'd made the safe decision. Crespi read a great deal about crime scenes and knew of the nearly miraculous discoveries made by the Scientific Police. It was very, very risky to move impulsively. You needed plenty of time before the event, to plan, and plenty of time after, to clean up and destroy evidence.

Five minutes past. Then ten.

Where was she?

Emily was not a girl who slept around, nor was she one, he'd learned, who would stay over with friends, especially on Sunday night; she'd have an early start tomorrow, as her company opened at 8 a.m.

So where the hell are you?

To rest his legs he crouched, keeping hidden from passersby by the container. Crespi drew from his pocket the lengthy, stained fileting knife, which was silent and fast as a wraith. This was the weapon with which he'd sliced the throats of his four victims. He recalled the delicious memory of their thrash about in death throes, reaching vainly out to him, perhaps for mercy.

As if there'd be any of *that* forthcoming . . .

Crespi had watched them die fast, and in relatively little pain. Draining blood, he'd read in a story, brought euphoria then unconsciousness quickly. Not a bad way to die, once you took away the absolute horror of the five preceding minutes.

He peeked out now and had a good view of Emily's front door. The building she lived in was four stories high, built during the Sixties. The doorway was in an alcove, in which she'd be completely hidden when she unlocked the door. He could be on her in seconds.

And here—different from London or New York, where CCTVs were everywhere—there were no security cameras. In several of the murders committed by the Sunday Killer, he had had to wear a ski mask, since there was a danger of being filmed. Tonight, he could reveal his face to Emily French during the entire course of the murder. It was somehow fitting—no, *exciting*, to think that his face would be the last thing she would see when the story reached its denouement. He smiled at this word, which he decided fit perfectly.

• • •

The hour was nearly 22:00.

Detective Inspector Rinaldo Tosca was pacing through his office, his carefully polished shoes stepping one in front of the other.

Minions, in the form of Scientific Police and Flying Squad officers—men and women—came and went. So did State Police homicide investigators, both uniformed and plain-clothed, assigned to the Sunday Killer case. There were even several federal Carabinieri. While the latter organization and the State Police had a well-known rivalry, Tosca was careful to maintain a friendly working relationship with his military-police counterparts. One of these in particular, on the Sunday Killer taskforce, was a young officer new to the force, Ercole Benelli, a former Forestry Corp policeman. He was a friend . . . and as talented a law enforcer as you'd find anywhere, even though his training had been investigating counterfeit truffles certificates and cattle thefts.

But none of the reports and suggestions and queries these individuals provided shed any light on who the Sunday Killer might be or whom he would target next.

The murderer had now gone three weeks without a kill. On instinct only, Tosca believed today was the day he would strike again. After decades in the homicide investigation business, he had a sense of when the perpetrators he pursued were growing desperate to satisfy their lust to take a life.

The Sunday Killer, he believed, was poised to slice another throat today.

Of course, it was possible that he already had. The fifth victim, someone living alone and not expected in an office until Monday morning, might be lying still and cold in a thickening pool of blood somewhere.

Tosca's eyes took in the map of Milan.

Somewhere, anywhere . . .

Damn. He ground his teeth together. His wife, Anika, texted to ask about supper. He was not in the mood for a conversation so he replied that he would miss the family meal tonight. This was a pity—he enjoyed the large family gatherings on Sunday. But he needed to remain here.

It was then that his phone—the landline—rang. He picked it up. *"Prego?"*

"Inspector, this is Officer Morelli at the front desk. There's a woman who wishes to see you. It's about the Sunday Killer case."

"A reporter?"

"No. She says she thinks she has some information."

"What's her name?"

There was a pause as the desk officer posed the question. Then she said, "Signorina Gialla."

Curious name. The color yellow.

"Send her up."

Three minutes later a uniformed officer escorted the visitor into the office, as protocol dictated. She was of indeterminate age, with a handsome face, lean figure, blond hair. Her blue dress was stylish, but not flashy, and she wore impressive high heels. A golden scarf encircled her neck. A black leather jacket was over her arm. Her eyes radiated humor and confidence.

She approached Tosca and, surprising him, gripped him by the shoulders and kissed him hard on both cheeks. He was taken aback.

"Well," he began, "what can I—"

"Inspector," Signorina Gialla said, but her eyes were not on him. Rather, she stared at the charts on the wall, the photos of the victims in particular, it seemed. This made Tosca uncomfortable and he realized he should have covered them, or met the woman elsewhere. The photos were not for public consumption. Still, she seemed unfazed and turned away to face him again. "I must apologize.

"Apologize from the bottom of my heart. But the truth is that, while I heard something about the Sunday Killer weeks ago, I didn't pay attention to certain facts. I wish I had. Perhaps some of the victims would still be alive, if I hadn't been so remiss."

"Who are you?" Tosca asked sternly. "Do you know the killer, or suspect his identity?"

"No, no, but I do know who the next victim will be."

Tosca tried to understand this. "Yet you claim you don't know the murderer? You realize this casts suspicion on you."

The woman sighed. "Ah, Detective Inspector, here I am, if you want to arrest me for . . . I don't really know what. I am clearly not a man—as is your suspect. And if you wish to arrest me for withholding information, aren't I 'guilty' of just the opposite? Since here I am imparting information?

"Now I recommend we not waste any more time with digressions, and enlist every officer in the building—no, every officer in Milan—to follow up on my suggestion." Her lips tightened into a grimace as she looked at the wall clock. "Although it is my fear that we are already too late."

• • •

Emily French loved Italy.

As a fashion industry consultant, the young woman had lived in a number of different countries—Japan and France among them—but no one took style as seriously as the Italians. Yes, she worked for an American clothing company, and she'd thought that, as an outsider, she'd experience some prejudice against the "Yankee" outsider.

Not a bit.

She was welcomed into the arms of the fashion world, where people were more than happy to work with her to create the best and most stylish garments and accessories they could offer to consumers.

She was now walking down dimly lit, deserted Via della Moscova, headed back to her apartment.

Loved the country. Oh, when she'd first come here, central Milan had seemed overwhelming. Busy, sprawling and—frankly—a bit dingy and pedestrian. But, she learned, that was only on the outside. Within those dun-colored buildings and vertical windows covered with metal shutters, were warm, spacious and stylish homes, jeweled with avant-garde décor. And the friends she'd met tonight for cacio e pepe and wine . . . what a wonderful group of people. Funny, cultured, warm.

And her assignment was for five years! She still had so many wonderful evenings in Italy to look forward to.

Emily was now approaching the dim alleyway in which the massive recycling container sat. She passed it and walked into her front door alcove. She inserted the key and turned it, hearing the satisfying click that meant she would soon be enjoying a late-night glass of wine and a phone conversation with her boyfriend, who was finishing an assignment in Switzerland and would be here late tomorrow. Oh, how she missed Phillipe!

Just as she opened the door, she heard a rush of footsteps behind her and arms were wrapping around her chest. A man was tackling her and she tumbled to the hard lobby floor, the breath knocked from her lungs.

"No, get off me!" she gasped.

The man whispered, "Quiet, quiet!" In Italian.

She was going to die! She recalled those press stories about the man they called the Sunday Killer!

Was this him? Was she about to be stabbed to death?

"Please!"

"Shhhh."

And then she heard another man's voice, also urgent, speaking in Italian, from about fifteen feet away. "He's there in the alleyway! . . . You, stop!"

Another voice: "Police, police! Don't move."

Emily turned and noted that the man on top of her was not an attacker but a police officer, a Carabiniere, wearing the distinctively posh uniform jacket and the blue slacks with the red stripes on the outseam.

He was climbing off her and blushing, it seemed, helping her up. Not far away, in the mouth of the alley, near the recycling bin, was a small, wiry man. He was staring at her with mad eyes, utterly insane. In his hand was a knife. The blade was splotched dark in places, perhaps from dried blood.

Two State Police officers were pointing their weapons his way, as was a second Carabiniere.

"Drop the knife! Or you'll be shot!"

The assailant seemed not to hear. He remained as focused on Emily as a fox on a rabbit.

But then clarity filled the man's eyes and he realized his goal of blood would not be fulfilled. He dropped the knife and turned to flee—but was promptly tackled by the officers, who then bound his hands.

From the shadows up the street came a low voice, calling out, "Report!"

"Sir, the assailant is down. In handcuffs."

The low, melodic voice again: "Get him to the lockup." The man speaking stepped into the light. He was heavy-set and wore a rumpled suit, but his shoes were perfectly polished to brown mirrors. He wore a badge on a lanyard around his neck. "I am Detective Inspector Tosca, Signorina French. You are unhurt?"

"Yes," she answered breathlessly. "But . . ."

"But shaken, of course." The tall, boyish-looking Carabiniere said, "Forgive me, Signorina French, for leaping upon you. There was no time to explain. The Sunday Killer, we saw, was very close."

Emily whispered, "So it *was* him."

"Yes, indeed it was," said Tosca, who was watching the man being led off to a police van. He turned to the Carabiniere who'd protected her and said, "Officer Benelli, would you and your colleague find out where he lives and search the place carefully?"

"Yessir," Benelli answered and the two officers slipped into the night.

"Now, Signorina, will you accompany me to the Questura, please? I'll need you to make a statement. And waiting there is someone you will want to meet."

"Why is that?"

"Because she's the person who saved your life."

• • •

Scores of paparazzi clogged the front of the Questura as Tosca led Emily French through the throng and into the building.

Video and still cameras rolled and flashed and questions fired from mouths, as the media wished to know more.

There would be a press conference later, Tosca called, and the two disappeared into the building.

They encountered another cluster outside Tosca's office in the Homicide Squad: police and city officials, present to congratulate Tosca for preventing the fifth Sunday Killer attack and arresting the man. And to ask their own questions. (Many seemed curious, as well, about the blond sitting quietly in a chair beside Tosca's desk, reading a book contentedly, as if she were sitting before a flickering fireplace with a glass of grappa in hand.)

Tosca announced that he would be filing all the appropriate reports and would discuss the case later. At the moment, he had another matter to attend to. He closed the door and lowered the blinds over the smudged glass windows facing the squad room.

"Signorina Gialla, this is Emily French."

"Ah, Ms French," the woman said, in lightly accented English. She rose and they embraced.

They sat down in office chairs, facing one another, and Tosca took a seat at the desk. He said, "Why don't you explain to Signorina French how you happened to learn that she was at risk."

"Yes," Emily said. "I don't understand it. I have never heard of this man . . . what's his name?"

"Crespi."

"Ah," Signorina Gialla said, "you may not have heard of him but he's heard of you. Or I should say, your namesake . . . from the book."

"The book?" Emily blinked. Then it seemed she understood. "Yes, the character from Agatha Christie's *Witness for the Prosecution*. Emily French. My boyfriend joked about the name when we saw the movie."

Signorina Gialla said, "Emily French was the murder victim in the story. *That* is why he targeted you. For your name only, not you as a person."

Emily asked, "And his other victims? They too were characters in crime novels?"

"Exactly. And not just any characters, but ones who died tragically."

Signorina Gialla rose and walked to the charts on Tosca's wall. She pointed to each one in order. "Percy Glyde—*Sir Percival* Glyde was a character—and not a very nice one, by the way—in

Wilkie Collins's *The Woman in White*. Becky de Winter, well, Rebecca, was, of course, the central character in the famous book of that name by Daphne du Maurier. Camile L'Espanaye was a young victim in Edgar Allan Poe's *The Murders in the Rue Morgue*—she died in a quite unpleasant way, murdered by a large ape, no less. And Lucy Ferrier was the girl who died in the Sherlock Holmes novel by Conan Doyle, *A Study in Scarlet*."

Tosca said, "Signorina Gialla became aware of the names earlier this evening, and hurried here to say that someone named Emily French was to be the next victim."

Emily frowned and said, "How on earth could you know that?"

"Ah, the answer to that is also the answer to the fact he killed on Sunday. You know the newspaper *Il Mondo Nuovo*, here in Milan?"

"Sure, of course."

"Every Sunday they run a special book supplement. About six months ago the editor wrote a column in which he presented his top five classic crime novels. The fifth on the list was *Witness for the Prosecution*, with the victim being Emily French." She glanced at Tosca. "The inspector here enlisted hundreds of officers to comb public records and the internet. They managed to track you down. Just in time, apparently."

Emily said, "So the killer became obsessed with those books. But why kill people with the characters' names? What would his point have been? His motive?"

A rapping on the door. "Inspector?"

"Ah, Officer Benelli, come in." To the others he said, "We may have some insights on those very questions."

The Carabinieri officers he'd sent to search Crespi's home entered.

Benelli nodded to the women and then said, "Inspector? We've completed the search of the premises. A *preliminary* search only, I must say. It will take weeks for a full inventory. The place was a complete warren. A fire hazard, in fact. Piled high with a thousand books. And tens of thousands of pages he had written himself. Or was attempting to write, I should say. Much of it was nonsensical. He tried the same passage a hundred times. Then often tore or crumpled the pages up and threw them in overflowing waste bins."

His fellow Carabiniere added, "And the extent of his madness was obvious: many of the pages, easily two or three thousand, were signed by him as if autographing fans' books. He would practice, 'To my dear, devoted fan, yours, Crespi.' Or 'Bless you for your support, Crespi.' He was truly deranged."

"Ah, yes," Signorina Gialla said. "That explains his motivating force."

"That he was driven to kill by his frustration as a writer," Tosca said.

"Precisely," she replied

Benelli continued, "And he had a list of names beside his computer—dozens. They included the names of the five victims."

"So," Tosca said, "he would have spent hours and hours searching for real people whose names were the same as those from each of the five books. That must have been quite a chore."

Benelli said, "Apparently he worked only a few hours a week and had no relationships or family. Plenty of time to prowl the internet and find suitable victims."

The second Carabiniere added, "Oh, and he was a particular fan of crime novels, especially those that dealt with forensics."

"Ah," Tosca said. "So that's where he learned how to avoid leaving forensic evidence."

Emily asked, "What did he hope to gain by the murders?"

Tosca shrugged. "Maybe he felt he needed to 'murder' the old generation of fiction to make way for him. If he did that, the ideas would flow. But, who knows? I'll leave that to the psychologists to answer. My job is to stop evil, not explain it."

Signorina Gialla glanced at her watch. "I must go. The hour is late."

"Thank you!" Emily French embraced the woman again and added, "Please, who exactly are you? A private eye, like Miss Marple?"

The older woman shook her head. "No, no. I'm just a simple shopkeeper. I happen to have had an insight about this case and thought I would share my ideas. That's all."

"Shopkeeper?" Tosca asked. "Where is your store?"

She answered evasively, "Here, in Milan."

"And you'll say nothing more about it?"

She shook her head.

"And I assume that Signorina Gialla is not your real name?"

"No, certainly not. I prefer to stay out of the limelight."

Tosca then had a thought. He said, "I can't help but note that your name is the female version of Giallo." To Emily he said, "Giallo is the Italian name for a crime novel." He turned back to the older woman and said slowly, "So it would be accurate to say, I suppose, that you are a true woman of mystery."

At this Signorina Gialla laughed hard. "Yes, indeed you might. Good night to you all." The stately woman pulled the golden scarf around her neck and stepped into the squad room and glided elegantly toward the exit.

Ninth and Nowhere

I. Jamal

Two of them were outside the apartment because there were always two of them outside.

Jamal Davis couldn't remember their names. One skinny, one less skinny, but both mean-eyed, like they'd practiced it. He'd heard the skinny one's dad'd been a famous OG, who'd made it to all of thirty-seven before he didn't make it anymore.

The block was brownstones, fronted by fire escapes, all rusting except for 414 West. Fresh paint on ironwork, fresh paint on the door, fresh paint on the window frames. Garbage and recycling clean and lined up perfect. The crew's apartment on the second floor was free because Lester told the landlord they'd watch out and make sure nothing happened to the building. But the funny thing was that, because the building was the crib of the DS-12s, nobody moved in to the other units. Lester took the rest of them over.

Jamal spotted Skinny and Less Skinny eyeing him from a distance. Nothing about him could give them much to worry about: a bulky olive-drab combat jacket that kept out most of the March chill. Jeans with cuffs, orange Reeboks—nice ones, more than he could afford. But sometimes you just had to. His hair was short and his body was round. Which he didn't like, the round part. But his grandmother had always given him food and he had always kept eating it. When he was in high school, sometimes somebody had made a comment. Jamal was only five seven, a regret, but God gave him muscle and after he broke a jaw or tore an ear or sent somebody on their fours, puking, the comments stopped.

To the two wall-leaning outside 414, round and waddling Jamal was just any other nineteen-year-old in the 'hood. He kept his hands outside his pockets, of course.

He joined them. "Yo."

"You Jamal?"

He nodded and when he wasn't looking around he looked at the two. Less Skinny didn't seem quite right, talking to himself and playing with his joint in a twitchy way. Jamal didn't want him to go off. Skinny was just smoking a cigarette. Calm.

"Let's see some ID. Gotcha passport, right?"

Jamal blinked. Less Skinny giggled.

Skinny: "Fucking with you. Do Jesus."

Jamal extended his arms, crucifixion-like, and got frisked.

"Go on up. Second."

As he stepped through the door, he was jerked to a stop. Less Skinny had gripped his collar. He whispered, pot breath, "Careful, son. Don't fuck up."

Son? He was Jamal's age.

The door to 2A was open. Jamal supposed if you had the whole apartment building to yourself, why bother to close it, let alone lock it.

Still, he knocked.

"Yeah?" a voice called.

"Jamal." He took a deep breath and stepped inside.

He'd been in crew cribs before and this was like any of them. Table for cards and business and meals. Some matching chairs, some that didn't match. A couch and two armchairs that looked years old, weird plaid, gray and tan, not even his grandmother would've liked it. A big-ass TV, of course. CNN was on, crisp and bright and silent.

One bedroom door was closed. Another was ajar and through that one he could see a man sleeping on his back, snoring. He wore cargo pants but no shirt. A house-arrest monitor was attached to his ankle.

Jamal heard the sound of pissing and noticed an open bathroom door, the shadow of somebody inside.

Should he sit or stand?

He stood.

A flush. The sound of water from a faucet.

Lester appeared in the doorway, drying his hands on a paper towel. Sleeveless white tee, cargos, Reeboks of his own, silver.

Lester was as skinny as Skinny downstairs. But shorter. And he was muscled, rippling muscles. Jamal heard that at an initiation beatdown, Lester had cracked a kid's skull with one punch, not the concrete he fell on. But the knuckles. Maybe it was the gold rings too. Lester wore four of them, two on each hand. They had to weigh a quarter pound total.

"Appreciate this, you know, you getting up early for this," Jamal said.

"Shit, dog. You think I get up for you? Ain't been to bed. We in an hour ago. My girl, she in that room there, the door closed, so keep your voice down."

"Sure, man. Yeah."

Lester's hair was cropped close and razor-cut along his forehead, then ninety degrees straight down to his temples. Like the barber'd used a ruler. On his chin was a long, stringy goatee.

"But I ain't got leisure time here, you know what I'm saying? So let's do this or not do this. My boys downstairs, they check you out, but I'ma ask you to strip."

Jamal didn't move.

"You mean—"

"Fuck, dog, strip mean strip. So . . ." He lifted his palms impatiently.

Jamal took a deep breath. He glanced at the closed door. Lester laughed. "She out for the count. And even she wakes up, you got nothing she ain't seen before. Do it."

Jamal did. And though Lester didn't ask, he turned around because that's what he'd seen people do in the movies to prove they weren't wearing a wire.

Lester looked over the round body, saying nothing, not joking about the belly and thighs and man tits.

"'Kay."

Jamal got dressed quickly. He was in fact terrified that Lester's girlfriend would walk out of the bedroom and laugh.

"I'ma ask you, dog. What you want it for?"

"I just need it."

Lester's eyes went dramatically wide. "Well now, that don't answer my question, you think?" He walked to the fridge and pulled a beer out, drank half of it. Didn't offer anything to Jamal.

"All about the green. It's a shit time for us. My grandmother, she got laid off. Doing cleaning now. She's a smart lady but she's sweeping and dusting like some Lat bitch snuck up here from Honduras. Fuck that. I send MT what I can."

Lester sat down, stretched out his legs. "Why you never jump in with us?"

Jamal kept standing. "Dunno. Guess 'cause I couldn't risk getting fucked up. MT's away for five more, even they give him the benefit of everything. And he's got himself into trouble inside already. Hit a screw tried to feel him up."

Lester winced. "Aw, man, let 'em feel. Don't hit. Thought your brother knew the rules. Bought him another year?"

"Six months, one sol."

"Fuck solitary." Lester's face screwed up tight. "But here you come, dog, asking what you asking, which'll put your ass right into the system, too, if you fuck up. Then what'll Granny do?"

Jamal's voice nearly broke as he said, "I didn't want it to go like this. I don't have any fucking choice."

Lester finished the beer and pulled a toothpick from his pocket. Not a wooden one. Plastic, white. Or maybe ivory.

"How much you got?"

"Three."

Lester was frowning. "Three won't get you shit."

"It's all I got. Maybe three twenty." He was going to add, "*If I didn't want to eat today,*" but Lester might say not eating today'd be a smart move. The weight and all.

Lester glanced at the TV—CNN, always busy. Rumor was he had a glass eye, or fake eye. Jamal didn't know if they were made out of glass or what. He watched a minute of breaking news. A little boy had gotten lost in a construction site, a huge mall somewhere. Had he been kidnapped, fallen into a foundation? His name was Robert but the newscasters called him Bobby.

Lester walked into the kitchen and crouched below the sink. He emerged with a brown paper bag. He collected a roll of paper towels and spray bottle of Windex. He walked to the card table and set everything down. He opened the bag and spilled out a pistol and a dozen bullets. The gun's wooden handle was nicked and the blue metal parts were worn and uneven.

"Three Cs ain't buying you a Glock or anything fancy, dog. You didn't think that, did you?"

"I didn't know." He reached for the small revolver.

Lester waved his hand abruptly and Jamal froze.

The gangbanger picked up the gun using a paper towel, sprayed it with the window cleaner and then wiped it down, his flesh never coming in contact with the weapon. He set it down and did the same with each bullet. Jamal's eyes slid to the TV. More about the missing kid.

Lester plopped down the last bullet. "'Kay, dog. The green?"

Jamal dug the money out of his pocket and damn if Lester didn't pick up the money, too, with a paper towel and put the wad in his pocket. He didn't count it but Jamal supposed nobody ever in the history of the universe had shortchanged Lester.

"You mention my name and you're gone and Grandma's gone too, you know what I'm saying?"

"Sure, Lester." Jamal started to load the gun.

"Later. Not here. Now, get the fuck out."

When he was at the door, Lester came up close and said, "Dog?"

Jamal looked back.

"Don't never do a bank or check-cashing shop, 'less you get somebody on the street after they been in. You jack a car, I know a place'll pay good green. Only cost you ten points to me. You do a house and end up with merch, I'll move it. Give you fifteen points there—riskier'n shit from cars, you know what I'm saying?"

Jamal nodded, then swallowed.

"Phone-card stores're good. And remember, convenience stores, lotta times, put up cameras, you know, security? But they fake, to save money. An' one last thing." A nod toward the pocket where the gun rested. "Don't use it 'less you absolutely got to. Bullets—they change everything. But if you do, it's pop, pop." Lester reached up and poked Jamal hard in the temple twice. "Two. The head. Don't bother no place else. You good with that?"

"I can do it," Jamal said.

Lester looked him over and laughed. "Damn, dog, I b'lieve you can. Now, out."

2. Lester

"He say where he going?"

"Nothing," Sharpe told Lester Banks. "Punk ass looked me in the eye, like pushing me, you know."

Lester figured that Jamal could take Sharpe, skinny as an old rooster, one on one. Beatdown. Except if it came to metal, Sharpe had his Glock and Jamal had the Shit and Wesson.

They were on the doorstep of 414 West, Lester and Sharpe. Doug too but he was hanging back. Lester scared him. Lester was watching Jamal's receding form. Easy to spot. The orange shoes.

Lester said, "I got some intelligence is interesting."

Sharpe asked what it was.

"His brother's in medium sec at Burlington."

"Yeah. His brother, MT, he solid."

"Do I care?"

"Well, you—"

"You don't gotta answer." Lester was thinking. "You see his face?"

Sharpe was silent.

"*That* you can fucking answer."

"Jamal, yeah. I see his face."

"He got something in mind. Something big going down. I think his brother tipped to something, heard it inside. Told the dog about it, and he comes here playing close-mouthed. Boy don't want to share. Only reason I gave him that piece, find out what he's about."

"I wondered why," Sharpe replied. "That's smart." Then fell silent under Lester's probing gaze.

Lester asked, "What's on about town?"

"The Flatland?" Sharpe asked. "Only thing big I know about."

Lester hadn't thought about that. There'd been talk of a crew across town getting a load of fent and oxy, a big load, up from North Carolina. They were in the Flatland neighborhood, near the docks. Bad fuckers.

"Damn, punk takes the fent, tags the courier and anybody nearby. Worth, what? A couple hundred large."

Sharpe said, "Man, we could move that shit fast. Market always want it. But might be something else."

"Then I'll cap his ass and take what he got. Get my Smittie back. Punk boy got no business playing with that. Something 'bout that dog I don't like. Gimme yo Glock."

Sharpe instantly handed over the pistol.

Lester checked the magazine to make sure it was loaded and a round chambered. He looked up the street, where Jamal was turning the corner. He slipped the gun in his pocket.

"Later."

And started in the direction where dog had disappeared.

3. Adam

The crack in the plaster ceiling was different things at different times.

It might be a map of an interstate, it might be a mountain range, it might be a woman's voluptuous body.

This morning, as he lay in his sagging bed, what Adam Rangel saw was something he'd never characterized the crack as in his eight months of living here: a pirate ship.

Well, any old-time ship, he supposed, but for some reason Adam thought of it as a pirate ship. He remembered seeing that movie with Christie, *Pirates of the Caribbean*. Maybe that was it. Maybe he'd had a dream about the date.

No, it wasn't Christie.

He couldn't recall. Somebody blond. Christie wasn't blond.

Sometimes, lying in his rickety twin bed, looking up, Adam wondered if the crack was a risk. It looked pretty deep. Did it mean that the ceiling would come tumbling down on him? The building was ancient, constructed with plaster. Sheetrock didn't fall. It rotted. And even if it did fall, it wasn't heavy. Plaster *fell* and it weighed a ton.

But was it worth calling the landlord?

Probably not a good idea. Adam hadn't been so good about paying rent on time. The checks somehow hadn't stretched the way they should. The fewer waves he made, the better. No lease here. He could be kicked out anytime. He knew he couldn't find anything this cheap and he sure wasn't going to pass a credit check for anything else. Just keep it down and keep it low.

Sometimes Adam Rangel walked a very fine line.

Besides, he'd never heard of anybody getting crushed to death by a plaster ceiling.

He rolled upright, planting his feet on the green linoleum

floor. He massaged his calf. This was out of habit, not to temper the pain. The five-year-old wound didn't ache at the moment. Hadn't for a long time. But massage it he did.

Adam slept, as always, in boxers. And he glanced down now, over his forty-one-year-old body, which was in good shape. Unfair, considering he got very little exercise and his diet was a joke.

Last year, Priscilla—he was sure it was Priscilla—had a chance to see virtually every square inch of that body and she'd told him she thought he was in his twenties. Sometimes he missed her and wondered where she was now. She'd traced her finger over the tattoo on his neck, an arrowhead in which a skyward-pointing sword was crossed by three lightning bolts.

"Special Forces," he had told her in answer to her question.

"Oh, is that where that thing came from?" She had massaged the bullet-hole scar too.

Thing.

"Did it hurt?"

"Did. Doesn't now. Usually."

"Was it the Taliban?"

"Friendly fire. Happens a lot. More than you'd think."

"No shit."

Yes shit.

He slipped his feet into loafers and walked into the bathroom to pee. Debated brushing his teeth and decided to. Today the effort wasn't too much.

Pay attention to the little things, accomplish the little tasks. What doctor had told him that?

Adam could remember former girlfriends' names better, if only slightly better, than doctors'.

He checked text messages. None.

This both depressed and relieved him. When he had to respond he sometimes got tense. He might get it wrong, people might ask him to explain what he meant, might ask him more questions whose answers didn't come easily to him.

He went online.

Several emails but they didn't bother him. Emails were in a demilitarized zone. Texts were immediate, high-pressure, front line. Emails you could stack up and let sit. You answered them on your terms.

One was a response to an email he'd sent to a big drug company that'd run an online ad looking for new hires. Adam had a BS degree, with some chemistry classes. For someone with his education, though, all they could offer was entry-level sales. And that meant desk, pushing paper and talking to people. Fuck.

Delete.

One was from his mother, no subject line.

Delete.

Another:

Dear Adam:

Thanks for your email. I of course remember you. I appreciate your candor. I wasn't aware that you were having some personal difficulties back then. No worries not getting back to me. We sometimes have openings for someone with your skills. Please contact Helen in our HR department. And thank you, too, for your service to our country.

Adam was handy. When he was ten, he and his father had framed and drywalled a couple of rooms in their and his grandparents' house. He had a talent for it. After the service, he'd worked for a couple of contractors. They'd liked his work. But then he'd started not showing up. Fired. He'd gone to day labor, cash. That was better. For a while.

Delete.

He pulled on his gray slacks, a T-shirt and a plaid short-sleeved shirt, which he left untucked. As he dressed, he looked out the window. A typical March day, overcast and dim. He could feel the chill coming off the grimy glass. The weather cheered him. He hated the sun, hated heat.

For such obvious reasons that it pissed him off. It made him predictable, made him a slave to the past in all the worst, clichéd ways. Almost funny.

Then the wasp started. No, two of them.

Two wasps. Little fuckers.

Adam reached between the box springs and mattress and took out a Colt .45 semiautomatic pistol. It was an old military sidearm, though not the one he was issued in Afghanistan. The army made you give your weapons back. Anyway, he'd flown home commercial, so there was that. He'd bought this one on the street. For protection. And just in case.

He pulled the slide back to put a round in the chamber and slipped the muzzle in his mouth. He tasted metal and oil and smelled gunpowder from the last time he'd fired it, at a range, a year ago. He'd never bothered to clean it.

He turned slightly so that when the bullet exited the back of his skull, *if* it exited, it would slam into a thick, structural riser of the apartment and stop there, so no one outside his apartment would be hit.

Five . . . four . . . three . . . two . . .

Then, aiming the weapon elsewhere, he looked at it, admiring the shape, the feel, the weight. He pushed a button to drop the magazine out the bottom of the grip and pulled the slide to send the bullet that was in the chamber cartwheeling to the bed. He picked the slug up, slipped it back into the mag and reloaded the Colt. Set it on the unsteady table.

Adam walked into the kitchen—that is, the five-by-ten-foot area divided from rest of the single-room apartment by a half-high wall. He hadn't changed the ceiling bulb, so he used a flashlight to see if the pizza from last night was presently home to anything with six legs. It was not. He felt a thrill.

And to drink . . .

Oh, shit. Disaster.

When he'd gone to bed last night around eleven, he'd left his second bottle of cabernet of the night on the counter. He'd poured only one glass, he was proud to say, and he was looking forward to the rest to have with the pizza for breakfast. But Adam's hearing had been damaged during the war and he must have bumped the bottle, not hearing it fall, as he staggered to bed. Almost all had spilled onto the floor; only a mouthful of the cheap, tangy red wine remained.

Fuck.

He lifted the bottle, and with what was left took his morning meds. He was about to fling the bottle across the room but controlled himself. There'd been enough complaints.

Sitting on the bed, he massaged the scar on his calf again.

And, naturally, here it came . . . What replayed a couple of times a day in his thoughts: he's hunkered by himself behind a low wall, rising sometimes to look for a target. Others in the platoon behind their walls, or flat on a crumbling driveway or in the sand.

Rising, squeezing off rounds, then low once more.

And when that happens, utter fucking hell. The incoming, thunk, snap, snap . . . the bullets everywhere. From thirty or forty guns. Hitting the front of the wall, skimming over it, slamming into the ancient building behind. Stone cascading, fragments zipping. So fast, so fast, snappy and stinging and loud.

The platoon is in a vast open space, with only two goatherds' shacks and three or four stone walls, three feet high at the most, for cover.

Adam rises and fires some bursts.

"Where's the fucking air?" somebody shouts.

"En route. Medevac too."

One of the guys in the patrol'd been hit, bad. He rose at the wrong time. Face and shoulder.

Bad.

More bullets. They zip like steel wasps, they fall like red-hot fragments of meteorites.

Adam is thinking:

If it weren't the fourth day of the relentless snap, snap, snap . . .

If he didn't wake up every morning trying to keep a big breakfast down, just so everybody thinks he's just one them . . .

If they could just take a few klicks of land in this god-awful outpost and hold it . . .

If he hadn't signed up solely for the sake of his father . . .

If not for all those things, then he might not do the unimaginable thing he's about to do.

But he has arrived at the end of the line.

Adam has never been shot or hit by shrapnel moving fast enough to break the skin. But today he knows he's going to be wounded. Because he's going to do the wounding himself.

He's not stupid about this. He knows he'll be suspect because it will be a non-lethal puncture of his flesh exactly in the place where someone wishing to shoot himself to escape duty would shoot himself. (The calf is number one.) This is among the most serious offenses in the military. The crime is malingering, which sounds as tame as loitering, but it's not. If you self-inflict an injury in combat, you'll face ten years of military prison and a dishonorable discharge.

So Adam looks about to make sure no one can see him. His weapon—your basic black assault rifle—has three modes: single semiautomatic, three-round bursts and fully auto. He clicks his rifle to single—one trigger pull, one bullet—because he doesn't want his flesh turned to gravy. Adam pulls a large bandage from his MOLLE backpack; he presses this against his calf, so that if CID is in the mood to play forensics, they won't find gunshot residue on his uniform or skin and will think the slug must've come from a distance. He'll discard the bandage later.

With no further prep, he shoots himself in the leg. The rifle he's been issued fires a small bullet, a little under a quarter of an inch. But it moves fast as the dickens, two thousand mph, far faster than the jets that are coming to pound the enemy and drive them, temporarily, to cover.

There's a sting but no terrible rush of pain. The nerves are traumatized. Still he cries out, "I'm hit!" And he hides the bandage in a pocket.

"Ahhh, ahhh . . ."

Adam freezes.

And looks behind him.

There was a gap in time from when he looked to see that he was alone behind this wall and when he fired his weapon.

And in that gap, a fellow soldier crawled up behind him.

His best friend in the unit, Todd Wilshire. They joked, they played cards, they shared books and stories about women, snuck illegal hooch.

The bullet slowed somewhat as it passed through Adam's leg. But it still traveled fast enough to zip into Todd's throat and neck and tidily open a vein.

His eyes lock on Adam's as he grips his neck, pointlessly, the red cascading, cascading.

"Ahhhh . . . Ah . . ."

For a moment, Adam debates. Todd saw, Todd would tell. But then: *No, I can't do it.* He cries, "Medic! Medic!"

Soon a shuffle of feet and the young man, hunched over, rolls into the spot between Adam and Todd. He glances at the wound on Adam's leg and assesses it minor and then turns to the hemor-rhaging solider.

Who can't be saved.

As his shivering death approached, Todd tries to say something to Adam.

The lips seem to form a *P*. But then he goes still.

Every day for the past five years, Adam Rangel thought of the incident, thought of his friend's eyes, thought that if he'd called for the medic sooner, Todd would be alive. What was he going say that started with a *P*?

He looked at the Colt sitting on the table.

Then: fuck. Out of wine.

Most places that sold liquor weren't open yet. He then remembered the Quik Mart on Ninth Street. He'd only been there once—it was a long hike—but he had a soft spot for the place, because the Indian clerk, Kari, the name badge said, used eighty cents of his own money when Adam couldn't come up with the full amount for his bottle and the Hot Pocket. Kari was a huge fan of the Beatles.

Quik Mart it would be.

4. Arthur

"I'm Patrol, yeah. Sure. But I haven't been *on* patrol, lower case *p*, in years."

Fifty-nine-year-old Arthur Fromm was speaking to the watch commander of the 19th Precinct. A man who was twenty years Fromm's junior. Short, intense, precise, as scrubbed as squash before going into the pot.

The man was confused. "*On* patrol?" But only for a moment. "Patrol Division, upper case. Being on patrol, lower case."

Fromm nodded his long head.

"That's funny." Though the watch commander wasn't smiling.

Fromm was tall, and because he never seemed able to gain weight, he was as slim as the day he graduated from the academy, eons ago. A fact that irritated many a fellow officer. His uniform was perfectly pressed. He sent it out. For years, Martha had ironed and rolled off lint every morning. The last time she'd tried, the fire department got involved.

The two men were in the hallway of the precinct house. Both started when a blast of March wind rattled the windows behind them. The building was 117 years old.

"I wouldn't ask this of you if it wasn't important, Arthur."

"Yessir, I'm sure." The commander was a captain and even though the man resembled an middle school Eagle Scout, Patrolman Arthur Fromm was respectful of authority. Always.

"I'm down two people in Riverside. We have to have it covered. The POS-Seven."

This was a requirement by some pencil pusher in headquarters, stating in clunky bureaucratic prose that every district in the city had to have a requisite number of "personnel on site," the count varying depending on population, but never less than one.

In this day of internet-connected squad cars, the requirement seemed antiquated. But there it was.

"Only for today. Mahoney and Juarez'll be back tomorrow."

It would be a black mark against the commander to let a district go unpatrolled.

"All right, sir. Yes."

The commander thanked him, though it had been an order, more than a request.

"Riverside."

Also known as the Nowhere District. Gentrification had largely passed the grim, pungent neighborhood by.

"That's right. Larkin from the bridge to the park and Ninth Street. There'd been some car break-ins. Graffiti. Muggings. Drugs. Don't sweat it. It'll all come back to you, Arthur. Do the things you used to do. Talk to shopkeepers. Ask kids why they aren't in school. Drugs? Don't bother unless it's packaged for sale. Or it's fentanyl. You know how to run a test?"

"No. It wasn't a big drug back then."

"You suspect that's what it is, call it in and somebody from Narcotics'll get right over there with a kit. Don't touch it. A microgram can kill you. Or milligram or something. It doesn't take much."

"Yessir." What he knew about fentanyl he knew from Discovery Channel true-crime shows.

"You checked out on the new Motorolas?"

"How different are they from the old Motorolas?"

The commander thought for a moment. "Supply'll let you know."

"I'll get my coat and weapon."

Fromm walked to the large cubicle he shared with another officer, a squat, cheerful African American woman named Delores.

"What'd Butch want?"

The nickname for the watch commander, thanks to the buzz-cut hair, which in Fromm's opinion was a bad fashion idea.

"He's sending me out."

"For coffee?"

"Hilarious. On patrol."

He opened the drawer and pulled his utility belt out. It held a Glock 9mm pistol, a Taser, extra magazines for the gun, handcuffs and a flashlight. The flashlight worked fine. He'd get new batteries for the Taser. He put the belt on. The weight was both familiar and disturbingly alien.

He asked Delores, "What's the story on body cams? I read a memo but I don't remember."

"Optional for now."

Fromm decided to pass. There was enough to think about with the rest of the gear.

As he left, she called, "You be careful, Arthur."

He grunted her way and smiled.

In Supply he got the Motorola, which worked exactly like the older version, though the sound was better. He swapped out Taser batteries. Then put his coat on, heading for the precinct's front door.

Walking away from the comfort of his desk, he thought: Damn, damn, damn. I do not want to do this.

In his career as a beat Patrol officer, Arthur Fromm had had his share of run-ins with all sorts of perps. Druggies—they were called "cluck heads" back then—and muggers and bank robbers. None of the incidents troubled him more than one would normally be troubled by talking a crazy-eyed perp into setting down the knife he was brandishing.

But then, four years ago, Martha had started failing.

Little things at first, just forgetfulness. Then worse and worse. Dangerous too. The burning-uniform incident. Boiling eggs without putting water in the pan. Cleaning the living room walls with gasoline.

Of course, it was a complicated disease, layered. And there were the moments of crystal clarity and—eerily—memories of their early days together in far more detail than he could ever summon.

But good symptoms or bad didn't matter. She was his wife of thirty-six years and he was going to make sure that she was taken care of until the end.

And so he'd transferred to Administration, where the odds were virtually nil that he'd be shot by a mugger or a husband in a domestic or one of the gangbangers from the crews that were moving into the precinct in increasing numbers.

Fromm had one month and six days till retirement, with a nice pension. He'd be home all the time and could dispense with most of the expensive full-time day staff.

Not religious by any means, he nonetheless occasionally prayed and he did so now.

Please, let me get to the end of watch today alive and unwounded.

Please, let me do nothing that would get me fired or brought up for conduct.

Let me get home to my bride . . .

He stepped outside into the damp, cool air, reflecting that at least the watch commander didn't exactly cut him a break. The man could have juggled personnel and stuck Fromm anywhere in the precinct. But he'd given him Riverside. Part of Fromm's job in Administration involved compiling statistics and he knew that the Nowhere District was one of the meanest in the precinct—in the whole city, in fact. There'd been a murder there just last week—one gangbanger had killed another right in front of a middle school.

He tried to think if a police officer had ever been shot in Nowhere.

Three years, Arthur believed. The cop had lived but he'd be in a wheelchair for the rest of his life.

He now headed for the Larkin Street Bridge, which would eventually take him to Ninth Street. Fromm recalled there used to be a great breakfast spot there, an old-fashioned diner. He hoped it was still open. That was one thing about walking a beat. If you didn't get shot or beaten half to death, you got to know the best places to eat.

5. Lanie

She lay in bed, on her back, thinking of Michael.

Picturing him.

He was a handsome man—looking a bit like a younger version

of the actor Harrison Ford, thick, dark hair, a solid face, broad shoulders. He was her age—mid-thirties—and in good shape; he, as she did, enjoyed running and working out. He did some kind of martial arts but one of the unusual ones. Not karate or tae kwon do.

Michael wore stodgy suits and his shirts had too much starch in them. They were like the dry marker boards Lanie used when she was brainstorming with the copywriters at her ad agency. Brilliant white and almost shiny. She'd teased him about it.

Lanie Stone, though, didn't always think this much about Michael's appearance. She thought more about his kindness. His eyes, which radiated confidence and care. His calm nature.

Calm.

During this time in her life, which was very, very un-calm.

A snore from beside her. She eased away from the warm, heavy body of her husband. Henry had rolled onto his back during the night. Hence the guttural snort.

She climbed from bed and walked silently over the thick carpet, comforting under her bare feet. And white as . . . white as the shirts that Michael wore.

Stop that.

Lanie slipped into the bathroom and pulled off the T-shirt she slept in, the cotton panties. In the mirror, she performed a fast examination of her profile. A pinch of the belly. A half inch more than she would have liked. But she wasn't too hard on herself, not at the moment. She indulged in a sweet now and then. Why shouldn't she? This was, hands down, the hardest time of her life.

No. No tears.

She had someone to save her.

Michael would save her.

Into the shower, the hottest water she could stand. Then she toweled off, dressed in a robe and blow-dried her short hair. She'd cut it recently. Michael said she should, and she had. Henry had blinked when she'd returned from the salon. "Oh. Short." He didn't know whether he liked it or not. "Why'd you do that?"

She said only she wanted a new look.

"Good. It's nice."

Which made Lanie feel particularly guilty. She almost told him about Michael right then and there. But no.

As she dressed in a blue silk blouse and a navy-blue skirt and jacket, she wondered what today would bring.

She'd told her secretary that she wouldn't be in today, she had a doctor's appointment—which was a good lie because you could always be a bit vague when it came to medicine, as if you didn't want to go into personal details. Something private. Something *down there.*

As for Henry, she hadn't told him she'd be away from her desk. But he never stopped into the agency and he rarely called during the day. He was a busy man himself, doing IT security, working long stretches to keep the computers of major corporations hack free. If he did happen to call and Rose told him she was at the doctor, he'd probably bluster that he'd forgotten, so as not to be embarrassed. And because his brilliant mind was always churning, he might very well believe she *had* told him.

A glance at her phone. Her stomach did a flip.

Ms Stone, the holiday ad proof will be ready at 8:30.

Which really said something else altogether. It was a message via code that she and Michael had laughingly come up with. It meant they would meet at the Holiday Inn on Tenth Street at the designated time. They'd agreed.

She texted back.

Thank you, sir. I'll look forward to reviewing said material.

She did her makeup, just a bit of blush, pale-brown shadow, pink lipstick. A waft of perfume, not much today, never very much. She used the fragrance solely for herself; the perfume triggered memories of a time before all the un-calm.

She looked at herself in the mirror.

You're really going through with this?

And nearly lost it. Tears started to well. Some sorrow, some guilt.

But mostly fear.

This was so fucking risky. She stood on the precipice of disaster, the very edge. The smallest of incidents could tip her over. A coincidence, being spotted in the street where she should not be. A roving reporter catching her on video in the background of an Action8 story about the Secretary of Transportation coming to town. Being hit by a car crossing the street. Police, phone calls, questions.

Disaster . . .

But, breathing, she got herself under control.

She started out the bedroom door. She had to leave now. Her husband's alarm was to buzz in three minutes.

Lanie looked at his sleeping form.

"I'm sorry," she mouthed. Then the cloud lifted.

She stepped to the front hall, pulled on her camel-colored wool overcoat. She locked the door behind her and hurried to the bus stop, looking forward to picking up a muffin and a latte.

But mostly looking forward to seeing Michael.

6. Carlos

Carlos stood at his kitchen window, overlooking the pleasant side of Carlyle Street.

Over there, the houses were beautiful brownstones, built a hundred years ago when attention was paid to detail. The structure directly opposite him was crowned with a scrolly façade inlaid with a mosaic of a fox. People living in *those* apartments, the rich folk, had to look at the scuffed yellow siding and aluminum frame of Carlos's building. Poor souls.

The five-foot-six Carlos Sanchez was wearing what he usually did: jeans and a shiny jacket in a sports team's colors. This was his trademark look. Today it was the Chicago Bulls, red and black. This was his favorite jacket, ever since he'd been told he looked like a younger Michael Jordan, though much, much shorter, of course.

His favorite and, he hoped, lucky jacket.

Lucky enough to keep him out of jail.

As he looked out the window into the gray, gritty morning, he was gripping his mobile, on which he'd tapped in nine/tenths of a phone.

The iPhone waited patiently.

Finally, he tapped the tenth and final number, "4," and then "Call."

The man answered on the third ring. "Yes?"

Carlos identified himself. "So. Can we meet? You said we could meet?"

Silence.

Please.

The man said in a harried voice. "I've got a nine o'clock."

A nine o'clock? Oh, appointment, he must've meant. Alfonse Webber was an attorney and like many of them, he existed in a whole different world from Carlos's, who was a foreman at an industrial plant on the waterfront. And he spoke a whole different language.

And what did the sentence mean? That he wanted to meet Carlos, or was he backing out?

"Should I—?"

"Be at my place at eight thirty. After that, I'm gone."

"That'll work fine. I'm going to my daughter's dance recital at school at—"

Click.

He turned from the window.

Carlos stared at the TV. The CNN story, he noted, was about a child, a boy of about five, who'd wandered away from an older brother on their way to school. The mother was working. The boy was lost in a jobsite where a mall was being constructed. They thought he might be trapped somewhere, maybe in a foundation pit. Carlos shut the set off.

He thought, naturally, of Luna. Twelve. Presently on the bus to her middle school, nervous about her recital but excited too.

He walked into the bedroom and sat on the bed, staring at the brown paper bag. The sack was identical to the one Luna had taken from him and slipped in her backpack. Hers contained a turkey-and-cheddar sandwich, a baggie filled with tiny carrots and a Little Debbie coffee cake.

This bag contained something very different.

Am I really doing this?

Then he zipped up the lucky jacket. He stuffed the bag into the pocket and stepped outside into the chill morning, the air fragrant with exhaust.

7. Brett

"It'll be fine. Imagine it's an audition for a part in a play."

"Oh, that's not making me feel any better," Brett Abbott said.

"You acted in high school."

"I hated it and I was terrible."

"I'm sure you were great." The petite blond kissed her husband hard.

"Ick," said Joey. Twelve. Soon he'd be more interested in the ick, though Brett supposed when it came to your parents, there was a perpetual ick factor.

Bev gave the baby some more glop. Brett thought: *Now, that's* ick for you.

They were in the kitchen of the family's split-level, in a subdivision just on the edge of town. Brett was polishing his shoes, which he did every morning before he left for work. He hadn't done this for two months and four days. It felt good.

Bev said, "Mr Weatherby seems nice." The couple had met Brett's new boss—*potential* new boss—several times, at a fundraiser downtown, the country club. And the charismatic man had taken Brett and Bev out to dinner once, as a sort of get-to-know-the-new-employee thing.

Potential new employee.

Bev said, "Maybe he can help us with a loan."

Brett's coffee paused on the way to his mouth.

"I'm joking, honey."

Weatherby owned W&S Financial Services and made good change from loans. And Weatherby himself made good change from W&S. He and the wife had driven a new Tesla, the fancy one, to the steak house.

Brett shrugged. "Ah, he'd laugh, you told him something like that."

Bev fiddled at the sink. "You're looking nervous."

"Really." Brett Abbott, thirty-eight, generally didn't give off nervous. He was six two, two-hundred-plus pounds, wide shoulders. He had a slow-moving way about him. He might look upset or angry and cagey at times, but didn't think he ever looked nervous.

"What's Dad nervous about?" Joey asked.

Brett had learned that nothing gets past kids but when your wife phrases something so out there, well, of course he was going to ask.

"It's like your first day of school. You're never sure how it's going to go. Your dad's trying out for this job."

Weatherby hadn't gotten to be a multimillionaire by paying money to people who weren't good at what they did. He offered Brett a probationary period, and they'd both see how it went. If he performed well, he could look forward to good pay.

Joey said, "Your last job, you took me on that sixteen-wheeler."

"That was fun."

"What're you doing for this new job? Something neat?"

"Do you know what 'vet' means?"

"Yeah, where we take Babe and Coffee." He nodded toward the two labs presently chowing down breakfast in the corner.

Bev and Brett laughed. "That's true. But it's a verb too."

"A word that means to do something," the boy said.

"Good. Right. 'Vet' as a verb means to check people out and make sure they can pay back loans before Mr Weatherby's company lends it to them. Have they paid money back in the past, how big are their assets . . .?"

The last word drew a snicker from the boy.

"Joey!" Bev said.

"Dad said it." Then the boy was losing interest—financial services couldn't compete with a big truck—and he returned to typing out texts.

You're looking nervous . . .

Because he was.

Nervous as hell.

The family was in trouble. Joey didn't know it—and the surprise arrival, Cindy, his sister, certainly didn't—but Bev had a problem, one that Brett had learned about only after they'd been married a few years. A problem that threatened to derail the whole family.

She was a compulsive shopper.

Buying things, it turned out, was an addiction too. Like gambling, like drugs, like drinking. She'd run up tens of thousands of dollars in credit card debt. Finally, facing bankruptcy, he'd convinced her to go into a program, like AA. That had been three years ago and it was working. With the help of constantly combatting her urges and some gentle medication, she'd had things under control for eight months.

But the aftermath of her prior bingeing remained. Brett had worked out agreements with banks and credit card companies to pay off the crushing sums that were owed. Bev was working too, two jobs. But then recently—two months and four days ago—Carelli Transport went under. Brett had looked at bankruptcy, but decided no. He would never do that.

He had to do something. There was no margin in their life; they'd just been making ends meet with what Carelli paid him—and even that meant eating lousy food, driving junkers and having no health insurance, neither he nor Bev.

But he was optimistic about today. He'd pulled in some favors from people he'd met through the transport company and got a meeting with Ed Weatherby. They'd met one on one, and then the couples got together too, and the matter-of-fact man said he liked the cut of Brett's jib (he'd had to look it up later). Weatherby would try him out. If it worked, he'd sign on full-time. One thing in his favor, Brett knew: he was very, very good at his job.

Brett looked at his watch, a big gold one that his father had given him for high school graduation. "Better go. Can't be late for this."

Bev followed Brett out of the kitchen. They stepped into the front hallway and Brett pulled on his navy-blue wool overcoat.

Coyly, Bev reached behind the other coats in the closet and handed him a shopping bag. It was heavy. "Got you a present."

He pulled out an alligator-skin briefcase. Beautiful.

His first thought, he was ashamed to say, was; how much had she spent?

"Don't worry," she whispered. "I got it on eBay for seventy dollars. I held my breath for the last ten minutes of the auction."

He kissed her hard. "Thanks, babe. Gotta go." He looked her in the eyes. "It's going to be okay. I'm going to nail this thing."

"I know you will. Wait, you didn't have a bite to eat, only coffee."

"There's a place on the way that's got breakfast sandwiches. I'll pick one up there. How do I look?"

He turned up the collar of his coat, held the briefcase at his side and cocked his head.

"You can vet me any day," she whispered.

8. The Quick Mart

Adam Rangel had been on the job for a half hour.

The fruits of his labor were not stellar.

He'd been standing outside in the cold, on Waterview Street, with his favorite paper cup and looking hopeful, saying, "God bless," and, "If you can, please." People who eyed him may have taken him for a soldier because of his age, build and haircut but he didn't play the veteran card when begging for money. Never would.

For more than one reason, of course.

He was still a few dollars shy of wine money. So near, so far. The Quik Mart was around the corner on Ninth Street, just three blocks away. Well, he'd keep at it.

This was supposedly a good corner to beg on. It was part of

the up-and-coming Riverside District. Businesspeople, some artists, restaurant and shop workers. This morning they'd all treated him as invisible. He'd also tried, "I'm hungry," which was true, and, "I'm trying to get some breakfast," which was also true, though the sustenance he wanted wouldn't involve bacon or eggs.

No generosity from the rich folks or the middle-class folks or the whatever-class. Adam never felt he was owed anything, not a single penny. Those people earned their money and deserved to keep it. They had no obligation to give him anything. But it was simple: he wanted to get drunk and he didn't know how else to do it.

Maybe he was putting people off because he was a little edgier than normal, fidgety.

This was because of an incident a little while ago.

He'd automatically lifted a cup toward somebody approaching. It turned out be a stocky Black kid, late teens or early twenties, wearing a combat jacket and jeans. His shoes were bright orange. The kid had seemed edgy. He'd walked past Adam, then paused and glanced back. Looking at Adam but not seeing him, focused instead on the street in the direction he'd just come from. Frowning. Adam felt uneasy himself suddenly. The look was like the kid wasn't completely here, freaked out. Dangerous.

Then he blinked and saw Adam, for the first time, it seemed. He dug into his pocket and pulled out some change, dumping it in the cup. Not because he wanted to, but, Adam's impression, because he didn't want to draw attention to himself. Why had he stopped, somebody might wonder? Oh, just to give the poor asshole some coin.

"Bless you," Adam said, cut by the fact that the kid was a lot younger. He didn't respond. Just continued to Ninth Street and turned right, with one more glance back.

But that wasn't what really troubled Adam and set the wasps

loose. That occurred just after the kid had disappeared. A man in his thirties, a compact Black man in a hoodie, strode along the street. The same direction the kid had been walking. While the youngster's shoes were orange, the older guy's were silver. Both of them joggers.

He paused beside Adam, glanced at the cup and then looked around the sidewalk.

"Yo, dog. Punk-ass kid come by here? Orange shoes. Orange like McDonald's."

The man's eyes were snide and cold.

Adam said, "No."

"He come this way. Why you ain't seen him? Fucking orange shoes."

"I didn't see him."

The man had marvelous gold rings on. One of them bridged two fingers. Adam saw an opportunity. He pointed the cup toward Hoodie Man.

"Fuck." Hoodie Man continued on and, pausing at the intersection, turned on Ninth in the direction the kid had walked.

Something was going down.

The wasps were hovering next to Adam's ears. Not a buzz but the whine of a power saw cutting fragrant pine.

He controlled his breathing and thought: I need my bottle. He returned to the task at hand. He was tallying in his mind. He had seven dollars and twelve cents. He needed only three fifty-two more.

The pedestrians came and the pedestrians went.

"Please, can you help me out," Adam said to their turned-away faces.

"Have a blessed day," he said to their receding backs.

• • •

Lanie Stone was walking down Ninth Street, her heels making a snappy sound on the concrete.

If it weren't for meeting Michael here, she wouldn't come to Nowhere—the name a take-off on other cities, which would shorten neighborhoods to be chic: SoHo and NoHo in New York or LoDo in Denver. But Nowhere was just that: run-down, scruffy. Like you wanted to take a power washer and scrub the dirt and grime off the sidewalks.

Lanie was always aware of her surroundings. Looking about, seeing nothing of any concern, she was pleased that there were people nearby. Not far away a tall police officer in his late fifties or early sixties walked into a coffee shop across the street. On the same side she was on, a short, stocky Latino, wearing a red-and-black satin sports jacket was walking toward her, a block away. His face seemed troubled. At the curb, a handsome businessman in a blue coat sat in the front seat of his Toyota, looking over what seemed to be a spreadsheet or other business document. He was on his cell phone, jotting notes. She noted beside him on the passenger seat something she'd never seen: an alligator-skin briefcase. She didn't really approve, though she guessed it was probably fake.

Lanie now walked into the Quik Mart and said good morning to the clerk, who smiled in return and went about his task of putting bakery goods into the glass case next to the register.

She was examining the delicacies. Chocolate chip? Walnut? *Indulge* . . .

She received a text from Michael, asking when she'd be arriving. She texted she'd be there soon. She was getting coffee and a muffin. Did he want anything?

He texted back:

The Eagle has landed . . . and needs caffeine.

• • •

Carlos Sanchez was walking down Ninth Street on his way to a nondescript office he'd been to several times before.

His hands were in the pockets of his Chicago Bulls jacket. This was both because it was cold and because he wanted to keep a grip on the paper bag.

It contained five thousand dollars in cash.

Am I really doing this?

The money amounted to the vast majority of his life savings. He'd had more at one point but Valeria's problem had taken much of it. And when she'd decided that she didn't want his advice or intervention with the drugs and drinking, most of the rest of his money went to fighting the custody battle to keep Luna out of his ex-wife's household.

The battle was like World War One, a standoff. Trenches on one side, trenches on the other, no-man's land between.

Oh, it was obvious that Carlos was the better parent: he didn't drink and had never done drugs. Since the divorce, he'd dated only sporadically and never brought a woman home when Luna was there.

Val, on the other hand, went to AA meetings for show and would stop in a bar on the way home. Her bed was occasionally occupied by a man she'd known for all of twenty minutes. Even when Luna was home.

But she was also smart as a snake. She played the mother card, the woman card, the how-can-a-man-raise-a-daughter card.

His lawyer had told him the odds were about fifty-five per cent that he'd ultimately prevail in the custody battle. But you never know about magistrates.

Except that Carlos had a secret weapon.

Alfonse Webber. The lawyer. The man who had "nine o'clocks." Not *meetings* at nine.

Carlos's life had taken an interesting turn a few weeks ago when he got a call from Webber. In his blunt style—the phone call this morning was typical—he'd said he had information that maybe Carlos could use. Webber had apparently met Valeria, Carlos's ex in a bar. They'd had drinks and Carlos supposed other stuff happened but Webber didn't go into it.

Just as well.

They saw each other off and on for about a month, then they parted ways. Webber had said he'd heard about the custody battle. "You know, Carlos, I could testify I'd seen her doing drugs and driving your daughter to school while she was drinking." And he'd learned that the man she was presently seeing was known to be "inappropriate" around young girls.

"Mio Dios!"

"Relax," came the gruff voice. "I said I could testify. You miss that part?"

And suddenly everything was clear. Webber hadn't seen Val's sins at all. But he was willing to lie on the stand to tip the balance of the custody decision in Carlos's favor.

Carlos guessed the parting of the ways between Webber and Val had not been so amicable after all.

And, Webber continued, because of the risk he was taking that perjury would cost Carlos five thousand dollars. Cash, of course.

He'd debated for several weeks, knowing that there was a small possibility that Webber and Valeria were setting him up. Bribing a witness would probably guarantee that he'd lose custody.

But in the end, he'd decided to go ahead with it. He knew in his soul that Valeria was toxic to the girl. Only he could save her from a mother who would drag the girl down with her.

He was looking ahead on Ninth Street, noting a convenience store. Quik Mart. A moment ago, a blond businesswoman with a pixie haircut had stepped inside. As he passed, he slowed to catch another glimpse of the pretty woman. What caught his eye, though, was a display of cut flowers. He and Luna had watched a concert on TV a few weeks ago, an Aretha Franklin tribute, and her eyes had glowed when she'd seen people leaving flowers on the stage for the singer.

Would she be embarrassed if her father brought a bouquet up to the stage at her high school?

He debated.

Whatever. He'd do it anyway.

He started inside.

A businessman in a dark overcoat carrying a fancy briefcase—what was that? Alligator, crocodile?—arrived at the same time. The man smiled and opened the door for Carlos. "After you."

"Thank you, sir."

Carlos stepped inside, beelining to the flowers and, with only a fast glance at the businesswoman, lost himself in debate: What would it be, roses or lilies?

· · ·

After opening the Quik Mart door for the short Latino in the Bulls jacket, Brett Abbott walked into the convenience store and looked around.

He noted the Latino heading straight for the fresh-cut flowers and the clerk behind the counter making a coffee.

Brett looked outside into the street. Deserted.

Let's do this.

He opened the alligator attaché case—such a sweet present from his sweet wife, a woman who in her bubbling innocence knew nothing about his real job. He withdrew the Glock pistol, a silencer screwed into the tapped barrel. He stepped forward, aiming the gun toward the person he'd been hired by Ed Weatherby—his *potential* new boss—to kill, Lanie Stone.

After her, he'd take out the clerk and the flower man, poor sucker . . . wrong time, wrong place. Then he'd rip out the video-cam drive, clean out the register, and leave.

Just another convenience store heist gone bad. Nobody would know the truth.

Brett stepped through the aisle of packaged candies and crackers and raised the gun to the back of Lanie's head.

• • •

Behind the counter of the Quik Mart, Jamal Davis was fixing up a latte for the nice woman with the short blond hair. She'd been coming in regular every day, this time, for the past week.

He turned from the espresso machine and froze.

The businessman in the blue coat—Jamal had seen him here earlier too—was walking up on her with a gun.

Breathing hard, his heart pounding so loud everybody in here had to hear it, he reached beneath the counter and grabbed the gun he'd bought from Lester just an hour ago. The businessman was concentrating on the lady and didn't see him.

Jamal had never fired a gun in his life. All he knew from movies and TV was that to shoot one, you aimed and pulled the trigger.

So he aimed and he pulled the trigger.

The roar was astonishing, shaking cups and napkins and the lottery cards and straws. The kick stung his hand and he winced in pain.

The businessman blinked in shock and touched the side of his chest, where the bullet had struck him. Jamal could see a tiny hole in the side of his jacket. No blood. Just a hole.

The woman screamed and dove for the floor. The man at the flower stand dropped into a crouch and covered his head with both arms.

The businessman pointed the gun toward Jamal but he ducked and the two shots hit the wall. Then the businessman fired toward where the lady had been. The guy was staggering around in pain, though, and couldn't aim very well. Jars and glass cases and bags of chips exploded. Jamal thought she screamed. But he was pretty deaf at this point.

More angry than scared, Jamal rose to his feet and aimed and pulled the trigger again, twice. Damn, his hand stung. He hit the man at least once more, because he winced and, looking dazed, turned toward the door and pushed outside.

It was then that Jamal realized he'd forgotten Lester's advice. He'd been so frightened.

It's pop, pop. Two. The head . . .

The man was alive and he still had a gun. He could still kill somebody outside.

Jamal scrabbled clumsily over the counter and ran toward the front door.

. . .

Carlos Sanchez rolled to his feet.

He felt damp. Maybe rose water, maybe lily water. He might also have peed his pants, probably did. He didn't care.

He was watching the man in the overcoat out in front of the Quik Mart, the man who'd been going to shoot the pretty blond woman. He was on the ground, hurt but still holding his gun. The clerk, a pudgy African American kid, had just dived over the counter and, holding a gun of his own, flung the door open and stepped outside.

Carlos glanced out the window, across the street.

Then back to the clerk.

No, no . . .

Carlos, too, ran to the front door, then pushed outside.

. . .

With a stain of fried egg on his police department uniform slack, Patrolman Arthur Fromm was standing in front of the Ninth Street Diner.

In front of the Quik Mart, a businessman, white, about six feet tall, dropped to his knees, shot, his back to Fromm.

Somebody was running in Fromm's direction, a black kid in a sweatshirt. And before Fromm could react, the kid doubled tapped him in the head. The businessman went down hard.

Jesus! No!

The kid had been knocking over the place, and the white guy had probably tried to stop it.

Fromm drew his Glock and aimed. "Freeze! Drop the weapon."

The boy stared. He did freeze but he didn't drop the weapon, an old-style .38. It was pointed toward the sky but wavering.

Shoot, Fromm told himself.

"Drop it, or I will fire!"

The boy was numb. Wide rabbit eyes. His arm was quivering, the muzzle going everywhere.

Oh, how he didn't want to do this. He'd never shot anyone in all his years on the force.

Goddamn Nowhere District . . .

He aimed at the boy's chest and began to squeeze the trigger.

Then he stopped, as someone else, a Latino, about thirty-five, in a basketball jacket, ran from the Quik Mart and stepped in front of the boy. His hands were up, his eyes were wide.

"No, no, don't shoot him! Don't!"

"Get down. I will fire!"

It was a team, Fromm thought. He'd read a report about that, Latino and Black punks joining up. The older guy was an OG, the younger one was part of the crew. Maybe it was an initiation. They'd knocked over the store together.

Just shoot Basketball Man, Fromm raged to himself. The kid working with him still had the piece in his hand.

But: you nail an unarmed person of color, that's seven ways of bad. Even if the Latino was in the worst crew in the city, Fromm'd pay.

If he didn't shoot and the boy nailed someone else . . .

Crouching, chest tight as a knot, Fromm stepped to the side, looking for a clear shot at the boy.

The kid still seemed paralyzed. Which didn't mean his trigger finger was.

Take him out. One dead already. No more.

But just as he was about to aim and shoot, the Latino covered the kid again.

"Get down. I will shoot!"

If the kid's muzzle moves one inch toward me, they're both going down.

Then: "He's the one!" Basketball Man yelled, pointing at the dead businessman, blood circling out from his head. "He's a fucking hit man, he tried to kill this lady inside."

Now, *that* was a bullshit story if Fromm had ever heard one.

But just then the door opened and a blond woman, a stunned look on her face, stepped out.

She spoke to Basketball Man, who kept his hands up, and continued to cover the boy, who they were both speaking to.

Motion of some kind . . . What . . . What was happening?

Then Basketball Man, hands still raised, stepped away. The gangbanger kid was lying on the ground with his arms outstretched. The woman was holding the gun. She carried it in two fingers to the curb and set it down, not near either of them.

"You," he snapped to Basketball Man. "Down too."

He complied, with a grimace toward the woman—the white woman—as if to comment: *I* have to lie down in the trash, but not you, of course.

It was then that Fromm realized he hadn't called the incident in yet. He reached for the transmit button of the Motorola, then recalled that, while he remembered how to work the radio, he didn't recall the code for shots fired.

He decided to go with 10-13, the universal code that meant "officer needs assistance."

Because, Lord knew, he did.

9. Aftermath

Arthur Fromm was slowly piecing together the facts.

Eight official law enforcement vehicles were present. Six squad cars from Central. And two unmarked. Ambulance, of course. Ten officers. But no detectives yet. Given his seniority, Fromm discovered that he was in charge. He struggled to recall procedure as the younger cops looked his way.

He tried, "Secure the scene, canvass witnesses."

Which apparently were the magic words. They scattered to do just that.

Fromm almost smiled.

So what do we have? He considered the cast:

A man with a silenced Glock, Brett Abbott, with suspected mob ties.

A woman advertising executive, Lanie Stone, whose interest in the whole big tsunami wasn't yet known, aside from the fact Abbott had tried to kill her.

Another customer, Carlos Sanchez, who was the stupidest, bravest and luckiest man on earth, having saved the life of the fourth individual involved:

The clerk at the Quik Mart, Jamal Davis, no record or warrants. He was the only one of the living participants still handcuffed, because he alone of those participants had pumped three, possibly four, rounds of .38 special ammo into a man.

Fromm crouched beside him.

"Hey."

The boy nodded. He was miserable.

"I'm not arresting you. Not yet. Just tell me what happened. You don't have to. But it'll go a long way in your favor if you do."

"I'll talk. I don't mind. Okay. That white guy." A nod to the medical examiner's tarp covering the body. "He come here every day, the last couple days. He bought some shit. But it wasn't like he really wanted it. I can tell. Us clerks always know. He was going to rob us. Pretending to buy some shit but really checking out the cameras and watching who come in and when. I told Mr Friedman, he's the owner, and he said what's he look like?"

"And you said a white guy in a suit. And he didn't believe you."

"Yeah, man. That's word. But that dude, he comes back and jacks the store or customers? It'd be my ass Mr Friedman'd get down on. I can't lose this job. I'm helping out my grandmother, she got laid off. And sending money to my mother. She in the system. Meth, you know. And my brother's doing time too. So, hard for a black kid like me get a job pays like this. I been there for three years. I'm the manager." This was said proudly. "I wasn't going to let nothing happen to my store. A brother hooked me up with the piece. The thirty-eight."

"Hurt your hand to fire it, right?"

"Like a bitch," Jamal said, then shook his hand. "Had to convince the brother I was a mean-ass fucker. I'ma perp somebody, jack some wheels. Otherwise he wouldn'ta given me shit. But, hey, I'm not givin' up his name. That ain't going to happen."

"I wasn't going to ask."

"I'ma go to jail?"

There were two witnesses—Carlos Sanchez and Lanie Stone—

who could testify that the shooting was in defense of others, and self-defense.

The problem was the gun.

Possession of an unregistered weapon was a felony.

"So where exactly on the street did you find the gun this morning?"

"Where—?"

"Because if you found it and just held on to it so no little kid'd find it and hurt himself or somebody with it, and you were going to call nine one one and report it but you didn't have a chance, I don't think you'd have anything to worry about."

"Yeah?"

"I don't think so. So where'd you find it?"

"Uhm." Jamal was looking around. "The curb?"

"Good." Fromm noticed a man walking in long, steady strides up the street. It was someone he recognized, Michael Garth, the top organized crime prosecutor in the city. The man was built like the football player that Fromm believed he had been at state university.

He nodded. "Officer."

"Prosecutor Garth."

Lanie Stone noted him and walked up fast and they hugged briefly. She'd been crying.

"How are you?" he asked.

"It was terrible . . ." she said.

Garth's face was dark with regret. "I don't know how the hell he got on to you. We screwed up. Should've had better protection detail on you." He noted Fromm was looking on with, understandably, some confusion. He said, "Ms Stone is the key witness in a homicide prosecution we're running against Edward Weatherby."

"Don't know him."

"Money launderer for the organization. Moves cash in and out, makes it look like loans. Mrs Stone here saw him murder a prostitute, some dispute over the price, we assume. The forensics was fifty-fifty, but she was an eyewitness. We've been meeting for the past two weeks to put the case together."

He explained that he'd had her cut her hair and change her appearance as much as she could. They'd never met in his office at the DA's, but at hotels and motels around town. They'd change the meeting place every few days.

Should've had better protection detail on you . . .

Guess so, Fromm thought.

She said, "Michael even came up with a code, so my husband wouldn't find out."

"He doesn't know?"

Garth said, "We had to keep it as quiet as possible." He nodded at the bloodstains where the hit man's body had been. "You can see Weatherby was going to do whatever it took to find her." He grimaced. "I should've thought about Abbott. He's one of the best. He used to work for Carelli, the East Side. But the truck company went under a few months ago, after old man Carelli ended up under a Peterbilt that accidentally on purpose slipped the jack. Abbott was out of work. He talked his way into Weatherby and got this job. He was good. Never thought anybody'd find you." A nod toward Lanie, then he glanced toward Jamal. "His story?"

Fromm explained about Abbott checking out the Quik Mart. About how the clerk was worried what the guy was up to, but the owner didn't believe him.

Garth said, "What part of the street did he *find* the thirty-eight in?"

Fromm said, "The curb, I'm pretty sure."

"Damn weapons just falling from the sky. Well, *my* department won't be going after him."

"Good of you."

"Not enough heroes in this world."

Fromm said, "Amen."

A car was pulling up. It had been moving fast, drawing the attention of all law enforcement present.

Fromm turned to the Acura. Two uniformed officers from the local precinct did too. One cop, a rookie, lowered his hand to his holstered weapon as the car eased to a stop nearby.

Fromm's eyes narrowed. But Lanie Stone nodded to the Acura and said, "It's okay. It's my husband." To Michael, she said, "I told him."

"Now, doesn't matter. We can put Abbott with Weatherby. Add a few other counts. Probably even hang felony murder on him for Abbott's death."

A round man with thinning hair climbed out of the sedan. His face, with flushed cheeks and concern in his eyes, took in everyone.

Lanie turned toward him and stepped forward fast. They hugged hard.

"Honey," the man said, looking around. "I got your call. What's going on?"

Lanie introduced Fromm and Michael to her husband, Henry Stone. She took his arm and they walked to a quiet corner of the sidewalk to have their talk.

Michael Garth wandered to the medical examiner's bus to talk to the tour doc.

Fromm helped Jamal to his feet and undid the cuffs. The young man rubbed his wrists. "Okay if I clean up my store? Mess in there."

"Have to leave it as is for now. Crime scene's got to process it."

"Yeah. Like *CSI*. Was a fine show."

Fromm then turned to Carlos, who was rubbing his wrists from the temporary cuffing. He'd been frisked and Fromm now gave him back the bag. It contained thousands of dollars in cash, twenties mostly.

"You understand this never looks good?"

Carlos sighed. "It's mine, Officer. I can show you the checks from my bank where I took it out."

"Not a crime to have money, son. But I'm going to ask you why you have it. What were you up to?"

He was thinking drugs, a disappointing prospect—though Carlos had come back clean when he'd checked his record.

The man sighed. "Was gonna buy something." He glanced at the bloodstains on Ninth Street. "But I changed my mind. I'm putting it back in the bank."

"Well, do it soon. You don't wander around this 'hood with that kind of green on you."

Fromm wondered if that was still street slang for "money."

"Yessir. Uhm, any chance I can go, sir? My daughter's got a recital. I can still see the last half."

Fromm debated, looking into the man's imploring eyes. Now he was thinking: family. "I'll need a full statement but, yeah, just call me later today. I'll hook you up with the detectives." He wrote his number on a slip of notebook paper and tore it off.

The man took it. "Yessir."

He walked off, circling wide around the bloodstains.

Fromm looked at the scene. He noticed Jamal was flexing and unflexing his hand. The gun had been a small-frame .38. Stung like hell to shoot.

There was another convenience store up at the corner. He'd give the kid some money and have him buy a cup of ice and some baggies. That would help with the pain.

Fromm sent a text to Martha's caregiver, explaining that he might be home a little later than planned. Something had come up at work.

Esmerelda texted back that was fine and he could take his time. Martha was having a good day. Another line followed.

She say to tell her handsome husband she loves him.

• • •

Finally.

Some kind soul had given him a ten.

The woman, mid-fifties, trim and wearing shoes that matched her beige raincoat, explained that her son had served in Iraq. She'd deduced Adam was a vet too. Was she right?

"Yes, ma'am."

He'd endured her rambling discussion of her son's PTSD, how it slowed his advancement at an investment banking firm on Wall Street. He didn't get the bonus he'd hoped for.

"But he's coping," she'd said.

Adam had struggled for patience, even asking polite questions about her son and successfully reining in his urge to scream. A ten is a ten.

Ah, the things we do for the things we need . . .

With Hamilton in his pocket, the wasps didn't go silent, but the keening buzz dipped a few decibels. Ever frugal, Adam slipped his paper cup into his jacket and walked toward Ninth Street, and the Quik Mart, where his breakfast wine awaited.

But when he turned the corner, he stopped fast. The street was blocked off by police cars and ambulances and there were a number of cops milling about, along with reporters and camera people and spectators.

A shooting.

In the center was the kid who'd given him the money, talking to a uniformed cop, an older guy. A sign in the door said, "Closed," though that wasn't really necessary because the police had strung yellow tape all around it. And there were bloodstains on the ground.

A body too.

Adam felt his breath coming a bit faster, his heart tapping urgently. And, of course, the wasps were back, a whole fucking hive of them.

God, I'm sorry, Todd.

Tears welled.

Breathe, breathe, breathe . . .

Okay. Got it. Barely.

Wine detail now. Quik Mart was out. But at the intersection where he stood was a chain convenience store. Much more expensive. His money wouldn't go as far but at least he'd get his bottle.

He walked in, made his selection, paid and started out, glancing at a TV behind the clerk. He stopped fast, staring at the story, a local report of a shootout on Ninth Street—at Quik Mart!

On the screen was the kid in the orange shoes. He was Jamal Davis, the daytime manager of the shop. How our prejudices stay wound tight as a wet knot. Adam had been sure the kid was a gangbanger. Davis had shot and killed a man who'd been about to murder a customer. Possibly a robbery, possibly some other motive. The police were still investigating.

Adam was thinking: Damn. If he'd gotten enough money for the bottle at Quik Mart forty-five minutes ago, he would have been inside when the shooting happened. Fate is one bizarre fucker.

He stepped outside, unscrewed the bottle and had his first glorious sip of the day.

Okay, one more.

As he was about to turn and head back to his begging station, he glanced across the street and noted some movement in an alleyway. Somebody was there, a man, in the shadows, hiding.

Did this have anything to do with the shooting?

The man stepped to the entrance of the alley. Well. It was the skinny black guy—Hoodie Man, the one who'd asked about the kid Jamal.

Hoodie Man stuck his head out and looked toward Quik Mart. Adam saw Jamal taking some money from the cop and walking this way. Maybe to buy something at the convenience store where Adam had just scored his bottle. Jamal was on his mobile, not looking around. Hoodie Man ducked back into the shadows and drew a pistol from his pocket. A Glock, it looked like.

He was going to kill the young man. Maybe he was a witness? Maybe the man Jamal had shot was Hoodie Man's friend.

Adam closed his eyes briefly. And he thought of what was sitting on his table in his apartment. His own gun, the Colt. Often, he carried it with him, just in case the moment came when he was in a park, at night, or the by the river. Alone. The wine gone, the wasps buzzing louder and louder and louder . . . And he'd kiss the muzzle for real.

Today he could've used it for something else.

Ah, well . . .

Go ahead, he told himself. What've you go to lose?

He took one long sip of wine and, as he charged toward Hoodie Man, flung the bottle into the alley, beyond him.

It crashed onto the ground, and Hoodie Man turned toward the sound. But only briefly, then the wiry man's instincts seem to kick in. He spun toward Adam, who was shouting, "Jamal, run!"

Whether the boy ran or not, he couldn't tell. Hoodie Man fired at Adam as he dove forward. He felt the hot gas on his cheek as he crashed into the man.

In the army they teach you that hand-to-hand combat is nothing like the karate fights you see in the movies. It's grappling, wrestling, struggling to use a weapon or take a weapon away. It's kicking, biting, gouging.

This is what Adam did now, fiercely gripping the man's shooting-hand wrist, digging nails into his skin and flaying away with his left hand.

The gun fired again.

Again, he didn't know if he'd been hit or not; like with the gunshot in his leg, all those years ago, his face and neck were numb. From the fierce muzzle flash? Or had the 9mm slugs actually torn into his body and opened significant vessels?

No matter, he decided. To his own surprise, he still had strength, from some reserve somewhere, and his grip was sure. He controlled Hoodie Man's shooting hand and kept the weapon pointed safely to the ground.

"Motherfucker," Hoodie Man muttered, then yelped in pain as Adam's left fist collided with his nose. The gun fell to the ground and Adam dragged the man away from it. He smelled pot and sweat and some kind of biting aftershave lotion. His own unpleasant body scent too.

He took a few oblique hits to the ear and cheek, then subdued Hoodie Man completely with an elbow to the face. But then the police were all over them, dragging them apart and cuffing both.

Medics attended to them. Adam had not been shot, though he did have burns from the flash and powder embedded in his cheek. His right ear sang—though a tone lower than the wasps. A young med technician, a woman, sat close, ignoring his why-bother-to-shower odor, and dabbed salve on the spot. After the treatment, he sat on the curb while the older police officer—a nice-enough guy named Arthur Fromm—checked his and Hoodie Man's records. He listened to Adam's story and ordered him unshackled. Jamal walked up and thanked him, looking him straight in the eye and shaking his hand.

Adam nodded but gave no other response.

Hoodie Man, whose name turned out to be Lester Banks, was apparently the head of a gang in a neighborhood not far away. He'd done time but had no current warrants, Adam heard. He was arrested for a handful of offenses.

Officer Fromm asked Jamal, "You ever see him before?" And

he asked it in the kind of way that told Adam that Fromm was absolutely certain they'd seen each other before.

"No, sir."

An answer that, Adam was sure, Officer Fromm was absolutely certain he'd hear.

"Okay," the cop said. "Ice that hand."

"Yessir."

With a look of utter hatred at Adam, Lester was escorted to a squad car and deposited in the back seat.

Adam was mentally counting the remaining cash in his pocket, and the tally indicated a deficiency in the wine department. Hell. He started back to his begging station.

"Rangers," Officer Fromm said to him.

Adam turned, frowning.

The cop touched his own neck. "The tat."

"Oh. Yeah."

The officer was silent for a moment. Then he said, "My grandson was deployed."

Adam didn't ask where. That was a question that he might have asked a long time ago. Now, no. He didn't care.

Officer Fromm said, "Had a rough time, Derek did. Rough. There, well, obviously. But back here too. Was worse in some ways. Got divorced, lost his job. He's good now. Was in kind of a group thing. Veterans. You've heard this all before. He heard it too, and it took him a couple of years to take the step. He can put you in touch with somebody. You have a phone?"

Adam pulled it out. Fromm blinked. It was a flip phone. He'd be thinking: They still make those?

No, they didn't.

The officer dictated the number and Adam put it in. Hit "Save."

Without another word on that subject, Officer Fromm asked, "You have any money for breakfast?"

The enticing smell of the spilled wine was strong in the

heavy, damp air. Officer Fromm did not glance the way of the stain.

"Not really."

"I'll stand you to twenty," Fromm said.

"No, I—"

"You pay it back. We've got to meet anyway. I need a statement for the prosecutor." He was nodding toward where the squad car, containing Lester Banks, had been.

After what seemed like a long debate Adam slowly reached out and took the bill.

Adam nodded thanks. He walked back into the convenience store and picked up another bottle of wine and two breakfast tacos. As the clerk rang him up, he glanced at the TV news again. Another story was on, about a youngster who'd gone missing in a big construction site. The boy, a five-year-old named Bobby, had just been located, unhurt. He hadn't been abducted or fallen down a pit, as feared; he'd just gotten lost in the huge site. A tearful reunion.

Adam stepped outside the store and walked toward the Larkin Street Bridge, eating the tacos fast, four, five, bites. Then gone. It was maybe the best meal he'd had in his life.

He walked halfway across the bridge, one of the older ones in town, stone, ornate. He stopped. He unscrewed the wine bottle and drank several mouthfuls. Then he leaned over the railing, looking down.

The river was wide here, moving steadily, if not fast. It was a rich gray. He enjoyed watching a tugboat and barge muscle past, upstream.

Another hit of wine.

Thinking about the scar on his leg. Thinking about the pirate ship floating in the ceiling above his saggy bed. Thinking about the *P* word his friend and fellow soldier Todd had been trying to say as he died in a flood of crimson.

This was the moment, Adam reflected, when he would climb the railing and swan dive into the chill water.

Or when he would pitch the bottle into the river, feeling his heart tighten with vibrant resolution.

He chuckled to himself, not a mad laugh but a real one, and did neither. He took another sip, slipped the cabernet back into the bag, and continued across the bridge, then turned onto the street that would take him home.

Unlikely Partners

I

March 13

"The meeting's finished?"

"It is," Bil Sheering said into his mobile. He was sitting in his rental car, your basic Ford, though with a variation: he'd fried out the GPS so he couldn't be tracked.

"And you're happy with the pro?"

"I am," Bil said. The man on the other end of the line was Victor Brown but there was no way in hell either of these two would utter their names aloud, despite the encryption. "We talked for close to a half hour. We're good."

"The payment terms acceptable?"

"Hundred thousand now, one-fifty when it's done. Hold on."

A customer walked out of Earl's Emporium for Gentlemen and made his way to a dinged and dusty pickup, not glancing Bil's way. The Silverado fired up and scattered gravel as it bounded onto the highway.

Another scan of the parking lot, crowded with trucks and cars but empty of people. The club, billed as an "exotic dance emporium," had been a good choice for the meeting that Bil had just had. The clientele tended to focus on the stage, not on serious, and furtive, discussions going on in a booth in the back.

He had left the place but was now in the parking lot, scoping out the cars, to see if anything looked suspicious.

Not so far.

Another customer left, though he too turned away from Bil and vanished into the shadows.

Bil, of medium build, was in his forties, with trim brown hair and a tanned complexion from hunting and fishing, mostly in a down-and-dirty part of West Virginia. "Bil" had nothing to do with "William." It was a nickname that originated from where he was stationed in the service, near Biloxi, Mississippi. The moniker was only a problem when he wrote it down, B-I-L, and people wondered where the other "L" went.

"Just checking the lot," Bil said. "Clear now."

Victor: "So, the pro's on board. That was most important thing. What're the next steps?"

"The occurrence will be on May six. That's two months for training, picking the equipment. A vehicle that'll be helpful. Lotta homework."

They were deep into euphemism. What "equipment" meant was rifle and ammunition. What "vehicle" meant was a car that would be impossible to trace. And "occurrence" was a laughably tame name for what would happen on that date.

There was silence for a moment. Victor broke it by asking, "You are having doubts?" A moment later the man's slick voice continued, "You can back out, you want. But we take it a few steps further, we can't."

But Bil hadn't been hesitating because of concerns; he'd just been scanning the parking lot again, for prying eyes. But all was good. He said firmly, "No doubts at all."

Victor muttered, "I'm just saying we're looking at a lotta shit and a really big fan."

"This is what I do, my friend. The plan stands. We take this son of a bitch out."

"Good, glad you feel that way. Just exercise extreme caution."

Bil hardly needed the warning; extreme caution was pretty much the order of the day when the son of a bitch you were being paid to take out was a candidate for president of the United States.

II

May 6

The Gun Shack was on Route 57, just outside Haleyville.

The owner of the well-worn establishment was a big man, plump with fat rolls, and tall and ruddy, and he wore a Glock 42—the .380—on his hip. He'd never been robbed, not in twenty-one years, but he was fully prepared, and half-hoping, for the attempt.

Now at 9:10 a.m. the shop was empty and the owner was having a second breakfast of coffee and a sweet bear claw Danish, enjoying the almond flavor—almost as much as he enjoyed the aroma of Hoppes gun cleaner and Pledge polish from the rifle stocks. He grabbed the remote and clicked on ESPN. Later in the day, when customers were present, taped hunting shows would be looping. Which, he believed, goaded them into buying more ammunition than they ordinarily would have.

The door opened, setting off a chime, and the owner looked up to see a man enter. He checked first to see if the fellow was armed—no open carry was allowed in the store—and concealed weapons had to stay concealed. But it was clear the guy wasn't carrying.

The man wasn't big but his shaved head, bushy moustache—in a horseshoe shape, out of the Vietnam War era—and emotionless face made the owner wary. He wore camouflaged hunting gear—green and black—which was odd, since no game was in season at the moment.

He looked around and then walked slowly to the counter behind which the owner stood. Unlike most patrons, he ignored the well-lit display case of dozens of beckoning sinister and shiny handguns. There wasn't a man in the world came in here didn't glance down with interest and admiration at a collection of firepower like this. Say a few words about the SIG, ask about Desert Eagle.

Not this guy.

The owner's hand dropped to his side, where his pistol was.

The customer's eyes dropped too. Fast. He'd noted the gesture and wasn't the least intimidated. He looked back at the owner, who looked away, angry with himself for doing so.

"I called yesterday. You have Lapua rounds." An eerie monotone.

The owner hadn't taken the call. Maybe it'd been Stony.

"Yeah, we've got 'em."

"I'll take two boxes of twenty."

Hm. Big sale for ammo. They were expensive, top of the line. The owner walked to the far end of the shelves and retrieved the heavy boxes. The .338 Lapua rounds weren't the largest-caliber rifle bullets but they were among the most powerful. The load of powder in the long casing could propel the slug accurately for a mile. People shooting rifles loaded with Lapuas for the first time were often unprepared for the punishing recoil and sometimes ended up with a "Scope-eye" bruise on their foreheads from the kicking back telescopic sight, a rite of passage among young soldiers.

Hunters tended not to shoot Lapuas—because they would blow most game to pieces. The highest-level competitive marksmen might fire them. But the main use was military; Lapua rounds were the bullets of choice for snipers.

The owner believed the longest recorded sniper kill in history—more than a mile and a half—had been with a Lapua.

As he rang up the purchase, the owner asked, "What's your rifle?" Lapuas are a type of bullet; they can be fired from a number of rifles.

"Couple different," the man said.

"You compete?"

The man didn't answer. He looked at the register screen and handed over prepaid debit card, the kind you bought at Walmart or Target.

The owner rang up the sale and handed the card back. "I never fired one. Hell of a kick, I hear."

Without a word, the sullen man walked out.

Well, good day to you too, buddy. The owner looked after the customer, who turned to the right outside the store, disappearing into the parking lot.

Funny, the owner thought. Why hadn't he parked in front of the gun shop, where empty spaces beckoned? There'd be no reason to park to the right, front of Ames Drugs, which'd closed two years ago.

Odd duck . . .

But then he forgot about the guy, noting that a rerun of a recent Brewers game was on the dusty TV. He waddled to a stool, sat down and chewed down more of the pastry as he silently cheered a team that he knew was going to lose, five to zip, in an hour and a half.

• • •

Secret Service Special Agent Art Tomson eyed the entrance to the Pittstown convention center.

He stood, in his typically ramrod posture, beside his black Suburban SUV and scanned the expansive entryway of the massive building, which had been constructed in the Eighties. The trim man, of pale skin, wore a gray suit and white shirt with a dark blue tie (the accessory looked normal but the portion behind the collar was cut in half and sewn together with a single piece of thread, so that if an attacker grabbed it in a fight, the tie would break away).

Tomson took in the structure once more. It had been swept earlier and only authorized personnel were present but the place was so huge and featured so many entrances that it would be a security challenge throughout the nine and a half hours that Searcher would be at the center for the press conference and rally. You could never scan a National Special Security Event too much.

Adding to the challenge was the matter that Searcher—the Secret Service code name for former governor Paul Ebbett—was at this point a minor candidate, so the personal protection detail guarding him was relatively small. That would change, however, given the groundswell of support. He was pulling ahead of the other three candidates in the primary contest. Tomson believed that the flamboyant, blunt, tell-it-like-it-is politician would in fact become the party's nominee. When that happened, a full detail would be assigned to nest around him. But until then, Tomson would make do with his own federal staff of eight, supported by a number of officers from local law enforcement, as well as private security guards at the venues where Ebbett was speaking. In any case, whether there were a handful of men and women under him or scores, Tomson's level of vigilance never flagged. In the eighteen years he'd been with the Secret Service, now part of Homeland Security, not a single person he'd been assigned to protect had been killed or injured.

He tilted his head as he touched his earpiece and listened to a transmission. There was a belief that agents did this, which happened frequently, to activate the switch. Nope. The damn things—forever uncomfortable—just kept slipping out of the ear canal.

The message was that Searcher and his three SUVs had left the airport and were ten minutes away.

The candidate had just started to receive Secret Service protection, having only recently met the criteria for a security detail established by Homeland Security, Congress and other agencies in the government. Among these standards were competing in primaries in at least ten states, running for a party that has garnered at least ten per cent of the popular vote, raising or committing at least ten million dollars in campaign funds and, of course, declaring your candidacy publicly.

One of the more significant factors in assigning Ebbett a detail was the reality that the man's brash statements and if-elected promises had made him extremely unpopular among certain groups. Social media was flooded with vicious verbal attacks and cruel comments, and the Secret Service had already responded to three assassination threats. None had turned out to be more than bluster (one woman had called for Ebbett to be drawn and quartered, apparently thinking that the phrase referred to a voodoo curse in which the governor's likeness would be sketched on a sheet of paper, which was then cut into four pieces—not to an actual form of execution, and a very unpleasant one at that). Still, Tomson and his team had to take these threats seriously. Adding to their burden was intel from the CIA that, more than any other primary candidate in history, Ebbett might be targeted by foreign operatives, due to his firm stand against military buildups by countries in Eastern Europe and Asia.

Another visual sweep of the convention center, outside of which both protesters and supporters were already queuing. Attendance would be huge; Ebbett's campaign committee had booked large venues for his events months ago—optimistically, and correctly, thinking that he would draw increasingly large crowds.

He glanced across the broad street, the lanes closed to handle the foot traffic. He noted his second in command, Don Ives, close to the rope, surveying those present. Most of the men and women, and a few youngsters here, had posters supporting the candidate, though there were plenty of protestors, as well. Ives and a half-dozen local cops, trained in event security, would not be looking the protesters over very closely, though. The true threats came from the quiet ones, without placards or banners or hats decorated with the candidate's name or slogans. These folks would have all passed through metal detectors, but given the long lead time for the event, it would have been possible for somebody to hide a weapon inside the security perimeter—under a planter or even within a wall—and to access it now.

Tomson much preferred rallies to be announced at the last minute, but, of course, that meant lower attendance. And for most candidates—and especially fiery Ebbett—that was not an option.

"Agent Tomson."

He turned to see a woman in her thirties, wearing the dark blue uniform of the Pittstown Convention Center security staff. Kim Morton was slim but athletic. Her blond hair was pulled back in a tight bun, like that favored by policewomen and ballet dancers. Her face was pretty but severe. She wore no makeup or jewelry.

Tomson was unique among his fellow Secret Service agents, he believed, in that he always "partnered up" with a local officer or security guard at the venue where those under his protection would be appearing. No matter how much research the Secret Service detail did, it was best to have somebody on board who knew the territory personally. When he'd briefed the local team about how the rally would go, he'd asked if there were any issues about the convention center they should know about.

Most of the guards and municipal police hemmed and hawed. But Morton had lifted her hand and, when he called on her, pointed out there were three doors with locks that might easily be breached—adding that she'd been after management for weeks to fix them.

When he described the emergency escape route they would take, in the event of an assassination attempt, she'd said to make sure that there hadn't been a delivery of cleaning supplies because the workers tended to leave the cartons blocking that corridor, rather than put them away immediately.

Then she'd furrowed her brow and said, "Come to think of it, those cartons—they're pretty big. They might be a way somebody, you know, an assassin could, you know, hide in one. Kinda far-fetched, but you asked."

"I did," he'd said. "Anything else?"

"Yessir. If you have to get out fast, be careful on the curve on the back exit ramp that leads to the highway, if it's raining. Was an oil spill two years ago and nobody's been able to clean it up proper."

Tomson had known then that he had his local partner, as curious as the pairing seemed.

Morton now approached and said, "Everything's secure at the west entrance. Your two men in place and three state police."

Tomson had known this but the key word in personal protection is "redundancy."

He told her that the entourage would soon arrive. Her blue eyes scanned the crowd. Her hand absently dropped to her pepper spray, as if to make sure she knew where it was. That, a walkie talkie and a mobile were her only equipment. No guns. That was an immutable rule, for private security on a detail like this.

Then, flashing lights and blue and red and white, and the black Suburban SUVs sped up to the front entrance.

He and Morton, along with two city police officers, walked

toward the vehicles, from which six Secret Service agents were disembarking, along with the candidate. Paul Ebbett was six feet tall, but seemed larger, thanks to his broad shoulders (he'd played football at Indiana). His hair was an impressive mane of salt and pepper. His suit was typical of what he invariably wore: dark gray. His shirt was light blue and, in a nod toward his individuality, it was open at the neck. He never wore a tie and swore that he wouldn't even don one at his inauguration—if he was lucky enough to win the nomination and the election, he added modestly.

Emerging from the last car was a tall, distinguished-looking African American, Tyler Quonn, Ebbett's chief of staff. Tomson knew he'd been the director of a powerful think tank in DC and was absolutely brilliant.

The candidate turned to the crowd and waved, as Tomson and the other agents, cops and security guards scanned the crowd, windows and rooftops. Tomson would have preferred that he walk directly into the convention hall, but he knew this wasn't the man's way; he was a self-proclaimed "man of the American people" and he plunged into crowds whenever he could, shaking hands, kissing cheeks and tousling babies' hair.

Tomson was looking east, when he felt Morton's firm hand on his elbow. He spun around. She said, "Man in front of the Subway. Tan raincoat. He was patting his pocket and just reached into it. Something about his eyes. He's anticipating."

In an instant, he transmitted the description to Don Ives, who was working that side of the street. The tall, bulky agent, who was a former marine, and a state patrol officer hurried up to the man and, taking his arms, led him quietly to the back of the crowd.

Tomson and Morton walked to the candidate and the agent whispered, "May have an incident, sir. Could you go inside now?"

Ebbett hesitated, then he gave a final wave to the crowd and— infuriatingly slowly—headed into the convention center lobby.

A moment later, Tomson heard in his headset: "Level four."

A non-lethal threat.

Ives explained, "Two ripe tomatoes. He claimed he'd been shopping, but they were loose in his pocket—no bag. And a couple of people next to him said he'd been ranting against Searcher all morning. He's clean. No record. We're escorting him out of the area."

As they walked toward the elevator that would take them to the suites, Ebbett asked, "What was it?"

Tomson told him what had happened.

"You've got sharp eyes, Ms Morton," the candidate said, reading her name badge.

"Just thought something seemed funny about him."

He looked her over with a narrowed gaze. "Whatta you think, Artie? Should I appoint her head of the Justice Department after I'm elected?"

Morton blinked and Ebbett held a straight face for a moment then broke into laughter.

It had taken Tomson a while to get used to the candidate's humor.

"Let's go to the suite," Ebbett said. He glanced at Tomson. "My tea upstairs?"

"It is, sir."

"Good."

The entourage headed for the elevator, Tomson and Morton checking out every shadow, every door, every window.

• • •

Ten miles from Pittstown, in a small suburb called Prescott, the skinny boy behind the counter of Anderson's Hardware was lost in a fantasy about Jennie Mathers, a cheerleader for the Daniel Webster High School Tigers.

In his imagination Jennie was thoughtfully wearing her tight-fitting uniform, orange and black, and was—

"PVC. Where is it?" The gruff voice brought the daydream to a halt.

The kid's narrow face, from which some tufts of silky hair grew in curious places, turned to the customer. He hadn't heard the man come in.

He blinked, looking at the shaved head, weird moustache, eyes like black lasers—if lasers could be black, which maybe they couldn't but that was the thought that jumped into his head and wouldn't leave.

"PVC pipe?" the kid asked.

The man just stared.

Of course, he meant PVC pipe. What else would he mean?

"Uhm, we don't have such a great, you know, selection. Home Depot's up the street." He nodded out the window.

The man continued to stare and the clerk took this to mean: If I'd wanted to go to Home Depot I would've gone to Home Depot.

The clerk pointed. "Over there."

The man turned and walked away. He strolled through the shelves for a while and then returned to the counter with a half-dozen six-foot-long pieces of three-quarter-inch pipe. He laid them on the counter.

The clerk said, "You want fittings too? And cement?"

He'd need those to join the pipes together or mount them to existing ones.

But the man didn't answer. He squinted behind the clerk. "That too." Pointing at a toolbox.

The kid handed it to him.

"That's a good one. It's got two little tray thingies you can put screws and bolts in. Washers too. Look inside."

The man didn't look inside. He dug into his pocket and pulled out a debit card.

Hitting the keys on the register, the boy said, "That'll be thirty-two eighty." And he didn't add, as he was supposed to, "Do you want to contribute a dollar to the Have a Heart Children's Fund?"

He had a feeling that'd be a waste of time.

• • •

The hallway of the penthouse floor of the suite tower at the convention center was pretty nice.

Art Tomson had learned, in his advance work, that in an effort to draw the best entertainers and corporate CEOs for events here, the owners of the facility had added a tower of upscale suites, where the performers, celebrities and the top corporate players would be treated like royalty. Why go to Madison or Milwaukee and sit in a stodgy greenroom when you could go to Pittstown and kick back in serious luxury?

Paul Ebbett was presently in the best of these, Suite A. ("When I'm back after November," he'd exclaimed with a sparkle in his eyes, "let's make sure they rename it the Presidential Suite.") It was 1300 square feet, four bedrooms, three baths, a living room, dining room, fair-to-middling kitchen and a separate room and bathroom actually labeled "Maid's Quarters." The view of the city was panoramic, but today that had to be taken on faith, since the shutters and curtains were all closed, as they were on the entire row of suites, so snipers couldn't acquire a target or deduce which rooms Ebbett was in.

In lieu of the view, however, one could indulge in channel surfing on four massive TVs, ultra high def. Tomson was especially partial to TVs because when he got home—every two weeks or so—he and the wife and kids would pile onto a sofa and binge on the latest Disney movies and eat popcorn and corndogs until they could eat no more. Special Agent Art Tomson was a very different man at home.

Only the candidate was inside at the moment. Chief of staff Quonn was on the convention center floor, testing microphones and sound boards and teleprompters, and Tomson and Kim Morton now sat in the hallway outside the double doors to Suite A. Tomson looked up and down the corridor, whose walls were beige and whose carpet was rich gray. He noted the agents at each of the stairway doors and the elevator were attentive and concentrating on their jobs. They didn't appear armed, but each had a fully automatic Uzi under his or her jacket, in addition to a sidearm, and plenty of magazines. Although armed assaults were extremely rare in this personal protection business, you always planned for a gunfight at the OK Corral.

Kim Morton said, "Wanted to mention: acoustic tile's hung six inches below the concrete. Nobody can crawl through."

Tomson knew. He'd checked.

"Thanks."

Tomson cocked his head once more, as transmission about security status at various locations came in.

All was clear.

He told this to Morton.

She said, "Guess we can relax for a bit." Eyeing him closely. "Except you don't, do you?"

"No."

"Never."

"No."

Silenced eased in like an expected snow.

Morton broke it by asking, "You want some gum?"

Tomson didn't believe he'd chewed gum since he was in college. She added, "Doublemint."

"No. Thank you."

"I stopped smoking four years and three months ago. I needed a habit. I'm like, 'Gum or meth? Gum or meth?'"

Tomson said nothing.

She opened the gum, unwrapped a piece and slipped it into her mouth. "You ever wonder what the double mints were. Are there really two? They might use just one and tell us it's two. Who'd know?"

"Hm."

"You don't joke much in your line of work, do you?"

"I suppose we don't."

"Maybe I'll get you to smile."

"I smile. I just don't joke."

Morton said, "Haven't seen you smile yet."

"Haven't seen anything to smile about."

"The two-mint thing? That didn't cut it?"

"It was funny."

"You don't really think so."

Tomson paused. "No. It wasn't *that* funny."

"Almost got you to smile there."

Morton's phone hummed with a call. She grimaced.

Tomson was immediately attentive. Maybe one of the other security guards had seen something concerning.

She said into the phone, "If Maria tells you to go to bed, you go to bed. She's Mommy when Mommy's not there. She's a substitute Mommy. Like the time Ms Wilson got arrested for protesting the removal of the Robert E. Lee statue and you had that substitute teacher? Well, that's Maria. Are we clear on that . . .? Good, and I do *not* want to find the lizard out when I get home . . . No, it was not an accident. Lizards do not climb into purses of their own accord. Okay? Love you, Pumpkie. Put Sam on . . ."

Morton had a brief conversation with another child, presumably younger—her voice grew more sing-songy.

She disconnected and noticed Tomson's eyes on her. "Iguana. Small one. In the babysitter's purse. I stopped them before they uploaded the video to YouTube. Maria's scream was impressive, man oh man. The boys would've had ten thousand hits. But you've got to draw the line somewhere. You have children, Agent Tomson?"

He hesitated. "Maybe we can go with first names at this point."

"Art. And I'm Kim. By the way, it meant a lot when I met you? You didn't hit the ground running with my first name. The woman thing. Lotta people do."

"The world's changing."

"Like molasses," she said. "So, Art. I'm looking at that ring on your finger. You have children? Unless that is a terrible, terrible question to ask, because they all wasted away with bad diseases."

Finally a smile.

"No diseases. Two. Boy and girl."

"They learned about lizard pranks yet?"

"They're a little young for that. And the only non-human in the household is a turtle."

"Don't let your guard down. Turtles can raise hell too. Just takes 'em a bit longer to do it."

More silence in the hall. But now, the sort of silence that's a comfort.

Inside the suite, he could hear, Ebbett had turned on the news—every set, it seemed. The candidate was obsessed with the media and watched everything, right and left and in between. He took voluminous notes, often without looking down from the screen at his pad of paper.

Morton nodded to the door and said, "He's quite a story, isn't he?"

"Story?"

"His, what would you say? Road to the White House. Reinventing himself. He went through that bad patch, drinking and the women. His wife leaving him. But then he turned it around."

Ebbett had indeed. He'd done rehab, gotten back together with his wife. He'd been frank and apologetic about his transgressions and he'd had successful campaigns for state representative and then governor. He'd burst onto the presidential scene last year.

Morton said, "I heard he came up with that campaign slogan himself: 'America. Making a Great Country Greater.' I like that, don't you? I know his positions're a little different, and he's got kind of a mouth on him. Blunt, you know what I'm saying? But I'll tell you, I'm voting for him."

Tomson said nothing.

"Hm, did I just cross a line?"

"The thing is, in protection detail we don't express any opinion about the people we look after. Good, bad, politics, personal lives. Democrats or Republicans, it's irrelevant."

She was nodding. "I get it. Keeps you focused. Nothing ex— What's the word? Extraneous?"

"That's right."

"Extraneous . . . I help the boys with their homework some. I'm the go-to girl for math but for English and vocabulary? Forget it."

He asked, "You always been in security?"

"No," she answered. A smile blossomed, softening her face. She was really quite pretty, high cheekbones, upturned nose, clear complexion. "I always wanted to be a cop. Can't tell you why. Maybe TV shows I saw when I was a kid. *Walker, Texas Ranger. Law and Order. NYPD Blue.* But that didn't work out. This's the next best thing."

She sounded wistful.

"You could still join up, go to the state police or city academy. You're young."

Her eyes rolled. "And I thought you agents had to be sooooo observant."

Another smile appeared.

"Anyway, can't afford to take the time off. Single-mom thing."

Then Tomson saw Don Ives approaching quickly. Tomson and the younger agent had worked together for about five years; he knew instantly there was a problem. Kim Morton too tensed, noting the man's expression. "What?" Tomson asked.

"We've got word from CAD. Possible threat triad."

Tomson explained to Morton, "Our Central Analytics Division. You know, data miners. Supercomputers analyze public and law enforcement information and algorithms to spot potential risks."

She nodded.

Ivers continued, "About an hour ago, there was an anonymous call about a white male in a red Toyota sedan, the plate was covered with mud. The driver was standing outside the car and making a cell phone call. The citizen who called nine one one heard this guy mention, 'Ebbett' and 'rally.' That's all he could hear. But he saw there was a long gun in the back seat. It was outside a strip mall in Avery."

Kim Morton said, "About five miles south of here."

Ivers continued, "That put all red Toyota sedans on a watchlist."

"The caller say anything more about the driver?"

"He was in combat or camo, medium build, bald with an old-time moustache. Like gunslingers wore, droopy. The computers started to scan every CCTV—public, and the private ones that make their data available to law enforcement. There were two hits on the target vehicles. At nine this morning, one was spotted in a parking lot near a gun shop in Haleyville."

Tomson turned to Morton, his eyebrow raised.

She said, "*Twenty* miles south."

Ives then said, "He parked in front of a closed-up drug store in a strip mall. The closest active store was the gun shop. We got their security video. The first customer of the day was a bald white male, thirties to forties, with a drooping moustache." Ives sighed. "He bought forty Lapua rounds. Prepaid debit card he paid cash for. Owner said he was a scary guy."

"Brother," Tomson said, sighing. He added to Morton, "Lapuas are high-powered sniper rounds."

"And he didn't park in front of the shop," she said, "to avoid the camera in the gun shop picking up the car."

"Probably."

Ives added, "Then another hit. Two hours ago, the Toyota was videoed parked near—but not in front of, again—a hardware store in Prescott, twelve miles away. He bought a toolbox and six three-quarter-inch PVC pipes. No CCTV inside, but the clerk's description was the same as the others. Same debit card as before."

"Where'd he buy the card?" Tomson asked.

"A Target in Omaha, a month ago."

"Been planning this for a while."

Morton grimaced. "Those towns? That's a straight line to where we are now: Haleyville, Prescott, Avery."

Tomson asked, "Status of vehicle?"

"Nothing since then. He's taking his time, probably sticking to backroads."

"What would he want the pipes for?" Morton asked. "To make bombs?"

Tomson said, "Probably not. That's pretty thin. You couldn't get much explosive in them."

"A tripod for his gun?" she suggested.

An interesting idea. But when he considered it, that didn't seem likely. "Doubt it. Anybody with a gun that fires Lapua rounds would have professional accessories to go along with it. And in an urban shooting solution, like here, he could just use a window-sill or box to support the weapon for a distance shot."

Tomson said, "Put out the info on the wire. Let's advise Searcher."

Ives nodded, pulled out his phone and stepped away.

Tomson knocked on the candidate's door. "Sir. It's Art."

A voice commanded, "Come on in."

The man was jotting notes on a yellow pad. Presumably for his speech that night. He'd do this until the last moment. A transcriptionist was on staff and she would pound the keys of the computer attached to the teleprompter until just before the candidate took the stage. Open on the table was Barbara Tuchman's brilliant—and disturbing book—about the First World War, *The Guns of August*. One of the first items on Ebbett's agenda as president would be to revitalize the US military—"make a great army even greater!"—and stand up to foreign aggression.

Tomson said, "Sir, we've had some information about a possible threat." He explained what they'd discovered.

The candidate took the details without any show of emotion. "Credible?"

"It's not hunting season, but he could be a competitive marksman, buying those rounds for the range. The camo? A lot of shooters wear it as everyday clothing. But the license plate was obscured. And he's headed this way. I'm inclined to take it seriously."

The candidate leaned back and sipped his iced tea. After he'd reinvented himself, this was the strongest thing he imbibed.

"Well, well, well . . . Hm. And what do you say, Ms Morton?"

"Me? Oh, I'm just a girl who spots tomato throwers. These men know all the fancy stuff."

"But what's your gut tell you?"

She cocked her head. "My gut tells me that with any other candidate this probably'd be a bunch of coincidences. But you're not any other candidate. You speak your mind and tell the truth and some people don't like that—or what you have planned when you take office. I'd say take it seriously."

"She's good, Artie." A smile crinkled onto his face. "And I like it that she said, 'when' I take office. Okay. We'll assume it's a credible threat. What do we do?"

"Move the press conference inside," Tomson said. "It's been in the news and a shooter would know that's where you'd be."

The conference, planned for a half hour before the candidate's speech at the rally, was to be held in an open-air plaza connected to the convention center. The candidate had wanted to hold it there because clearly visible from the podium was a factory that had gone out of business after losing jobs overseas. Ebbett was going to point to the dilapidated building and talk about his criticism of the present administration's economic policies.

Tomson had never been in favor of the plaza; it was a real security challenge, being so open. The choice had been Tyler Quonn's, but Ebbett had liked it immediately. Now, though, he reluctantly acquiesced to moving the conference inside. "But I'm not changing one thing about the rally tonight."

"No need, sir; the center itself is completely secure."

"The press'll probably like it better anyway," Ebbett conceded. "Not the best weather to be sitting outside listening to me spout off—as brilliant as my bon mots are."

Tomson noticed that while Kim Morton got the gist of what he was saying, she didn't know the French expression, and this seemed to bother her.

English and vocabulary? Forget it . . .

He felt bad that his partner was troubled.

Tomson called Tyler Quonn and explained about moving the press conference. The chief of staff apparently wasn't crazy about the idea, but agreed to follow Tomson's direction. Then Ives opened his tablet to a map and they studied the area, setting the iPad on the coffee table. Tomson explained to Morton and Ebbett: "Assuming he was going to try a shot at the press conference, we'll locate where a good vantage point would be. Get undercover agents and police there to spot him."

Then Ives added, "I keep coming back to the pipes. The PVC. And the toolbox."

"He could slip into a construction site, fronting he was a worker.

You know, bundle the gun up with the pipes." He shrugged. "But there's no jobsite with a view of the plaza."

"Three's construction's going on there," Morton said, her unpolished nail hovering over the screen. She was indicating a block about a mile from the convention center.

"What is it?" Ives asked her.

"A high-rise of some kind, about half-completed. All I know is the trucks screw up traffic making deliveries. We avoid that road commuting here."

Tomson picked up the tablet and went to three-D view. He swept his fingers over the screen zooming and sweeping from one view to another. He grimaced. "Bingo."

"Whatcha got, Artie?" Ebbett asked.

"You'll be inside the convention center for the rally. But the only way to get into the hall itself is along the corridor behind this wall." He zoomed in on a fifty-foot wall, with small windows at about head height. The windows faced the jobsite.

Ebbett chuckled. "Artie, come on. It's nearly a mile away. At dusk. Who the hell could make that shot?"

"A pro. And shooting a Lapua round? It's so powerful, what'd just be a wound with another gun would be fatal with a slug like that. Sir, this is a level two threat. I'm going to ask you to cancel, if we can't find him."

Ebbett was shaking his head. "Artie, just let me say this: my enemies, and the enemies of this country, want to make us afraid, want to make us run and hide. I can't do that. I won't do that. I know it makes your job tougher. But I'm going to say no. The rally goes on as planned. Move the press conference inside, okay. That's as far as I'll go. Final word."

Without a hesitation, the agent said, "Yessir." Then, given his orders, he turned immediately to the task at hand. "Don, you get a team together. I want eyes on every CCTV from here to that jobsite, looking for that Toyota and the suspect. And I want two dozen tac officers inside and outside that site. And I need to come up with a different route to get Governor Ebbett into the hall, one that doesn't involve any outside exposure. Even a square foot."

Ives said, "I'm on it. I'll call in when I'm in position." He hurried down the corridor.

Tomson said, "I'll find a covered route to get you to the hall, sir."

As he and Morton turned to leave, Tomson glanced down once more at the coffee table, where the book, *The Guns of August*, sat. It hadn't occurred to him earlier, but now he remembered something; the cause of the First World War, in which nearly twenty million people died, could be traced to one simple act—a political assassination.

• • •

In conclusion, my fellow Americans:

This country was founded on the principles of freedom and fairness. And I would add to those another principle: that of fostering. You may remember someone in your youth, who fostered you. Oh, I don't mean officially, like a foster parent. I mean, a mentor, a teacher, a neighbor, a priest or minister, who took you under his wing and saw your inner talent, your inner good, your inner spirit.

And nurtured your gifts.

Freedom, fairness, fostering . . .

Together you and I will invoke those three principles to make our nation shine even brighter.

To make our strong nation stronger.

To make our great nation greater!

God bless you all, God bless our future, and God bless the United States of America.

• • •

Governor Paul Everett looked over his notes and rose from the couch. He practiced this passage a few more times, then revised other parts of the speech. Little by little he was closing in on the final version. He still had a couple of hours until showtime.

He smiled to himself.

Little by little.

Which was exactly the way he was creeping up on the presidential nomination. So many people had said he couldn't do it. That he was too brash, too blunt. Too honest—as if there were such thing.

A knock on the door. "Sir?" It was Artie Tomson.

"Yes?"

"Your dinner's here."

He entered, along with the woman who had saved him from the tomato target practice. He liked her and was sorry she was only a security guard and not on his full-time staff. They were accompanied by a white-jacketed server, a slim Latino, who was wheeling in the dinner cart. Under the silver cover would be his favorite meal: hamburger on brioche bread, lettuce, tomato and, since the first lady to be was not present, purple onion—the sandwich accessorized with thousand island dressing.

And his beloved sweet tea.

The man opened the wings of the table and set out the food.

"Enjoy your meal, sir." He turned to leave.

"Wait," the candidate commanded.

The hotel employee turned. "Sir?" His eyes grew wide as Ebbett pulled his wallet from his hip pocket, extracted a twenty and handed it to the man.

"I . . . oh, thank you, sir!"

Ebbett thought about asking, as a joke, if the man was going to vote for him. But he didn't seem the sort who would get humor and he worried the server might actually think it was a bribe.

The slight man scurried off, clutching the money, which, Ebbett bet, he wasn't going to spend but would frame.

Artie Tomson was giving him an update about the potential assassin, which really was no update at all. They hadn't learned anything from the state police about local threats and hadn't learned from the NRO, NSA or CIA about foreign operatives. There was a full complement of tactical officers—some undercover in construction worker outfits—in and around the jobsite. But there was no sight of the bald, moustachioed suspect or the red Toyota.

As they spoke, Ebbett glanced across the living room and noted Kim Morton on her phone, head down, lost in a serious conversation.

Tomson received a call and he excused himself to take it.

Ebbett strolled casually to the table and plucked a fry from the basket. Nice and hot. He dunked it in ketchup and, salivating already, lifted the morsel to his lips, as he turned to the TV to check the weather and see if the predicted storm would come through, and possibly keep people away. No, it looked like—

Then a crash of china and glass and, with a sharp pain in his back, Ebbett tumbled forward onto the carpet. He realized just before he hit the floor that he'd been facing away from the curtained window and he wondered, with eerie calm, how the assassin, who was apparently across the street nowhere near the jobsite, had known exactly where he would be standing.

• • •

Art Tomson was in the hall, the hub surrounded by a half-dozen other Secret Service agents and local police, all facing him as he gave them calm, clear instructions on how to proceed.

One by one, or two by two, the agents and cops turned toward the elevator and headed off for their respective tasks.

Ives walked up to him and Kim Morton, who stood silently beside the senior agent. Ives's face was even paler than normal as he displayed his phone. "Here's the answer."

Tomson was staring at the words on the screen. Then he nodded to the door of Suite A. "Let's go."

They walked inside, Kim Morton behind them.

Searcher, Governor Ebbett, was sitting on the couch, a heating pad on his back.

That was the only medical attention he'd needed after being tackled while about to take a bite of French fry, dipped in what might be poisoned ketchup.

Tomson said, "Sir, we're awaiting the analysis of the food. But the substance in question is zinc phosphide."

"The hell's that?"

"Highly toxic rodenticide, used to kill rats mostly. When it's ingested, it mixes with stomach acid and a poisonous gas is released."

"Oh, *that's* pleasant . . . What's going on, Artie?"

He nodded to Kim Morton and said, "I'll let my partner here explain. She's the one thought of it."

With her eyes on Ebbett's, she said, "Well, sir. I was thinking that this guy . . . perp, you say perp?"

"We say perp," Tomson said.

"I was thinking if this perp really was some brilliant assassin, well, he didn't seem to be acting so smart. Conspicuous, you know. Parking suspiciously. Talking about the rally in public, while he had a rifle in the back of his car, and he wasn't too concerned if anybody heard him or saw the gun. Wearing camouflage. Buying the PVC pipes and toolbox so we'd think he'd be in a jobsite . . . I mean, it just seemed *too* obvious that he was planning to shoot you. And I looked at those windows in the hallway again. I mean, even if he was a pro, that'd be a hell of a shot.

"So what might other possibilities be? I thought I'd call the places we knew he'd been: the gun shop and the hardware store. We knew what he'd bought but what if he'd *shoplifted* something that could be used as a weapon—a tool or knife or a can of propane to make into a bomb? Nothing was missing at the gun shop, but at the hardware store—where there weren't any video cameras—I asked the clerk if anything was missing. They did an inventory. Two cans of rat poison had been stolen.

"When I saw you go for that fry, sir, I just panicked," Morton said. "I thought that if I shouted anything, you might still take a bite, so I just reacted. I'm sorry."

He chuckled. "No worries. It's not every day a beautiful woman launches herself into me . . . and saves my life at the same time."

Tomson said, "We've closed down the kitchen and concession stands, and analyzed the HVAC system. No sign of poison yet. But all of your food and beverages will come in from outside, vetted sources."

"Don't have much of an appetite at this point." He grimaced. "Had to be the fucking Russians. They love their poisons. Look at Litvinenko."

The Russian ex-pat murdered in London by Moscow agents, who slipped polonium into his tea.

"There was no chatter about it in the intel community," Ives pointed out. "Washington's been monitoring."

"Of course there's no chatter. They're not talking about it overseas—the communications would be picked up. No, they hired some locals to handle the operation—where the CIA can't legally monitor phones and computers without a FISA warrant. Tell the Attorney General I want the Bureau and the CIA to check out the known Russian cells and anyone with a connection to them. I want them to use a proctoscope."

"Yessir. They've been alerted."

"And the car? That Toyota?"

Ives said, "Never got close to the jobsite. Like Officer Morton was saying, it was a diversion, we think. A CCTV in Bronson, about thirty miles east, spotted it, headed out of the state. We're still looking but, after that sighting, it's disappeared. I've got one team going through the hardware store, looking for trace evidence and prints. Other teams are going over the convention center service entrance, kitchen, and talking to food and beverage suppliers. Maybe it *was* the ketchup or the food itself. But we're also looking at the tea."

"Bastard messing with my sweet tea?" Ebbett grumbled in mock rage. Then his eyes slid to Kim Morton. "A local security guard took on a pro assassin . . . and kicked his ass."

"Oh, I just had some thoughts. It was Agent Tomson and Agent Ives who did everything."

"Don't play down your role." He looked her over for a moment. "Artie was telling me a few things about you. How you always wanted to be a police officer."

"Oh," she said, looking down. "Well, that didn't work out. But I'm happy with my life now."

"That's good. Sure . . . But you know my campaign slogan."

She said, "Making a great country greater."

"So what if I could make your happy life *happier*?"

"I'm not sure what you mean, sir."

"What I mean is you did something for me; now I'd like to do something for you. Artie, leave us alone for a few minutes. There's something I'd like to discuss with Ms . . . I mean, with *Officer* Morton."

"I'll be outside, sir."

• • •

At exactly ten-twenty that night, Governor Paul Ebbett's speech concluded with "And God bless the United States of America." The last word vanished in the tide of screams, whistles and thunderous applause. Thirty thousand people were on their feet, waving banners and tossing aloft fake straw hats.

Art Tomson, who'd been on stage for the full event, now walked down the steps and joined Kim Morton, who was standing guard at the doorway that led to the underground passage through which Governor Ebbett would exit in a moment.

The evening had gone without a hitch. In a few minutes, Searcher would be in the SUV and speeding to the airport.

"Good speech," she said.

Tomson, who'd heard it or variations of it scores of times, simply nodded noncommittally.

Then she lowered her voice and said, "Thank you."

"For what?"

"Did the governor tell you what he's going to do for me?"

"No."

Morton explained what the candidate had said in their private meeting. "He's going to get me into the state police academy here. He's a friend of our governor, who owes him for something or another." Her face broke into a smile. "And he arranged for a stipend—almost as much as I'm making here. He said one favor deserves another. He did that all because you told him I wanted to be a cop."

"He was asking about you. He thought you were sharper than some of the people working for him." Tomson added, with gravity in his voice, "And the fact is, none of us came up with that idea about the poison."

"Just a theory is all."

"Still, in this line of work, better safe than sorry."

He tapped his earpiece and head and heard: "Searcher's on the move." Into his sleeve mike, he said, "Roger. Exit is clear."

Tomson shook her hand. She gave him a fast embrace. Never in his years of being an agent had he been hugged by a fellow personal protection officer. He was startled. Then he hugged her back and peeled away to join the candidate, now moving quickly to the waiting SUV.

III

May 24

The main room at Earl's Emporium for Gentlemen wasn't smoky, hadn't been for years.

Even vaping was prohibited. But the aroma of tobacco persisted, as the owners of the place had made no effort to clean the smell away. Because men, alcohol and semi-clad women somehow demanded the scent of cigarette smoke—if not the fumes themselves.

Bil Sheering was at the bar, nursing a Jack and Coke, looking at the scruffy audience sitting by the low stage and at unsteady round bistro tables. While he knew they all could figure out "exotic dance," he was wondering how many had a clue what an "emporium" was. He wondered too why Earl—if there was, or had been, an Earl—had decided to affix the word to his strip joint.

Then his attention turned back to Starlight, the woman who was on center stage at the moment. Some of the dancers who performed here were bored gyrators. Some offered crude poses and outsized flirtatious glances. And some were uneasy and modest. But Starlight was into dancing with both elegance and sensuality.

Enjoying her performance.

Then his attention slipped to the TV, where an announcement was interrupting the game, which no one, of course, had been paying much attention to, given the competition from the stage. On the screen was a red graphic: "Breaking News."

Somebody beside him chuckled drunkenly. "Don'tcha love it? 'Breaking news' used to be a world war or plane crash. Now it's a thunderstorm, vandals at a 7-Eleven. Media's full of shit."

Bil said nothing but kept his attention on the grimy TV. A blond anchorwoman appeared. She seemed to have been caught unprepared by what was coming next. "We now bring you breaking news from Washington, DC. We're live at the campaign head-quarters of Governor Paul Ebbett, for what he has said is an important announcement."

Bil watched the man stride to the front of the room. Cameras fired away, the thirty shots per second mode, sounding like silenced machine guns in a movie.

At Ebbett's side was his wife, a tall, handsome woman on whose severe face was propped a smile.

"My fellow Americans, I am here tonight to announce that I am withdrawing from the campaign for president of the United States." Gasps from the crowd. "In my months on the campaign trail, I have come to realize that the most important work in governing this country is on the grassroots level, rather than inside the Beltway. And it's in those local offices that I feel I can be of the most benefit to my party and to the American people. Accordingly I will be ceasing my efforts to run for president and returning to my great home state, where I'll be running—" He swallowed hard. "—for supervisor of Calloway County." A long pause. "I'm also urging all of my electoral delegates and other supporters to back a man I feel exhibits the best qualities of leadership. Senator Mark Todd."

Another collective gasp, more buzzing of the cameras.

The governor took his wife's hand. Bil noted she didn't squeeze it but let him grip the digits the way you might pick up a gutted fish in a tray of shaved ice to examine it for freshness.

"Senator Todd is just the man to lead our party to victory and—" Ebbett's voice caught. "—make a great nation greater.

Thank you, my fellow citizens. God bless you. And God bless the United States of America."

No applause. Just a torrent of questions from the floor. Ebbett ignored them and walked from the room, his wife beside him, their hands no longer entwined.

The scene switched back to the brightly lit newsroom and the anchorwoman was saying, "That was Governor Paul Ebbett, who just yesterday seemed unstoppable on his route to his party's candidacy. But there you heard it: his shocking news that he was dropping out of the race. And his equally stunning endorsement of Senator Mark Todd. Todd, considered a far more moderate and bipartisan politician than Ebbett, has been the governor's main rival on the primary campaign trail. Although Todd avoided personal attacks, Ebbett rarely missed the chance to belittle and mock the senator."

Reading from what had to be hastily scribbled notes on the teleprompter, the blond anchor said, "A lot of people were surprised by the success Ebbett enjoyed in the primary campaign, which played to the darker side of American society. His positions were controversial. Many in both parties thought his nationalist-charged rhetoric was divisive. He openly admitted that his campaign phrase, 'make a great country greater', meant greater for people like him, white and Christian. He promised to slash social spending to education and the poor.

"He alarmed those both in this country and abroad by stating that one of his first acts in office would be to mass American troops along Russia's borders.

"Some pundits have said that Ebbett might have targeted Russia not for any political or ideological reason, but because he believed a common enemy would solidify support around him. Much like Hitler did in 1930s Germany.

"We now have in the studio and via ZOOM hookup our National Presidential Campaign panel for an analysis of this unexpected announcement. All right, panel, the big question, of course, is why? Do you think the governor's reason that he would prefer to practice politics at the grassroots level is legitimate? Let's start with—"

"Hey, Bil," came the woman's voice behind him.

Bil turned to see the dancer who'd just been up on stage sidling up to him, pulling a shawl over her ample breasts. Bil wasn't completely happy she'd donned the garment.

He knew she went by Starlight here in Earl's, but he couldn't help but think of her by her real name: Kim Morton.

She smiled to the bartender, who brought her a Scotch on the rocks. The headline dancer began to pull bills out of her G-string. As tawdry as Earl's was, it looked like she had been tipped close to two hundred dollars—for twenty minutes at the pole. She sipped her drink and nodded at the screen, talking-head city, dissecting Ebbett's withdrawal. She said, "You did it."

"*Me?*" Bil asked, smiling. "*We* did it."

She cocked her head. "Guess I can't really argue with that one."

We did it . . .

They sure as hell had.

Six months ago the national party committee had become alarmed, then panicked, that Paul Ebbett was picking up a significant number of delegates in the primary contests, beating out the candidate that they vastly preferred, Senator Mark Todd. They were astonished that Governor Ebbett's bigoted and militant rhetoric was stirring up a groundswell of support.

The committee, headed by chairman Victor Brown, knew that Ebbett was lose-lose. If elected, Ebbett would destroy not only the party but probably the economy and perhaps even the nation itself—if he was responsible for the Third World War, which seemed more than a little possible.

Victor wanted Ebbett out and Todd to be their nominee. But

backroom attempts to negotiate with the governor to drop out were futile. In fact, the effort incensed him and fueled his resolve to win . . . and purge the ranks of those who had questioned his ability to lead the country.

So, extreme measures were required.

Last March, Victor had called in Bil Sheering, who ran a ruthless opposition political consulting company in Washington, DC. Bil had hurried back from his hunting lodge in West Virginia to his M Street office and got to work.

For the plan he came up with, he needed a "pro"—by which he meant a call girl based in the region of the Midwestern state where Governor Ebbett would be holding a big rally in May. After some research he'd settled on Starlight, aka Kim Morton, a dancer at Earl's, with an escort business on the side. He'd found her to be smart and well spoken and without any criminal history. She also had a particular contempt for Ebbett, since her husband had been killed in Afghanistan, which she considered an unnecessary war, just like the one Ebbett seemed to be planning.

Victor had given Bil a generous budget; he offered Morton a quarter-million dollars to take a hiatus from her dancing and hooking for two months and get a job as a security guard at the Pittstown convention center. She used her charm and intelligence to talk her way onto the security team working with the Secret Service at the rally, earning the trust of the senior agent, Art Tomson.

The day of the rally, Bil, who'd grown an impressive moustache and shaved his head, dressed in combat gear and smeared mud on the license plate of an old hulk of a Toyota he'd bought at a junkyard. He'd made his way toward the convention center from Haleyville to Prescott to Avery, making intentionally suspicious purchases: sniper bullets and PVC pipes and a toolbox. He'd also made the anonymous call about a man having a phone conversation about Ebbett and the rally, with a rifle in the backseat of his car.

Meanwhile, Morton continued to ingratiate herself into the Secret Service operation . . . and get the attention of Ebbett himself. She'd spotted the suspicious man in the crowd, armed with two rotten tomatoes (the kid was an intern from national party headquarters given a bonus to play the role). Finally, she'd offered her insights about the sniper attack being a diversion; poisoning might be the real form of assassination. (There never was any toxin; at the hardware store Bil had not stolen the rodenticide, but had merely hidden the cans on another aisle, so that when they were later discovered, the Secret Service would conclude the attack was a product of the security guard's overactive imagination.)

The script called for Morton to tackle Ebbett to "save his life." Following that intimate and ice-breaking moment, Kim Morton had fired enough flirtatious glances his way to ignite latent flames of infidelity. After he'd asked her to stay, and Art Tomson had left the suite, Ebbett slipped his arm around her and whispered, "I know you want a slot at the police academy. An hour in bed with me and I'll make it happen."

She'd looked shocked at first, as the role called for, but soon "gave in."

The ensuing liaison was energetic and slightly kinky, as Morton told him she was a bit of a voyeur and wanted the lights on. Ebbett was all for it. This proved helpful, since the video camera hidden in her uniform jacket, hung strategically on the bedroom doorknob, was high def and required good illumination.

She'd delivered the video to Bil, who uploaded the encrypted file to Victor Brown. The head of the national committee had then called Ebbett last week and gave him an ultimatum: withdraw or the tape would go to every media outlet in the world.

After a bit of debate, in which Ebbett had apparently confessed to his wife what had happened (the fish-hand thing suggested this), the man had reluctantly agreed.

Eyes now on the screen, Morton said to Bil, "He's actually running for county supervisor?"

"That's the only bone they'd throw him. He's up against a twenty-two-year-old manager at Farmer's Trust and Savings. The polls aren't in Ebbett's favor." Tomson leaned close and whispered, "I have the rest of your fee."

"I've got one more show. I'll get it after."

Bil had an amusing image of himself, sitting in the front row and, as Starlight danced close to him, tucking a hundred and fifty thousand dollars into her G-string.

He then asked, "This worked out well. You interested in any more work?"

Morton squinted his way. "You've got my number."

Bil nodded. Then he lifted his drink. "Here's to us—unlikely partners."

She smiled and tapped her glass to his. Then she shrugged the silky wrap off her shoulders into his lap and walked back to the stage.

Selfie

Flowers.

The flowers tickled his memory.

What was it?

Kyle Wallace was sitting at his favorite outdoor table at Maude's, best breakfast in the neighborhood, if not all of Nashville. He'd ordered his usual—his *Monday morning* usual, the heartiest of the week—and was glancing up Hopkins Street. From here he could see the side of his girlfriend's small house in this pleasant area south of downtown, just outside 440.

A purple bouquet was leaning against the side door. Elle had just left, to drive her former college roommate to the airport. Janie, a Chicagoan, had spent the weekend here, and the two had seen the sights of Music City, hitting some country concerts and, Kyle supposed, doing what former roommates in their twenties always did: gossip and chat and talk about men and enjoy girl drinks and ice cream.

Just like old times in the carefree days of higher learning.

Despite her interest in the world of entertainment, Elle Margolis had never strayed far from education.

Kyle now leaned forward, squinting toward the bouquet. He was some distance away, so it was just a dot and he couldn't tell what kind of flowers they were—not that he'd know even if he'd seen them up close. Kyle enjoyed the neighborhood garden that abutted Elle's property, he enjoyed their walks through Vanderbilt University's groomed grounds, but those times he'd been paying attention to *her*, not horticulture.

Carlotta, the harried waitress, brought him the over-easy eggs, toast, coffee and cheese grits. He lifted the laden fork and began to eat, still staring at the tiny dot that was the bouquet of flowers.

Something familiar. But what?

The glint of sun told him they were encased in plastic, like the bouquets you'd buy at Food Lion or a drug store, pre-assembled for a last-minute gift. It sat in an odd position, leaning at a sharp angle against the side door, not in a vase. Which somebody would have provided if it was a real present. The pose, for some reason, suggested a body, stiffened in rigor mortis, propped against a battlement.

Kyle Wallace was a big *Game of Thrones* fan.

The tall, stocky young man, whose round head was topped with sandy hair that had a mind of its own, sat forward and continued to eat.

Bite of eggs, bite of grits, bite of toast.

Slug of black coffee.

Hearty . . .

A glance at his phone. Five minutes till he had to leave for work.

Back to breakfast. The most important of the Three Squares a day, his mother always said. He then looked up from his egg-runny plate and stared once more toward Elle's bungalow, hearing the indistinct conversation from the young millennials and workman around him, hearing the distant wet hiss of rush-hour traffic off-gassed by the expressway. He wiped his face with his napkin. Nashville, June. Warm already and soon to be a lot warmer.

Curious. Flowers.

Were they in fact a present? From who? They weren't from Janie. She'd arrived with a carry-on suitcase and a backpack. A hostess gift inside, surely. But no flowers.

And when had they been left?

It was twenty minutes till eight. Had they been there all night?

He understood how Elle could have missed the spray of purple. She and Janie had left for the airport by the front door, the one painted in green enamel, with a window marred by a crack the shape and size of a turkey wishbone. They'd walked to her Volvo, parked at the curb to the right of her house, and headed straight into traffic so they'd had no opportunity to see the side yard.

Finishing breakfast. Mopping light yellow with dark brown toast. Maude's got toast right.

Kyle paid and drove to Elle's house, glancing toward the side door, as he cruised slowly past. Yes, a large bouquet of purple flowers with some sprigs of white. *Those* he recalled. Baby's Breath. Pale, little delicate buds. When he'd bought Elle flowers not long ago, pink roses, the florist had suggested he fill out the spray with some of them. Only a dollar extra. He'd agreed.

He noted now that there was no card or note accompanying the flowers.

Accelerating away, he frowned. He *knew* he'd seen something just like these recently.

Hm.

He'd have to think about it. Get the old gray troops in the brain hiking, hup, hup, hup.

Kyle hit the accelerator and headed to work. He liked his job.

And he was good at it. A customer service specialist, he took happily to the many challenges the vocation presented and didn't let a single glitch or question or error or confusion get by. People spent their hard earned money and they deserved to be helped . . . and respected. Not every employee felt that way, of course. To them a job was something to endure. They weren't partners, the way Kyle looked at customers. He felt sorry for workers like that. He recalled hearing Wednesday referred to as "hump day." At first he'd thought it was dirty, but then someone explained it meant the middle of the week, a mountain summit, so that once you'd passed it, you were headed downhill to the glorious weekend. But Kyle liked every day of work. Good job, good fellow workers, near to Elle's house and his apartment.

He knew Elle hadn't had quite the same luck with careers. In the year since they'd met, she'd seen her dreams postponed, if not derailed. The slim, sultry brunette had hoped to be a model and actress—there was a lot of film and TV production in Nashville. But a first audition wouldn't lead to a call-back; an actual job ended up a one-off. Elle was now an administrative assistant in the School of Engineering at Vanderbilt, thinking of getting a degree in computer science. Several times he'd offered to support her, if she wanted to spend more time auditioning, but she'd declined. He supposed the reality was creeping in that while she was beautiful, no doubt there, maybe she wasn't quite talented enough for the big time. Kyle knew from the TV shows he watched that acting was a very special set of skills; not everyone could do it.

He pulled into the employee parking lot, climbed from the car and clicker-locked the door.

Thinking again: Flowers . . .

What the heck was the memory?

And then, walking inside, he happened to glance at a computer, whose screen a co-worker was cleaning with an anti-static rag. It was then that the tiny gray troops came through. Yes! He'd seen the flowers on a screen. That still could have been from a number of sources, though: TV or computer. In addition to his Netflix subscription, Kyle loved video games—what 28-year-old didn't? So the fact that he'd seen the flowers in pixels didn't narrow down the possibility a great deal.

Still, it was a start.

He actually paused and closed his eyes. Trying to picture the scene of the flowers. No, nothing more came up. But he'd have to consider it later; he got to work, concentrating on "isolating tasked challenges," noting "stratified objectives" and making sure he was "responsive to the ask." Yes, he enjoyed his job, but that didn't mean he didn't have a skeptical view of corporate mentality, as reflected in such phrases from the memos that fluttered down from management. (Kyle collected them and would forward them to Elle; she had a wicked sense of humor herself.)

And thinking about her, as he often did, pushed the gray troops one step farther.

Yes! There was some other connection between the purple flowers and his girlfriend. Was it that movie they'd seen? The one about the superheroes? There had been a scene in a garden. Was that it?

No, he didn't think so.

And, finally, the troops stood to attention.

Got it!

Kyle knew exactly where he'd seen the flowers. But the action of "achieving the optimal finalization of goal" was mixed with a vague sense of concern. He wasn't sure why that was the case— his subconscious, surely, but something troubled him. Yet there was nothing more to do at the moment; the image had been on a computer screen. But Kyle couldn't check online now; Mondays were always busy.

At five o'clock, he hurried to the parking lot, leapt into the car and sped home, as best he could, through rush-hour traffic. In a half hour he was in his townhouse. Grabbing a Sam Adams and bag of chips, he headed into his bedroom and dropped into the comfortable armchair in front of his computer. Kyle shoved aside dozens of DVDs and disks of computer games and went online.

The memory that had clicked, thanks to the little gray soldiers, was of Elle's Facebook page. Kyle now logged on and scrolled through her photo album, which is where he was sure he'd seen the purple flowers recently. The weekend's pictures documented the former roommates' sightseeing. While Kyle had binged all Sunday on last season's *GOT* and *Outlander*, the girls had done the town, seeing the famous Nashville sights and attending two concerts, one in the afternoon and one in the evening. They'd taken a dozen selfies, which Elle had posted.

He found the flowers in the sixth picture.

Janie & me at Woodlawn Cemetery. Resting place of LOTS of famous CW singers. George Jones and Tammy Wynette, JD Summers (he sang with ELVIS!!), Eddie Arnold, Little Jimmy Dickens and here we R @ Marty Robbins' grave!

The picture showed the two girls standing over a large metal grave marker in the ground, bearing the name *Martin David Robinson*, and the raised signature of his stage name.

Elle was more into country music than Kyle but even he knew about Marty Robbins. He now heard clearly in his head Robbins's voice singing about doomed love in the West Texas town of El Paso, a song his grandfather had listened to over and over.

But Kyle wasn't paying much attention to the nostalgia. The picture took his full attention. Elle and Janie were not centered in the picture—they hadn't used a selfie stick—but were in the left side of the scene, so there was a good portion of background in frame. Kyle could see a man in a dark jacket—probably black or navy blue—and a forest green baseball cap. He wore sunglasses—the mirrored aviator style that seemed to be coming back in vogue. The man was white and about Kyle's height and weight. The brim on the hat was long and his face was in shadows.

He was standing near another grave site about thirty yards away. And he was holding a bouquet of purple flowers that looked just like the one left on Elle's side doorstep that morning.

Coincidence?

That seemed impossible. In the picture, the Stranger—that's what Kyle called him—was too far away to be with the girls but there was no doubt he was focused on them, not looking down at any of the nearby grave plates.

Could he be a friend of Janie's? She'd arrived at the airport alone but he supposed she might have another friend in Nashville. Still, if they were friends, why was he standing so far away? And why looking so . . . well, grim—that was Kyle's impression.

Then the little gray soldiers began hiking again, as Kyle looked at Elle's other posts.

Here we are @ the Parthenon—an EXACT replica of the one in Greece. Same size and everything! In Centennial park. Beautiful. Janie and I decided: Greek food tonight . . . though maybe bbq will win out!

Kyle stared, feeling his mouth slacken as he scanned the screen. The girls were in front of the structure and again she'd gotten plenty of background in the shot. To the right were rows of bushes and beyond them a stand of trees. He couldn't be absolutely positive but it seemed to him that in a shadowy spot between two of the trunks was a man looking toward the girls, possibly in sun glasses and a dark baseball cap.

Yes, no?

Scrolling once more, Kyle was aware of his pulse tapping

quickly. He felt a throbbing in his head, matching the twisting in his gut.

The next selfies were of the women at the Belle Meade plantation, a beautiful antebellum estate that Kyle didn't much care for because his mother would drag him to the place on holiday and summer afternoons. Always a dull outing. It was a women's tourist site, for mothers and grandmothers, linens and china and delicate paintings. There wasn't enough space devoted to the only neat part about the place: its having been a Civil War battleground. Of sorts. A skirmish was fought between Yankees and Confederates right in the front yard.

Kyle examined the first picture closely: the two girls were in front of a reconstruction of the plantation's slave quarters. There was no caption accompanying this image. A second shot—near the main building—was described:

> *Beautiful gardens at Belle Meade! Saw gravestone of Enquirer, the #1 stud horse in America a while ago. (Think he never raced . . . he just made baby horses. Nice job if you can get it, guys!!)*

Despite his concern about the mysterious Stranger, Kyle had to smile. Elle was never crude but she could be charmingly suggestive. He loved it when she was.

Neither of these pictures revealed the Stranger.

Relief began to flow.

The next image was of the girls at a Starbucks across the street from the Vanderbilt campus; Kyle knew it well. He'd spent hours there; it was near the building where Elle worked. They'd often go for walks on this portion of the pretty grounds.

Elle and Janie were drinking some frothy beverages. Kyle didn't care for those much. He drank plain coffee, black. Not these sugary, whipped-creamy concoctions. Partly this was because he had to watch his weight like a soldier on patrol—he stayed slim because he worked at it (Elle could eat pretty much whatever she wanted). Partly to save the pennies; the fancy stuff at Starbucks could really set you back.

Kyle was beginning to relax. The Stranger was a creation of his imagination. It had to be. He scrolled back to the Parthenon selfie. Squinted. Might be a sunglassed man. But might just be shadows, and sunlight on leaves.

The next pictures were of Music Row—not a single street but a neighborhood, honky tonk, loud and brimming with that uneasy blend of touristy and genuine. These shots were busy, revealing crowds of people, a lot of traffic, bikes, walked dogs. Kyle saved them to his Personal Pix file and then blew them up with a photo view app. He scanned everyone. No sign of the Stranger.

So, *had* to be his imagination. But how to explain the flowers? He could—

No! He'd just scrolled to another selfie on Music Row and found himself looking at the girls, cheek to cheek, in front of a club that featured a huge guitar sculpture done in neon tubes, bright red.

And behind them, about a hundred feet away, yes, the Stranger. He carried two things: One was a small shopping bag, blue, with the initials H and T on it.

The other was a cup of Starbucks. So he *had* been to the coffee shop.

He plowed ahead with his investigation, now examining a selfie of the girls with another woman, taller, thin, wearing a plunging plaid shirt and a white cowboy hat. The pretty woman was smiling, a practiced grin, like she'd posed a thousand times before.

Rockin' out at Lake Watauga, listenin' to the Kelley Jones band. Here we are with Kelley! She's the best!! Check her out on Twitter!

Looking past them, scanning the concert-goers.

And, hell, yep! He saw—couldn't be sure but *thought* he saw—

the Stranger half-hidden by the crowd clustering near the stage on the shore of the beautiful lake in Centennial Park. Still clutching the shopping bag.

There was one more selfie documenting the ladies' tour of the city: Elle and Janie in front of the red-brick Ryman Auditorium, home of the Grand Ole Opry.

"The Mother Church of Country Music." Isn't it bee-autiful? Imagine everybody who's appeared here. Love it!

No Stranger in this scene.

At least, Kyle didn't see him at first. But then he began focusing on the *reflections* in the windows. In the third one from the right, yes, it was possible that one cluster of light and shadow was a man in a dark hat and aviator sunglasses.

What exactly was going on?

It seemed unlikely that Janie was the object of the man's attention. She had no Nashville connection and, to be honest, she was frumpy, a plain-looking woman.

No, the person he was interested in had to be Elle, beautiful, charming Elle.

She had always attracted men (a few women too), some nice, but some not so. Twice Kyle had had confrontations with guys who wouldn't leave her alone. He wasn't a large man but he was strong and, more important, he could have an intense, even scary gaze (he often thought of himself as a character back in medieval days, not as massive as some knights but more fiercely intimidating). It didn't help either that Elle didn't have the best judgment in people. Ones she thought were harmless were clearly manipulative and dangerous. Others, innocent and friendly, she was suspicious of. And he knew she had a tendency to adopt people, to trust them, even the bad ones.

Who was this guy? How exactly was this going to play out?

Examining one of the clearer images of the Stranger . . .

What do you have in mind? One answer was obvious but he needed more facts. He began to keyboard again.

As it turned out, however, only one more piece of the puzzle was necessary, before everything fell—shockingly—together.

He shook his head in dismay, staring at the screen.

He'd been looking for what the Stranger had been shopping for at the H & T store. The answer chilled him.

H&T Sporting Goods
The finest hunting and combat knives in the South.

If you want a blade for cookin', go to Macy's.
If you want one for . . . something else, we're the place for you!

Kyle picked up the phone and said to Siri, "Call Elle."

The call went right to voice mail.

He left a message, then called her office in Vanderbilt. He got another assistant and asked for Elle.

She replied, "Hold on . . . Hold on. No. Don't see her. Her desk is all straightened up. Probably means she left for the night. Can I take a message?"

"Do you know if she was going straight home?"

A hesitation.

"It's all right. I'm her boyfriend."

"She said she was, yes."

Without another word, Kyle disconnected the call. As he rose, fishing for his car keys, another thought occurred to him. Picturing the bouquet once more, he wondered: Wasn't purple the traditional color for funerals?

• • •

Kyle was at Elle's house in fifteen minutes.

He noted that her red Volvo was parked on the street. A half-dozen other cars were too. Some he recognized. Others he didn't. He passed by her place and parked at the end of the block and returned on foot. He checked the side of the house; the flowers were gone.

On the front porch he rang the bell and received no response. He knocked.

Still, nothing. The front door was locked.

He returned to the side door, which was also barred. Then he continued to the back.

This door was not only unlocked. It was open. He looked around, then pushed it wide and walked inside.

"Elle?"

No answer.

He stepped into the kitchen, a small, hot room that Elle didn't use very often. A single woman millennial didn't have much cause to cook, other than nuking Lean Cuisines and making Keurig coffee. He passed through the room. It wasn't very clean.

"Elle?"

Silence but for the buzzing of a large fly.

The den, also tiny, was unoccupied. He glanced at the book-shelves, which were filled mostly with textbooks. Her Mac computer, closed, sat on a rickety table she was using for a desk.

Back to the hall, moving softly, taking in the amalgams of floral scents—shampoos, deodorants, soaps, perfumes. Sachets maybe. He knew Elle had been very close to her grandmother, whose hobby was making such dainty things, along with hankies, scarves, potholders, needlepoint wall hangings and a myriad of other cloth creations every day of her adult life. Kyle could smell mold too; this was an old house, and Nashville, even in early summer, was as humid as any Southern locale could be.

The back bedroom was dark and empty, so he continued on.

At the front bedroom he paused. The door was partly open and he could see the end of Elle's bed, a four poster.

He also saw two bare, unmoving feet.

"Elle?" he whispered. He pushed the door all the way open. A creak of hinge, and the heavy slab of wood swung slowly into contact with the rubber buffer on the wall, meant to keep the knob from damaging the old plaster.

Kyle froze, looking down at Elle, lying atop the cream-colored chenille bedspread. Her head was on the pillow, dark hair a tangled mess. Her mascara had run and her pink lipstick was smeared around her mouth, all the way down to her chin. There was a bruise on her cheek and her palm bled from a shallow slash. The knife that had probably made the cut lay on the floor.

"Elle!"

On the second pillow was the purple bouquet.

Her eyes focused on him. "Kyle," she whispered.

"Are you all right? What happened? Was it that guy I told you about in my message? The one in your Facebook posts?"

Then her eyes went to the bathroom.

A man of about Kyle's age and build stepped out, holding a small pistol. He aimed it at Kyle.

"What, what is this?" Kyle gasped.

There was a moment's pause. The man stepped closer to Elle, looked down.

And handed her the pistol.

She took it and aimed directly at Kyle's chest.

"I'm sorry," she whispered. "I am. Really."

• • •

"Wait, what are you doing?" Kyle stammered. He started forward.

"Don't move, no. Stay right where you are."

"Keep the gun steady," the man said.

She did.

Kyle stopped fast. He then noticed that the man was holding the *H & T* bag from the posts. Then he squinted. "You. You're Todd Bendix."

Kyle recalled that he and Elle had dated in high school and off and on for a year or two after, Elle in college, Todd at Preston Ford.

Eyes wide as those of a child watching an adult horror film, Kyle said to Elle, "What is this? I . . . What are you doing?"

Elle whispered fiercely, "You just wouldn't listen, Kyle. You just . . . You just wouldn't listen. I gave you every chance! Every chance to back off, to save yourself all the grief."

"What grief?" he asked, genuinely perplexed by her words.

"The arrest, for one."

"Oh, that wasn't so bad. The officers were pretty nice. The hard part was seeing you go to all that trouble to keep me away from you. Those restraining orders. *Those* were harsh, true. But I knew, knew in my heart, that you didn't mean it. You were confused."

She laughed aloud. "Confused? *Confused?* You'd sit on the curb in front of my house hours on end every night, every weekend. Then we modified the order to move you a hundred feet away, and you started sitting in the garden across the street. And then we got a *thousand* feet and you moved up to Maude's, that same corner table, every morning, every night, every time you had a day off. Staring at the house. Staring, staring, staring."

"Had to prove to you how much I loved you. Convince you we were meant to be together."

Elle echoed once more, "Meant to be together? How could you think that?"

Even in her anger, she was so beautiful.

Todd shook his head, grim faced. "Pathetic. Sick."

Kyle knew he came from a tough part of Nashville, what'd be

described as the other side of the tracks. Redneck, drunk, weed smoker, if not worse. Ran with a tough crowd in high school. But even the crude ones can lay a pretty line on the girls. He'd surely put some hard thoughts into Elle's head about Kyle.

A tendency to adopt people, to trust them, even the bad ones . . .

Elle continued, "Kyle, listen to me! We had one date, you and me. *One* date. A year ago! We went to the Cineplex and saw that stupid movie. Had coffee after. That was it."

He was mildly offended. "The movie wasn't that bad."

Kyle liked his superheroes.

"We didn't even sleep together!"

"We kissed, and it was like a kiss from an angel."

"Oh, Jesus," she said in disgust. "I kissed you *good night.* That was all. On the cheek."

"And we emailed and texted."

"I sent you two, three texts, then stopped. But you didn't. Fifty a day sometimes."

"One of us has to work at the relationship. Until you come to your senses."

It was only a matter of time, he knew in his heart.

"We're not in a relationship, Kyle, whatever you post on Twitter or Facebook."

"There's a word for that, Elle. Denial."

"*Denial?* No, that's *you*, Kyle. You're not in the real world! You follow me, a hundred feet behind, on campus, and you post that we went for a walk. You send me flowers twice a week I don't want. You email me jokes and YouTube clips, and you change email addresses so often my spam filter's useless. This weekend! Take this weekend! You followed me to the airport and hid on the other side of baggage claim when I went to pick up Janie! You got that job at the Shop-More up the street, just so you could be closer to my house! You left management track at Ferguson Manufacturing so you could be a greeter at a big box store. *That's* denial!"

"I'm a customer service specialist."

Her eyes closed. Then they sprang open and bored into him once more. Such a lovely brown shade. Gold flecks. How they sparkled!

So lovely . . .

"Kyle, I tried. I really tried. But you wouldn't listen. And now look what it's come to."

Then Kyle was gazing around the room, at the gun, the cutlery store bag. In a soft, resigned voice he said, "I get it now. It was all a plan. All a set up. *He* couldn't stand it that you dumped him and that you loved me. And he's seduced you with this idea how to get rid of me."

"Oh, Kyle, you're that far gone?"

Todd said, "Listen, asshole: You've screwed up her life. She told me what kind of psycho you are. I'm just helping her out."

"Oh, I'm sure," Kyle said sarcastically.

Elle was crying now but the gun had not slumped one millimeter. It was still pointed at Kyle's chest.

"I gotta give you credit. It's pretty damn smart. Getting him in those selfies so it looks like you and Janie were being stalked." He looked Todd up and down. "You're about my build—so in the hat, sunglasses, jacket, it could've been me." He frowned. "Was Janie in on it? . . . No, she wouldn't be. But still you invited her here to use her. So you two could walk around town, see the sights, and get those selfies, post them. The cops could see quote 'me' following you. See the flowers at the cemetery, flowers on your porch, for the neighbors to see. Everybody would think I'd come to your place."

He gave a grim laugh. "And I didn't have any alibi that it *wasn't* me. Which you knew, since I texted you that I'd be binging on TV all Sunday at my place."

She repeated, "Fifty times a day . . ."

"You left the flowers out, figuring I'm remember them from the pictures on Facebook."

"You're on my page more than I am, Kyle."

"I'd see the bouquet by your side door this morning, and look at your other selfies and decide you were in danger. And you'd know I couldn't go to the police. If I told them anything, they'd arrest me for getting close to you and violating the restraining order."

Todd and Elle shared a glance.

Kyle continued, "You knew I'd risk the court order to come here and warn you. When I called and left a message, that was a sign you should get ready. You were going to make it look like I'd tried to assault you and you'd shoot me. Then dress me up in that jacket. Plant the sunglasses and baseball cap on me." He scanned her face. The bruise was real. Todd had probably inflicted it. And she would have cut her palm herself—it would look like a defensive wound from Kyle's knife attack.

Todd didn't seem to take offense. He said, matter-of-factly, "Okay, Elle. That's all we needed to know. He said he didn't go to the cops." He walked close. "It's okay. Do what you have to. He deserves it."

Elle inhaled deeply. "I'm sorry, Kyle. I have to get my life back." She looked down at the gun, and pulled the hammer back. It made a solid click.

"No! Please!" Kyle dropped to the floor, huddling, turning away from them, choked sounds coming from his throat.

Todd said coldly, "You son of a bitch. Stand up."

"The plan won't work if you shoot me in the back," Kyle shouted.

Todd stepped forward, "I'll just turn you around—and beat the crap out of you when I do. We'll tell the police I came over and found you trying to assault her. We struggled. Elle had to shoot you when you went to stab me."

Kyle glanced over his shoulder.

How beautiful was her face! All heart shaped, creamy skin.

Then he was smiling. And only partly because of the gorgeous vision that was Elle Margolis. Mostly the smile was one of relief. It accompanied the sound that emanated from his hands—an electronic *whoosh*, not unlike the sound of rush-hour traffic from I-440, the soundtrack of his breakfast.

It was the tone of an iPhone sending an email off into space.

Todd stared the mobile in Kyle's hand and he quickly touched Elle's arm, lowering the gun.

"What?" she whispered.

Todd said hesitantly, "He . . . Did you just send something?"

"I did, yes, that's right. A recording of the conversation we just had. I emailed it to myself."

Todd and Elle regarded each other. Kyle couldn't tell whose face was the paler.

In a calm voice he continued, "Some people love makes stupid." A glance at Todd. "Some people it makes smart. See, I knew there was something off about those selfies. My little gray troops—I've told you all about them, Elle. They were saying something wasn't right. You made sure you and Janie were only taking up part of the frame; you always got plenty of background too. You wanted to make it clear somebody was following you, somebody dressed up like a killer from a bad '70s thriller. I mean, it was pretty obvious, don't you think? And carrying a bag from a knife store? Did you really think it was credible for the stalker to buy a weapon on the same outing where he was following you? Seriously? Did I mention stupid?"

A natural eye cut toward Todd. "So I figured somebody—turns out to be Pep-Boy here . . . whoa, take it easy! I figured somebody'd poisoned your mind against me. And had come up with a plot to take me out. So I called, left the message you were at risk and then came over. Sure, I took a chance. If I was wrong I'd get arrested for violating the RO. If I was right you might just shoot me as soon as I walked into the door. But I doubted that. You needed to find out if I'd called the police about the stalker. If I had, well, it wouldn't be *me* doing the stalking, would it? But I delayed long enough before I mentioned that to get everything I needed on tape."

He held the phone up like an Olympic medal. "Anything happens to me, the police'll get a warrant and read all my emails. It's standard procedure. You'll both be indicted for conspiracy to commit murder. Years in prison."

"You son of a bitch," Todd muttered.

Kyle felt indignant. "Wasn't me about to lay somebody out on a slab in the coroner's office, now, Todd, was it? Now, Dexter, why don't you run back to your carburetors and grease pit?" He stepped forward and took the gun from Elle's trembling hands. He'd never shot one but you couldn't watch a half hour of TV now, any channel, without becoming an expert in firearms. He pointed it toward Todd. "Oh, and leave the jacket and the rest of the disguise. Knife too. I'll hold on to those." He'd just seen a marathon session on the Discovery Channel about the miracles of DNA evidence.

"Elle," Todd began.

"Go on, leave. We'll talk later."

"Probably you won't," Kyle said. "But take the first part of that advice: 'Go on, leave.'"

At a loss for words, Todd summoned a glare—it looked silly—and stormed out the door.

Kyle lowered the hammer of the gun and slipped it into his pocket. He smiled. "No serious harm done, Elle. I understand that Mr Todd worked his way into your skin. The way a tick'd do. Hardly even notice until long after the poison's inside. But that man is gone now. It's okay, it's all right. We can focus on mending our relationship. We've got a strong enough foundation to survive this. We do."

She was crying softly.

Tears of joy, tears of relief . . .

"Tomorrow we'll get that pesky restraining order lifted." He took her hand. It was no longer trembling but limp as silk. "You'll do that, right?"

Eyes down, she nodded.

"Good. And now, I'm thinking we should celebrate. Go to that fancy dining room in Opryland Hotel, what do you say? There's a plan. Now, get on into the bathroom, and put your face on, my mother used to say. And slip into something pretty. How 'bout that little lacy yellow dress you picked up last week at the mall? Nordstrom's. I didn't exactly see what you bought at Victoria Secret, but if you want to wear that too, I wouldn't object."

Elle slowly rose. As she walked to the bathroom he said, "Oh, and make sure to bring your phone. We'll want to get some nice pictures, now, won't we?"

Bibliography

'The Babysitter' first appeared in *Playing Games*, edited by Lawrence Block (LB Productions).

'Forgotten, a Colter Shaw Story' was published as a standalone digital novella by HarperCollins in 2021.

'Hard to Get' first appeared in the July/August edition of *Ellery Queen's Mystery Magazine*.

'The Writers' Conference' first appeared in the 2014 Bouchercon Anthology *Murder at the Beach* (Down & Out Books, 2014).

'A Matter of Blood' first appeared in *The Big Book of Jack the Ripper*, edited by Otto Penzler (Vintage Crime/Black Lizard 2016; audio edition by Highbridge, a Division of Recorded Books 2020).

'An Acceptable Sacrifice' first appeared in *Bibliomysteries Volume 1* (Myst Press, 2012, audio edition by Brilliance Audio).

'The Adventure of the Laughing Fisherman' first appeared in *In the Company of Sherlock Holmes*, edited by Laurie R. King and Leslie S. Klinger (Titan Books, 2015).

'A Significant Find' first appeared in *Alive in Shape and Color*, edited by Lawrence Block (Pegasus, 2019; audio edition Tantor Audio 2021).

'Where the Evidence Lies, a Lincoln Rhyme Story' first appeared in Strand Originals (Mulholland Books, 2016).

'A Woman of Mystery' has not appeared in print before.

'Ninth and Nowhere' first appeared as a standalone digital novella and audiobook (Amazon Original Stories, 2019).

'Unlikely Partners' first appeared as 'Security' in the anthology *Odd Partners*, edited by Anne Perry (Ballantine Books, 2019).

'Selfie' has not appeared in print before.